Tennyson the poet said it best:

"Tis better to haved loved and lost, than never to have loved at all."

...to the reader I make this promise: I have written out of love and have followed this story from the perspectives of those who have participated in it...
I offer you the dreams of one who first loved long ago, and lost, but triumphed in the end...
There are many kinds of love. Read between the lines and enjoy the journey. There are secrets waiting for you there. And as you do, with the poet Moore say:

"Oh, there is nothing half
so sweet in life
as love's young dream!"

From: *The Last Valentine*

The
Last Valentine

For fifty years she waited for him to return until...
The Last Valentine!

James Michael Pratt

WINDSONG
WS
FICTION

***

For Jeanne, who has walked with me through

"the tunnel of love."

***

The Last Valentine

Copyright © 1995
by
JAMES MICHAEL PRATT

Library of Congress Catalog Card Number:
In Progress
ISBN 0-9651163-1-X

DISTRIBUTED BY

Origin Book Sales
6200 South Stratler
Salt Lake City, UT. 84107
1 (888) 467-4446

PUBLISHER

Windsong Communications
2524 Townsgate Rd., Suite "G"
Westlake Village, CA. 91360
1(888) 375-2059

For speaking engagements please call 1(888) 375-2059.

IN LOVING MEMORY

The power of love transcends time. *The Last Valentine* is especially dedicated in memory of my friend, the late Lieutenant Michael Moore, fighter pilot, United States Navy. His powerful advocacy for principals of freedom, God and country, and his loyalty to the highest of Christian moral virtues and values, affected me deeply.

His profound love and devotion for his wife, Marilyn, and their two children, Teresa and Michael Jr., was expressed to me two days before his death. It was fitting that his final expressions of life were melodious. They can be summed up in the three most elegant, yet simply powerful words found in the English tongue when used in harmony. As he lay dying in his wife's arms I muse at the poignant phrase he uttered. It is one we all long to hear. He said simply: "I love you."

We all desire to leave a legacy. Mike did. The legacy of love lives on in all who knew him. Here's to you Mike! May the reader possess the lofty dreams of love which you believed in!

And here's to you, the reader. May you love and overcome the thorns of life to forever hold the rose!

INTRODUCTION

Once in a while our thoughts drift and fade back...back into the recessed hiding places where our memories are safely stored. At times, we recall them; the memories of our loves, of our youth, of our life experiences. In day or night dreams they appear before us, and for seconds, minutes or hours we are there once again.

Memory. Our mind's powerful possessor of personal events. Powerful enough to remind us, teach us, hold us slaves, or free us. Memories of the past are forever suspended in our minds for instant recall. And instantly they may employ the authority to possess our present lives.

Memories of love—no matter how distant the scene—can once again bring to us the sweet joys of youth, just as it was "then." And, no matter our age, all of us at times long for it as it was— *then*. Then, when there were so many possibilities, when life was beginning, and anything seemed ours for the taking.

The Last Valentine is a story about memories of love—love, the romantic kind—love, the brotherly kind—love, the kind which endures trial and in devotion becomes never ending in its loyalty.

And, in the end, it's about a love that gains an immortal stature. Like a torch that cannot be extinguished, this kind of devotion is the keeper of the flame.

Along with our memories of loving relationships, there are often special places—public and private—that captivate and hold a sacred meaning for us. In recall of these sites, our memories invoke reverent feelings; not because the place itself is a holy sanctuary, but because something wonderful—heavenly—happened there.

So it was with Lieutenant Neil Thomas Sr., USN, and his wife, Caroline. So it is with the story of *The Last Valentine*.

CHAPTERS

PROLOGUE

<u>UNION STATION—Los Angeles, February 14, 1945</u>

Caroline's heart beat wildly as she entered the revolving doors which opened to the cathedral-like hallways of Union Station. Soldiers, their wives and girlfriends, filled the walkways. That old feeling came back to her. It was as if she felt him close to her, as if he were there, leaving her again. The feeling of desperation had consumed her one year earlier as she held onto her husband's arm...as she held onto the last touch of his strength before sending him off to the hostilities raging in the Pacific.

This was the place. Two years earlier they were reunited here by strange fortunes of chance, and then they married. They chose Valentine's Day, 1943, for their wedding. One blissful year followed, with Neil stationed as a Navy flight trainer in Southern California. Then his combat assignment came and he shipped out, by a quirk of fate, on their first wedding anniversary, February 14, 1944. Now she was hoping against all odds... Hoping to see him walking down the train ramp and then racing into her arms as he promised he would.

Back—he said he would be back for her...back for her at the very place where they last held each other close—Union Station. With their embrace, she had also held onto a hope that he would come back from combat and they could start their third year of marriage by this very time, the lovers' holiday and their wedding anniversary. She loved him; she had loved him since grade school. And now she loved a man declared by the War Department as "Missing in Action."

She walked alone, her mind heavy in thought. Forward she moved—alone and forward through the mass of humanity, some greeting their returning loved ones from war, others sending their loved ones off to war. Forward towards gates G and H and then into the tunnel which led to Track Twelve—the last place she had seen him.

Tears welled up in her eyes as she reminisced. Caroline sought for control over the tender emotions which enveloped her. Even if Neil was "missing," she wasn't; she was there. They had promised each other to be there, to hold each other again at the station by February 14th. Maybe it was a silly promise, an unrealistic expectation, but it was something for both of them to hope for, live for. She could keep her promise even if...even if he couldn't.

Lost in her tender reflections, she proceeded past the throngs of people and up the center aisle towards the departure gates. She stared straight ahead, not wanting to see the happiness reflecting from the faces of returning servicemen in greeting their girls, nor the sadness shown by the girls who held tightly to their departing warriors. It hurt. It was as painful as that day one year before.

Her wistful memories were suddenly interrupted by a hand reaching out from the crowd. A strong, manly hand on her shoulder caused her to shudder as she slowly turned in an anxious, vain hope that it could be...it might be him.

The young Navy pilot had noticed the young woman surging past with the crowds. He was there, Ensign Bobby Roberts, at Union Station to keep a promise, to visit the wife and son of his missing comrade and flight commander. He needed to catch a cab and head out for Pasadena to keep his promise and be back to catch his train later that evening. But he had to stop. The glimpse of the young woman sparked a recognition in him that he couldn't immediately place. He had seen that face before, but had never met her. He dropped his duffel bag on the highly polished tile floor and worked his way back through the crowds until he caught up with her.

"Excuse me, ma'am," he said reaching for her shoulder. She stopped and turned around, staring at him with an emotionless, blank look. An ambivalence showed from an otherwise beautiful face that he sensed could be captivating, if happy.

"Yes?" the young lady answered.

"Excuse me. I know we don't know each other, but...well, you look so familiar, and I..."

She cut him off, "Look, I'm married. If this is what I think it is, I'm not interested."

Prologue

"Oh...no...no...that's not it...please forgive me... I thought you might be...well." An awkward pause followed. "Well, you must be on your way to meet your husband. I'm sorry." Roberts turned to head back towards Alameda Street and to the waiting taxis.

"Wait," she called. The young woman wore a flower-patterned dress and her petite frame belied a certain strength in her graceful carriage. Her auburn hair was neatly put up in a bun, and her brown eyes, though sad, could beguile any man—under different circumstances. She made her way back towards the young Navy pilot and stopped, staring at the gold wings pinned to his uniform. She gawked at them unabashedly, then her eyes filled with tears and a small cry escaped from her throat.

"You're a Navy pilot," she sobbed in a soft, trembling voice. "Welcome home," she whispered. "I'm sorry I was so sharp with you." She searched her purse for a handkerchief, the one her husband had given her the year before. "My husband...I don't know if...when he's coming home," she struggled. "I just came down here in hopes...well, he left one year ago, and it's our anniversary, and I'm a little upset. Anyway, I'm sorry for being rude."

A smile creased the lips of the young Navy pilot as she struggled to finish offering her apology. She wondered why he was taking time with her and her story anyway, and was embarrassed at his apparent amusement. He just didn't get it, she thought.

"Caroline?"

Startled, she flashed him a deep questioning gaze revealed by the furrowed brow and eyes that searched his face for some explanation.

"Caroline? Caroline Thomas?"

"Yes," came the carefully posed response. "Have we met?"

"Not officially," he replied, extending his hand in greeting. "My name is Bobby Roberts. Ensign Bobby Roberts. I've seen your picture many times, on the wall of my quarters aboard ship...the cabin I shared with your husband, Neil."

She let out a faint gasp and drew her hand to her mouth. She felt suddenly weak and gaped at him with eyes that questioned... eyes that searched.

Roberts reached out to support the quivering wife of his shipmate. He had plenty of things to share with her. Hope, courage, belief and the words that his flight leader, Lieutenant Neil Thomas, had asked him to deliver to her if anything should happen to him. Guiding her out of the center of the large waiting area, he motioned to a table at the nearby cafe. "This is for you, Skipper," he whispered under his breath.

***

FEBRUARY 14, 1945 Behind enemy lines—Bataan Peninsula, Philippines

"Tomás! Japs coming down ridge. Maybe one hour we finish them off. We go in five minutes," Rios called. Filipino guerrilla commander Ernesto Rios squinted into the cave where downed Navy fighter pilot Lieutenant Neil Thomas Sr. crouched, putting the finishing touches on a homemade Valentine card.

"Yeah, sure. Just a minute more, Ernesto," the young pilot coughed weakly. The Valle de Sombros—"Valley of Shadows" in English—was a long way from home, Pasadena, California. He wondered if Ensign Bobby Roberts had been able to keep his promise they had made to each other aboard ship the night before he was shot down—a pact that if something happened to one of them the other would contact his family and give them a message...a final declaration of his love.

"Ernesto!" Neil called out in a muffled tone. "Ernesto, I need to speak to you."

"Yeah. What you want Tomás?"

"Ernesto. Can you make me a promise?" Neil's voice showed signs of strain from constant sickness.

"Sure, Tomás. No sweat." The Filipino approached from the opening of the cave.

"Good. This card and these letters," he said pointing to the metal thirty-caliber ammunition box. "These letters in here...if something happens to me today...will you make sure an American officer gets this box?" A desperate look greeted Ernesto as Neil glanced up from his prone position on the sandy floor of the cavern.

Prologue

"Yeah, sure. No sweat, Tomás." The Filipino reached down and laid his hand on the thin shoulder of the scruffy-looking, bearded American. "Nothin' gonna happen to you today, Tomás. We set trap, kill enemy, Americans come and you go home. No sweat. We gotta go. Just a minute more. I wait for Morang and then we go."

"Thanks, Ernesto. They'll make you a general someday." Both men grinned at the remark.

Neil held the picture of his wife Caroline in his hand for one last, hard look before he joined the guerrillas for the ambush laid out for the Japanese patrol closing in on their position. His tour in the Pacific should have been up. He had flown over a hundred combat missions up to the day his plane was hit over Manila. He was due to get rotated home. Getting shot down on the opening day of McArthur's promised return to the Philippines didn't allay the feeling that he had failed his wife. He had failed to keep his promise; his promise to return home by their anniversary, February 14, 1945.

Now it was one year to the day when they stood together at Los Angeles' Union Station. He could still picture Caroline in his mind, poised on the wood-plank boarding walk at Track Twelve, and watching as the outline of her figure disappeared as he perched himself on the platform of the train's last car. She was waving to him as he yelled those words out to her...words of love...words he knew would contain to her the depth of his love. They were words from their early childhood together; words from the first time he had ever told her how he really felt.

Words. He pondered their significance; " 'I love you' isn't good enough! Not for you Caroline!" A smile lit up his face as he sat there in the dim light of the cave looking at the well-worn black and white photo of her and his newborn son, Neil Jr. He wasn't there when his son was born. He wondered what his little boy looked like now. Neil returned the photo to his shirt pocket where he could reach for it easily if he wanted.

The thudding sound of artillery fire could be heard in the distance, awakening Neil to the fact that the American Army was slowly advancing towards him and his motley band of Filipino guerrilla fighters. He reckoned the fight was no more than fifty to sixty kilometers west, up the road called Zig Zag Pass. Zig Zag—the winding route which commanded access to the Bataan Peninsula from the western coast over the Zambales Mountains to Manila Bay. Neil's musings were suddenly interrupted by a voice from outside the cave.

"Tomás! Morang coming. We gotta go. Get ready!" called Rios from the mouth of the low ceiling cave.

"Morang," he thought. He loved his little Negrito rescuer and friend. "Morang...sounds like a desert," he thought with a smile as he slowly pulled himself up from his sitting position. Maybe it was "Moran," or "Morange," he wasn't sure of the spelling. He looked towards the cave opening for his teenage-fighter friend to appear. Turning, he knelt next to the ammo box and fastened the lid shut. His last Valentine and the letters were stored safely—at least securely. Now if he could just get them into Caroline's hands when the Army arrived...

The diminutive Negrito scout shuffled into the cave, out of breath. Neil watched as the tribesman carried on a conversation with with Rios in their native Tagalog. Finishing, the leather-skinned mountain native sidled over to Neil to visit with him one last time. The pilot was taking in every second of rest he could before following Rios out into the humid jungle and to the ambush location below the cave, on the small rivulet called Rio Sombro.

"Go home. O.K., Tomás? Americans come. Japs...we..." he drew his hand across his throat. The little Filipino had been Neil's personal protector and bodyguard for the three months since his downing; he had tended to the needs of his weakening and ailing American pilot friend the best he could.

"Yeah, Morang. Maybe this last fight, then I go home," Neil returned with a cough. The dank and musty air carried a sickening scent that made it hard to breathe.

"Morang fight. Tomás no. Tomás be low," he motioned with his hand indicating he wanted Neil to keep his head down when the fighting started. "Go home. O.K., Tomás?"

Neil's guerrilla fighter friend was trying to be reassuring. Neil chuckled at his effort and reached out his hand as Morang helped drag Neil up from his kneeling position, after which Neil cupped both hands over his friend's and slipped a small personal gift into them. Morang smiled broadly at the ivory-handled pocket knife. Neil just nodded his head as he looked into Morang's eyes.

"Morang! Tomás! Time. We go!" It was Rios from the mouth of the cave.

"Rios. Please... Can you tell Morang about the ammunition box...you know, if something happens to me? Could you tell him in Tagalog that an American officer must get this... Please?" An anxious expression covered Neil's face as he pointed to the green metal container.

Rios called Morang over and rapidly repeated Neil's instructions to him as Neil stooped down, picked up the ammunition box, and held it up for him to see, then pointed to the boulder behind him by the wall of the cave.

Morang listened to Rios and then turned to Neil. "No sweat, Tomás. No Jap hurt Tomás. Morang take care." With that the small diminutive fighter hurried out and down the jungle path under the instructions of Rios.

"Be careful, my friend," Neil called as he slowly rose to his feet. Rios, at the mouth of the cave, was apparently giving last minute instructions to another guerrilla who suddenly appeared.

Neil knew all he had to do was make it through this last ambush, this last skirmish and then wait—hold out with his Filipino comrades for twenty-four, perhaps forty-eight hours. The Japanese were tenacious fighters. Although they were no match for the fresh and well equipped troops of the U.S. Army Sixth Corp, they wouldn't make it easy for them either as the Americans fought their way up the mountain pass. Neil had been with the thousand-ship Armada that delivered the Allied Forces to Philippine shores just months before. He knew the disparity in strength between the invading Allies and the Japanese Army was great. It gave him hope of a quick conclusion to this part of the war. And the conclusion would take him home...home to Pasadena and his wife and son.

He slid the box behind the massive stone that covered a small opening in the wall of the cave. He was sick. Sick and tired. Just moving seemed a chore. Malaria, dysentery and lack of food had plagued him even more than the Japanese. He wished he could just lie down and sleep—sleep until the Army arrived—but he couldn't. He couldn't let his Filipino friends down. He pulled out the photo from his shirt pocket. He had to make it back. He had to hold out!

"Tomás!" came the voice of the gangly Ernesto Rios. "Tomás! We go now! Japs up on ridge. Trap is all set."

"Right. No sweat, Ernesto," Neil returned with a weak cough as he pulled out his Colt .45, checking the ammo clip and tightening the rope that held the rotting leather holster to his worn out trouser belt. Then he caught sight of the crucifix that swung out from under his tattered shirt.

"Ernesto. I need a moment...alone. Just a few seconds...a few seconds to..."

"Yeah, sure Tomás," Rios nodded. He understood.

"I be outside. But hurry!" Rios muttered as he made his way outside the cave.

Neil stood there gazing down at the crucifix that hung with his dog tags on the loose chain around his neck. He held it up to the dim light penetrating the cave's opening. He rubbed his thumb across it and felt the crown of thorns on the figurine of the cross, his mind transfixed as a dozen thoughts from his past flashed by in an instant. He pulled it down to his lips, kissed it, and fell to his knees to pray.

As he whispered, he felt a strange foreboding, still...

"Dear God, Father who art in Heaven," he began:

"Hallowed be thy name. Thy Kingdom come—thy will be done, on earth as it is in Heaven. Give us this day..." Neil stumbled on the words and coughed heavier now, *"...give us this day our daily bread."* He brought the crucifix once more to his lips and quietly, deliberately, enunciated each word, *"...and forgive us our debts, as we forgive our debtors. Lead us not into temptation..."* his voice wavered, *"but deliver us...me...from evil. For thine is the kingdom and the power and the glory, forever. Amen."*

Then, remaining on his knees, he spoke from the heart:

Prologue

"I also need to pray for some special things today. But first...first I want to thank you. I thank you this day for my life and for those I serve with. I want to go home now. Please protect me and this group of soldiers, my friends. Help me make it through this battle and get home to Caroline and my little boy. Please let me keep the promise I made to Caroline a year ago.

"I promise to seek your will the rest of my life... I just... I just want to make it back home. But God, if I don't... If I don't make it back, then your will be done. And Father, please let my wife get these letters if something happens to me...so that she will know. So she'll know how much I loved her. And please? Please..." His frail voice broke with emotion. *"If this is the last time she receives something from me, let this **last Valentine** reach her. It's all I'm asking. Amen."*

He brought his right hand to his eyes and squeezed the moisture filling them as he slowly raised himself to his feet.

"Tomás! No time to lose. We gotta go. Now!" Rios called from the mouth of the cave.

"I'm coming, Ernesto," he responded, tired—so very tired.

He squinted back into the darkness one final time to make sure the ammo box was securely stored behind the boulder. A strange penetrating warmth filled him, calmed him. Maybe God would answer his prayer. Maybe he would get back home. Or maybe, at least maybe, Caroline would get his letters and know how much he loved her. Maybe her eyes would one day look upon the last symbolic gesture of love he could offer her from the desperation of a dirty war... *The last Valentine!*

***

The Last Valentine

Captain Osamu Ito—Japanese Imperial Army. Rio Sombro February 14, 1945 01200 hours

Captain Osamu Ito peered through his binoculars to the valley floor below and the flooded wood bridge with the single column rope-crossing hanging over the river. The sand bars on both sides appeared deserted enough. He stole a glance at his watch. He couldn't wait for nightfall. He had orders to secure the bridge. His regiment would be falling back from the attacking Americans and the bridge was vital for their defensive purposes.

No sign of enemy soldiers. But...he knew that was exactly how the enemy operated. The thick jungle canopy and the high mountain ridges above the bridge offered excellent hiding for the Filipino guerrillas who had tormented his decimated company for one month now. If they were there... If they were waiting... If his men were attacked as they attempted to cross the footbridge and secure Zig Zag Pass from the far side of Rio Sombro, surely they would all die. For fifty meters surrounding the bridge there was no effective cover, and there was no other crossing.

He was tired. His men were slowly being killed off by sickness, fatigue, guerrilla snipers and ambushes. He knew he was probably being watched—even now—and there wasn't a thing he could do about it.

He had his orders. They were to take the bridge, hold the high ground overlooking the pass and fight to the death—to the last man or until reinforcements arrived. He wished he could just surrender and spare his men the fate he knew deep down inside awaited them.

His men. They huddled together in the underbrush, staring back at him with empty gazes. To Ito, hidden within their eyes were stares of resignation—death with sixty eyes; all awaiting his command, resigned to die by the oath they had taken to the Emperor! Eyes of death, he thought.

Captain Ito breathed a heavy sigh, delaying its release as if he could rid himself of the stress he was under. His thoughts went to his wife and son in Osaka. He knew it was likely only a matter of hours before he would be dead. But still Ito held onto one last hope, a wish. He reached into his pocket and felt the crucifix tucked next to the last letter he had written to his wife.

His men didn't know his secret, the secret of his faith, his Catholic faith, his conversion six years earlier when he was sent to study at a Catholic University in Los Angeles, California.

Now he would die and never do the one thing he longed to do for the three years he had suffered through war in the Philippines. It was such a simple thing, the thing he desired: to talk to a priest, hold a confession, speak to someone who understood, anyone—it didn't matter. He was alone, all alone... An anomaly, a religious renegade in command of a desperate band of thirty soldiers, with only God to hear his heartfelt pleas.

Inching away from his men into the brush, Ito withdrew the letter and the crucifix from his pocket and unwrapped the wax type paper protecting them from the constant jungle moisture. Then Osamu bowed his head and silently prayed.

When the Americans found his body, he prayed that they would find and spare the letter, pictures and the crucifix and somehow see that they were forwarded to Japanese authorities and then to his home. He knew the war had to end—someday.

Ito withdrew a fountain pen from his leather satchel and wrote in English on the back of the envelope asking that an American priest "please get my letter." Then he, Osamu Ito, would leave it up to God. God would have to see that Kyoko and his little son, Takeichi, got his letter, expressing all of his deep love and concern for them.

He gently rubbed the crucifix between his fingers, noticing the crown, the thorns and thinking about the words he had written in the letter to his wife: バラにはとげがある

She would understand the hidden meaning of the words. Kyoko would know he loved her and, though his life was taken from him, no one could kill his love! No one could take that away! No one!

"THE LAST VALENTINE—A LOVE STORY"

January 2, 1995 Pasadena—CNTV interview, Neil Thomas Jr. author, 'THE LAST VALENTINE—A LOVE STORY'

The reporter, Susan Allison from the Cable News Television Network, listened attentively, taking notes, as I finished unfolding my parent's love story to her. It had been two hours and she hardly looked up from her steady writing. The atmosphere in the room was warm and inviting. Her being there, in my mother's old home remodeled in the forties, helped make it all the more comfortable. A small fire of pine logs blazed in the stone-faced fireplace that gave the modest living room a cozy feeling.

The rain began to come down again. I looked out the front living room window and down the drive towards California Avenue. This was my second visit with Susan. The first time we met was two months earlier. I had been invited to CNTV's studios for a "get to know you" session between the producers and the author. They were committing a great deal of resources to the promotion of my book, *The Last Valentine—A Love Story.*

I thought about the last statement I made to her as I finished recounting the tragic, but inspiring end to the lives of my father, Lieutenant Neil Thomas Sr. and the Japanese Captain, Osamu Ito. The statement, "There are many kinds of love," typified my feelings at the moment. The heroic last stand of goodness and mercy played out by my father for a stricken Japanese soldier on the field of battle, fifty years earlier, was one type of love. The way I wanted to feel about a woman...the way my father had felt about my mother, was another kind of love. I quietly mused upon the whole story and how it had come to this—this meeting with CNTV's, charming Susan Allison, when the pleasant pondering was momentarily interrupted.

"Mr. Thomas?" Susan asked without looking up from her writing.

"Yes, *Ms*. Allison?" I hoped she caught on to the stressed "Ms." with my tone of voice. I wanted us to call each other by first names...become more at ease with each other.

"A statement you made. The one in which your father's letter from the war used the words, 'the rose always rises above the thorns?' And then 'even roses have thorns?' "

"Yes, Ms. Allison?" I respectfully returned.

"I take it that those phrases held deep meaning for your mother?"

"Yes. Yes, they did," I replied. "That brief statement carried a world of meaning. The secret the message alluded to was the essence of my mother's outlook on life forever after...for the last fifty years."

"Could you elaborate on it a little more for me?" she asked.

"Yes, I'd be glad to."

For the next several minutes Susan listened and wrote with a seriousness and intensity which caught me somewhat by surprise. I knew that the message of my father's *"last Valentine"* to my mother carried strong messages of hope, and love, but I didn't expect it to have the effect that it seemed to be having on CNTV's representative, Ms. Allison.

I finished my explanation of the metaphor. She continued to write, pausing for a moment and then picking it up again. I remained quiet, out of respect, as she thoughtfully pressed forward with her note-taking.

I sensed that there was more than a physically attractive cable show host in her. There was an intriguing intellectual mystery about her and it was hidden both behind her enchanting mask of beauty and in thoughts she exposed through conversation and writing.

I admit it. I couldn't seem to help it, when on my first visit with her, I developed feelings—the butterfly type a boy gets—for CNTV's top anchor and host.

Now as I observed her at work I was even more certain of those feelings. I clearly didn't want my interest in her to overshadow the love story I was relating to her, but there was a certain something. What would you call it? A recognition? Like a familiar connection that sometimes occurs between two people. When it happens a person knows there is a kinship of thought, yet neither he nor she can

put their finger on what the feeling means. That's how I f̶
though I never intended it, or even wanted it.

"Naw!" I said to myself. The thought came to me that ̲ ̲ ̲̲̲
how I felt around my deceased wife, Diana, and my mother,
Caroline Jensen Thomas. It caused a stirring inside me as I
watched Susan write. I tried to hide my growing interest. The
silence seemed filled with that familiar sensation.

My mind wandered mental passageways from my past as I sat
across from Susan. She continued writing, then abruptly turned her
attention towards me.

"Mr. Thomas? I hope you don't mind a personal question."

"No. No, I don't mind. Please, go right ahead," I motioned
towards her as I snapped out of my daydreaming state of solitude.

"I like to know a little bit of family background on the people
we feature. May I?"

"Sure. Yeah, of course. What would you like to know?"

"Children?"

"Yes. Two. Eric and Rachel. Both teenagers."

"Uh huh." She nodded and wrote with my reply. "Married?"

"Once," I stated. "She...my wife Diana...well, she passed away
two years ago. Cancer."

"Oh. I'm sorry! Please forgive me for the intrusion. I didn't
mean to..."

I cut her off. "No need to feel like you're intruding. Your question is fine. I'm over the rough part."

Susan looked around her as if she had lost something. She was
looking for words. "I feel sorry...well—you've lost two women in
your life over two years?" She seemed genuinely touched by the
thought.

I smiled weakly in reply. "Yes I did. And my children lost as
well. We lost the two greatest women in the world." I wanted her
to know that I was sincere and that relationships do mean a great
deal to me. Ms. Allison cocked her head at an angle with the kind-
est look of sympathy I had seen in awhile.

"I hope you don't mind if I jot down a few more thoughts before
finishing?" she asked tenderly.

"No, please, go right ahead. I'll just sit here and relax." She s capturing a part of me I hadn't surrendered since...since feeling Diana close to me... Since being in love.

I pondered upon it. It had been a long time since I felt the tenderness of an understanding woman in my life and I was growing accustomed to a barrier building up around me, a shell of protection. It had been two years since Diana's death. Watching her slowly waste away from cancer about killed me. I didn't want to ever go through that again—risk the grief again.

There is a loneliness that consumes the partner of the one dying. I was with Diana for eighteen months from the time she was diagnosed, yet I wasn't. It wasn't the same Diana. She was different. It was a gradual change that overcame her. Her perky, bright outlook on life was more measured. It became measured by the effects of chemo, pills, headaches, small joint pains, then general body pain. Medicine—drugs to help her cope with the pain—subdued her ever-present enthusiasm for life. Cancer kills more than *one* when you are in love.

Could anyone ever fill the void created in my life by Diana's cancer, by her death? I hadn't dated anyone but my wife for twenty-five years. I hadn't loved anyone since marrying Diana. How would I know, learn to recognize, trust my feelings for another woman?

And now? Now I was sensing a spiritual elation from having written the story about my parents' tender and lofty love affair of the wartime 1940s. Now with financial stability coming my way I knew that I could take more time with my two kids, Eric and Rachel. I even felt strong desires to return with full commitment to the faith, to God. I had temporarily abandoned my trust in divine help during the bitter months of life and death struggles faced by Diana. She, of all people, deserved a miracle, a second chance.

Diana was the heart and soul of our family and many others. She was as devoted to the care of others as my mother had been. She and my mother were as close as mother and daughter could ever be. Life was good, very good. I blamed God for not hearing me. Or, maybe I blamed myself for not praying hard enough. I'm still not sure where my anger was directed, only that I checked out of the hospital waiting room when word was given me of her death that fall day two years ago. I also checked out on checking back in with God for almost one year after.

Then all this news about my father's remains being discovered, the *last Valentine* he had meant for my mother Caroline Jensen Thomas to have, the additional letters. It all caused me to wonder at his strength of character, his belief in a God who sustained him through tremendous crisis and adversity caused by World War II. I couldn't deny, either, that my mother never wavered in her devotion to their love and to her God. It all compelled me to rethink my unhappiness, my bitterness.

I returned from my mental wandering and watched Susan as she finished writing and now spent her final moments reviewing her notes. I wondered what my feelings for her meant. A part of me didn't want to allow the feelings; another part of me shouted so loudly to do something about them I felt equally uncomfortable trying to bury them.

What could finding out a little bit about her hurt? Was she single? What kinds of things did she enjoy? Was she actually enjoying our visits...the book I had written? Where did she live? It wasn't every day a man in my position got the chance to get to know one of the most popular cable show hosts in the country. I finally decided it couldn't hurt at all. It couldn't hurt to reveal a small amount of interest in her. Everyone enjoys being noticed in a positive way. That's how I would do it.

I knew my boundaries, my limits, the wall that surrounded my inner estate and I could be dignified about showing interest. Gentlemanly. No one could take offense as long as a man was behaving like a gentleman.

She would be leaving as soon as the interview concluded. I needed to find a way to make her decide to stay longer. I wondered if the rain would make a difference. The freeways could be a mess. Maybe Susan would consider taking a later flight. Well, I'd give it my best shot...look for a reason that she could agree to so that I could get her to stay...to get to know her better.

I noticed she had stopped writing and was bent over, focusing on her yellow legal pad as if searching for a final thought. She finally looked up at me, stretched her arms and shook her hand that must have become tired from the constant note-taking.

"It's packed with love. A special kind of love," she said softly.

"There are many kinds of love," I replied in reference to a statement found in my book's "Introduction." Susan looked up at me with an inquisitive glance, but said nothing. The question was written on her face. I sensed I had touched a nerve. A sensitive button had been pushed and the fact that she was mentally reviewing something in her own life in those few seconds was apparent. She shook her head up and down as if in agreement with my statement and began to write again. I sat there in silence.

I watched her. I was deeply concerned with my parents' love story. It was the reason she was here in my mother's old home. But from the moment she entered the door I struggled to keep my mind entirely focused on the reason for her visit. Now her inquisitiveness suspended any thought I had about protecting myself behind my inner barrier-like wall. I wanted to reach out and know what was touching her, making her pause, causing a child-like look of vulnerability to come over her.

I was fascinated by her demeanor, professionalism and class. She was good at her work and it was impossible not to notice her physical attributes as well. She possessed a natural beauty, an attractiveness that all adjectives I could think of would fail to fully address. There was a distinctiveness to her character, to her intellect, that made her all the more intriguing. She dressed conservatively...tastefully. The light-colored two piece pantsuit molded comfortably to a slender figure, yet without over emphasis given to obviously flattering dimensions. Men like that. I definitely liked it. It added a mystery to her and a quality rarely found in today's world.

Her long and full-bodied black silken hair fell around her slender shoulders. Her light complexion, hazel eyes, offset by the intensity of thought noticeable in her furrowed brow, held me captive. Her full red lips parted as she wrote, as if in speaking to herself. Her high cheekbones added to an unusual glamour that accentuated the sharp lines of soft skin that noticeably narrowed to a delicate chin.

Everything about her seemed natural, yet unusual. I couldn't quite peg it. She possessed a "light look" in her countenance, a genuineness, an innocent vulnurable appearance.

I finally decided it was the same "old fashioned" goodness that my mother Caroline Jensen Thomas possessed. Susan was as comfortable, positive and unpretentious in behavior as I could ever hope to find in a woman. And her interest in the Valentine story I related was portrayed through a sensitive method of probing, asking questions.

I was definitely falling for her. I even thought my mother would highly approve of my growing personal interest in her, my fantasizing about possibilities that might exist or become created. There was much to like about this woman, Susan Allison.

I watched as she added some finishing touches to her writing. She looked up and the spell was suspended by a quick but furtive smile that brought me back from my musings to the topic at hand. I cleared my throat and quickly looked away to the coffee table that separated us. I picked up the packet of old letters and began to speak once again.

"My father, Navy Lieutenant Neil Thomas Sr., had poetry in him. You could see it in the letters he wrote to my mother during the war. And now, fifty years after being declared 'missing in action,' a military historian for the Smithsonian uncovered these." I handed the packet of letters to Susan. I had saved them for the end of the interview.

"You say these were kept safe for fifty years, in a cave in the Philippines?" she asked.

"Yes. The story surrounding these letters and this special one, here"—I handed her the *last Valentine* he had written during the war—"was uncovered by retired Army Colonel David Jackson, whose part played in the drama I briefly touched on earlier. As I had mentioned, he was engaged in the research of facts surrounding little-known battles and skirmishes of World War II. His research took him to a mountainous jungle region of Luzon Island in the Philippines. The Zambales mountain range courses through the famous Bataan Peninsula. The story relates how my father was rescued by Filipino guerrilla fighters when his Navy Hellcat fighter went down during the opening days of the American invasion.

The Last Valentine

After joining the guerrillas in the Zambales he helped to liberate a key section of road from the Japanese. The securing of the road was vital to saving time and lives of the advancing American Army."

Susan handled the thick paper with the poetry and the drawing, enclosed in a plastic sheet protector, with an almost reverent awe. "Military operations and war stories don't normally interest me, but..." She stopped in search of words. "But this story really doesn't make much sense without probing the crisis the war created by interrupting your father and mother's life. How he handled it, how she responded, his stirring account of three and one half months as an airman downed and behind enemy lines. He really lived to come back...to return to your mother from the war, didn't he?"

"Yes, he did. The conflict of war—the contrast of hate versus love—was the catalyst for my father that helped him discover tremendous secrets of a better way to live. And the single most impressive idea to come out of his letters was that his heart became more tender and sensitive as the war progressed. He was able to focus on the most important things in life...the things which *really* matter. Knowing *what really matters* and then spending time accordingly is the key to happiness, I suppose."

Susan looked at me as if she were staring right through me. Now she was the one locked in a temporary suspension of continued conversation. I wondered what she was thinking. By the look on her face and because of her furrowed brow, I surmised that her thoughts were indeed of a personal and serious nature. I waited for several anxious seconds. I noticed that she finally broke her stolid stare and then quickly looked down to pen some sort of note to remind her of something.

"Then someone kept these safe for all these years until this Colonel Jackson discovered them during his research?" She looked back towards me and carefully placed the aged Valentine back on the coffee table in front of us.

"That's correct. A villager, a former guerrilla fighter, was apparently instructed by my father to give them to the first American officer he met. Unfortunately, it took fifty years for the Negrito tribesman to meet one. That's the strange part of this love story between my father and mother."

Susan was clearly animated by the story. CNTV, the newest of the cable television giants, had created a new program called "American Diary." The program aired in weekly segments and examined human interest stories similar to other popular "tabloid" television news shows.

She put the legal pad beside her on the sofa. Reaching for the stack of love letters, she carefully opened one and read for about two minutes with intense concentration. I remained silent. Her mouth was open as she read and I thought I caught a hint of her lips moving as she studied the words. I wondered if she always took such a deep interest in the stories she researched. Or, was it that she was hungry, as hungry as I was for the secrets hidden for fifty years...secrets in the Valentine and in the letters that promised to offer enduring and powerful answers to the mystery of the bond my parents felt for each other.

Susan's deep interest attracted my attention until I became almost too comfortable trying to read her body language. My mind wandered until she caught my stare as she had before. She finished the letter and put it back into the envelope. She offered a more lingering smile than the last, which I returned as naturally as I could.

"Whew," she breathed as she straightened her back and glanced down at her watch. "You had a romantic for a father. I'd love to have some time to read all of these letters, but I've got a flight in two hours and I need to make sure I beat the traffic to LAX."

"It's raining pretty hard out there. Perhaps I could drive you later when the rain stops. I'm afraid our L.A. freeways can become dangerous. If you would like to stay longer, I could..."

She gently raised her hand to stop my pursuit. She was tactful. "I have to be back in D.C. tonight for an early-morning interview. I'd love to take you up on your offer, but I must go."

"I understand," I replied in an agreeable tone, trying not to show how disappointed I was. "Oh, about those love letters, and my father's Valentine—I thought you might like copies." I handed her a large manila envelope.

"Thank you, Mr. Thomas!" she exclaimed, as she reached across the coffee table. "Oh, I almost forgot. You mentioned yesterday, as we talked on the phone, that you now have a revised copy of your manuscript, *The Last Valentine—A Love Story*. I'm hoping to spend some productive time on my return flight to Washington. I'd enjoy reading the additions you talked about."

"Here it is," I offered, handing her the file folder of one hundred and eighty pages.

"Thank you! That's wonderful. You are really prepared, aren't you?" she smiled.

"The Boy Scout in me I guess," I returned, hoping for another smile. "I still have some final editing to do," I continued. "Just a little reworking that Phil Stanwick at Warren Publishing suggested. I've employed a writing style of moving back and forth in time as I describe my mother's reminiscing and recollections of the past. It's her devotion to the ideal of love that spans fifty years and makes the story. The story necessarily moves back and forth from 1944 to 1994. I did my best to smooth it out without diluting the impact I felt it should have. I look forward to your comments."

Susan responded courteously, "I'm sure that the periods of reflection—time travel from the perspective of your mother and father's lives—will make the story that much more interesting. I've found the love story to be very moving, and well, to have letters and this Valentine..." she held up the file folder and pointed to the stack of yellowed papers on the coffee table... "Well, to find this fifty years later is like bringing someone back from the dead...like resurrecting them. Moving, very touching." She gathered her papers and enclosed them in her briefcase.

Her use of the word "resurrected" sounded so familiar, like something my mother would say.

"I hope you'll find it as moving to read as I found it to write. I'm afraid that your questions today have piqued new thoughts and I may make some minor additions or changes. I promise to hold strictly to the facts and say precisely what happened. Thank you for your interest, time and kind comments."

"Listen, there's no need to thank me—I want to thank you. Mr. Warren loved the *Reader's Digest* condensed version of the story. And I know that our editors at Warren Publishing will look forward to your longer rewrite. I'm looking forward to seeing it in print."

I was flattered. After twenty years of freelance writing I had finally secured a major publishing contract. Mr. Bruce Warren owned CNTV and the fastest growing publishing company in the country, Warren Publishing. Then, with the advantage of his popular cable shows, like American Diary, he spotlighted the stories and their authors. With an estimated weekly audience of twenty-five million viewers, American Diary's spotlight segments virtually ensured him of a bestseller with every book he took to print. He was smart. He was calculating, market driven. I didn't regard myself the best writer in town. I was merely lucky to have a unique love story to share with the world.

"Mr. Thomas, I personally think this is ideal for our show," Susan began again. "Our producers will see this as I do, I'm sure. It's dramatic, warm and has the element of triumph over tragedy. It's definitely the type of story we are looking for. You wouldn't mind setting a schedule this month for videotaping our interviews, would you?" she asked as she closed her notes, the manuscript, and the copies of the Valentine and letters in her briefcase.

"I'd be delighted, Ms. Allison," I answered. She arose to leave and extended her hand. I couldn't help but notice: No wedding band.

"I have your two telephone numbers correct, I hope," Susan queried.

"Here, let me check." I took her day planner as she extended it to me and I flipped to the address section. "Yes, you have them. The second one is my work phone at West City High were I coach football and teach English."

"Great! I'm looking forward to this, Mr. Thomas." She smiled and realized how formal we had been. She added an extra gentle squeeze with her handshake and said, "Please forgive me if I seem so formal. Please call me Susan. May I call you Neil?"

"I was hoping you would. I would feel more comfortable." I smiled as we walked to the door. She was slowly gathering mental notes of the old home as we exited onto the covered porch.

"Neil," she paused, "this place has a feeling to it. It really grabbed me as I sat here, and then walking out, I noticed how neatly "forties-ish" your mother preserved her home. We should shoot the interviews here. You wouldn't mind, would you?"

I was surprised she had even asked. I had just assumed we would use the old house for that purpose. "Of course not. I sort of expected it," I answered.

"Good. I've got some more research to do. I want to contact Colonel Jackson and set up a schedule with him. I also want to integrate that Japanese soldier's letter found with your father's. We will try to locate the soldier's wife or surviving relatives in Kobe and Osaka, Japan. I'll need some time to follow up on that lead. Do you mind?"

Susan made sure to ask for permission to every detail involving the story. I was taken back by both her courtesy and professionalism about the entire affair. "Susan, you have my permission to do anything you need to do to tell this story as it really happened. I trust you."

"Good," she again stated as she extended me her hand a second time. "I'll get back to you next Monday."

The rain had let up to just a drizzle and she ran out to the car, holding the briefcase over her head. I noticed every step she took. She made me feel something...something I hadn't felt for a long time. Then suddenly I realized that I could at least be a gentleman and open her door. I took a few leaps and met her at the car.

"Here let me get the door for you. I guess you're anxious to get back and spend time this weekend with...your family?" I quizzed tactfully as she slid into the driver's seat of her gold Lexus rental.

"Well, if you could call Daisy, my cat, family, then yes." She smiled and offered a quick wink as she closed the car door. I just stood back with my hands in my trouser pockets and made sure she handled the long driveway backing out to California Avenue. She waved. I returned the gesture.

I stared at her as she drove off. I was glad she was handling the story and looked forward to our next meeting. There was an energy to her personality that intrigued me. As she exited the driveway and turned towards Orange Grove Avenue, my mind reflected on the memories this place, my mother's home, held for me.

Things now seemed right. Even with all the things that had

gone wrong in my life in the preceding two years, I sensed a strange assurance. It was hard to put a finger on, but an assurance, a feeling that things were heading in the right direction with me, my life, my kids, and this story, seemed to sweep through me. I'd been disappointed before. But somehow this felt different.

I thought about the woman who had just entered my life and now was gone as quickly. I felt like a kid again. "Like a kid again" was how I felt twenty-five years earlier when I met Diana. I thought about it as I stood there kicking at the gravel next to the walkway.

Here I was. Just turned fifty. Everything I had hoped for, every dream of having my own solid family ties..."the good life"...had crashed around my ears. Just when everything seemed to be coming together. Then the discovery of my father's remains and the letter was made. Just when my mother's joy was complete, mine seemed to be a full circle, from bitterness to a measure of joy—but without a woman in my life, without a mother for my kids, a wife for a companion.

I still loved Diana. Could I ever love someone else in the same way? True, I had been angry about it all. The strangest part of the anger was that I knew I should be thanking God for twenty-five wonderful years with her, yet I felt justified. Justified even though a gentle voice seemed to knock on the hardened door to my soul. It knocked and I shut it out. The voice seemed to quietly whisper to me: "It's all right. Everything's O.K. You'll be together again." I didn't want to hear that. Now I know I was wrong.

The story. I wandered around the side of the house to the porch steps and stopped. I ran my hand up the smooth stem of a growing rose bush. The barbs were tender, not prickly as they soon would be. There was the harshness to thorns but also the silky smoothness of the petals. I just smiled at the metaphor running through my mind.

Renewal. I needed a fresh start. I needed to let go of the past. I needed to recommit myself to principles of reality, truth, hope. I needed to live in the "now." Living in the past had become a trap. It caused my "today" to go by as if it didn't exist. It was a destructive course. Again, it was the circumstance surrounding the story I had just relayed to Susan Allison which caused me to finally fully understand. I realized the past could still be part of me, but today was all I had. It's all any of us have, I suppose.

With all of this new understanding, an emptiness still seemed to plague me, fill me, even though I had this bestseller on my hands. I thought again about my excitement at meeting Susan. I wanted something—a relationship to fill the void. But I also longed for something more. And I knew what that something was. I knew that if I made the commitment to find out, to open up to God—the former source of my strength—I must forever remain committed.

Looking up into the sky I saw the clouds had parted and the last rays of sunlight illuminated the western horizon. Did He care? If there was a God, then why? If God was there, why did I feel so alone? I had to find a way to get over my feelings of abandonment.

Susan. She possessed that rare ability to make people feel good. It would certainly be a step in the right direction if...

Would she even take a second look at me after the story was taped and aired? The thought ran through me that this was just her. She made everyone she talked to feel good. I admired that—but dared I indulge in wishful thinking?

At fifty, some had said I appeared more like forty. I worked out daily with my high school teams. I ate right and felt young. Age was a chronological thing to me. "You're as young as you feel," they say, and I felt young. I wondered if Susan Allison saw me that way.

I wandered back around to the front yard, deep in thought. Susan was probably thirty, maybe thirty-five. Could she be interested in an old guy? Ah, well, I'd better let it go, I thought. I needed to get back to my writing. Writing was difficult enough even when I remained focused.

It was a pleasant evening to be outside. With the clearing clouds the air was crisp and clean smelling. The roses would bloom soon. The garden my parents had planted together was famous even by Pasadena standards. My mother had tended it like it was a memorial. I guess it was in a way. It seemed to be both a memorial to my father, who planted the first rose bush, and to their love, that never died.

The Last Valentine—A Love Story

Romance. Their love was more than that. It was a devotion, a sacred duty to keep a promise. The words on one of his last letters to my mother came back to me. I mused upon the words as I gathered in all of the memories that were caused by staring at the garden she had loved so much: *"The rose always blossoms above the thorns. So does true love."*

They were poignant words. Hard words for me now. But, I felt as though I had always known him. Maybe writing this story would perform the healing miracle I hoped for—healing from the sorrow and the wounds caused by my wife's death. My lips parted in a couched smile, more a grimace really, as I pondered on it all and turned back into the quiet of my mother's memory ridden home.

The room was still. It smelled like her. There was a fragrance to her life. I missed her. "Caroline Jensen Thomas," I thought, "I'll miss you, Mom." Her sudden passing away the year before had not ended the drama their special fifty-year romance had become. Death completed it, sealed it, finished it. She finished a journey in love. How many people end life like that, I would never know. But, one thing was certain: To know her was to become a believer in dreams, in hope, and in love.

Faith. I considered my mother's. Her youthful energy and excitement for life seemed renewed daily because of it. She had always possessed a passion for life, for teaching the school children for forty years, and for her roses. I thought she could never die. Not with her vitality, her beliefs, her faith. Her faith in God—it was personified in her conduct, how she treated others. Because of her I never really doubted that there was a God. But I wondered if he knew me, and if he cared about me.

I grew up knowing my mother cared. She was a living angel. I watched her give cheerfully all her life as if she had this secret, a secret which gave her the gift of a positive nature. Others noticed. They would ask how she did it all. Her service at church, to youth groups, at school, raising a boy on her own.

She would smile, and if the person asking was at our home she would cut a long-stem rose and give it to him. Her lecture followed but was always kind, brief, to the point. Sometimes a story about enduring hardships, trials and always....always her *"Valentine Story."*

Her *"Valentine Story"* was something I grew up believing in. She would tell a tale of the very first "Valentine" ever given, and the origins of the holiday named for "Saint Valentine." Maybe that's part of the reason I was blessed with such a rich marriage to Diana. I believed in the secrets of Saint Valentine as my mother would recount them. I employed those secrets then. Maybe, because I had it so good—a good marriage—I wasn't ready for fate to interrupt my well-laid-out plans. I didn't want challenges. I didn't want to lose the love Diana and I had built. I guess it's only natural to become suddenly angry when a loss like that comes.

But then, after the discovery of my father's remains and his *"last Valentine"* to my mother, I understood her better, more fully. Her character. Her graciousness. She had lost a spouse and for fifty years endured the loneliness, the challenges. She never really lost her steadfast hope, or her focus on what really mattered.

Yes, I did see more clearly. She was a wonderful guiding light in my life. She was a strength to me, right up to the delivery of the news by the Department of the Navy that my father—his remains— and his personal effects had been found.

It was then I noticed a change—a change in my mother. Gradual at first, it started to affect the way she handled everyday things. Her interest in life seemed to be fading like autumn leaves. I had never seen less than a vibrant, strong woman. Although she was "growing old," I never thought she would actually "get old." She started to miss days of taking care of the flower garden. When the rose petals started to fall, it hit me. She was dying inside. She missed my father and she desperately needed him. Though time inflicted its unkindness on her physical body, she still held the thoughts of him close. And, her spirit inside was young again—as young and as sweet as their love once had been.

My mother. With the exception of her three months' bad health near the end of her life, I was sure she could live to be a hundred years old. Three heart attacks nearly took her from us. Now I know she had a time appointed, a date with death. I guess that sums up the dramatic element to a story that illuminated her final days.

The Last Valentine—A Love Story

I mused upon the scene of my mother reading the fifty-year-old love letters the Navy had delivered. She held the special war-worn Valentine card to her breast. She wouldn't eat. She rarely left the sacred pages written in my father's hand. She had lived for others her entire life. Now, as I recall, all she wanted in those last few days of her life was a small piece of the past, of love...just for herself. She wasn't asking too much. She had been an exceptionally loyal and wonderful woman.

It would take an exceptional woman for me to ever feel deep love again. Someone like my mother. Someone like Diana would be fine, too, but it just needed to be someone with hopes, dreams, or belief in the never-ending nature of love—my mother's *"Valentine Story"* type of love.

I wondered about Susan again. Perhaps there was more to the comfortable feeling I possessed being around her. Perhaps...

The story. I walked over to the old sofa covered by the quilted Afghan that seemed made for it. I sat there pondering upon the events of the last year. It really was something that the world desperately needed. I felt that the secrets to a love such as theirs should not be lost. If this story came out as my parents had written in letters, and as relayed to me by my mother, then they wouldn't be.

I pulled out my writing pad and continued the rewrite I had almost finished. The interview with Susan allowed me to review the details with a freshness which stirred new thoughts for the book deep inside of me. I could feel the words coming together rapidly. Experienced writers call the feeling "inspired." It happens when the pen and ink can't keep up with the mind and heart.

I examined all of my mother's reminiscings, especially those which occurred each year on her wedding anniversary, February fourteenth. Her annual pilgrimage was like a step back in time for her. It had a magic that allowed her to hold him once again, even if briefly, as she savored the memories. The past became revisited there, at the special place.

The special place? Union Station, the old downtown train depot in Los Angeles. It was there she would spend the entire Valentine's Day each year. It was there they touched for the last time. And now, it seemed right that she would hold the *last Valentine* in her hand in that place where she took her last mortal breath.

It was as if the hand of destiny reached out and linked their hands once again, that last day of her life, February 14, 1994. She went there to find him. Did she? I have a note that expresses her last words...final words written in her shaky cursive hand as she sat there in her daydreaming solitude. Were the words that described what she was seeing in her final moment a fantasy or were they real?

At best her life ended exactly as she wrote it. At worst her's is a very special Valentine's Day story.

The silence seemed to sing with thoughts. My pen flowed freely until I had exhausted all of them. After a couple of hours, I reviewed the first chapter for one final edit.

There was nothing grandiose, really, about their relationship in the world's way of looking at things. It was just a simple, never-ending bond between two people who cherished one another more than life itself. What could be more simple than that?

That afternoon, aboard American Airlines flight 1530

"There are many kinds of love." The words seemed to haunt her. Words from the author of *The Last Valentine—A Love Story*. It was 5:30 p.m. as Susan settled into her firstclass seat aboard American Airlines flight 1530 to Washington National Airport. She was anxious to look over the latest copy of Neil's manuscript. She felt drawn to the story somehow. She liked the author as well, she decided. She hoped it hadn't shown too much. He was soft-spoken and had a command of the language that impressed her. He was as much a romantic as his father, she thought.

He was tall, maybe six feet, physically strong looking, and had a toothy smile she found charming. His light auburn hair, combed back with light streaks of gray running through it, waved along the sides. His blue eyes seemed to sparkle along with his smile and his facial features exhibited strength. He looked and acted dignified, in control, manly. And there was something else. He possessed an inner integrity, a sense of peace. Yes! That would describe him well.

"No!" she thought. The last thing in the world she needed right now was to fall in love with anyone. She had done that once before and it still hurt. Even though her ex-husband, Rick, had made and broken promises, even though she could lay most of the blame for a failed marriage at his door, still...she was not without fault, not without culpability. And if she failed once, it could happen again. She wouldn't let her heart or peace of mind be lost on someone again!

All the years of hope. All the years of patience. All the years of yearning to have her dream of children, a happy home, a full life, were blown apart by Rick leaving her for someone else. Her faith and trust and hopes had been shattered. Still, she could have done better, kept him more interested in her. Maybe...

She was reminded of a powerful thought which had occurred to her earlier in the day. It had come unexpectedly while listening to Neil reply about the role of war that played such a heavy part in the love and devotion his parents developed for each other. She remembered having felt struck by it. The thought's sudden impact was so forceful that she remembered stopping and just momentarily staring into Neil's face. But she was thinking about the words, not about him.

The words. What were they? She had written them down. Opening her briefcase, she found the yellow pad and leafed through the pages. Finding the quickly scribbled note, she leaned back to ponder upon the words...

"And the single most impressive idea to come out of his letters was that his heart became more tender and sensitive as the war progressed. He was able to focus on the most important things in life...the *things which matter most...*"

Then Neil had said something that hit her squarely between the eyes—in a personal way. *"Knowing what really matters is the key to happiness."* Neil's father had written it long ago. How, why, was he, Neil's father, able to discover the key to happiness? Looking back at her notes she saw the words...

The Last Valentine

"The conflict of war—the contrast of hate versus love—was the catalyst that helped him discover 'secrets' of a better way to live."

"Secrets" of a better way to live? Conflict? Through conflict? She had always dismissed the torture of conflict as an unnecessary annoyance. Things should flow along smoothly for happiness to be achieved, she had thought.

She thought about a statement made by a motivational speaker she interviewed the previous month. His book was just another on *"How to Achieve Success Through..."* He had stated, "Happiness is found all along the way, in the journey and not at the end of the road."

Hyperbole. She had considered the statement pure hype. Just another high-paid speaker living in "la-la land," she had considered. She had even thought, "He's probably never really been tested. Words come easy..."

But this story. It was pure and undiluted in its simple "boy meets girl, girl and boy fall in love, get married, war takes boy away" turns and twists of fate. Irony, conflicts, yes...but...

She wondered about *"the things which mattered most"* in her own life. Then she looked down at her notes again. Neil's statement. *"Knowing what really matters is the key to happiness."*

She had been bitter because of the conflicts in her life and at times wondered why love couldn't just continue unabated, without all the snares, traps, roadblocks—"conflicts."

Then, as Neil was speaking, something clicked inside her mind. It was as if a light, a powerful spotlight, like a neon billboard flashing in her mind was speaking to her, for her, saying:

"Conflict is the necessary experience in life. Because of it we rise or fall, but without it we never rise at all."

She had quickly written those few, almost poetic words down. She had no idea where they came from, only that they were there. She appreciated the impact of choice, succinct statements. Instinctively, she had culled a good line for later use on a broadcast. But it was more than just a "good line."

Was Caroline and her Navy pilot husband's love increased,

intensified, because of World War II's tragic call? Why didn't Caroline of *The Last Valentine* story become angry and embittered? Why didn't Lieutenant Neil Thomas die with words of hate for his enemy instead of those which were reportedly his last?

"What really mattered most?" The thought repeated itself over and over in her mind, for minutes it seemed, as she sat pondering on the interview with Neil Thomas Jr. She was in search of something. Something more than her big paycheck or fame. She wanted to answer *"what really mattered most"* in her *own* life. She thought about the man she had met with that morning. How, by the afternoon, she had felt something...something almost tangible about the scene. The place where they sat, a sense of love—strange as it may sound but there came a feeling to her that Caroline was right there in the room. It gave her a rush of comforting chills just recalling it.

Then there was something about this Neil Thomas Jr. The feeling of excitement that ran through her—was it just infatuation? Yet, this man had a familiar something about him. He was kind, gentlemanly, soft spoken, and his looks accentuated the other positive qualities she sensed. But there was something else. That familiar feeling which she sensed in the old home, a serenity which seemed to surround their interview. A man that seemed at peace, as if he possessed a secret. Could it be part of the answer to the question of what "really mattered most?" She weighed it.

Another of Neil's statements came to her again: *"There are many kinds of love."* She mused on the simplicity of the phrase... the complexity of the implications.

She remembered noticing something else during the interview. It was a picture of Christ over the fireplace mantle. Then down on the end table next to the sofa on her right was what appeared to be a family Bible. She had glanced to the opposite end table and noticed another book. It was a thick leather-bound volume. She moved down the sofa and picked it up. Neil had left the room for a minute to get some pictures he wanted to show her. It was a book of poetry: *One Hundred and One Classic Poems.* Caroline was a romantic and deeply religious.

The Last Valentine

Suddenly things began to make sense. The feeling. It was always the same around romantics; they seemed possessed of strong convictions and faith in a divine being—God—and she liked it. Her aide, Kathy Clark, was full of an almost child-like zeal, a faith; not just in her views but in her daily living. She could trust Kathy. Never pushy. She just lived her talk. Caroline Thomas obviously was cut from the same cloth. If Neil Thomas was like his mother had been, then maybe she could trust him... Maybe she could let her guard down a bit.

She sensed he had taken an interest in her. "Be careful, Susan." It was like an inner voice putting up a wall for her whenever she sensed a man might be drawn to her. She had to be careful. It would only add more challenges to her life...and she had been through it before. She decided to control her feelings. She could like him and be guarded at the same time. She had her work, her career to consider.

She stopped and pondered on her successes. They weren't that convincing. Her life was a mixture of business balanced by a sense of personal failure. Success, because she earned the position of top editorial director and anchor for an award winning television show, American Diary. But that didn't mitigate the feeling of failure. She had failed to realize her childhood dream. The cozy home with a white picket fence...the children gathered around her, and the security of a lasting love. It eluded her.

"What mattered most." The thought came on stronger still. So many intriguing ideas came to her from her morning interview. She had sought to convince herself that her successes were all that really mattered. "Perhaps," she thought, "romance was meant for others. Still..."

The plane had taken off, and the "fasten your seat belt" light went off. She pulled a blanket and pillow out of the overhead compartment and turned on the reading light. Reaching into her briefcase, she pulled out the folder with the manuscript. *The Last Valentine—A Love Story.* She smiled as she looked at his name on the cover page.

THE
LAST VALENTINE
A LOVE STORY

by

NEIL THOMAS JR.

Susan turned the page and read the introduction:

INTRODUCTION

I will start from the beginning with a premise for a rare but true love story. The premise is this:

All love stories that are weighted with tragedy possess equivalent hope for the opposite—triumph. As a pendulum may swing high in one direction, the laws of nature dictate that it must swing with equal force in the opposite. So it is with love. Love lost may yet be found, and love gained may yet experience loss.

But what are we to do? Should we never risk to grab hold of love when it is presented before us? Tennyson the poet said it best:

Tis better to have loved and lost, than to never have loved at all.

A more poignant love story could not be told than one in which a hunger, a need, a desire is so strong that the bond of love can never be broken...not even by death.

So, to the reader I make this promise: I have written out of love and have followed this story from the perspectives of those who participated in it. By telling it as it was passed along to me through conversation, by reading my father's lost letters and the contents of his *last Valentine,* I offer you the dreams of one who first loved, long ago, and lost, but then...triumphed in the end.

As you step back in time with Caroline, not once, but several times, gaze at the world through *her* eyes. From the viewpoint of an aging woman who once risked to love, to hope and to dream.

There are many kinds of love. Read between the lines and enjoy the journey. There are secrets waiting for you there. And, as you do, with the poet Moore say:

Oh! There is nothing half so sweet
in life,
As love's young dream!

***

The Last Valentine—A Love Story

Reading the words of Tennyson and then the poem by Moore, Susan wondered if Neil really believed them or if he had inserted them because they sounded so good. She wanted to believe...to reawaken dreams she had lost and also to taste the love the author promised.

Putting her seat in a reclined position, she turned to the first page of Chapter One. "Roses have thorns..." she read.

CHAPTER ONE

THE PILGRIMAGE

"Roses have thorns." Words. Final words from the last letter my mother Caroline received from my father Lieutenant Neil Thomas' battle station, aboard an aircraft carrier in the Pacific during World War II. A strange way to reassure her. My mother understood the words, though. She couldn't have known it then, but they would be the last words she would hear from him for fifty years...until the *last Valentine*.

It all ended in a strange way. Some would call it tragic. It was at worst tragic, and at best the expression of a beauty rarely found, even in the most inspired and elevating art or music. The ending, surprising and unexpected, was melodious...like a crescendo rather than a diminuendo. But then surprise endings can be the happiest endings of all.

***

February 14, 1994—Union Station, Los Angeles,

The last time she saw him was February 14, 1944. He was home on leave before shipping out to the fighting raging in the Pacific. To her, he epitomized the word "handsome." Especially in his Navy pilot dress uniform, with his jet black hair combed in that carelessly meticulous Clark Gable sort of way. A perfect toothy smile complemented the blue eyes that always held her as easily as his muscular arms. But, with all her physical attraction for Neil, what drew her the most to him was his tenderness towards her, his thoughtfulness, and his wit. He made her smile through gloom and he laughed at his own mistakes and bad luck. "Bad luck can't be all bad," she could hear him say, "since I've never really had any luck at all. You can't have something *bad*, if you've never had it."

She loved his ready comeback to problems and how he worked

at something until it worked *for* him. She felt loved, not only for all the little things he did for her, but because he made her feel wanted and needed.

It wasn't just this place, the old train station, that made the flood of memories return, but it was that they touched for the last time here, as the train pulled away. And touching him was something the like of which she had never experienced since. When he held her, she felt safe and the world seemed right. She knew life would be good, and she felt complete.

She imagined she could see him there, just as it was then, waving to her as he boarded the train, in the now almost deserted Union Station.

She clutched his *last Valentine* in her hand as she walked through the glass doors and into the massive lobby of the old depot on Alameda Street. The station was cathedral-like, a California Spanish colonial architecture with an old Catholic "mission" flavor to it. The old missions had been built by Catholic priests in the late seventeen and early eighteen hundreds, dotting the California coast. Their influence was felt in much of the building which had gone on in Southern California for over fifty years now. It felt like home to her.

Union Station was brand new then, fifty years ago, when she entered these same doors to send her husband off to war. It seemed even larger now, now that it was so empty... Now that the crowds had diminished... Now that so few take trains to their final destinations. She liked it though. It was as if her special place was "theirs," hers and Neil's, and that made it even more special to her now...this place that seemed frozen in time.

She slowly shuffled past the photo gallery that occupied the lower walls of the fifty-foot-high lobby with its massive beams and huge candelabra lights. The subdued glow from the overhead circular lighting mixed with the suffusion of light from the outside. The shafts of light made the high, polished mosaic tile floor glisten, encouraging visitors to linger at the entrance and take in the photographs.

The old photos, encased in glass-covered frames, displayed a history of the years of construction, especially the war years when

The Last Valentine

Union Station was at its peak capacity for travelers—particularly soldiers embarking on their journeys into the unknown.

She stopped, as she always did, at the final photo on the north wall, by the old ticketing booth area, now closed. There it was. Mobs of soldiers, sailors and marines, and their girls, heading out to gates G and H and the tunnel that led to track Number Twelve. There she was, if one looked at the photo hard enough. Caroline, age twenty-three and Neil at twenty-five. He was turned to one side looking down at her. They were packed so tightly with other servicemen all around that they could hardly move.

A photographer had captured a moment she would relive over and over again. She ached for him as she reached her aged hand out to gently caress the old glass-covered photo, as if in touching it she could erase the fifty years that separated them.

But she was happy. He would come today—she knew he would. She had seen the swallow in the window the day before, and now she had the *last Valentine*. The yellow roses he had planted all those years before had survived. They bloomed early, just like they did when he went away on their wedding anniversary, the 14th of February in 1944. It was a sign to her that he hadn't forgotten, that he would come for her, and she dreamed of him. Even if it all were just a dream, she would be happy to be so deluded.

She stared at the photo with one last, hard look. She was remembering how heart-rending it had been to finally say "goodbye." She hadn't made it easy for Neil. He tried to leave her gently, not once, but several times with tender body language. She remembered feeling like an emotional wreck. As she thought back to that day; she thought she could hear his voice again. She closed her eyes, if only for a second, to savor the memory, and in it pretend that she was touching him. Mentally, she was there again, revisiting the past, saying goodbye, February 14, 1944.

The Pilgrimage

February 14, 1944—Union Station, Los Angeles, California

"Come on honey. I know it's hard. It's hard for me too," Neil said as he tenderly held her tearful face between his hands. By sheer fate it was February 14th, 1944, and their wedding anniversary. Departing for the war on that day only made it more difficult.

Caroline tried to look happy for him. It was no use. "I don't want you to go. I don't care about duty. I'm afraid, Neil. Hold me," she begged as they held tight to each other.

The attendant was opening the metal doors at gates G and H leading into the tunnel. "Announcing first boarding call for Union Pacific Number 71 leaving at track Number Twelve. Number 71 departing for San Francisco in thirty minutes. Non-passengers may accompany ticketed passengers to the tracks." The attendant repeated the announcement two more times.

"Come on, honey, let's go into the tunnel," he said in a quiet, gentle voice. She held onto his arm and pressed herself up against him with a grip that he knew represented fear. Neil felt his heart would break. He couldn't do anything for her. He struggled to find the words to cheer her up. He had to be strong for her. If she only knew how hard it was for him to remain stoic—outwardly calm—in control.

She was ordinarily a strong person...an independent person. But then shipping out for war was not an ordinary thing, and whatever he did affected her. He knew that she wasn't feeling well with the pregnancy. Maybe that had something to do with it... But there was something else. A deep, gnawing, uneasy feeling centered in the pit of his stomach. He knew she felt it too.

He was a man, and he was surrounded by hundreds of other servicemen who must act like men. He didn't want to be cavalier, but the final thing he could do for her would be to summon his strength to buoy her up.

They walked slowly along with others through the tunnel, passing several boarding ramps to the other tracks. There were girlfriends and their uniformed boyfriends, husbands, maybe, and the place was overflowing with emotions. There were oceans of heartache, the kind found when called upon to endure a future replete with uncertainty.

"The tunnel of love," he whispered in her ear after what seemed like a long silence. He had his arm around her slender waist and, stopping her with a grasp, looked down at her. She raised her sad brown eyes to him and he repeated what he had just said as he pointed to several couples along the walls, kissing. "The tunnel of love," he breathed once again. This time he pulled her to him in a long, hard embrace and allowed her to join him in all of the inner-most feelings they had for each other.

"I love you," she said, pressing her head against his chest.

"I love you, too," he returned in a shallow voice. "Let's go," he gently urged as he took her hand and stood erect, mustering the strength to fight back the moisture welling softly in the corners of his eyes.

At the base of the long boarding ramp, Caroline stopped abrupt-ly. She felt as if her legs were tied to weights fastened to the floor.

"What's wrong, sweetheart?" he asked, knowing full well what it was. "Are you afraid I can't fly good enough to come back to you?"

"You can fly good enough, Neil," she replied, fighting back the tears. She struggled to speak. She opened her mouth but the words were weakly straining through her lips. Almost inaudible, the throaty sound finally offered, "I'm trying, I'm really trying...it's just that...it's just that, I'm afraid that..." She was gasping against the heavy sighs in her breath.

He held her to him at the foot of the concrete ramp as other peo-ple passed by. She struggled to gain some control and finally released her feelings. "I'm afraid if we leave this tunnel, we'll leave it for the last time. I'm afraid I won't see you coming back through it to get me." She looked up at him with imploring eyes, eyes that looked for his assurance, eyes that searched every part of him...to tell her that her feelings were all wrong.

"I know," he said quietly as he tried to imprint every detail, every feature of his beautiful young wife into his memory. There came a deep gnawing feeling. It came stronger still. These were frantic last seconds of time together. It caused his jaw to clench tight and his hands to squeeze shut into hard fists as he sought for composure. "I've got to be strong! Be strong for her!" he commanded himself silently. As he looked into her eyes, the dam broke which held back the tenderness. Suddenly he lost control.

Tears came now, and he didn't fight them. To her, this proved that he understood. He needed her, too. She threw her arms around his neck and held him tighter than she ever had before.

"We've got to go, Caroline." His voice was soft and low as he tenderly pulled back and reached for her hand.

"I know," she said as she gripped his hand and slowly walked up the ramp with him.

CHAPTER TWO

"THE VALENTINE STORY"

Union Station lobby—The present - February 14, 1994

"Excuse me madam, are we intruding?" asked the young man in a courteous tone with a distinctively British accent. "May we see these World War II photos with you?"

The old woman came to herself, standing in front of the 1944 photo display and realized she had been daydreaming. She drew her hand back from caressing the glass-covered images. Others had come to view the historic gallery. She flushed with embarrassment.

"Oh no...no, you are not intruding at all. Please, come ahead. I was just remembering...just remembering..." Caroline's voice trailed off as she mustered a smile and patted the young man on the arm.

She began to walk again, forward to the waiting area and the high-backed wooden benches. They were the same well-cared-for leather seats. The whole place was as it was then. People dressed differently in 1994, but the place never changed.

She found the seat and the location where they waited for his boarding call on that long-ago Valentine's Day. She slowly turned and sat down in the brown leather chair that was stiffly rigid and high in the back. She laid her arms on the solid oak armrests that curled at the ends so one could hold onto the seat comfortably. She gazed above her. The same high ceiling dressed in massive beams, stained to appear dark oak in color, stared back down at her. The exquisitely finished wood-paneled walls surrounded her. The shining tile floors welcomed her. Her bench-like chair, "their chair," was facing the gates.

If she sat there—she fantasized—surely he would recognize her. Although she knew she was an old woman now, Neil would come through gate G or H and find her there.

As she sat there, she wondered: "Fifty years...where did it go?"

The Valentine Story

The old woman sighed as she rested her tired body in the cushioned seat.

She looked down at the card, still clutched tightly in her hand. "His *last Valentine*...in time for our anniversary," she mused. Caroline now finally knew the truth about him, what happened to him during the war.

Looking down at the handmade fifty-year-old Valentine caused her to think back. She thought about the meaning of Valentine's Day. Each February fourteenth for forty years she had taught her school children about the lover's holiday. Gazing up at the high, darkly stained wooden ceiling, she pictured herself standing in front of her fourth grade class at Woodland Elementary and telling them the Valentine story.

***

"Class, your attention please. Who can tell me what we are celebrating today?" The entire classroom of children would raise their hands.

"It's Valentine's Day," they would respond in a happy chorus.

"That's right, children. And I want to tell you who Valentine was. There once was a man who, long ago, died for his beliefs. His name was Saint Valentine. The legend goes that Saint Valentine was a prisoner of an evil king because of his belief in God. He would not deny it," she told her pupils. "Then God sent a miracle," she followed.

"Saint Valentine had a great love for his wife and he wanted to let her know one last time. He prayed to find a way to tell her. Then, a strange thing happened. A certain pigeon appeared at the prison window. It was one of the pigeons he recognized from his home. He and his children loved to feed the birds and this was a special one that would eat right out of his hand. It brought him comfort to have his little friend there with him and he shared his food every day with the white and black-spotted pigeon. He wondered about his problem as he fed the bird some scraps of his prison food.

"There was also a rose bush that grew near to the prison window and it had one beautiful red rose on it. It was close enough to touch and to smell its fragrance. It reminded him of the love he felt for his wife as he would feed the pigeon and contemplate upon its beauty. He wondered how he might get a message to his wife as he looked at the rose. He didn't have any paper or pen to write the message with. Then an idea came to him. He could share the rose with his wife! He reached out and gently plucked the rose from the stem. The thorns caused his fingers to bleed, but he didn't care.

"He looked around in his prison cell for something hard and pointed and he found a piece of straw from the pile the guards gave him to sleep on. He decided to write the words about his love for his wife on each petal of the rose and then give it to the pigeon. He hoped the bird would take the petals and fly away to his house. Maybe his children would find the petals or maybe even his wife would find them. He had to take a chance. He decided to place his message on the rose so that his wife would have it and know that he loved her.

"He used the sharp end of the piece of straw and began to write the words, 'I love you,' pressing the words out on the petals of the rose. He sent the message, one petal at a time, by way of the pigeon that would land on the window ledge each day. The pigeon would take the rose petal from his hand and quickly fly away. It continued to do the same thing every day until all of the petals were gone.

"Then came the appointed day for his execution. Again, the King's emissaries asked him if he would renounce his beliefs in God. He would not do it. The guards took Saint Valentine and cut off his head. He had been true and faithful: true to his love for his wife; true to his love for his God. *True love* demands a price be paid, an effort made."

The children would always gasp at the part about Saint Valentine's execution, but one brave little soul would always seem to ask, "Do I have to have my head cut off if I love like Mr. Valentine?"

Caroline would chuckle at the query and respond, "Oh no, dear! But I tell you this story, children, so that you see the importance of trying, of making an effort for love. It is easy to *say* you love someone. It is sometimes not so easy *doing* it."

The Valentine Story

"Oh," the little one asking the question would agree in a way that let her know the children couldn't possibly fully understand the implications of loving, making commitments, the efforts involved, yet... Yet, she was determined to instill in them *values*. Love did not come cheaply. Not *true love*.

She would continue: "The prison windows had great iron bars to keep the prisoners in, but the bars did not keep Saint Valentine from sending his love out. Saint Valentine was free!" Invariably the classroom of children would furrow their brows and gaze at her strangely because of the puzzling paradox in her words.

Then the one, brave, inquisitive child would again raise his or her little hand and ask, "If there were bars on the windows, and he was in prison, then how was he free?"

"Because when you love," Caroline would answer, "and when you tell someone you love them, and then when you believe in something as strongly as Saint Valentine did, no one can lock away your love. The jailer can imprison you, but not your *feelings*. You must always keep them safe. Safe, right here," and she would point to the center of her chest.

"No matter what bad things happen to a person, if they feel love for someone and believe in something, then they too are free. The Valentine Card is the symbol of love for others and the rose is the symbol of hope and of sharing that love. When you see a rose, think about how Saint Valentine loved his wife and family so very much. And as you grow, look for someone you can love in the same way. And then, every rose will remind you of your special love. It's one reason your daddies may give a rose to your mommies along with a Valentine Card."

Again the children would appear a little bewildered, but just as surely, one would also ask, "Did you get a rose from your husband, Mrs. Thomas?"

"Oh yes," she would answer. "Yes...yes I did, a very long time ago. And I knew he loved me then and I still believe he loves me now."

***

The Last Valentine

Returning her attention to the old train station waiting area, Caroline fumbled with the tattered Valentine card in her hand. The memories were strong. Forty years of teaching. It was fifty years ago when she said goodbye to Neil here. She believed in the Valentine story she had taught each of those forty years to her school children. She also believed in the power of the rose...and the promise of her faith. Once she only had the symbol of love...a flower. Now she had the promise of eternal love...

But she was still just a girl inside, still longing to be held, still loving him. It didn't matter anymore. Just as long as he came back for her. Maybe some would say or think she was just a silly old woman for living in the past. But she didn't feel that way. If she felt better there, with him in the past, what was silly or wrong with that?

She felt the mascara washing away. The mascara so fastidiously applied in that same girlish hope that somehow, someway, she would see him there, walking, then running towards her. Maybe she could awake and find that the loneliness from missing him had been a long, bad dream. Maybe he would be running down the walkway toward her.

It was a dramatic fantasy that she came each year to play out in her vain hope it could become real. Caroline knew that she was a dreamer. She had to be—she had to hold on to hope. Romance, after all, was for dreamers.

She bent her head forward to reach for the black cloth purse she had dropped to the floor beside the chair. Reaching inside, she removed a handkerchief, the same one he had given her on the day he departed. It came with her every year, on the pilgrimage. It was something his hands had touched and she sought for it in comfort, for her eyes and also her lips.

She rested her aging head against the cane positioned between her legs. She looked down at the flower-patterned dress and the square-toed shoes and it seemed like 1944 once more. With a deep sigh and a recomposed look on her face, she straightened up and then leaned back with her head against the corner of the padded leather-seat and softly whispered as she closed her eyes: "I'm here darling. I'm here where I said I would be waiting."

The Valentine Story

Worn out from the day's bus trip from Pasadena to the Los Angeles train station, she nestled back, using her shawl as a pillow and the corner of the bench to rest her head. Her long silver hair was put up neatly in a bun. It was just the way he liked it, the way it was that day when they last held each other...fifty Valentine Days before.

To dream asleep or awake...it didn't matter. Some might consider it overly sentimental. But she was keeping a promise. She came there to think about him, to dream about him, and for one day, their wedding anniversary, she was, as if transformed into a girl—back in time to that day, February 14, 1944.

CHAPTER THREE

"GOODBYE"

February 14, 1944 - Union Station, Los Angeles

The conductor called for final boarding. Soldiers streamed by Caroline and Neil as they struggled to say their last goodbye.

"Caroline, I need you to be brave for me, O.K? Come on baby, O.K?" Neil looked down at her as they stood near the steps to the last car on the train. They clung to one another so long that Neil found it imperative to board now.

She was wearing the red and white flowered dress that clung just the way he liked it. "You are such a doll," he said to her with a nibble on her ear and a little growl that usually made her laugh. He held her by the waist, waiting for a smile.

"Come on now," he prodded softly as he lifted her chin up with his hand. "How could a guy get so lucky?" He kissed her on the forehead, wearing his smile she found so irresistible, even though she was determined not to return one.

Staring into his eyes, she put her arms around his neck. "I thought you didn't believe in luck," she said with a searching look.

"I said that I didn't believe in bad luck when you didn't have any luck at all. That only applies to marbles, crap shoots and horse shoes. You are my luck, and I've felt that way since the first time you kissed me back at Adams School. Remember?"

She was smiling through the tears. He pulled out a handker-chief. "I almost forgot, I bought this over at Olvera Street today and meant to give it to you. You got a minor in Spanish at Pasadena City College. Look. Look right here. What does this word written in red thread mean?"

"Felicidades. Felicidades means...it means 'happiness to you,'" Caroline replied begrudgingly.

"See, what did I tell you. It's a sign of good luck. And look. It's got the little flower patterns in the corners. Cute, huh?"

"Just like you," she returned with struggling attempts to speak, to be happy.

"That's my girl, Caroline."

The conductor's voice sounded, "All aboard!"

Neil only had a second left. The crowd pulsed with the final goodbyes as the train's engines noisily built for departure.

He raised his voice above the noise, "I've loved you since Adams School, through the years of growing up in Eagle Rock, through all the good times, and I now can't remember any bad. I think I've just always loved you!" He scooped her up into his arms as they melted into one final kiss and embrace.

He pulled back to face her and grabbed the carry-on bag he had dropped on the ground beside him.

As he pulled away, he let go of her weakened grasp and said, "No matter what happens Caroline, I promise before God, as I stand here, I will come back for you. I will! And we'll hold each other again, right here! I promise."

"I'll be here waiting," she called in a quivering voice as he broke away and turned his back to board the train, disappearing into the jostling crowd. She waited, hoping to see him one more time, as the train began to move.

Caroline struggled to see above the crowds for a last glimpse of her man. "I love you!" she shouted, above the noise of the crowd and the train's engines, even though she knew he couldn't hear her. The crowds pushed...girlfriends, parents running alongside the train.

The place reverberated with frantic waving and shouting. She called out again—the three most treasured words of the English tongue—"I love you." She cried them softly as the train slowly disappeared into the distance. She turned to walk away, then bolted suddenly and looked back. She thought she had heard his voice...those words...the ones he had always used...the ones that made her feel so wanted.

Neil had run out onto the back platform of the last car fighting his way down the aisle, through the rows of soldiers and sailors to the back door of the passenger car. He wanted to know that he had done everything...everything he could to reassure her. He opened the door and found himself looking back towards her. He shouted it. "I love you isn't good enough—not for you Caroline! I'll see you Valentine's Day 1945. Be here!"

They held their hands up in a final wave as if the space separating them could be touched, and by grasping with interlinking fingers, they could hold on forever. Caroline stood there until she could see the train no longer.

Slowly, she turned back into the station, down the ramp from Track Twelve and into the crowded tunnel that led underneath the tracks and into the main waiting area.

Passing through the turnstile doors, there were more soldiers and their sweethearts. She knew she wasn't the only one to feel the pain of separation, yet it hurt, personally, like a stab wound. It was sharp, penetrating, anxious.

"Excuse us," a young soldier with his arm around his girl said, as they quickly slipped past her. The look on the girl's face told the story.

Finding herself out in the front lobby, she headed for the exit and cringed as the newsboy hawked his papers for a nickel with the cry, "Read all about it, Marines take Marianas Atoll. Seven thousand Japs die. Americans land at Anzio!" The announcement also meant American boys wouldn't be coming home.

The paperboy's barking sales pitch sent a shiver up Caroline's back. Her heart was suddenly drawn out to the only source of help to which she could appeal. "Dear God," she silently prayed, "protect my sweetheart! I believe that you will. Please protect Neil!"

She found her way to the tan-colored 1938 Ford V-8 sedan and put the keys in the ignition. Leaning her head against the steering wheel, she breathed heavily, seeking to dismiss the stressful feelings that had consumed her. She felt sorry for herself and didn't care if anyone saw her or not. She knew anyone watching could understand, for as much heartache was going on around her.

But the opposite was true, too. Boys who had been gone for two years were starting to rotate home, and it hurt to see the joy they were experiencing. A squeal of delight would come from a girl as she caught the first look of her husband or boyfriend after two agonizing years.

She tried to gain the composure to pull out and see clearly

enough to drive the ten miles on the new Arroyo Seco Freeway and back home to Pasadena. Sitting there, she pondered as she scanned the scene around her. She rested her light auburn hair against the black leather-padded driver's seat, asking herself a question. "When did I start loving him?" The scene played out in her mind as if it had been yesterday. Smiling, she said to herself, "My little girl better never kiss boys on the playground!"

The memories playing out in her head slowly turned her broken heart into tears of laughter as she revisited her sweetheart's shocked eight-year-old face when she bussed him on the cheek behind the old Adams School...and in front of his new-found friends!

Neil had asked her, "Caroline, why did you kiss Richard yesterday over there by the drinking fountain?"

Caroline answered, "You mean like this?" as she giggled, kissing him on the cheek and hugging him tight until they both lost their balance. He tried to pull away but fell backwards instead, sending them both sprawling to the ground. She found herself lying right on top of him.

"Naughty little girl!" scolded a clearly upset Miss McCullough as she reached down and picked Caroline up by the arm and began to march her towards the office.

She could still see him...the little boy in the red and white striped T-shirt, the jeans with holes in both knees rolled up at the bottom, and those silly suspenders. She smiled, thinking about it. He always wore those suspenders—until the Navy made him take them off. He never needed them. He was as solid and slender as could be. "He just wanted so much to be like his Dad," she thought.

Caroline remembered turning around, when Miss McCullough opened the door to the office at the old country school, and she blew Neil a kiss.

The other children were hooting and howling and starting to push him with teases, "Neil has a girlfriend... Neil has a girlfriend!"

"The poor kid," Caroline thought, as she came to herself and turned the key, starting the engine on the old Ford. It was a short trip back to Pasadena, but her heart would ache every mile.

CHAPTER FOUR

"I LOVE YOU... ISN'T GOOD ENOUGH"

Caroline pulled into the driveway to the small white frame house, which sat on an acre of land in back of California Avenue. She and Neil had purchased it in 1943, just one week after their marriage. Caroline's uncle had given them a bargain they couldn't refuse. It was his wedding gift, of sorts, to them. The home, built in the 1920s, needed a little work. One hundred dollars down payment, take over the monthly payments of fifty dollars, and continue paying until the five thousand still owed was paid in full.

She was home. She sat in the car and thought back about the wonderful year they were married and the miracle it was to have him there, even though he was in the service. She stared at the house. She loved their fixed-up two-bedroom bungalow with the unfinished upstairs. It was a lovely yet suddenly lonely place. She was expecting their first child, and maybe being occupied as a mother would help fill the time in the quiet place. She wondered if it could.

She had loved to see Neil there. He would smile as he worked up a sweat, whistling a tune or imitating Frank Sinatra as he methodically took the house room by room, and with her help, sanded, painted, and turned it into a place to be proud of. His Navy assignment as flight training officer at the Santa Monica and Long Beach airfields was almost too good to be true. Most nights he was home while serving in the war effort at the same time. She had always known down deep...something had always told her that it was too good to be true...too good to last. But she didn't want to believe.

She thought about the hand-carved sign Neil had hung over the entry on the inside of the front door. She could still hear the sound of him driving a nail through it's center and calling her to come and see.

"Caroline, can you come and see if this thing is level?" He was standing on an old wooden step ladder, holding onto it.

"Neil! Where did you get that? I like it!"

"Had an old-timer friend of mine from the train station carve it. He used to work for my Dad in the shipping department. Does it look level to you?"

"Not only level but very well thought out! Did you think that up or did some famous person say it?" Caroline laughed.

"Both. I thought it up over the door and my mother used to quote some famous guy named Paul from the New Testament," Neil responded through his teeth with two extra nails hanging from his lips.

"Belief is the substance of things hoped for; the evidence of things not seen," Caroline read aloud as Neil finished nailing the small sign into place.

"He stood back to inspect it. "Yep. Level the first time. Belief, Caroline. That's all you need. Then like magic, as you work for it, the miracle happens. Just like a blueprint that your uncle followed to build this house..." He turned towards her and unexpectedly found her arms around his neck. He received her warm lips on his.

"Whew, baby! See...just like I said, the substance of things hoped for. Turn out the lights, chicken. It's time to hit the sack."

She did. They did.

***

That was just one year before he was called up. Caroline's mind viewed the porch and the front door as she sat daydreaming in the car. She thought about all the nights he was home. It was a warm beginning. No one could have been better for her than Neil.

A porch was built to surround the little house. On evenings he came home from the airfield, they would sit on the porch swing, hold on to each other, enjoy the views of the San Gabriel Mountains looming upwards to a star-filled sky...and just talk. Playing a few records on the old Victrola or listening to the Philco broadcasts of Radio City Music Hall added to the romantic simplicity of it all. The war seemed a million miles away—and just as well for Caroline.

The Last Valentine

The hardest part of being with him was when the war news came on over the radio. Neil would be suddenly alert, anxious, and put his entire attention to the events taking place on the battle fronts. Caroline knew what he was thinking. He should be there. Not with a cushy flight training job that let him leave the airfield two, three and even four times a week to go home to his wife.

He was cheating death without honor...at least those were his hidden feelings. She could tell. It was written all over his face each time the news came on. Even some of the neighbors made a point of it. They had let her know how nice it must be for her to not have to worry about the fate of her husband while their husbands or sons were risking their lives overseas.

Sitting. She was just sitting there in the car caught up in visions of how it had been. She was home but didn't feel like getting out of the car. Not just yet, anyway. A empty house awaited her and she was enjoying her recollections of an exciting year...a year in which her dreams began to take shape...the "things hoped for." She pulled the handkerchief out of her purse, the one he had given her hours before, and played with it in her hands. She stared at the design and then the word *Felicidades*—"happiness to you." She smiled at the thoughts racing through her mind.

She thought back one year earlier to January 30, 1943. Back to when she found a love that she thought was lost. She hadn't seen him for six years. The scene played like a movie in her mind. She was the main character and Neil was her leading man. She was one of three USO girls serving free coffee and donuts to servicemen. The place? Where she had just said goodbye: soldier-filled Union Station, January 30, 1943.

***

Twenty-four-year-old Navy Lieutenant Neil Thomas was back home in L.A. It had been six long years since his father was transferred by Union Pacific Railroad to the Ogden, Utah station. It was in the midst of a depression and although the Thomas family didn't want to leave the Los Angeles area, it was take the transfer or lose the job. And since jobs were hard to come by, they moved to Ogden. He thought about all that had happened since he left and how the hand of fate had had its way with him.

Walking down the wooden ramp, he entered the tunnel which led underneath the tracks and into the main waiting area. It was packed with servicemen, most of them shipping out to the fronts — and here he was being shipped out to Long Beach to flight training school as an instructor. He never dreamed that he would be assigned stateside duty during the biggest war the world had known. He wanted in it and silently was resentful of the soldiers, sailors and marines shipping out. It bothered him. The guilt ate at him. It was like he was training and sending other guys to fight — and maybe die — in his place. Both of his brothers had already shipped overseas. Even though Billy... He shook his head and released a heavy breath of sadness.

"Billy. Ah, Billy. Why did he have to die. He had a wife and kid. I should have gone in his place. Lousy dumb luck," he sighed.

Neil had a two-week pass and wasn't sure what to do. His uncle John still lived in Santa Monica. He would be welcome there. Perhaps he could borrow the car and go visit friends out in Eagle Rock and Pasadena...that is if any were still around and not at war.

Neil's bags brushed against passing servicemen and their girls. No one seemed to mind. It was jam-packed and everyone had too much on their minds to be bothered with a little jostling or pushing. As he worked his way up the tunnel he was doubly resentful. Love... Most of these guys had a girl hanging all over them. Neil not only was headed away from the war but he didn't even have a girl. "Man, of all the dirty rotten luck," he whispered to himself.

He had liked a Mormon girl once in Ogden, but she married another guy. A Mormon. What was he to do? Become a Mormon just to get married? He liked his Mormon friends and all, but Thomases were Catholic. Always had been, and Neil guessed they always would be.

Maybe he could hurry and goof up as a flight trainer — then the Navy would send him overseas. Maybe he could meet a USO girl or something so he'd have someone to write to him.

The Last Valentine

Passing through the turnstile at Gate H, he entered into the main lobby. It was good to be back. When his family had moved, in '37, the station was still under construction. The lobby was a beautifully dressed room with a high wooden-beamed ceiling and mosaic style tiles surrounding the walls and covering the floors. Brass handrails and doorknobs, leather-backed chairs and benches.

"The place was a one hundred percent class act. But then what was one to expect from Los Angeles?" he thought.

Neil noticed the USO tables. Free coffee and donuts for servicemen—with pretty, young girls serving. He was in no hurry to go anywhere. Coffee, donuts and a little conversation sounded good right now.

He waited in line. It was hard to get a good look at the girls serving, since a large group of loud and obnoxious sailors were monopolizing the front of the table.

"Uh humm." Neil cleared his throat loudly. He tapped one of the sailors on the back. "Sailor, what's your name?"

The sailor turned slowly, and then, noticing an officer, saluted and answered, "Peterson, sir."

"Peterson, you coming in to L.A. or shipping out?" asked Neil in a commanding tone.

"Shipping out, sir."

"Quite a group of you here. All on the same ship assignment?"

"Ah, yeah. I mean, yes sir."

"I just heard the boarding call's had been changed for one of the trains heading out. Looks like it's leaving at Track Eleven in a few minutes. What's your train number?"

"Forty-nine. It's forty-nine sir."

"Well, sailor. I think you may be missing your train. I sure wouldn't want to be missing my ship. Would you?"

"No...no, sir. Hey, fellas, this officer says he heard our number called. Departure time was changed. Hey! Come on!" The group of sailors grumbled and grabbed at extra donuts as they left the front of the table, leaving it open for Neil to advance.

She was an attractive girl, even with her head bowed as she searched for something on the floor. She possessed a familiar profile. Two of the three girls looked like they had lost something.

"I Love You . . . Isn't Good Enough"

Neil wasn't sure why his heart was pounding so rapidly, but he decided to find out. He offered to help by stepping around the table while the one USO girl continued to serve coffee.

"May I be of help to you?" asked the brunette closest to him.

He couldn't help notice her petite figure and the blue buttoned blouse hanging open, revealing more than the girl probably meant to. "Oh, I, ah wondered if I could be of any help," Neil returned.

The voice sounded familiar to her. She whispered to her sister, Jenny, "Just my luck to have someone I know show up now. Naw, it's probably another grabby sailor. They all sound alike."

The petite brunette quickly put a hand to her blouse, realizing the need. Standing up to greet the man, she had a clearly perturbed look on her face. The sailors had been unruly and crass, and when one had reached over the table to try to kiss her, he caused an earring to drop off her ear and onto the floor. She was ready to belt this one if he tried to make a pass at her.

Her face suddenly changed from angry red to ashen as she stared into his face. Eye to eye, she realized the Navy man looked very familiar! Someone she thought was lost; love that had been hers years before.

"It can't be...you're not..." She stuttered and backed up with her hand still clinging to her blouse.

Neil smiled broadly. He couldn't believe his luck. Maybe there was a God after all.

"Caroline? Caroline Jensen? I mean Caroline Terry. I heard you were married. I heard you married Fred Terry. What are you doing here?"

Neil took off his officer's cap, revealing his military cut but wavy black hair and stood waiting with the same boyish grin she had remembered when she waved goodbye to him six years before.

"Neil? It can't be. I, uh...I'm still just Caroline Jensen. I... Fred and I didn't get married." She was flustered at the suddenness of her childhood sweetheart standing in front of her. She hadn't heard from him for more than two years.

"I was told you were dead. Someone told me you were killed over Europe in a bombing raid. No..." She put a hand to her mouth. "Is it really you?" Her lips quivered, and moisture caused by a thousand questions came suddenly to her eyes.

"It's me. I'm alive. My brother Bill...he was killed in a B-17 raid a couple months ago." He said it soberly, reassuringly. "Hey, how about a hug for a resurrected dead man?" Neil decided to try to put her at ease. He held his arms out to her. He had been in love with her once and now the years that separated them seemed to melt away.

"Neil! Oh my... Oh!" She threw herself into his arms and they held each other for one long, happy moment. Others watched. Servicemen waiting in line cheered and helped themselves to the donuts and coffee. The other two girls stood back and watched as one excitedly seemed to be explaining to the other what she understood had happened.

"How, why?" Caroline asked as she pulled away to look up into his face.

Holding her hands in his, he could read the questions on her face and gave her a gentle kiss on the right cheek.

"Got orders for stateside duty. I'm a pilot. Navy flight training officer. I'm going to be working with pilot trainees at new schools opening up in Long Beach and Santa Monica. Not bad, huh?" Suddenly it didn't seem so terrible that he was missing out on the war action. He felt seventeen again. His heart flipped the way it did back then, before the family had moved away to Utah.

"Neil, I'm shocked! Stunned! You'll have to forgive me," she said as she turned to her sister, who was happily taking in the drama. "Jenny, it's Neil, Neil Thomas."

"Yeah, I can tell," she replied with a grin. "Neil, it's so good to see you!" Jenny walked up to him and gave him a warm embrace. "You look...well, so good!"

Stepping back and turning to Caroline, she whispered, "My gosh he's handsome! You'd better not lose him this time. You do and I'll be after him."

Caroline gave her sister a little push on the shoulder at the tease and wiped away the remaining moisture that had come suddenly to her eyes. The shock was a joyous startle and her questioning look had been replaced by a smile that welcomed him...home.

"Hey, uh, I'm kinda hungry...and donuts won't do the trick. Jenny?"

"I Love You . . . Isn't Good Enough"

"Yes!" She could tell what he was going to ask even before he did. "You two go and get reacquainted. Sally and I are fine. Besides, these guys seem to be helping themselves just fine," she laughed. The other girl at the table nodded and winked at Caroline.

"Thanks guys!" She grabbed Neil's arm and asked, "Where to?"

"Mexican food sound O.K.? It's been a long time since I've had real good L.A.-style Mexican cuisine. Utah hasn't discovered it yet. Across Alameda at Olvera Street?"

"Sounds good to me. I've got a favorite place."

"My bags. Jenny? Are my bags O.K. here for awhile?" Neil asked.

"Sure, just scoot 'em under the table there." She pointed with her elbow as she continued to pour coffee.

"Thanks," he said with a smile and a wave as he turned to escort Caroline out of the station.

"I can't tell you what this means to have you with me. I was kind of down, and then seeing you, well... I guess we have a lot to catch up on...me being dead and all, and now...well, you know what I mean." He laughed nervously.

"Yes, I think I do." She held his arm close to her as they exited through the front doors leading to Alameda street and to the place called "Pueblo de Los Angeles—Olvera Street."

"I never quit thinking about you, Neil," Caroline offered softly as they walked arm in arm.

Neil looked down at her and suddenly felt the urge to say it. The words that he blurted out all those years ago at a Rose Parade when the two had gone on a date...their final one before he moved. He stopped her—there on the sidewalk leading to Alameda Street.

"I love you...isn't good enough... Not for you, Caroline."

He held her by the waist as they stood on the sidewalk. She let her smile and eyes reveal her thoughts to him. Slowly, carefully, he moved his lips towards hers. Then they embraced.

Caroline welcomed him home.

CHAPTER FIVE

MEMORIES

Back in Pasadena, Caroline sat in her car for at least a half hour, remembering how she had found Neil in the train station that day, one year before.

Memories. She had just seen Neil off to war and now faced an uncertain future. Memories of being so in love. Nothing interrupting the flow of it. A mixed blessing, Caroline thought. That was one year before. One year and two weeks before today.

Today. Today was their first wedding anniversary—February 14, 1944. Today she tearfully said goodbye to him at that same place. Today he got his macho wish: he was off to war. She hit the steering wheel with her hand as she sat there in the driveway of their home, not wanting to go inside. She was alone and felt empty as she sat there...thinking, remembering. Memories could be so sweet—and now?

The scene that replayed in her mind, now one year old, weighed on her. She stepped out of the car and off the runner to see something laying on the driveway. Bending over to pick it up, she saw it was a copy of a picture, a wedding photo taken one year earlier. She was in her wedding gown and Neil was dressed in his Navy officer white dress uniform.

Finding it there sent a chill through her body. "Bad luck!" The thought came suddenly to her. "No, just silly superstition," she voiced, seeking to convince herself by mumbling the words aloud. She fought to put it out of her mind as she walked up to the porch. She stared at the photograph intently, wondering how it had gotten there. The last time she had seen it, it was in with the others she was arranging for the family album. Maybe Neil had picked it up, meaning to take it with him, and it had dropped out of his hand somehow, she thought.

She was glad she had found it. Turning it over, she read his writing: "Lieutenant Neil Thomas and Caroline Jensen Thomas,

Memories

Husband and Wife—Forever. February 14th, 1943." It brought a smile to her face, a smile on a face that had so recently flowed with tears. She was glad she was home, safe in their home—even if he couldn't be there. Just moments before she hadn't wanted to go into the empty bungalow. Now? She couldn't seem to control the rollercoaster of emotions she felt.

She opened the screen door and fumbled with the keys as she unlocked the solid oak raised-panel door with the small picture-frame window in the center. The small window was at eye level, and it let light into the entry hall with a small coat closet and a mail drop. She took her coat off and hung it there.

Picking up the mail from the box, she found the letter from Neil. Hurriedly, she walked into the living room, set her purse down on the end table and fell back into the cushion padded sofa. Anxiously, she opened it. "He must have slipped it into the box as they left the house," she thought. She read the words on the card:

Feb. 14, 1944
Dearest Caroline,

It's hard for me to leave you, especially on this day, our wedding anniversary. You know that I felt it was my duty to volunteer. I couldn't keep sending other guys off to fight and maybe die without the guilt hitting me...hitting me hard. I would never leave you. But so many of them are in the same boat we are. Please understand. I love you! It will all work out right.

Bing Crosby says it better, in that song you and I danced to as we listened to the radio last night.

"Because you speak to me—I find the roses 'round my feet, and I am left with tears and joy of thee...
Because God made thee mine—I'll cherish thee, through all life and darkness and all time to be.

And pray his love may make our love divine... Because God made thee mine!"

The Last Valentine

I left you a fresh rose by the bed on the nightstand before leaving today. I even created an original poem. Not as elegant as Bing's verses, but I like to think of you smiling, so here goes:

"Roses are red, violets are blue. This poem isn't perfect, but my love is for you...
The flower I leave, with the card, here behind, is a symbol of beauty—a picture of mind...
And the picture I'll hold in my thoughts are of those—your face, your love, and this symbol...the rose!"

'I love you' isn't good enough. Not for you, Caroline! I'll come back...you'll see! I love you more than words can say. Forever is a promise to keep!

Your faithful husband,

Neil

***

She could still feel him close as she held the card to her breast. She leaned back into the cushioned sofa, her eyes closed. Even the smell of the greasy cloths thrown on the floor of the laundry room was evidence that he had been there just hours before. He had used the overalls to tune up the car once more—"good enough to last one full year," he had said.

She got up, weary from all the energy she had used in her anxiety to make the last few hours with him meaningful. Entering the small bedroom, she looked out through the bay window to the rose garden they had planted together.

She turned back towards the dresser. The smell of his aftershave still lingered in the room. "Old Spice" she mused as she went over to the white cologne bottle with the picture of the sailing ship on it. She uncorked it and held it up to her nose with her eyes closed. It was as if he were there. It smelled like him, clean, smiling, holding her in his arms Neil...

Memories

Hearing the undeniable sounds of B-29 Superfortresses flying overhead, she put the bottle down and peered out the window. They were heading northwest, probably to the Burbank Army Airfield, she thought. As she strained to watch them disappear over the hills, which created the little valley where the famed Rose Bowl sat, she thought about Neil's excitement to be able to fly. He was looking forward to a career after the war. "Aviation was the future," she could hear him say.

She looked over at the roses, once the planes had passed out of sight. Spring was just around the corner and the first intimations of leaves and buds were showing. It had made perfect sense to her when Neil had suggested it. A rose garden, some gardenias, carnations and chrysanthemums. Gradually as they cultivated them, the plan to sell them annually to Rose Parade float designers could pay off. Neil called it their "retirement account." He had put a lot of care and love into those first roses.

She filled herself with a deep breath of the fresh, spring-like air that filled the empty house, laid the card down on the nightstand next to the queen-size posterbed, and picked up the single-stem rose. Smelling it, she left the room to wander outdoors.

More planes appeared, high overhead. "The gentle noise of war," she whispered. "It never seems to end."

The engines weren't frightening, rather comforting, she mused. Perhaps it was that they were "friendly" sounds...sounds of an entire nation geared up, turning out equipment and machines and everyone seemed to have something to do behind the scenes for the war effort. They planted "victory gardens," collected scrap metal and rubber, and everyone was united, bound together in a sense of pride. The ugliness of war was distant, and only as close as the theater screen.

You could go down to her uncle's cinema, the Jensen Theater on Raymond Street. Every Saturday the latest film clips from the battle fronts would be shown. But it all seemed so far away, and the patriotic sounds and music behind the announcer's commanding voice made it feel somehow "right." It was like the war was a good cause, and this was a "good" war, and the boys would be marching home soon. With their tokens of battle, proud, they would be standing erect as they marched shoulder to shoulder, victorious, and after all was said and done, all would be right with the world.

Looking up at the war planes, it was hard for Caroline to envision the flying machines being used in desperate attempts to kill other people in anger. Neil killing in anger, others trying to kill him... The thought made her shudder.

Focusing back to earth and to the rose garden, she thought, "They'll be blossoming soon." Then she whispered, "Every rose, every carefully planted flower will remind me of him." She took another deep breath, then walked back into the house...to pray.

CHAPTER SIX

GOLANDRINAS

It was evening. Caroline sat in the living room, waiting for her sister Jenny to arrive. She had a fire going and had turned the small table-size Philco radio on. Dialing the tuner, she found the CBS Radio Network. The music made her smile. She was listening to the broadcasts from Radio City Music Hall in New York. One of the songs reminded her of their first anniversary. She remembered the hotel and the beach near Santa Monica as the announcer presented Captain Glenn Miller and his Army Aircorp Orchestra.

"And now we are pleased to present Sergeant Johnny Desmond and the Crew Chiefs...take it away Sergeant!" The crowd applauded and Desmond started to sing:

Good night, wherever you are,
May your dreams be pleasant dreams...wherever you are,
If only one wish, I wish was true, I know the angels will watch over you!

Caroline sat there curled up on the sofa holding a pillow to her as she stared into the glowing fire, listening:

Good night...I'll be with you ,dear, no matter how near or far!
With all my heart, I pray to God on high, wherever you are...good night!
Dream of me...And I'll dream of you, wherever you are!

She wondered how long, how many days or months it would take, before missing him got any easier. The songs continued when she heard the knock at the front door.

"Hi, doll face," Jenny said, peering through the small window in the center of the door.

The Last Valentine

"I'm glad you're here," Caroline returned as she hurriedly opened the door and gave her older sister a big hug. "I need someone to talk to. Come on over here to the couch." Jenny left her overcoat in the hall closet and followed Caroline over near the fireplace and sat next to her on the sofa.

After a short silence, and with the radio on low, she finally invited her sister to say something.

"O.K. Sis, how'd it go today? I mean, what did you do, before seeing Neil off? I guess it was kinda hard?" Jenny offered in a soft, inquiring tone meant to be comforting.

Caroline tilted her head back and gazed at the ceiling, searching. "Yeah, real hard!" came the reply with a heavy sigh. "Oh Jenny, it's got me so scared! I'm afraid! I'm afraid he won't be coming back. I keep thinking about Tommy Jones, Phil Johnson, Neil's brother...some of the other boys who've been killed...it's got me scared, real scared!"

Jenny drew herself closer and put her arms around her younger sister. She knew it wasn't realistic to say that he would be sure to come home, but she knew she had to reassure Caroline. "Hey, sweetheart, come on now, he'll be O.K. You'll see. He was a top flight trainer. He's tough. He's smart."

Caroline looked up at her sister and implored, "He may be superman to me, but he can't stop bullets... Jenny he can't stop bullets!" She looked into the eyes of her sister with a pleading look that said, "Please tell me I'm wrong—tell me that he *can* stop bullets!"

Jenny couldn't say anything to comfort her, other than, "It'll be all right. You'll see, Sis. It will be all right."

They sat there, bathed in the music. Gradually, Caroline composed herself and they started to talk. Jenny said, "It's normal...the way you feel I mean. You're afraid. We're all afraid. The best thing to do is write letters, send things, and plan for the future. If you plan for the future, then you have hope. You can live in the past, Sis, when you want to be alone with him, but look to the future. See him coming back to you, there at Union Station. And Caroline, remember what Mom always told us before we went to bed?"

"Yeah," and they both repeated it in unison: "Don't forget to say your prayers, girls." They were holding hands and a smile came to both of them as Caroline wiped away the last tears staining her face.

"That's what's holding me together, I think." It was more than words to Caroline. She meant it.

A quiet pause in their conversation followed as they listened to the radio that was now turned down low. The crooner, Frank Sinatra, was singing. Jenny decided to try to get Caroline to open up.

"So, Caroline, tell me about today. What did you do before Neil boarded the train. The place is always packed. Did you guys go out or something?"

"We had a good time," she responded in a quiet tone as she reached towards the hearth and added a small log to the fire. "We walked around town a bit. We went up to Chinatown and then back to Olvera Street. You know the place, just across from Union Station. It has all those souvenir shops. Well, we had lunch at La Golondrina Restaurant where Neil gave me the ring two years ago. The old Catholic Church built in the late seventeen hundreds was open. Neil stopped there. He asked me if I wanted to join him...to go inside and pray. I shook my head and left him alone for a few minutes. When he came back out, we bought some souvenirs and I tried out my Spanish. I drove some hard bargains. It was fun."

Caroline twisted and played with the handkerchief as she stared into the fire, recalling the afternoon. Her sister sat quietly, giving her the time she needed to get her thoughts together and talk things out. Then she seemed to suddenly brighten at a particular thought.

"Oh, Jenny, you've got to hear this. We were sitting in La Golondrina, waiting for our order to arrive. The Mariachis were playing. Neil got up suddenly and took my hand, leading me out to the dance floor. He started to dance, pretending to do the cha cha or rumba or something like that. He had me in hysterics. People started to clap and whistle. Pretty soon, every sailor, marine and soldier who could find a girl was up and dancing. The rest sat there cheering and clapping to the rhythm."

"Neil—always the life of the party," laughed Jenny.

The Last Valentine

Caroline continued, "Neil had this Mexican Sombrero on his head. I guess I really got into it then. I started to whoop it up. I began to stomp my feet and some sailors began to whistle, which egged me on even more. I really didn't want the day to be all doom and gloom. Well...then I did that skirt thing...you know how the Mexican girl grabs the skirt and starts to fling it around from side to side?" She held up the handkerchief. "Then Neil got this handkerchief out and started waving it over his head."

"The sailors started yelling, 'go Lieutenant, kiss the girl,' and then the whole place chimed in as they clapped. Neil finally yielded and did the movie thing where the leading lady bends backwards as the leading man makes his kissing move. They all whistled, clapped, and then pretty soon guys were kissing girls all over the place. It was a riot. We left the dance floor laughing until the tears flowed. Then, after finishing our meal, we went over to Union Station."

Jenny was enjoying the laughter and the light side it was bringing out in her younger sister. They talked for hours after that about the gang and growing up in Eagle Rock, their home town just a few miles west of Pasadena. Somehow, the conversation got on the yearly trek they made as families to the Rose Parade and how the Jensens and Thomas' with a few other friends had turned it into a tradition.

"Remember the parade back in '37—or was it '38?" quizzed Jenny.

"It was January 1, 1937," returned Caroline with a smile. "The month before Neil moved with his family to Utah. For all of those years I had such a crush on Neil, and then I finally knew for sure how he felt about me."

***

Since childhood, Caroline, Neil and their brothers and sisters—along with hundreds of thousands of others—lined the route of the famous Rose Parade in Pasadena. The tradition had started in 1933. The families would find a spot on Colorado Boulevard the day before and camp out. Then they would celebrate.

Golandrinas

At midnight the bells of St. Andrews Cathedral, on Raymond Street, would ring out. When the bells would sound, the street would break out with horns honking, firecrackers exploding, and party whistles blowing. Sometimes a few cars would get together and turn up a radio station that would bring in the new year with big hits from the year before.

Colorado Boulevard and Raymond Street was a prime corner. It was within short walking or running distance—depending on the need—to St. Andrew's Catholic Church, where Neil and his family attended Mass. And it had one of the most important accommodations for a long evening of partying—restrooms, made available to the public.

It was also on Raymond, just two short blocks south from St. Andrew's, that the Jensen Theater, built in the 1920s, was located. Although it belonged to her uncle, it carried the name—and in her mind, the street seemed to belong to them.

Caroline remembered that first time, the Rose Parade, when she first thought she had noticed him noticing her. Soon they were making eyes and teasing. She had been sure Neil must have known how she felt about him. She had left plenty of hints.

On that 1937 Tournament of Rose Parade eve, the gang was huddled closely together. The boys had stoked a fire in a trash can and they were singing songs, but it was cold, and Caroline couldn't stop shivering.

They all had blankets, but Neil must have noticed. He brought his over and put it over Caroline's shoulders. He then stood back and warmed his hands over the fire with the other boys, who were laughing and cracking jokes. Caroline remembered smiling appreciatively and suddenly she sensed something different about Neil. He kept glancing over to her as if he was checking on her.

She wanted to make sure he knew how she felt. She decided that on his next glance she would risk it all. "Thank you, Neil!" she whispered, and then she added the words, "I love you," mouthed in silence.

He just stood there, staring back at her. Then he just blurted it out. Treasured words that became such a part of their growing love story. "I love you' isn't good enough... Not for you Caroline!"

The Last Valentine

Neil's brother, Bill, who was laughing it up with his other brother Johnny, and Caroline's brother Pete, caught the look and heard Neil's off-the-cuff romantic comeback. He wasn't going to let go of it for the rest of the night.

Finally, Neil had had enough. Instead of striking back, he sat down next to Caroline and pulled a part of the blanket over his shoulders and shared it with her. He turned to her and winked and reached for her hand as she eagerly reached for his in return.

There was silence for a minute. Neil's brothers had expected him to fight back a little or to leave to get away from the harassment. Instead, he put his arm around Caroline and she snuggled up to him, willingly and unabashedly, in front of the rest of the family.

The morning brought an event that would make even more memorable that 1937 Rose Parade. As the parade began and the Queen's float passed by the young group, a bouquet of roses that bordered the stand on the float fell off near the group. Seeing that a fast-approaching mounted police officer's horse was headed for the roses, Neil quickly ran out and picked them up. Returning to stand in front of Caroline, who stood to cheer with the other onlookers at the rescue of the roses, he bowed respectfully to her. Then bending, with one knee on the ground, he handed the bouquet up to an embarrassed but pleased young lady. The crowd cheered louder and a photographer from the Los Angeles Gazette caught the scene with the Police mount and the officer abruptly halted in front of them. Neil announced, "For a true Rose Queen," and the crowd roared with approval. The newspaper came out with the happy scene and captioned it with "Rescue of the Roses—Gentleman of the Court honors a Rose Parade Queen."

***

The glass-enclosed, framed photograph of that New Year's Day event graced the mantle over the small stone hearth of the fireplace. Jenny laughed with her sister as they relived that day and the other New Year's days they had spent together on Colorado Boulevard.

"How about some donuts? I made them fresh this afternoon. Maybe a cup of coffee too?" Caroline asked, getting up to go into the kitchen.

"Sure, Sis, anything you have will be fine."

"How I wish we could go back to those days, Jenny. It all ended with the attack on Pearl Harbor. Then came January 1, 1942, the first Rose Parade after war was declared, but the fun was over."

"I don't know, Jen, it kind of wasn't the same for me when Neil moved with his family to Utah that year. But I know what you mean about 1942." Caroline came back from the kitchen with the tray of donuts and coffee.

"Hey, Sis, what would you be doing right now if you hadn't been at the train station USO table serving coffee and donuts last year?"

"Huh? What do you mean, Jenny?

"You know...if you and I hadn't filled in for Mary and her partner...if we weren't there at the table. What's the chance that you would have gotten a marriage proposal on that day?"

Caroline grinned. "There is justice in the universe—there is a God, isn't there?"

"See, you're all happy just thinking about it. The risk of marrying a man who you knew—deep down inside, knew—could be shipped off to war, was worth it, wasn't it?"

"Uh huh," Caroline agreed as she bit into one of the homemade donuts.

"So, answer my question. What would you be doing, right now, this year, if you and Neil hadn't found each other again. You know. He would have thought you married Fred Terry and you would have thought he was dead."

"I never thought much about what I would be doing," she returned thoughtfully. "I just assumed it was the hand of God in our lives and that it would have had to happen—that it was meant to be. To meet him again, I mean," Caroline continued. "But, I guess I would have taken that teaching job downtown with the L.A. School District's Spanish speaking program. It's something I've always wanted to try. You know, the one working with immigrant children? I've been thinking of applying again anyway, now that Neil's gone. You know, to fill up my time, put a little money away, feel useful."

"Might help. Might be fun," rejoined Jenny.

The Last Valentine

There was a silent momentary pause. A warm feeling had displaced any gloom that might have attended their conversation early on.

"Caroline," Jenny initiated. "What did Neil say about Utah? Mormons. You know, living up there for six years. Did he say it was strange, him a Catholic and all?"

"I asked that once. I was curious."

"Well? What did he say?"

"Well, he shrugged his shoulders, looked up, smiled and said, 'Yeah pretty nice people. They're like everybody. Good people, bad people...but mostly good.'"

"They don't smoke, drink, don't do coffee," Jenny held her cup up, "I wonder what they do for fun."

Caroline just shrugged her shoulders. She hadn't wanted to get into any sort of divisive discussion. Neil had his religious preferences and she had hers, but they both believed and prayed to God.

Jenny wouldn't leave it alone. "So, Sis, what you guys going to do about religion? Bring your kids up Catholic, Methodist, what?" Jenny quizzed.

Caroline shrugged, "Well, we've been going to his church at St. Andrew's. I took him to our church up on Orange Grove—you know, just trying it out—and he came out pretty upset. I guess the minister was on a hell/fire/damnation binge. Neil said he thought ministers should be less "preachy" and more "ministery." I thought that was a good way of looking at it. Don't you?"

"Yeah, but you still haven't answered my question. You a Catholic now? What about the family? It's important you know."

"Look... I appreciate your concern, big sister." Caroline stood up and took the tray into the kitchen. "Maybe we'll sell this house, move to Utah and become Mormons!" she laughed as she called it out from the kitchen.

"Caroline, you wouldn't!" Jenny exclaimed with a forced cough to accentuate her disapproval at the idea.

She shrugged her shoulders again and let the quizzing die. She wasn't concerned about confusing things with denominational arguments. She just wanted it simple, and it had been. She finally reassured her probing sister with, "I'll be careful, Jen. I promise."

Golandrinas

It was getting late. Jenny was staying the night and decided to keep her sister talking until they both crashed. "So, before you saw Neil off today, you two ate at that same restaurant where he proposed to you? What's the name? La Goldrina? La Golrina?..Come on, help me out with it."

"La Gol-on-drina," Caroline said, pronouncing each syllable, slowly, clearly and distinctly for her sister.

"La Gol-on-drina," Jenny repeated aloud. "What does La Gol-on-drina mean in English, anyway? Is it food or something?" Jenny laughed at her own remark.

Jenny's question reminded Caroline of what she had seen in her window that day. She had seen a small bird. A robin, sparrow or...

She suddenly felt cold all over. The chilling sensation caused her to shiver. She couldn't help it. It caught her off guard.

Caroline's mind went back to another day, a year earlier. She had run into an old school friend down at the market near her mother's home in Eagle Rock. She was picking up a few things for a family birthday party. Her friend told her how a swallow had shown up one day on the kitchen window sill while she was doing dishes, and it just sat there. She broke down and cried when she revealed to Caroline that a Western Union telegram arrived three days later: Her brother had been killed the same day the swallow had appeared, killed in action on Guadalcanal.

"Superstition...silly superstition," Caroline muttered with her arms folded over her upper body trying to combat the chills that had suddenly over come her.

"Caroline, you're cold! You have goosebumps. Honey, what's wrong?" Jenny showed her concern by coming close and rubbing her shivering arms with her hands.

Caroline just turned to her sister, trying to suppress the look that caused her face to become drawn out in anxiety.

"Swallow...Golondrina means swallow in Spanish."

**

CHAPTER SEVEN

"JOSIAH—THE GUARDIAN"

Los Angeles—11:30 a.m. February 14th, 1994—Union Station

"Who's the old lady?" the custodian Armando asked his friend motioning toward Caroline sitting in the waiting station chair.

"That, my good man, is none other than Mrs. Caroline Jensen Thomas. She's a regular here. Like clockwork. I can always tell when it's February 14th even if I don't have a calendar. Come Valentine's Day an' she be here...no question asked," answered Josiah, the Union Station security guard. "We been good friends now twenty-five years. I kinda watch over her, wake her up a few times...jus' in case...makin' sure she's bein' O.K. She's one fine lady, I tell you that, Mando, a real sweetheart...yes sirrey."

Josiah reached over and tapped the old woman on the shoulder as Armando kept sweeping the high-gloss polished tile floor of the old train station lobby.

"Miss Caroline...Miss Caroline...you bein' O.K., sweetheart? Miss Caroline?" Josiah shook her gently to let her know he was there.

She slowly opened her tired eyes and reached for the glasses she had set down on her lap. Struggling to put them on, she finally focused as she looked up into the eyes of her affable Union Station guardian.

"Josiah! Oh Josiah, I'm so glad you're here. For a minute I thought that maybe it was Neil coming to get me." She dropped her brown eyes in a state of confusion mixed with a look of embarrassment.

Josiah chuckled, and seeking to displace her concern returned, "I understand, Miss Caroline. It's jus' old Josiah makin' sure you bein' O.K. I'm glad to see you still gettin' down here, little lady. Another year gone by an' you still comin,' for what be the number of years now, honey?"

"Josiah—The Guardian"

"Fifty years since I last saw him. I've come for fifty years, including Valentine's Day, 1944. It seems like yesterday. This place doesn't change, Josiah. Come and sit with me, won't you?" she tiredly replied as she patted the empty seat next to her.

He really shouldn't stop, but seniority had its privileges. Besides, he could chalk it up to good public relations. "Sure, little lady. Why sure, I'd like to take a minute," he answered as he sat down.

"You know this makes twenty-five years since I started workin' here, Miss Caroline. You rememberin' that first time I caught you sleepin' here on the bench an' thought you was some sort of bag lady?" Josiah laughed loudly at his own remark.

He continued, "You was the prettiest bag lady I ever seen though, an' I was determined to do my job good. You really straightened young Josiah out, didn't you, honey?"

Caroline's lined face broke out into a wide grin. "Pretty fancy dresser for an 'old bag lady' and pretty good with this walking stick," she said, raising her cane towards him as he faked blocking it. "I guess you startled me. I was too quick with my cane but it was good training for a new security man, right Josiah?"

She was happy to see her old friend. He had been so comforting to see during all those visits, year after year. He had watched out for her. He was new at Union Station back in 1970 and she had just turned fifty years old. Hardly an "old bag lady."

Josiah Williams relaxed a bit as he sat next to her. He reached over to her slightly trembling hand that lay on the arm rest. He turned towards her and cupped his hands gently over hers, and then reached over to give the tired old woman a kiss on the forehead.

"Thank you, Caroline. Thank you for what you did for me an' my Martha. If it hadn't been for you...well, she deals real well with our boy Charlie dyin' over there in Vietnam. I tell you this every year, don't I honey?"

She looked up at him with the compassionate smile of one who did understand and answered with a simple "Yes." Her voice had aged gracefully. It was slower and shaky, but each word was soft, deliberate.

"You remember me tryin' ta help you an' then feelin' that you been the one helpin' me?" he asked.

Caroline looked over at him with a smile on her lips that was linked to a gleam in her eyes. It hinted of a memory sparked to life from its safely stored hiding place in her mind. She added a nod in reply as she clutched his protecting hands.

"I wasn't sure what to make of you," Josiah continued. "Then you got up an' walked over to McCarthy's Cafe, an' told me to follow you. You waved me over to a table an', thinkin' I was jus' goin' ta have ta listen to a rambling old woman talking crazy 'bout somethin,' you told me to sit down."

"I told you to sit down and 'be quiet,' as I recall."

"I was jus' gettin' ta that," he laughed. "Then you told me to take a break an' bought me a cup of coffee. I'll never forget how it hit me when you said, 'I want to tell you some history, a war story.' It had been jus' three weeks since our Charlie had been kilt."

"I didn't know about the loss of your son, Josiah. I felt so bad," she replied.

"How could ya know, Miss Caroline. Ya know, what you said made so much sense as I listened about your husband bein' lost over the Philippines during World War II an' all. How ya knew he was probably dead, even though he'd been officially declared "missin' in action." Well, it sure did help to see how someone who lost a loved one was behavin'—you takin' life with a smile an' a song an' all. An' then you said:

"Josiah, as long as love is alive, the dead never die. It's not in the end alone that we love, but along the way. A love that endures the thorns of life calls out to us. When we listen, it lights the ground upon which we walk and we know that we are not alone. And, when the flame of life flickers out and is no more, the love you showed to others will light the ground for them to walk upon."

"Josiah, you sounded so eloquent. Did I say that?"

"You sure enough did. You wrote it down an' I been sharin' it with others all these years."

"Oh," Caroline returned with a quiet humility.

After a moment of silence, Josiah added, "He was a special boy, my boy Charlie was. An' now, 'cause you helped show us how we could handle it, we got dozens of kids callin' us 'Mom' an' 'Pop.'

That was real good you showin' Martha how ta reach out an' lose herself like that. She sees a hurt in other people's lives and she'll be there for 'em."

A hint of tears appeared as Josiah looked away and with his left hand squeezed his eyes to try to control them. He cleared his throat and continued, "She been a real good teacher too! Jus' like you, sweetie!" and he reached over and gave her another kiss on the forehead, as he got up to leave.

"I remember talking to you, and then having dinner with you and Martha, but my mind... Sometimes I think I leave it at home." She looked up at him with a questioning, puzzled look. "I'm having trouble remembering a lot of things, Josiah."

Caroline suddenly brightened and said, "I wish I could go see Martha one more time. You tell her that I said I love her and that I'm proud of her, will you Josiah? And tell her...tell her I'm sending something from me to the both of you. It's special. I left it with my son who will make the arrangements."

Caroline squeaked out her request with a gentle and soft high-pitched voice in an imploring tone and look that left Josiah baffled. He could see how worn out she appeared. It concerned him.

"Yes ma'am, but what you mean you 'wish you could see her one more time?' Miss Caroline, you're invited any old time. You goin' somewhere? Movin' maybe?" countered Josiah.

"No, not from here anyway. Josiah,"...she fumbled with the card that was in her lap, "this is from my Neil. He is coming to get me and take me home today." She weakly gestured with her hands to the old card sitting on her lap. She fumbled as she picked it up with trembling hands.

Josiah, standing up and positioning himself in front of her, knelt down to look her directly in the eyes. "You not meanin' your husband Neil. You be meanin' Neil Jr., don't you now, Caroline." It was not a question. Josiah said it like a statement of fact.

"No, Josiah. Neil Jr. is with my grandson Eric at his basketball game and won't be coming to take me home. Lieutenant Neil Thomas, he's coming today. I know he will." She stared off towards the windows by the old forties style wall clock that hung over the doors to the patio on the south side of the waiting area.

The Last Valentine

She watched the birds at play.

He looked over at where her vision was directed and asked, "What you be seein', honey?"

"Las golondrinas," she whispered with a smile on her face.

CHAPTER EIGHT

"EVEN ROSES HAVE THORNS"

She leaned back and smiled as Josiah said, "I be checkin' on you now, Caroline." He patted her hand and walked down towards the entry to check on a call that came to him over his two-way radio.

Up from the Alameda Street entry and passing Josiah, came a noisy group of school children, giggling, laughing and poking each other as their guide explained the history of Union Station. A smile crossed the pursed lips of the old woman as she watched the youthful display unfold before her. She rested again, with the sounds of the playful children resonating in her ears.

She watched them, and her thoughts went to daydreams of the days and years she worked as a school teacher. "How I loved the children," she mused, talking to herself in a low tone. She was truly a fortunate woman to have had her life and cares consumed in caring about all the children that passed through her classroom doors.

Her mind. Full of forgetfulness. Except for daydreaming—having a never-ending wandering mind—she felt it served others very little. At least not like it used to when she could teach.

Caroline fumbled with her purse lying on the floor between her legs. Her chest suddenly felt tight and breathing was a struggle.

"I forgot to take my pills when I left this morning...or did I?" she mumbled to herself in a low, soft voice. She found the prescription holder and flipped the long white top open. Her hands trembled as she did. The pills were all separated into days. Easy, so that she wouldn't take too many, or forget one day. The trouble was, she could barely remember what day it was. If the pain wasn't so great she would have to laugh, she thought to herself.

Her fingers trembled as she reached for the small white pills and brought them to her mouth. She let them sit on her tongue for a minute then reached back down for the small plastic juice container she had brought. The plastic straw was already inserted into the top. She drank. Coughing caused her to almost choke. She struggled for a moment and then relaxed back in the chair, seeking a steady rhythm of breathing to calm her.

Finally, she bent over to return the container to her large black purse. As she did so, her hand touched an envelope. She lifted it out to set on her lap with the last Valentine. Taking deep breaths, she partially recomposed herself and leaned her head back again to the corner of the chair.

She glanced over her right shoulder to the wall clock. The original old clock still accurately gave the time, as it had to hundreds of thousands of waiting passengers over the years.

It was eleven a.m. She gazed around her. The place was so much the same, but much less busy. Amtrak was the name of the trains now...they were called Union Pacific then...then, in 1944...and her mind wandered back again as she looked down at the last Valentine and the envelope she had brought from her purse.

Her husband, Neil, would need to come for her by three p.m. That's when the men from the Navy said he would be there. That's when they said his remains would be returned to the United States. Neil would keep his promise to return to her, "right here at Union Station." Those were among his last words to her, and although it took fifty years for him to keep his promise, she trusted him, and believed in the signs she had seen.

She thought about his first letter now that she had his last. She closed her tired eyes and breathed in steady, shallow breaths to try and regain her strength. The pain in her chest eased from sharp to slight. Caroline allowed her mind to wander back as she sought to calm her ailing heart.

***

"War of Nerves"—March 15, 1944—Pasadena

After one long agonizing month, a letter finally arrived from Neil. Caroline had had her own war to fight—a war of nerves. She anxiously removed the cloth gardening gloves she wore as she worked the soil around the roses. She had seen Mr. Myers, the postman, come up the street and hoped that he would turn up the long dirt driveway to her home.

She had been sure to be out working in the yard every day for the last week, at a quarter to twelve, acting like she needed to be busy around the yard. She was secretly hoping and praying that she would get her first letter from her husband.

"Hello, Mrs. Thomas. Well, lookie here," Mr. Myers said. "Looks like a letter from someone with the same last name," and he jokingly held it up into the sun to see if he could make out the contents. She tapped her foot nervously, impatiently.

"Says U.S. Navy Postal Service, San Francisco. Hum. Well, then it must be for you, Mrs. Thomas," and he smiled and extended his hand with its contents as she eagerly reached for the letter.

"Have a nice day young lady," he happily called as he headed back down the driveway to California Avenue.

"Thank you, Mr. Myers," she called back, and with anticipation that far exceeded her quickened footsteps, hurried into the house to sit down and enjoy Neil's first letter. Falling onto the sofa, she nervously opened the letter and began to read:

Somewhere in the Pacific

Feb. 28th, 1944

Dearest Caroline,

I miss you! We shipped out of San Francisco and made it to Pearl Harbor in seven days. The accommodations were spacious. We only had four pilots to a ten-by-ten bunk room. Because we're replacements, we are awaiting assignments to a carrier. I have a fair idea where we are headed.

The fighting right now is in the Marianas and Caroline Islands. The Marines are taking one island at a time, it seems, and the Navy is claiming the air and the sea, to cut off the Japs from reinforcing their strongholds.

We certainly can't let the Japs mess with your islands, can we?

The Last Valentine

The Carolines, I mean. It'll bring me good luck to fly out there, you'll see.

I guess you're keeping up on the news down at the theater. If I get onto a newsreel I'll be sure to wave by wagging the wings for you.

How's Johnny and Pete? Have we heard anything? It sounds like it's been real rough for Johnny over there in Italy. That Anzio place is really taking a beating, from what the Stars and Stripes have to say. Hope Pete is out here somewhere giving a hand in that submarine he got assigned to. I'll feel a lot better about floating around on a big flat top with him working below. We ought to have 'em licked soon, coming at the Japs from both angles.

Pearl Harbor is a sobering sight. The wreckage from the attack on December 7th, '41 is still visible and the Arizona is a tomb to a thousand sailors. It has made the war suddenly more real to me.

I can't think of a whole lot to say. I realize that it might take a while to get letters back and forth. Just write me often. I live to hear from you.

I made this little paper rose all out of napkins. Maybe I've finally found my calling...a florist. Well, it's the next best thing to our garden, and it doesn't need water.

I pray for you and our baby. I'm proud to have you for a wife, sweetheart. I love you more than I know how to say in words. That's why "love isn't good enough—not for you, Caroline."

Forever your loving husband,

Neil

P.S. You won't believe who I saw my first day in Pearl. Fred Terry. You know...your EX-fiance. He says hello. I think it still bugs him being such a big loser and all. I tried not to rub it in how he lost out on taking the prettiest girl from Eagle Rock to the altar. He's a typist at the processing center at Naval H.Q. Tell his folks I saw him and he looks great. (Why shouldn't he, the sun and the beach and a cushy job. He probably got the job by being the fastest typist who could write, "Now is the time for all good men to come to the aid of their country"... Man how do some guys rate?)

"Even Roses Have Thorns"

Caroline carefully folded and placed the two page letter back into the envelope and put it in the end table drawer. She had been sending letters through the Naval Post Office with his name, rank and serial number, and she hoped they were getting to him. He sounded good and it was soothing to her frazzled nerves to hear from her husband.

She was dealing remarkably well with the separation, she thought. It was good to be keeping busy every afternoon at the Jensen Theater. Working at the ticket booth gave her the opportunity to see a lot of old friends and exchange news on how things were going for all the boys.

It was weeks before she heard from him again. She was out in the yard, waiting and hoping, as usual, that the postman would bring her the letter she longed for. He always had some new quip about who was sending the letters from the Pacific. She had gotten used to knowing, by the look on his face, whether he was carrying a letter from Neil or not.

"How's the flowers, Caroline?" asked Mr. Myers soberly, as he startled her from her intent work on a new area of recently troweled soil. She had been on her hands and knees.

"Oh!" she held her hand to her chest as she got up from her kneeling position near the east porch, where she was making a new row for the flowers.

"How'd you sneak up on me?" she asked with a smile. She wore a full, blousy one-piece dress now that she was farther along in her pregnancy. Brushing it off at the knees, she quickly removed the dirtied gardening gloves.

"Practice," he replied simply with the mail outstretched in his hands.

"You don't look your normal cheerful self, Mr. Myers. Is something wrong?" Caroline's brow lowered as she reached for the mail. She quickly looked through it to make sure there was no telegram among the three pieces handed her.

"I've had to deliver three Western Unions today. It's almost more than I can take sometimes. I know all the people and their boys. I don't know why they all seem to hit at once, but they do. One of the boys was Ricky Bell. Killed over Germany in a bomber.

The Last Valentine

He was a gunner. That boy was really something. Only eighteen years old, too."

Caroline gasped at the news about the other two servicemen from Pasadena. One was Bob "Lightning" Richards, a star football player from high school and a good friend of Neil's. He was married and had one child, a daughter. It had a chilling effect on her. She felt for the families. She was sorry for them, but at the same time glad none of the telegrams were for her. Her eyes began to moisten as she listened to Mr. Myers tell about it.

"I'm sorry if I upset you, sweetheart. I didn't mean to," Mr. Myers apologized, but he, too, was clearly moved at the realization of the deadly business that had taken their best young men away from them.

"Looks like a letter from someone in there that you should probably go read. It will make you feel better. You have a nice day, young lady, and don't worry." He turned slowly to walk away.

Caroline liked him. He was clearly a sensitive man and there weren't enough of those in the world. "Thank you, Mr. Myers," she called back as he waved an acknowledgement. "Thank you for the letter." She hoped to never see him with a Western Union telegram.

Setting her gardening gloves on the porch swing, Caroline opened the front door and walked into the house, removing her shoes in the entry. Curling up on the sofa, she opened the letter and started to read.

***

U.S.S. Princeton
South Pacific
July 6, 1944

Dear Caroline,

You must know from the newsreels what's happening out here. We've been chasing Japs from island to island.

I guess you ought to know some other things. I've been holding a lot inside. Every time I think I've just about arrived at having the battle hardening experiences behind me, something new happens that humbles me. Flight training is one thing... I'm not going to try

"Even Roses Have Thorns"

to kid you sweetheart...dodging bullets is a totally different story. I wondered if I should talk about it to you or if I should just gloss over the fact that this business out here is a far different life-and-death struggle than one imagines, even if you're watching actual film footage shot from the front lines. (Keep watching the news-reels—maybe you will see me or something that I'm in. They put a camera on my plane the other day. I guess they think I'm good enough to not get it damaged. I hope so.)

I'm officially an "ace." That means that five enemy planes got in my way. I don't feel much like celebrating, though. War isn't the the glory thing Hollywood makes it up to be. It hurts a lot of peo-ple... _A lot of people._ When one of your friends gets it, there is no band playing, no bugler playing taps, no marches in parades, no speeches, no one waving a flag...nothing that can make up for the loss... When your buddy takes a hit he just goes down and disap-pears under the waves of the Pacific Ocean.

Listen honey, this thing is for keeps for a lot of guys. I just want you to not feel like I'm alone or that you're alone. There are a lot of married guys out here and a million men at war in the Pacific. The odds are on our side that I can come out of this O.K. Please know that I'm doing my best, but if something happens, it's no less fair than if it happened to another guy.

I know that you don't want to hear this, but I want at least one of my letters to be as honest as possible so that you know I believe...I mean—what I'm trying to say is—that I believe that there is a God who knows us and our situations, and if my time is up, well, then I believe He will make everything right for you and me. I'm not going to do anything stupid, but I've got to tell you that it's offended me more than once to have Japs shoot back at me.

The good news is—I've definitely been protected plenty and attribute that to your prayers. I feel them, and I am encouraged by it. Keep it up. We'll have this thing over with soon.

Things are heating up. The pressure is really on the Japs. We're leap-frogging from one island to the next and within one year we'll be knocking on Tokyo's door. The Japs are really getting clobbered. Even so, they put up a fight to the finish. Between March 30th and April 30th we took on half of their navy and their *island airfields. They haven't got much of a navy left. I guess I'm telling you all this because I've got to get it off my chest.*

Also, I want you to know that I believe we are engaged in a just cause. I couldn't do this if I thought for one minute that we were not.

From the time I saw the Arizona sitting on the bottom of Pearl Harbor with a thousand sailors trapped inside, until today, I know that what we are doing is fighting for peace. Ironic isn't it? Fighting for peace, I mean. Well, just be proud of us and pray for us.

I'll be more cheerful now.

How's our boy? I guess I just think that the baby will be a boy. Got the picture two days ago of you in front of the garden. You've really been working hard! It looks great! How come you're so beautiful no matter how big you get?

How I wish I was there with you through this. I want you to know that I pray for you. I want you to be at peace. I'll come home to you. Don't worry , sweetheart. I'll keep my promise and we'll plant flowers together and go to Rose Parades together for fifty more years. You'll see. You are my inspiration and I need you! I've got to close for now. You're the first thing on my mind when I awake and the last thing I think about when I hit the sack at night.

Caroline, don't let all of the stuff I've mentioned in this letter get you down. <u>Even roses have thorns.</u> I love you with all my heart! Take good care of our kid!

Forever your loving husband,

Neil

***

It bothered her, but she understood that he had to try to make it clear about his fear...that she might not understand if something happened to him. She had never heard him talk so openly about the dangers.

The words, *"even roses have thorns."* She knew what he meant. She knew that he was tough. Her man must be tough. It must really be getting to him or he wouldn't have been so brutally honest.

She continued to follow every bit of news from the Pacific theater. The enemy was tenacious. War. Thorns indeed. She wondered: Was he being shot at today? Was he shooting at someone else? Was he strafing an enemy ship with a hundred guns pointed at him? It was all too heavy to think about. She had to know, but, at the same time, she had to also shut it out of her mind.

Once the thorns were removed, they would own love and would never be separated again.

CHAPTER NINE

PACIFIC WAR

Oct 14, 1944   U.S. 5th Fleet - Task Force 58 - Aircraft Carrier U.S.S. Princeton

Lieutenant Thomas was taking his dinner at a relaxed pace while he read the *Stars and Stripes*. Things were swinging the Allies' way on all fronts. He reflected upon the ten months of war he had experienced. He considered how he had built up a shell around him to keep him from thinking about the killing and the loss of friends. He wondered about his surviving brother Johnny over in Italy and what he must be going through.

In ten months he had experienced more danger, more fear, more loss of friends and more involvement in killing than a hundred men his age could possibly experience, outside of the element of battle and war.

He pondered upon it. The killing ability of modern weapons was something the world had never experienced before. The slaughter of millions had taken place in World War I—"the war to end all wars"—and it was brutal, but the awesomeness of what destruction could be wrought upon an enemy force by a single well-armed plane was incomprehensible.

This war was hundreds of times more deadly from above than anything ever witnessed before. One good hit with a well-placed five-hundred-pound bomb or torpedo could cost the enemy hundreds, maybe even thousands of lives in a matter of seconds. With hundreds of planes moving in at each other with speeds of up to four hundred miles per hour, Neil and his comrades in their F6F Hellcat fighters were awesome in what damage they could inflict. The pilot seat was not only a seat in a deadly piece of machinery, but also in witnessing the course of war rapidly heading towards highly mechanized methods of killing.

Caroline. How was she doing? What was she doing? Their little boy had come a month early. How he wanted to be there.

Home. Home, the sweetest place on earth. The war. It was a just cause. It was for them, his wife and kid. If it wasn't for that thought, he could never do it. It *had* to be just. That's all there was to it.

"Hey Neil, ol' buddy, what ya say I join ya." Lt. Commander Chad Watson sat down at the mess table with his tray opposite Neil. "How's the war goin' for our comrades in Europe?" he asked.

Neil looked up from the *Stars and Stripes* and smiled, "The Nazis are getting their fannies kicked, Skipper. I've got a brother on the ground somewhere over there." He smiled as if in reminiscing he suggested that it was Johnny's boots doing the kicking. "If anybody can kick hard, it's my older brother," he laughed.

Commander Watson smiled, noting the affectionate look the memory of Johnny brought to the lieutenant's face. "I guess I owe you a congratulations. Some of the boys told me your wife gave birth to a son. I'm real happy for you, Neil."

"Oh yeah, I almost forgot." Neil reached inside his shirt pocket and pulled out a cigar. "I saved this for you, Skipper." He handed the red and white banded cigar over the table to the squadron commander.

"Thanks." He held it to his nose and asked, "Cuban?"

"The best," returned Thomas. "Bought 'em in L.A. the day I shipped out. I decided it would be good to have, you know, to celebrate with when the big day came. Funny, I don't smoke."

"A good smoke now and then would do ya good, Neil," replied the grinning commander as he put the cigar in his pocket and started in on the mashed potatoes and gravy.

There was a pause while they both worked at their food. Neil was just about done and was getting ready to head back to his quarters.

"You've got seven kills, Thomas. Today could of been your eighth. What's wrong, Neil?" Watson queried his wing leader. He noticed a seriousness to the lieutenant that smelled like stress, fear, and tightening up. He had seen it before. It could get a man killed if he didn't get a handle on it.

"I froze," he shot back, looking up at the commander with apparent ambivalence. "I don't know why. I just froze. I'm sorry."

"Is it your boy? Being a new dad?"

"No sir."

"Look, sometimes it happens. We start thinking about the wife and kids and we get cautious, tense, and lose the aggressive edge. Losing that edge has gotten good pilots killed."

There was a pause as the commander looked at Neil while continuing to eat. "I'm giving you some leave time," he directed with a mouth full of food. "Unwind. We need you, Thomas. We don't need you dead. No missions for a few days. I want you on the bridge. Work with Captain Keller. I've already talked to him about it. It will give you some good experience, besides."

"Listen, sir, I appreciate what you're trying to do, but..." Watson cut him off. "I don't need more dead pilots, dammit!" he responded using his fork directed to Thomas' face to make the point. "You deserve the break. I'm not picking on you, Thomas. It happens to the best of us, and, frankly, you're one of them. I'm the commander here and it's my squadron. If we get short and into trouble, then the leave is off. But for now, no missions for a week."

He glared at Neil sternly and shoveled another fork of potatoes into his mouth. "Oh, yeah, I almost forgot. Once this next campaign is over I'll be sending you and Bobby down to Australia. We've got some new F6Fs to pick up. Take some time. Have some fun. You know what I mean?" The commander winked at him.

"Oh, and Thomas," Watson looked up from his tray of food. "The brass says it can wait till we open the way for the Army Aircorp in the Philippines. It all starts in a couple of days. It shouldn't take too long before the Army has a couple of airstrips. Then we'll turn it over to them. Get some rest." He returned to concentrate on his food.

"Thank you, sir. Is that all?" Neil stood up with metal tray in hand to leave.

"That's all, Thomas. Loosen up, boy."

Neil saluted and left. Dropping his tray off, he headed out of the officers' mess and down the stairs to the pilots' quarters and the bunk room he shared with Ensign Bobby Roberts.

He was uptight and he recognized it. He hated what he was

becoming. "Yeah, sure," he reasoned. "It was a duty, it was war, that's all. Them or me." All that self-talk to try and keep him tuned up for battle. He was slipping. It was more than the battle taking place in the Pacific skies. It was more than that. It was the battle taking place inside of *him* that had him worried the most. Was he a softie? Was he afraid of something? Something bigger than dying?

What would he be when he returned home? How would he act? Would he be a psychopathic, hate-filled killer or just an ex-Navy pilot...a hero who did his job well...killed well? He couldn't figure out what was eating at him. But it was eating from the inside out.

Neil thought about the "Nip" Watson had splashed that day. He replayed the whole scene in a matter of seconds on his way to his bunk room. It was his kill, an easy kill. It would have been his eighth. He had the Jap on the run. Like a movie, he could visualize the fight. He could see the Jap "Zero" in his gunsights.

***

He not only froze with the Jap in his sights and his finger on the trigger of the six wing-mounted .50 caliber machine guns, he had some crazy thought go through his head when he should have been concentrating on combat. It had never happened before.

There was the enemy fighter, a Zero, the sole survivor of a group of six fighters Neil and his squadron had just tangled with. His thumb was on the trigger. He watched the Jap pilot maneuvering wildly, trying to escape. But Neil had him cold. The Jap would die in seconds when he let go with a burst from the machine guns.

Then...he couldn't do it. Something happened. The callous shell of protection a pilot must throw up around himself had been pierced.

Then he remembered. He saw an image flash into his mind, like the replay of a movie. It was Cameron. He could see Jim Cameron running with two Jap Zeros on his tail. It happened one month earlier over the island of Tinian. He and Jimmy, accompanied by a new guy, Ensign Roberts, had been caught off guard. Jimmy decided to try a maneuver to draw off one of the Jap fighters, but two followed him instead. Neil and the new guy, tangled up with two other Jap planes, got lucky and splashed the Zeros, and then went to help out Jimmy, who was frantically calling for backup. He could still hear Jim's voice over the radio:

"Damn, I can't shake these guys. Where are you Neil? Oh, man! I'm hit. I'm going down! May Day! May Day! ... You guys read me? Come on Thomas... You there?"

Neil called back, "We're on our way Jimmy! Hold on buddy... Go down if you're hit, maybe they'll peel off of you and we can pick 'em up... Jimmy?" No response.

Then he caught sight of the aerial duel—or what was left of it. They had Jimmy and he was going down onto the deck—flying just above the surface of the water followed down by the Zeros. He was smoking, fire coming out of the fuselage. The Tojos showed no mercy. No mercy at all. They fired at him again and made sure he wouldn't survive. Jimmy's plane was finished as it broke apart from the impact of hitting the water.

Suddenly Neil was filled with rage. A feeling of hate swept over him. He closed in from 12 o'clock, coming in on them out of the sun, Bobby Roberts right behind. He opened up immediately, nailing one Jap pilot cold. He saw him get hit as the .50 caliber bullets tore the canopy to shreds, and watched as bits and pieces of airplane exploded around him. He felt a satisfaction that he had evened the score. Payback. Payback felt good. He watched the Nip's plane, what was left of it, cartwheel and skip across the waves. Kill number seven.

Bobby was chasing the other one and, after a minute of dueling, the new guy made his second kill.

Neil turned back and flew over the spot where Jimmy Cameron had gone down, hoping beyond hope, that somehow Jimmy had gotten out of the cockpit and was down there alive. Nothing. No sign. His buddy had been swallowed up in the great expanse of ocean, as if nothing had taken place.

It was strange. His fellow pilot and comrade flying next to him one minute, gone the next. Not a trace he had even existed. A big gaping hole opened in the sea and ate him, swallowed him, and he simply was no more. Nothing to say. Nothing to do. Just fly back to the carrier.

Pacific War

Neil entered the deck hallway to his quarters, his mind far from that day when they lost Jimmy Cameron. Now his thoughts shifted to the scene during the dogfight on that day's morning mission. He could see himself with the enemy plane in his sights. He could see the moment—when he should have blasted the Jap out of the sky...but he froze instead. It came to him like a "flick," a movie scene playing in slow motion.

With his thumb on the stick's trigger he could down the Nip. More payback. But the thoughts of the two Jap pilots that didn't show mercy to Jimmy one month earlier had a sudden and unexpected effect on him. He saw Jimmy there, in his mind, instead of the enemy pilot, trying desperately to live, to survive, to get back home to his wife and little girl.

He had hesitated as that mental picture ran through his mind. He couldn't kill the Jap. If he did that, it would, in a sense, kill the man's wife, child, mother, father...

His meanness had suddenly vanished. The bravado—the "edge"—was missing. The will to kill wasn't there. His lack of action could cost another American his life, and he knew it. Then the Skipper moved in. Watson yelled over the radio for him to get out of the way or get shot down, then he moved in and splashed the Jap. It was over. The ocean took the Jap and his fighter and swallowed him, just like it had done with Jimmy.

Neil opened the metal door to his cabin and entered the small cubicle. He was confused. He was supposed to be a killer. That's what he was getting paid to do. It was his job, his duty, with a million other American men as well. It was war.

He sat on the edge of his bunk. Staring at the floor he knew the Skipper was right. He needed a break...to sort the strange feeling out. If he didn't, next time it might cost him his life, or that of one of the other guys.

He swung his legs onto the bed and lay back, hands behind his head, looking into the ceiling as if a movie was playing there for him. He saw the picture of Caroline and the rose garden on California Avenue. He pictured a little boy—his boy—playing there. He was suddenly sick of the violence. He was afraid of the prospects of growing stone cold, insensitive, mean.

Reaching over for the picture of his wife that he had pinned to the wall, he brought it down to him and laid it on his chest as thoughts continued to cause him an uneasy feeling. He had become a killer. He had lost everything gentle the last time he had touched her. He now was a killer in a just cause that people would be slapping him on the back over when he returned home. An ace... Five kills plus two. And what was more, he was good at it.

He tried to put the pity out of his mind. It was pity for himself, or was it sympathy for the Japs he had killed? No, it wasn't sympathy. They were trying to kill him and were just as dedicated to their job as he was to his. It was a fair duel when he tangled with an enemy pilot. The best, or luckiest, won. That was all. That was it. Nothing more. Killing just happened. It was war. It wasn't personal. "It was fair, wasn't it?" he asked himself.

If it wasn't fair, then it was when he splashed the Zero that killed Jimmy. He felt rage, anger, and satisfaction at downing the Jap and evening the score. That was what was eating at him. It was something eating at him from the inside, an anger and a fear. Anger that the war had taken him away from his wife and kid, anger that it had killed his friends along with his big brother Billy, anger that it was starting to become part of him—who he was—his personality. Fear? Fear that it was changing him. Maybe he would never be the same, feel the same about life, about love. Maybe it was a combination of the two.

A new preoccupation with a little inner voice he was battling had entered his life. The voice whispered, "Get ready..." He tried to dismiss it as a pure overactive imagination at work.

He had to fight it! He had to get back to the love that used to sing in his heart...the carefree spirit that made life so meaningful. Caroline, their new little house, simple dreams...peace.

War. He wanted to get it over with and get back home. He hoped to keep his promise to Caroline to be there at Union Station by their anniversary, February 14th.

After these many months the wind of war was blowing west...to the Philippines. Perhaps they could get this thing over with soon and all the foreboding, feelings and mixed-up emotions could be left out in the Pacific where they belonged. Buried. Buried in the Pacific with all of the dead pilots and sailors from both sides.

War. It could destroy men on the inside as much as it could kill them on the outside. He suddenly thought about that day on Santa Monica Beach back in February, just before shipping out. He and Caroline had gone there to be near the ocean and walk along the beach at sunset. He picked up a seashell and handed it to her. Lying on his bunk with his hands behind his head he could see himself with Caroline.

***

"Here. Listen, Neil," she handed it back to him. "What do you hear, honey?"

"The sounds of peace," was his poised reply.

"Don't you hear the ocean, the waves?" she teased, poking him in the ribs.

His mind was on his visit earlier in the day with Father O'Donnell. He looked down at her with a weak grin and simply said, "Peace."

What had Father O'Donnell told him when he went into St. Andrew's, there on Raymond Street, in Pasadena... What was it? And why did he say what he said? He had gone there looking for a benediction of sorts, not a philosophical lecture.

"Keep your head and your heart linked together, Neil. Don't fear the death of the body, boy." Father O'Donnell had always called him that..."boy." He went on, "Fear the death of love. No one can take that from you, Neil lad...no one. Only you can let it die...and you can't let it die! Fear hate and anger like it was a cancer... Take care my boy. Here's a scripture from Proverbs I want you to ponder on. You read the words aloud and then tell me what you think they mean."

Neil remembered reading them, almost with ambivalence:

Keep thy heart with all diligence; for out of it are the issues of life.

The Last Valentine

"No matter what happens, don't let any man take your heart," the priest continued. "Know what's most important and then do it. As you do, your life will be well spent. There is nothing more tragic than one who lives a life filled with petty and unimportant things. To know what matters most, you've got to keep your heart."

It was his last visit with his friend, the good Father. He shared other thoughts with him, reminding him of his good family and the catechisms, and prayed with him. Then there was a final confession before heading for combat.

But those words. Words about love, the heart, *what matters most*. The words seemed like idle banterings of a pious man who didn't understand how much Neil cared about the life of his body. He thought the old priest was just trying to do his duty.

But then...then he recalled that Father O'Donnell was an ex-Army chaplain. He had seen men die in World War I. Maybe the priest had seen something or knew something that Neil could only know after tasting the bitterness of battle. Now he knew that the old priest indeed was wise.

He felt the warmth of love through distant recall of memories. Could it die? Could the ability to love be hardened or lost because of the killing he was experiencing? He pondered long and hard on the questions.

He couldn't fathom love dying, then. Then, he felt so full of it. Then, before he had killed, before he had tasted war's ugliness... before he was an ace or a hero.

He respected the Skipper, but Watson was an ignorant man, at least about one thing, he thought... Watson winking to him about having fun down in Australia when he went to pick up the new planes. He knew what the Skipper meant. Loosen up. Get rid of the tension. Relax. Get a woman...or two. Forget about the war.

"Nobody is going to fill these arms but you, baby," and he kissed Caroline's picture tenderly and pinned it back on the small corkboard hanging on the wall. Being with her was what taught him about love.

Neil pondered upon the words of Father O'Donnell as he stared at the photograph. Love. Peace. War. One preceded the other. Which one, though?

Pacific War

He thought back to that day, ending there on Santa Monica Beach. He remembered Caroline's questioning look when he had simply repeated to her the word "peace," when she had asked him what sound he heard coming from the seashell. His mind was on what was out there, out there in the Pacific, six thousand miles beyond Santa Monica Pier.

"What does *Pacific* mean in Spanish, Caroline?" he recalled asking. He thought it meant calm or something.

"Pacifico," she said, "means peaceful. Tranquil." She had looked up at him with a confused look, wondering what he was thinking.

"Pacific. Pacific war." He turned to her. "Peaceful war," he joked in a quiet tone indicating the irony of it. They walked down the beach until it grew dark. His eyes were on the west, the setting sun. It was a rising sun for others. Soon he would be there.

CHAPTER TEN

"SUSAN AND CAROLINE"

11:00 p.m. EST January 2, 1995 - American Airlines Flight 1530

Susan looked up at the stewardess who was asking her if every-thing was alright. The plane had encountered some air turbulence.

"Yes, I'm fine, thank you," Susan replied. She looked at her watch. She had read steadily for two hours. She was engrossed in the manuscript, *The Last Valentine—A Love Story,* but the preceding chapter had made her pause to think deeply.

She thought about the man she had just come to know, the son of Lieutenant Neil Thomas. "Neil Thomas Jr. The son—the man I just met this morning. Could he be at all like his father?"

She liked what she had read about Lieutenant Thomas and could see why Caroline had stayed "in" love for so many years. "If the son of the World War II Navy hero was anything like his father, then..." She wondered at the possibilities.

The man portrayed as Lieutenant Thomas seemed to have it all. Warmth. Strength. Charm. Wit. Courage. Love. The blend that makes a true hero. They were enduring qualities. It seemed so unfair that man's brutality to man would cause lives like that to be snuffed out so easily. The world needed examples of the virtues that seemed to be so much a part of Lieutenant Thomas' life.

She felt fortunate to have a part in a story like this. It would be refreshing to tell, to broadcast. The gloomy world of violence, intrigue, corruption... The typical take of the video tabloid and talk shows, was too much a steady diet of depression for her. Mr. Bruce Warren, CNTV's owner, had the American public pegged right, she thought. American Diary provided them hope, a cause for celebra-tion, with the stories of courage and love acted out by everyday Americans.

It was a tribute to American viewers that the clean, non-gossip format was attracting so many millions of them. American Diary

"Susan and Caroline"

provided the viewer a "break" from the steady diet of "TV trash." She was glad she was given the chance, but she had no time for relationships. She was constantly on the road.

She thought about it. Would she be willing to give it all up for the right man? She drew a big paycheck and it was a dream come true for a professional working woman. "Money can't buy happiness, the saying goes," she thought. Those words came back, now haunting her. Words from fifty-year-old love letters. She heard them that morning. *"The key to happiness... The key to happiness... The key to happiness..."*

Like a drum beat they rolled through her mind. Why wouldn't the words leave her...leave her in peace?

"The key to happiness is knowing what matters most...what matters most...WHAT MATTERS MOST! "

Susan found herself staring out the window of the plane at the clouds...seeing right through them to visit the face of the man she had barely met. She was kidding herself to think she wasn't interested.

If this Neil Thomas Jr. was a religious man, what would it mean to her? She had known other religious men and woman. Her aide, Kathy Clark, was one. She always seemed to be so wholesome. Kathy—one of the funnest, yet totally committed people she had ever known. Committed to live what she preached. She walked her talk. All too many people seemed to live a life "saved" in their ways; not "saved" from them. Her "ex," Rick, was always preaching to her and then turning around and doing what he wanted. He was "saved," he had told her. She didn't know if she was or not.

She hadn't found...what? What was the right word? She searched her mental dictionary for the best word to sum up why she hadn't been impressed by most religious ideas. Substance? Yes. Yes, that was the word. "Substance."

"Substance?" She thought about the carved words on the wooden plaque over the entry door in the Thomas family home. That must have been some strong subliminal suggestion. She smiled at the whole affair of being so caught up in this Caroline Thomas' world. She had even fantasized of living in the 1940s and being in Caroline's shoes. Susan and Caroline...a world apart, yet...

The Last Valentine

"The words placed there five decades earlier by Lieutenant Neil Thomas, Sr.... The old Thomas home," she thought. She would be willing to give up freedoms, paychecks, her work, if... "If there could be substance to a relationship with Neil Thomas, the writer."

Still, she couldn't set herself up for another fall. Rick, had swept her off her feet—then dropped her down hard.

Promises. It would take a lot of courage for her to open up to another man.

Faithfulness. It was an integral part of her dream which included the country cottage, white picket fence, children.

Trust. It is a big part of marriage. Too big to dismiss.

Courage. She mulled upon the word. There was the courage of battle as typified in the life of Neil's father. Then there was another kind of courage. She remembered Neil relating to her the reason why Caroline never remarried. That was a different kind of courage. Her thoughts were interrupted by the rough ride the plane was encountering.

"Ladies and gentlemen, this is Captain Sorenson. We're heading into some weather patterns which may cause a few bumps in our approach to Washington National. We recommend you fasten your seat belts and relax. As soon as we are through it, we will turn off the 'fasten your seat belt' sign. Thank you for flying American, and have a pleasant remainder of your trip."

Susan put her chair back in the upright position and fastened her seat belt. She looked out the window and noticed the darkened sky and distant lightning. Rain started to streak across the window.

Courage, she thought. There are so many ways to show it. As she looked down at the page she had been reading she pictured the woman—a strikingly beautiful woman. She felt like she was beginning to know Caroline Thomas.

The picture Neil painted in the opening scenes was of a very sensitive woman, one who showed emotion easily. According to Neil in private conversation, there was a very strong woman under that tender exterior. There was a side to her as determined as she was gentle. She was, according to her son, a woman who wouldn't give up hope. A committed woman who kept her word. And, she was a proud woman who took care of her son through work and education.

Caroline was evidently a devout woman. Although Susan didn't know much about specific tenents of the various Christian churches, she did know they believed in all of the virtues described in the Bible. She also knew they believed in the sanctity of marriage and the family. That was a tenant that would be easy for her to accept, embrace.

What Susan knew about Caroline, she liked. It was unadulterated, old fashioned goodness. The kind of goodness so hard to find packaged in people today. It seemed to come effortlessly to her.

With many marriage offers, opportunities to find fulfillment and happiness, Caroline had refused them all. She remembered the way Neil had described her life, earlier that day during their interview.

Susan had posed the question—a natural question that would cause anyone to wonder: "Why didn't your mother ever remarry?"

"My mother was a beautiful woman with a sparkle in her eye that could grab you, take you in," Neil replied. "And when it did, you knew you were welcome. It was something that she could have done. Remarrying, I mean." Neil handed her a picture of his mother in her thirties, then one in her forties and fifties.

"Striking," Susan responded as she intently searched the black and white photos.

"Yes, yes she was, and in a regal way. She carried her age with a gracefulness and even a childlikeness—always kind, affable, ready to offer a smile at a moment's notice. You would have been greeted as if you were the only person in the room, *the* most important person. She would look at you with those brown eyes and you could see a depth and an innocence, all at the same time. If I sound like I worship my mother, well, you'd be right. As I grow older, I see clearly the sacrifices—her deferring of personal pleasures for those of others. Deferring love until..."

"Until your father returned?" Susan interjected with a question.

"I guess so. I've often thought so—to myself of course. You know, she did have many suitors, and once I thought she might remarry, but she never could. When I'd ask her why, she would answer, 'I'm still waiting...waiting for the right man.' Now, I think, she simply couldn't fall out of love with my father... I think the love grew with age."

Susan stopped. There was a pause in her questioning. Those words: "...She simply couldn't fall out of love..." What a feeling to have and to hold onto. She considered the deep meaning behind that kind of sensitivity. She wondered if it were actually possible to feel that way about a man. She returned to the conversation.

"And so, her annual pilgrimage to Union Station... Do you think she looked for more than memories there? Do you think, perhaps, she actually looked for him to keep his promise to return to her there?" Susan was probing, seeking to get a handle on the psyche of this woman, Caroline Thomas.

"My mother was an incurable romantic. Romance personified. But not just romance for the sake of romance... It was for love, true love. I have come to believe that it may not be a bad way to live. But, in addition to all that, she married him "until death do us part." She would remind me that "missing" didn't mean "dead." So, I guess she did harbor a hope that somehow he could return."

"Interesting." This woman was a dream come true to any man who would hope for a faithful companion to the end, Susan mused. She wanted to ask about the religious beliefs of the woman, Caroline Thomas, but the demeanor of the interview was directed in more disclosure of her love affair with her missing husband. She needed to continue to pursue that angle.

"Was there anything else, some other compelling reason which would keep your mother so loyal and true to your father's memory?" she probed.

"There was one other thing that kept her feeling close to him. It was the dream she had two nights in a row before she received the telegram from Western Union. And it was the powerful impact it had which caused such a resolve in her to be the buoyant personality that she was."

"A dream?" Susan perked up. "But that's not in your manuscript, is it?"

"No, not the complete version, anyway. Would you like to hear about it?"

"Please, go ahead. Yes. I want to hear all about it," Susan replied.

"Susan and Caroline"

***

My mother should have known. For two nights in a row he was there...there in her dreams, working next to her in the garden. He had his uniform on. He was happy, and he was home, but it seemed so strange.

Her dream gave her a warm feeling, as warm as his touch always gave her. He held her in his arms, among the roses. He brushed the back of his hand gently against her cheeks as she stood there, her eyes closed, feeling his tenderness. He spoke to her in the dream.

"I came to tell you that I love you, Caroline." He looked at her with an intensity that seemed to ask silently, "Do you understand?" He held her hands to his chest, cupping them in his.

"I've never loved you more, and I finally know the word for all of my feelings for you...I know the word..." and he would turn to the rose bush and pick a long-stemmed single red rose in full blossom.

"Your hands are bleeding, Neil. The thorns...they're hurting you... Let me go and get some bandages," she would say to him in the dream.

"No! Don't leave! Not yet! It doesn't hurt anymore. Nothing hurts anymore. Caroline, the thorns don't hurt. The thorns are a *very important* part of life!"

"Why?" she remembered thinking, and it was as if he could read her mind.

"Because, love means more, grows deeper, if you can overcome the thorns." He then kissed her softly and tenderly. "To overcome them means we must deal with them, even get hurt by them."

Looking at her, as he slowly pulled away, he would say, "The thorns appear to everyone. Can you do it, Caroline?" and he appeared to have an anxious expression on his face, a pleading look.

She melted into his arms for one final embrace and then she was left standing there as he disappeared into a bank of fog. He would turn, in the dream, and he would think the question so clearly that she would know he was asking, "Can you do it?"

The Last Valentine

She wanted to run to him but her legs were heavy, as heavy as lead. They wouldn't move.

"I'll be back for you," he seemed to call from the fog enshrouded field. "Forever... *Forever is a promise...to keep.*"

Somehow she felt right, even though she couldn't run to him. She felt a peace and a warmth, the way it always had been when he was there with her. She accepted it, but not without tears. She would awaken with moist eyes. But she knew he had to leave, as if it were a duty... Just as if one more mission needed to be flown before he could finally return home to her.

She was grateful to wake and feel as if he had been with her in the night. She prayed for the dreams to return.

Then the swallow came: "La golondrina." It appeared at her window on the morning of the second dream-filled night. She suspected the truth would lie in what the postman would be delivering to her that day.

***

Susan peered out the window of the 747 and realized that her mind had been wandering for over a half an hour, recalling that part of that morning's interview with Neil and the story of the dream. She had used some of the time to inquire about his personal family-marital status, as if it was just part of her job to know. She wondered if it had fooled him. It didn't matter, really. What mattered was this story, but the more she read, the more she thought about him.

"Thorns appear to everyone." She reflected again on the adage. "An appropriate way to describe my life," Susan whispered to herself.

It was 8:00 p.m. Pacific Standard Time, and she turned the hands of her watch forward to show Eastern Standard Time. Eleven o'clock. The plane had been bounced around by rough air. She glanced around her to see terror on the faces of several passengers. Their knuckles were white from gripping the armrests on their seats and the lightning show outside only challenged the resolve of most passengers around her to stay calm. Children started to cry. She was nervous, but didn't want to feel or show panic.

In an attempt to see if she could calm herself by getting back into the manuscript where she had left off earlier, she read the first words of the chapter titled "Western Union," and read: "Caroline awakened to the sound of a small bird outside her bedroom window..."

CHAPTER ELEVEN

WESTERN UNION

October 20, 1944 Pasadena, California

Caroline awakened to the pleasant chirping sound of a small bird outside her bedroom window. She wrestled with getting out of bed. For two nights in a row she had dreamed that Neil had come to her. She felt warm, good, loved. Little Neil hadn't stirred, so she just lay there, listening to the song of the bird. Then it hit her. There, sitting on a ledge, was a small bird—a swallow!

Caroline threw the covers off herself and angrily flung her arms towards the small winged creature. "Shoo—fly away! Shoo—leave!" She finally rapped on the window with her hand and covered her shivering body with her arms. She was shaken and her hands and feet felt weak.

"It means nothing. Absolutely nothing," she told herself out loud as she walked out of the bedroom and into the kitchen to start a pot of coffee.

It was 8 a.m. and time for the CBS morning news broadcast. She turned on the Philco radio that sat on the kitchen counter and began to work with the water on the stove. The announcer started with war news:

This morning, it was announced, the combined forces of the Allied Pacific Fleet and Armies, under the direction of General Douglas MacArthur, launched attacks against Japanese forces throughout the Philippine Islands. In what has been called the largest naval armada in American history, the Pacific fleet assembled at dawn, Philippine time, and began to engage the enemy on land and at sea. Reports of naval air attacks against the capital city of Manila have been confirmed. For more on the latest developments, stay tuned to this CBS radio network.

Western Union

The seemingly banal chatter and music of advertisements came on the air.

"Dear God...dear God..." Caroline cried aloud. Feeling suddenly weak, she grabbed hold of the kitchen table, easing herself down on the wooden chair. She understood what her anxious feelings had meant. And now, the dream of Neil coming to her, of his hands being cut, of his questioning her if she could "do it" as if it meant...

The bird... "It was a sparrow, not a swallow!" she told herself. The story her friend had told her—how a swallow had alighted on the window ledge when she washed dishes and how three days later a telegram came, a Western Union telegram, telling her family that her brother had been killed on Guadalcanal! The worst possible news came in Western Union telegrams! Telegrams prefaced by swallows! She put her hands to her head, trying to convince herself it was all a bad dream—or she was going crazy.

Caroline felt cold. She crossed her arms and slumped her head down on them. Her breathing was heavy as she sought to regain emotional control. The war. It controlled her life!

The news report came on again:

"People of the Philippines, I have returned!"

The announcer then continued:

The voice you just heard was actual radio transmission of words spoken by General Douglas MacArthur as he strode ashore today onto the Island of Leyte. His address, in part, carried a message to the Filipino people that he is in personal command at the front and has landed with his assault troops.

The battle for the liberation of the Philippines commenced earlier yesterday morning with attacks by aircraft of the U.S. 5th and 3rd Fleets. The planes struck at targets throughout the Philippines as American and Allied troops landed on the southern island of Leyte. The largest naval armada in U.S. history is pursuing what is left of the Imperial Japanese Fleet. There are no reports of casualties at this hour. We will bring you updates of this battle as we receive them. Now for the rest of the news. In Europe today...

Caroline switched off the radio and sat in stunned silence, staring blankly into the living room, a dark and oppressing feeling coursing through her. The news had been positive enough...but why then? Why did she feel this way?

She had been to the theater the Saturday before to watch newsreels. She had to know, to see what her husband was facing. She remembered looking on in tense silence as the camera mounted on the nose of a Navy Hellcat fighter bombed and strafed enemy ships in the Mariana Islands. She had seen footage of the "Battle of the Philippine Sea," or the "Marianas Turkey Shoot," as it was also called. American forces decimated Japanese air and naval forces, virtually eliminating them as a viable offensive fighting machine. She instinctively knew that Neil had been engaged in that combat. In fact, she imagined the footage being shown was shot from his plane.

Fear. She never had known such fear in all her life. The pilots and servicemen in the newsreels always smiled, as if they had no fear at all. Or were they just hiding it?...like Neil did...trying to bury his true emotions and feelings. They seemed to swagger with an ambivalence to the dangers around them.

She recalled the words in the dream so clearly. Neil's words: *"The thorns appear to everyone... Can you do it, Caroline?"* She didn't have any choice but to handle it. The thorns. They hurt, they cut, they made it so difficult to cling to the rose.

***

Three days had passed since that morning when the small bird appeared at Caroline's window. There had been no letters from Neil and the news from the Philippines showed American forces winning on land and at sea. There had been one American aircraft carrier, a destroyer, a cruiser and other American naval vessels destroyed by desperate Japanese "kamakaze" attempts to forestall the American invasion. She knew that more than a dozen aircraft carriers were attached to a fleet and there were two fleets engaged in the fighting. She hoped that it wasn't the Princeton, but she worried. No word was almost as bad as hearing the worst. It left her filled with anxiety.

Caroline tried to dismiss the coincidence of the dreams. Two nights in a row, the sweetest dreams she had known for all the time he had been gone. Then the happenstance of the swallow, or sparrow, appearing at her window. She tried to put it out of her mind.

She had gone to St. Andrew's Cathedral the day before to pray. She was a Methodist, but it was Neil's place of worship and she felt close to him—and to God—when she went there. No answers and no real peace came. But she had to turn to someone. She knocked on Father O'Donnell's door and he answered, looking older than she had remembered.

"Caroline Thomas! Come in! Come in, child!" The aging priest gave her a warm embrace. "What brings a good Methodist girl like you to our sanctuary this lovely October morning?" He knew what the look on her face meant. He gently took her by the hand and led her to a chair beside his small work table that served as a desk.

"I don't know where to go, Father...or what to do." She was in tears. She had little Neil with her in the stroller.

"What's wrong, child?" He knew, but he wanted her to tell him.

"Oh, I haven't heard from Neil for awhile, and this battle that's going on in the Philippines...I know he is there...and..." she couldn't go on.

The old priest came near to her and, kneeling down, let her cry it out. "I understand, I understand, dear," he said softly. "How can I help you feel better? Can we pray together?"

Caroline lifted her head, weakly smiled, and nodded as she struggled to contain the tears.

"O.K. then. You hold onto these beads and pray the words I pray. Then you come back to see me each day until you feel His strength, God's strength." They began to pray together. There was a pause, then the "Amen." A serene sense of well-being filled the small room.

The Last Valentine

"There, now. You come back any time, Caroline. My door is always open. I will pray for Neil. Look to God, child. Look to him in all your troubles. Please take this," and he handed her the crucifix with the prayer beads. "It is identical to the one I gave Neil on his last visit with me."

"Thank you! Thank you, Father O'Donnell. I feel much better. You'd make a good Methodist, Father."

"And you a good Catholic, child."

She returned home, comforted. With Neil Jr. down for a nap, she retreated to the bedroom to be alone. It was around noon when she began to feel the need...to pray. She knelt by the bed, but the words wouldn't come. Just thoughts. Just his words, from the dream...

"Can you do it, Caroline?" What had he meant by that?

There came a knock at the door. A cold chill swept through her. She didn't want to answer it. If it was regular mail, Mr. Myers would just put it through the mail slot and be on his way. She hadn't wanted to see him, not for the last three days, anyway.

She slowly rose and headed for the door, hesitating at the second knock. She mustered up her strength and remembered the dream: "Can you do it, Caroline?" The words kept returning. She had to do whatever it took, whatever Neil would want her to do.

Squinting through the window pane on the oak-paneled door, she could make out the shadow of a man. Perhaps it was a package from Neil; perhaps it was a special delivery letter saying everything was O.K. Perhaps... Maybe it's not Mr. Myers. She cautiously approached, opening the door as if in doing so any bad news would just go away. She grasped the door knob and slowly swung open the door to see his back to it.

"Yes, Mr. Myers. What can I do for you?" she asked weakly. Her heart pounded with fear. He turned around slowly and she could see the strain on his face, the tears gathering in the corners of his eyes. He couldn't speak...he couldn't move...he just looked at her.

"This..." he swallowed hard as he tried to finish the sentence. He looked down at the ground, trying to regain some composure. He held up the Western Union for her to see.

"This just came in, Caroline. I'm so, so sorry if..." He held it out to her nervously with an unsteady hand.

She looked at Mr. Myers and then down at the Western Union telegram with a sense of incredulity. Her mind rejected what was happening as she searched his face for any hint of a bad joke. He continued to hold the telegram in his outstretched hand.

Her body felt suddenly helpless as her legs seems to buckle under her. A stinging, white-hot feeling ran through her body that made her grip the door for support. Mr. Myers reached out to steady the young woman as she slid slowly to the floor. Letting out a faint gasp for air, she strained to control the emptiness that suddenly enveloped her.

"Caroline! Mrs. Thomas! Come on, honey, let's get you inside." The postman set his mail bag aside, gently lifted the sobbing young woman up and guided her slight, trembling frame to the sofa. He waited for some time to pass as she lay back trying to comprehend what was happening to her.

Finally looking back towards him, she whispered a throaty, "Please...please forgive me, Mr. Myers," and wiped away the moisture that coursed down her face. She fought for the courage to receive the telegram from his hand.

"I know how you must feel, Caroline," offered the gentle voice of her friend. "I'll just leave this right here on the coffee table and you call somebody and don't open it until they arrive. O.K., sweetheart?" He was kneeling down looking at her as she nodded through her weak gasps for air. He knew no one could console her, but at least family or friends could be there to support her.

"I want you to know, if there is anything, anything at all that I can do for you, I will. You'll be alright." He patted her hands that reached out to him as she struggled to speak. He was truly sympathetic, but now he, too, struggled for control as if he couldn't come to terms with the awful truth the telegram must hold.

Struggling to his feet, he finally said with a shaky voice, "I'm sorry, truly sorry, Mrs. Thomas. Call someone to come over. God bless you, dear," and he turned to go to the door. But as he reached for the door handle he heard her call out to him through a strained, tearful voice. "Mr. Myers, it will be O.K. It will be alright. Thank you, Mr. Myers."

He just shook his head in pity and muttered to himself as he opened the door to leave, "Such a senseless waste!"

Caroline stared down at the telegram. "Can you do it?" came the thought from the dream of the night before. She wanted to sleep, go back to the safety of the dream and hold him again. "Can you do it?" came the thought pounding in her head as a line from a song does...a line or verse that just won't leave until you change the tune.

She reached for the yellow Western Union and fingered it. Rising up, she walked over to the wall phone and put in the call to Richmond 9... A person picked up the phone on the other end.

"Hello, Jensen's," came the reply.

"Jenny?" asked a quivering voice.

"Yes... Caroline, is that you?"

"Yes," came the weak answer in a tone that at once spelled trouble.

"Jenny, can you come over? And Mom, can she come? O.K... Yes, I'll be fine. Please hurry." Her trembling voice hadn't fooled her big sister.

She hung up the receiver and staggered back over to the sofa. Reaching for the telegram, she slowly opened it.

1234 67 GOVT = WASHINGTON DC A.M. OCT. 23, 1944
MRS. CAROLINE THOMAS
CALIFORNIA AVE.
PASADENA, CALIFORNIA

THE NAVY DEPARTMENT DEEPLY REGRETS TO INFORM YOU THAT YOUR HUSBAND NEIL THOMAS, LIEUTENANT USN, IS MISSING FOLLOWING ACTION WHILE IN THE SERVICE OF HIS COUNTRY. THE DEPARTMENT APPRECIATES YOUR GREAT ANXIETY BUT DETAILS NOT NOW AVAILABLE AND DELAY IN RECEIPT THEREOF MAY BE NECESSARILY EXPECTED. TO PREVENT POSSIBLE AID TO YOUR COUNTRY'S ENEMIES PLEASE DO NOT DIVULGE THE NAME OF YOUR HUSBAND OR SHIP ASSIGNMENT.

VICE ADMIRAL JACOBS, CHIEF NAVAL ADMINISTRATIVE
SERVICES

"He's not dead! They don't know!" she exclaimed. Caroline
sunk to her knees on the floor. Coupling her hands together, she
offered a prayerful plea: "Dear God! Thank you. He's not dead.
Missing isn't dead!"

She looked up with tear-filled eyes, wiping at her stained cheeks
with the back of her right hand. The first thing she saw was the
hand-carved sign Neil had made when he was remodeling the
house:

*Belief is the substance of things hoped for, the evidence of things
not seen.*

The void in the silent room blended with Caroline's whispered,
"Thank you! Thank you, God! Help me to believe!"

***

11:30 p.m. EST January 2, 1995   Final approach - American Airlines flight 1530

Susan felt like she had been kneeling with Caroline as she read
the words of her heartbroken plea to God. She placed a marker in
the page, closed the pages of the manuscript and stared down at the
name on the cover page. A strange feeling of warmth swept
through her as she read his name on the bottom—"Neil Thomas Jr.
What are you doing to me?" she whispered almost inaudibly.

Due to heavy snowfall and storm conditions the plane had been
redirected to land at Dulles International Airport outside of
Washington D.C. Susan returned the manuscript to her briefcase.
She had hardly noticed the plane's rough ride over the previous thirty minutes. She was glad, however, to be almost on the ground.
Anxiousness, an impatient desire to touch down and make some
calls, consumed her.

The Last Valentine

Susan wanted to get back to Los Angeles within a week and that necessitated some quick scheduling with camera crews and her interview with Colonel David Jackson, the military historian for the Smithsonian. She decided to try to line up the interview with Jackson for the following day and stay the night in D.C. It was Jackson who had discovered the hidden fifty-year-old Lieutenant Thomas letters in the Philippines the year before. She could have camera crews there easily enough.

After landing, the passengers quickly exited. Everyone appeared relieved to have finally arrived on solid footing. Susan headed for the phones in the waiting lobby. The call to David Jackson went well and an interview time was set up for the following day.

She decided to make another call—a long distance call to Pasadena.

"Thomas," came the husky reply.

"Neil?" Susan queried in her best interviewer's voice.

"Yes!" came the animated response.

"Neil, this is Susan Allison. I had some time during my flight to rearrange my schedule to return to Los Angeles a bit sooner than I had expected. Some scheduling challenges caused me to ask if we can move our videotaping up to...let's say, January 9th. Will that be O.K. with you?"

"I'd be delighted, Susan." His reply was smooth and calm. He didn't want to give away his excitement at hearing her voice.

"Then, let's say, 8:00 a.m. Pasadena, January 9th and our crews will arrive an hour earlier to begin setting up equipment."

"Perfect. I look forward to it. Susan, I...I want you to know how impressed I am with your professionalism. I enjoyed every minute of our time together." He hoped she would catch his personal hint, the dual meaning that the enjoyment was more than just her professional tone.

"I feel the same, Neil. I read through most of the manuscript. Used up all of my Kleenex." They both laughed at the remark. "If any changes arise, I'll call you. Did I give you my telephone number?" she asked, knowing that she hadn't but wanting to make sure he had it in hopes...hopes of perhaps something more.

"I have your office number," Neil responded.

"Let me give you my home number, just in case, you know, you need to reach me and make any other plans. It's area code..." she gave him the number and said goodbye.

That went well, she thought. She could relax now. The tension of the meeting with him and the reading of the story had built up inside her all that day. Passing by the magazine racks at the gift shop and seeing the Valentine Card display, she smiled.

CHAPTER TWELVE

"VALENTINE DAY SPECIAL"

Pasadena, California. 8:00 a.m. January 9, 1995
Interview with Susan Allison and CNTV

It had been a long week. I looked forward to the taping of our interview highlighting the lives of my parents and their love story. But what had me anxiously watching out of the living room windows of my mother's old home on California Avenue, was the heart-pounding rhythm of my thoughts...thoughts about seeing Susan.

It was 8 a.m. and the camera crews were setting up for the interview. Susan hadn't arrived yet. Then I noticed a red Ford Thunderbird pull up into the long driveway and slowly come to a stop behind the video engineer's van. She was here.

"Welcome, Susan," I said with out-reached hands. "It's good to see you again. Come in...come in...the rain just keeps coming down." I eagerly motioned for her to enter as I held the door open.

"Well, I see the crew is here and setting up."

I smiled and nodded, reaching out to help her off with her overcoat.

"When is this rain going to stop, Neil?" she asked with a smile as she waited for me to guide her into the living room.

"I think it's here to stay." I found myself making small talk as I stared into an intriguing set of hazel-brown eyes and a soft-looking face with the features and mystery which had me momentarily beguiled. "I'm sorry...I didn't mean to have us standing here this long. Well, you know the way. Please...wherever you feel comfortable," I returned as I motioned with my arms to the sofas and chairs in the small but cozy corner of the living room. Warmth blazed from the fireplace. The ambience was as warm as I hoped the moods of my guests would be.

"Thank you," she said as she confidently entered, greeting each of the crew members by name. We took up seats opposite each other with the fire offering a backdrop to the comfortable setting.

"I've got to tell you, Neil. Your mother was an extremely devoted and sensitive woman. And your father...well he was one romantic man. And the ending to the story, if I have it all correct, is powerful. It's the tragedy that makes the triumph. It has all been very touching to document." Susan had been talking to me as she directed with her hands, pointing out to the crew what she wanted. She attached a 'collar mike' to her blouse and worked to get the adjustment right.

"I'm pleased, Susan. I can't tell you what this means to me, finding out about my father and all. It's become a special obsession to get the story right," I returned.

"Now, let me understand before we get started," she queried. "You freelance with the *L.A. Times* when you're not teaching high school English and coaching basketball, right?"

"Right," I replied.

"When all of this came together, you started to piece the events of what happened into a short story to sell in the Sunday edition of the *L.A. Times Magazine*, or was it *Reader's Digest?*"

"It was the *Times*. *Reader's Digest* picked up from there. I have some other publisher connections through a literary agent friend of mine back in New York, Phil Stanwick. He showed it to a couple of editors he knew at Warren Publishing and they wanted it. So here we are."

"O.K. I just wanted to mentally picture how we are connecting the American Diary segment with the publisher. Now the manuscript doesn't cover all of the letters. Do you have plans to make them public? A follow-up story perhaps?"

"Well, yes, Susan. I was hoping you might bring that up. It's a little bit early to be announcing another book, but the letters that were found with the last Valentine contain a history of his private battle for life behind enemy lines. And, I guess, more importantly they bequeath to us his soul's most cherished thoughts and philosophies on life. *The Last Valentine—Secrets of Love* is the tentative title. A sequel of course."

"Secrets, huh? I hope you'll have some more time to spend with me soon. I believe it would make a terrific follow-up story! Well that clears up the track your writing has taken to get us to this point. I just wanted to go through it once more. Let's get started, shall we?"

I knew she understood the story behind the manuscript. I guess I surprised her with the announcement of another book. I reserved my excitement at her suggestion of getting together again after this show was aired. I wanted that...needed it. I had to find out what made this woman tick. She had initiated our second meeting with a professional flare, I thought. Not giving into too much personal emotion. I secretly hoped that the outer wall of "TV persona" could be broken down by the end of the day.

"I'm ready," I nodded.

"Why don't we review the outline while the audio man tests the sound. We'll be at it for a few hours and take the best of the video and insert it into the half-hour piece." She handed me the script outline.

I took about five minutes to review it and handed it back to her with a question. "Susan, you might be interested in a part of my father's story that isn't covered in the outline."

"Oh?...What's that?" she asked.

I briefly went over one chapter in my book that told about my father's feelings at having frozen with his fingers on his plane's machine gun trigger when he had a clear "kill" on a Japanese fighter. I explained about his last flight and his struggle for survival in the Philippines. I emphasized again that the letters retrieved by Colonel Jackson with the *last Valentine* were all written with a special purpose in mind.

"Being based upon my father's most poignant sensitivities, they further described his beliefs and the emotions piqued during the war. He portrayed the distinct feeling that he wouldn't be coming back. I think some of those valuable insights may be useful in the script." I stopped and waited as she jotted down some notes.

"I'm sorry. His *last Valentine* to your mother and the information about the Japanese soldier's letter, found by Colonel Jackson, and then your general story, given at our last interview, was so thought-provoking that I didn't even consider that angle." She was still writing as she finished talking. "Neil, what do you say we start out here and then move to the chapter in your book describing his experiences, then shift into the script right here?" She pointed to the second half of the third page. "We'll tie it in here, where he encounters the Filipino guerrillas and then backtrack to the first two and a half pages." She looked at me for a response.

I nodded as the audio man announced; "We have speed. Ready, 5, 4, 3, 2, 1. We're rolling."

Susan began:

"We're in the Pasadena, California home of the late Caroline Jensen Thomas. With me is Neil Thomas Jr., her son, the author of *The Last Valentine - A Love Story.*" She picked up the newly designed jacket cover of my book and held it towards the camera. "The story you are about to see and hear is a modern love story that has taken fifty years to fully mature. It is an amazing tale of devotion, suffering, war, peace, the symbolism of a rose, and the fragrance of an enduring love that overcame the thorns of adversity.

"The story comes to its full and poignant conclusion in this, the anniversary year of the ending of hostilities with Japan. This year marks time in a special way. The warriors of World War II are aging. On both sides of the conflict they leave us with the drama of heroism, the stories of their love for families left behind and the memories of how they felt when, in their youth, they were called to fight for their countries."

She turned to the second camera, which allowed the camera man to zoom in on the wedding photograph of my father and mother.

"Tonight's story is their story. Its main cast of characters include Lieutenant Neil Thomas Sr., who, declared 'missing in action' for fifty years, has finally come home to rest. His wife, Caroline, with her special devotion, and the letters of love, lost for those fifty years, bring us a very extraordinary Valentine's Day story. You won't want to miss tonight's special edition of 'American Diary.' I'm Susan Allison. We'll be right back."

"Replay that for me will you, Andy," Susan called over her

collar "mike" to the video engineer in the next room. The introduction was replayed on the small monitor in front of us.

"We'll go with it," she called to the engineer. "O.K., let's have speed and start into the interview."

"We have speed," announced the audioman.

"Roll the cameras, Terry," she said as she straightened her blouse.

"Ready, 5,4,3,2,1. We're rolling."

Susan turned towards me and Camera One.

"Neil, you have just written a book titled *The Last Valentine - A Love Story.* Tell us, how did this all come about? And if you could, give us a little history on how the five-decade love story started here, in this beautiful old home."

"I'd be delighted, Susan," I returned with surprising comfort. Under other circumstances it would feel like an intrusion; the lights, cameras and four other people at work while I tried to create an acceptable feeling of ease for a smooth retelling of my parent's love story.

We taped for an hour and then we came to the story about my father's last flight and his fight for survival in the Philippine jungles. I took the interview from the chapters in my book, starting with the one titled "Missing In Action."

***

CHAPTER THIRTEEN

MISSING IN ACTION

October 20, 1944 Gulf of Leyte off the Philippine coast

He stopped writing and read back the words. It was "macho-man" talk. "How do you tell a woman about war? The way it really is, without depressing the heck out of her?" he wondered. The one thing he wanted most? To share what he was going through, not just the military stuff, but what he was feeling on the inside and what was causing it on the outside. But then...

Everything he felt on the inside had to do with the outside events. Aircraft coursing through the air at speeds of up to 400 miles per hour. So much enemy fire coming at you... It was all in the hands of God. All of it.

God. He knew God was real now. Not because of war...but in spite of it. "There must be a devil, too," he mused. Evil, hate, death, war. It all contrasted so diametrically with goodness, love, life, peace. The only person he could talk to was God... or Caroline.

He looked down at the letter again. He read the man-style writing...his attempt to get it all out. He knew if women could see this first-hand, war would probably end.

"They'd ban it! They'd hold out their most precious feminine offering from men until they all surrendered and signed peace treaties with each other." He smiled at the weird thoughts. Strange thoughts, but probably accurate. For him, women and sanity seemed to go hand in hand now. They had the sensitivity and instincts to find a better way. The ability to perceive the insanity of it all.

"It's a big operation, Caroline..." He frowned, crumpled the letter up, threw it in the wastebasket and walked out of the briefing room. "The censors would probably cut it all up anyway," he considered.

The Last Valentine

Lieutenant Thomas had an uneasy feeling. The attack against targets in Manila would commence at 0600 hours. The planes were on deck as he filed out of the briefing room accompanied by Bobby Roberts and a new pilot by the name of Tony Martinez. Tony was from Oxnard, California, just up the road from L.A. Neil liked him and vowed to take extra care of the new guy.

He didn't like it when that uneasy feeling came over him. It usually meant someone was going to die... one of his men or someone in the squadron. He knew the possibility existed it could be himself. Neil knew that he just had to suck it up and do his job. Everyone depended on each other. He'd be there for them.

It was big. The operation was backed by an armada of over a thousand warships. The 7th Fleet under Admiral Kincaid and the 3rd Fleet under Admiral W. F. "Bull" Halsey were out to crush the naval and land forces of Imperial Japan in preparation for the move against Japan itself. The first order of business was the "back door." The Allies could not afford to allow the Japanese to have over 300,000 men behind them as they approached the islands near Japan. They must wipe out the enemy's ability to reinforce troops from the Philippines.

It was coming soon, the big day the Filipinos had been waiting for. MacArthur, commander of Allied Forces in the Pacific, had promised he would return. Today he would do so after three long and bloody years of war.

The planes were on the flight deck. Pilots were headed towards their Hellcat F6F fighters. Each plane carried ammo for the six fifty-caliber machine guns and two five-hundred-pound bombs. Their primary mission was bomber protection and strafing of enemy targets, but today they were to be prepared to take on any enemy ship or target that could threaten the invasion—poised to lead the liberation of the Philippines from the air.

"So it's Manila and Clark Field," Lieutenant j.g. Billings commented to Neil.

"Yeah. You look out for yourself, Billings. By the way, congratulations on your promotion. The guys in Raven 2 are some of the best. You'll do fine as their leader." He could tell how nervous the young 21-year-old Lieutenant was. He felt the same way, but hoped he didn't show it.

Billings gave him the thumbs-up sign and split off to his flight division positioned ahead of Neil's group.

Neil's division was known by the call sign "Raven 3" and all of the flyers were under 25 years of age. He was the "old man" at 26.

"How you feeling today, Tony?" asked a confident acting and smiling Lieutenant Thomas to the new guy as he patted him on the back.

"A little nervous, Skipper," came the reply.

"You just follow Bobby and me. Remember what you've learned and you'll be O.K."

"Ay, ay, Lieutenant," returned the anxious young pilot with a look on his face that said, "if you say so."

"Every new pilot goes through the same thing. Just ask Bobby here. He splashed two Zeros in his first week. No sweat, right Roberts?" The Lieutenant was doing his best to bring some needed confidence to his men. Everyone seemed to look to the "Mormon" pilot and the "Skipper" for assurance and support.

Bobby was busily engaged in his chewing-gum and staring off towards the planes taking off. They would get their call any second to man their planes. "Yeah, that's right Skipper, no sweat," he replied as he continued busily chewing and watching. He, too, was nervous.

"O.K., gentlemen. Our turn. Let's go," Lieutenant Thomas called out above the cacaphony as they were given the signal to board their Hellcats.

"Every new pilot goes through the jitters," he was thinking as he ran to his plane. "Man, I go through this every time I take off. Every combat mission makes my hands sweat." That uneasy feeling he was trying to put aside was still with him. The older pilots had the same fears and anxieties as the newer ones, they just learned how to swagger through it. Becoming cavalier about facing death was a way to cope.

He pulled himself up into the cockpit. The wind was high and the noise from the engines was deafening.

"Hey, Lieutenant," came a shout from the deck. It was Johnson, the crew chief.

The Last Valentine

"Yeah, what is it?" Neil called back. The petty officer had something in his hands.

"You dropped something," he called over the noise, and held it up for the Lieutenant to see.

"Oh, yeah. Thanks." Neil motioned for Johnson to climb up and hand it to him.

Johnson handed the Lieutenant a small brown paper package and patted him on the hand.

"Good hunting, Skipper," Johnson shouted over the din and jumped back down to the deck. He gave him a salute, which was returned by Neil's grin and a thumbs up.

Lieutenant Thomas, his hand to his throat collar "mike," was now giving the flight command to his pilots. They began to taxi out.

He reached into his "Mae West" life-vest zipper-pocket, took the small brown package out and kissed it. Replacing it, he zipped the pocket securely and offered a silent prayer followed by the sign of the cross, his way of settling into the mission. Once he had done that, he focused. The small package contained a framed picture of Caroline and three-month-old Neil Jr. He didn't have time to read the letter. Mail call was just minutes after the briefing and he now had something to look forward to after their morning mission.

He taxied into position. That gnawing, uneasy feeling...he fought it through his mechanical flight check as he waited for the signal to take off. The flag came and he gave his engine full throttle. In minutes he was airborne, with his squadron alongside him.

"O.K. gentlemen, listen up. We will be on radio silence after this. Our objective is Red Bird. I repeat, Red Bird. Everybody got that?" They all acknowledged with a "Roger—Skipper." Red Bird was the code name for strafing Clark Airfield, the former U.S. Army air base before the fall of the Philippines to the Japanese. Planes from the Princeton were attacking with two objectives: One was Clark Field, the other, Manila itself.

Within thirty minutes they sighted the billowing smoke from the other squadron's attack on Manila fuel depots and shipping. They were headed northwest, over the Sierra Madre mountain range and into the center of Luzon itself. No enemy aircraft had been sighted.

They had caught the Japs flat-footed.

"O.K., boys. There's our target. Eleven o'clock. Let's knock 'em out with one big punch—then we go home. Follow me in." Lieutenant Thomas banked hard to the left and each of the Hellcats followed.

"Stay close in, Tony. Just follow Bobby."

"Ay, ay, Skipper," returned the new pilot.

They made two passes through heavy anti-aircraft fire. One of the planes was hit instantly. It was Wilkerson's.

"Looks like I caught some fire, L.T.," Wilkerson radioed. "My right wing flap. I've lost a little oil pressure, too."

"O.K., Wilk. Let's see if you can nurse your baby home."

"Roger, Skipper."

Their first mission of the invasion over the Philippines went better than he had expected. One plane hit but no losses. Not yet, at least. Lieutenant Thomas looked over to his right wing man. There was Tony Martinez with a thumbs up.

"Looks like we left 'em smokin', huh Lieutenant." It was Martinez.

"We sure did. A fine job, Tony. You get a couple of Zeros there on the ground?"

"Yes sir. Only three to go until I'm an ace, right Skipper?" the young pilot jokingly replied.

"Sorry, Martinez. They have to be airborne at least one foot off the ground. That's the rules of the game." It was Ensign Roberts.

"Yeah, them's the rules, Martinez," chimed in Wilkerson, as he guided his smoking Hellcat back towards the carrier. It helped calm him to be part of the on-going chatter.

"Raven leader to Raven 3... Raven leader to Raven 3, come in Raven 3." It was the squadron commander, Chad Watson.

"This is Raven 3. I read you Raven leader. Go ahead," Neil radioed back.

"Raven 3. What kind of shape you in?"

"All accounted for sir. Wilkerson hit, nursing it, and we're headed home."

"I've got a little change in plans. We need you to make a run against Black Dog. Over."

"Ay, ay, Skipper. Same coordinates per game plan?"

"Roger, Raven 3. Send Wilkerson home. We'll keep radio contact with him."

"Roger, Raven leader." Neil hated abandoning any of his men. They all knew the score. The mission came first.

"O.K. Listen up gentlemen. Raven leader gave us a little follow-up mission. The target is 'Black Dog.' I repeat the target is 'Black Dog.' Wilk, I hate to do this, but you're on your own. Maintain radio contact with Raven leader at ..." and he gave Wilkerson the radio frequency. We'll follow your flight path back home. You read me?"

"Roger. I copy that L.T." Ensign Wilkerson saluted as the group peeled off, heading south for Manila.

Within seconds they had Manila's docks in sight. The previous bombing runs had awakened the sleeping enemy and they had opened up with a fury from every gun emplacement not destroyed by the previous waves of American planes.

"O.K., boys, one run and we're home free. Let's make it a good one. Follow me in." Lieutenant Thomas peeled off to a hard two o'clock and headed into the firing which created puffs of black smoke around his cockpit. He was headed for the docks and the ships still afloat and returning fire at the American planes.

"Remember Pearl Harbor!" he voiced as he let go with every gun he had. He pulled up hard and felt a thud as his plane shook around him. He had been hit, but the plane was still manageable.

He glanced back at the ship he had just strafed as a ball of flames shot up into the air. "Bingo!" he exclaimed as the explosion was followed by a second and then a third.

They regrouped at 10,000 feet. A plane was missing.

"Were's Martinez?" Thomas called over the radio to Ensign Roberts.

"He was right behind me. Perry, did you see Martinez?"

Perry had just joined them. "Yeah. He got it. Saw him get hit and then he took it into the docks. No chance of getting out."

"Damn!" It was Thomas' voice. Instantly he was filled with the same rage he felt over the downing of Jimmy Cameron months before. Rage and violence go hand in hand. It was the only way he could make sense of the killing and destruction. He was glad he felt it... It was the only way for him to cope with the lunacy of it all, the confusion playing its bitter melody inside his head.

"Hey, Skipper, you don't look so good yourself. You got oil starting to make a mess of things. You got a good chunk of fuselage gone too."

"Yeah, I know." Neil had to get control of himself. They were over Manila Bay and headed west. He had only two options, really. He could try to make it back to the Princeton, 100 miles off shore to the east of Luzon, or he could ditch it in the bay. If he tried to make it back and had to bail out over Luzon, he would face capture from an enemy that beheaded their prisoners. If he ditched it in the bay, there was a chance he'd be picked up by a sub or rescue plane. He felt safer with the latter option.

"Looks like I'm a swimmer today, Bobby. You're Raven 3 now." Just then his plane stuttered and he felt a jolt. Oil engulfed the canopy.

"This baby just froze up on me. Can't see a thing. I'm going down. Get me some help, fast. You copy, Bobby?" Lieutenant Thomas opened his canopy for visual help...to pilot his fighter down towards the sea. He looking over at his wing-man, Roberts.

"Roger that, Skipper," the Ensign returned. "We're calling for the cavalry now, sir. You hang in there. If you can't, nobody can."

"Thanks, Bobby. Follow me down and then get back home," Neil radioed as he struggled to level out his plane now at five hundred feet. He didn't like the idea of "jumping out of a perfectly good airplane" as he had joked to his paratrooper brother, Johnny, two years earlier.

"Bobby?"

"Yeah, Skipper?"

"There are only two things that fall out of the sky. You know what they are?"

Roberts laughed nervously. "Yeah, Skipper. I think I do. Fools and bird..."

"That's right. I want to make sure no one thinks of me as

either." Thomas angled his plane into the surf below. Pulling hard on the stick, and with the engine freezing up, he was in a glider against the wind.

"Just a wet deck on a bobbing carrier," he reassured his fellow pilot. His tail hit the water first and dragged the plane to a skipping halt. The nose hit a small wave and the jolt caused him to strike his head hard against the instrument panel. He was bleeding, but alive.

"Roberts to Thomas," came the anxious voice over the radio.

"I'm O.K., Bobby. It's a rough ride down here. Breaking out the raft."

Ensign Roberts looked on as his comrade climbed up and out of the cockpit and onto the wing of his plane, still afloat. He saw the life raft inflate as he radioed a "May Day" distress call for his flight leader. His signal was received and he gave the ship the coordinant for the downed pilot.

"Good luck, Skipper," Bobby said to himself. "O.K. boys, we're going home." He swooped low over his friend Thomas and wagged his plane's wings to let him know he had called the "May Day" in. With a deep feeling of resignation, he offered a silent prayer for his friend.

***

"I've got to get out of this bird," Neil thought as he scrambled up and out of the cockpit onto the wing of his Hellcat, now bouncing on the waves. He inflated his life-raft and waved a hand signal to Ensign Roberts, who wagged his fighter's wings in a signal to him.

Easing into the rubber raft, he tried to paddle away, but the waves kept pushing him back towards the plane, which slowly started to sink.

"God, let me live," he mumbled aloud. He felt dizzy. The whack on the head must have been harder than he had thought. Blood strained down his face from a cut over his right eye. He pulled a handkerchief out of his trouser pockets and held it to the wound as he lay back.

"Let me get out of this and see my wife and kid. God, if you can hear me, I..." he blacked out and lay prostrate in the small raft.

He drifted for hours, coming in and out of consciousness while every now and then a swell would lift his body up and then send him and the raft down the other side. It started to rain. He wondered where the rescue planes were. He hoped for a submarine, seaplane, someone to see him. He knew the Navy would be looking for him. He had known one case where Admiral Spruance held up his entire task force for two hours while they searched for one downed pilot. That single thought gave him hope. The waves and the rain were getting stronger. He had to just hold on, just a little while longer.

"Got to keep myself alert, watch for the plane," he whispered under his breath. The storm grew more violent. It took everything he had to hold on.

Hours passed, as did the storm. As night fell, the moon reflected an eerie light that shimmered across a vast expanse of water. He was in Manila Bay, floating...floating among sharks, Jap patrol boats and, hopefully, a friendly sub.

He longed to be home. Home in Caroline's arms. Home with his little boy. Pasadena, California had the sweetest ring in the world to it, he thought. What he wouldn't give to be there with his wife and kid. But he couldn't think of that now, could he?...

Neil's mind wandered. It wandered in an effort to stay alert, alive. He was drained from his efforts to stay afloat, bail out water, paddle, keep alert and awake. He hadn't had real sleep for over thirty-six hours. He was glad for one thing, though. He was glad that the sea had become a calm surface. With the moon out now, he could see the silhouette of a mountain range above the distant shoreline. He estimated it to be only five miles away. With any luck, and help from the current and paddling, he could make it to shore before sunrise.

He began to talk to himself. "I've got to live! For Caroline. O.K. Think, Neil—you've got a kid now. For little Neil. Come on, man, you can do it." He put his effort into paddling and continued to talk to himself. He kept his thoughts on home, on Caroline and the baby. "Belief, the substance of things hoped for!" He thought of his home and the message of the sign nailed up over the front door. He wasn't going to think of anything else!

"Come on, Neil—they're waiting on the shore...come on man, if you just make it to shore... You can do it!" His thoughts weren't the only source of his strength. He believed in God, and the help he might get from his weak prayers, but he also called on his thoughts of home...the same thoughts he used every time he took off for another combat mission.

He visualized holding Caroline, there in the rose garden, next to their comfortable little home on California Avenue. He visualized handing her a rose. And he visualized asking her to be tough for him. *"Can you do it, Caroline?"* If he would ask that of her, to be tough and make it through the fire, the pain...then he must ask the same of himself. He would survive...if only for them.

Hours passed. He had lifted off the Princeton at 0600 hours. His watch showed 0400 hours. Twenty-two hours since he took off with his squadron from the carrier deck. He hadn't slept much the night before. He and Roberts had spent hours talking about God and religion. The questions and answers that conversation created had kept Neil up most of the remaining hours, thinking...until early morning. Over forty hours without sleep. His muscles ached and his lungs felt as if they were on fire. He could see the white foam glistening in the moonlight as it lapped in small waves along the beach.

His paddle hit something hard. It was coral. He was on a reef. He lifted himself over the side of the raft and began to walk unsteadily over a bed of jagged coral. It was awkward to stand, let alone walk on the stuff. He stumbled and staggered as he pulled the small raft along with him. He fell, several times, cutting his arms and legs on the sharply calcified sea formations. He must have fallen a dozen times before he realized that the shoreline was only fifty yards ahead. One hundred and fifty more steps and he would be on solid ground.

He stumbled onto the beach and fell into the sandy cushion. He lay there, physically drained, unaware that he had let his raft float back out into the surf. He knew that he must move...move into the palm grove a hundred feet or so off the beach. He couldn't move a muscle. His body wouldn't respond to his commands. He fell into

Missing In Action

a deep and complete sleep as he lay there, cut, bruised, motionless, but grateful to be alive.

***

Neil had no idea how long he had been lying there. The water moving over his body and the rays of the morning sun awakened him, along with the sounds of life coming from the jungle that sprung up just a few yards from the beach. He came to, long enough to struggle into a nearby grove of trees and brush. The jungle was alive with sounds of every type. The chattering of birds and monkeys mixed with the sounds of ocean waves, creating a surreal sense of life—like a dream you couldn't wake up from.

Neil opened his life vest pocket to take out his survival kit. He broke out some crackers and tried to eat them with a dry mouth. He still had his gear, a Colt .45 with 2 clips of ammo, and the package from Caroline. He was thirsty, hungry, and needed to get his bearings. Pulling out his compass, he guessed a location based upon his last look at Manila Bay before he hit the water. He guessed that he was on the Bataan Peninsula, the same one where MacArthur and his troops had made their last stand some two and one half years before. The place would still be crawling with Japs. And the way things looked, they were not likely to feed and keep him prisoner. No, they would interrogate and then kill him outright and be done with him. On the offense, they had been inhumane captors. On the defense, as was their position now, they would certainly be no less brutal.

He had to start moving. He couldn't stay on the beach. Taking his coordinates, he decided to head for the mountains, where he might find bands of loyal Filipino guerrilla fighters.

He needed to hold out until the American invasion of Luzon commenced. It was only a matter of time. Weeks, maybe months, but no more than that. The landing in Leyte Island to the south was just the first in a string of liberations the American forces would be making. He needed some time; just a little longer, then he could go home. Luzon, after all, was the prize and Bataan was a bitter memory for MacArthur. No doubt the General would attack the Bataan

The Last Valentine

Peninsula soon and pay the Japs back for the brutality they inflicted on his forces and the Filipino people. No doubt.

He began to trudge west, towards the Southern Zambale mountains. There were no trails and the jungle was so thick that it created a stifling humidity mixed with a darkness from the shadows of the plant-like canopy overhead. The jungle thickness blocked the sun but kept the heat in.

"It must be 120 degrees," he thought as sweat poured off him in buckets. He had wandered for hours, in circles maybe. His throat was parched and ached for moisture. He stumbled a few more feet towards a clearing and sat down under a palm tree utterly exhausted. He saw the coconuts overhead. They would have moisture, but he wouldn't be able to get to them. He didn't have the strength.

It started to rain. Perhaps the monsoon had saved him. He looked for a way to scoop the droplets into his mouth. At first he just lay there and opened his mouth, letting the kind moisture soothe his parched throat. Then he noticed the water running off the leaves. He eagerly gathered large palm fronds and positioned them to drain the drops into his mouth. But he couldn't save the water; he had lost his canteen somewhere as he got out of his plane. The moisture refreshed him and he lay there soaking in all he could as his exhaustion sent him drifting into unconsciousness.

How long he had been asleep, he didn't know. What day it was, he wasn't sure. He awakened to the noises of the jungle and his first thoughts were of food and water. He had to kill an animal if he could and then make a fire somehow... If he could just get his hands on the coconuts. The meat and the juice should last him awhile. As he pondered his dilemma he heard the sound of a click and a rustling in the bush behind him. He pulled out his Colt .45 and dove for cover. As he did, he felt the sharp point of an object in the small of his back. He dropped the gun and turned to face his captor—a diminutive Negrito tribesman. The mountain native pulled his spear back and smiled broadly at the lieutenant.

"You American! You American!" he repeated excitedly several times.

"Morang...Morang" came the words. He patted himself squarely on his chest to indicate his name. Two other Negritos, no more than five feet tall, appeared from out of the jungle. Smiling, dressed in nothing more than loin cloths, they chattered excitedly among themselves.

"Thirsty...Thirsty" Neil said as he made gestures with his hands to his mouth and throat.

"Tirstee...Tirstee," laughingly repeated the one who held the spear. Then, understanding, he was up the tree in a second, and with a machete dropping coconuts to the ground. The two others quickly grabbed them and took their machetes to open them for the American.

Neil sat and greedily drank the juice, then began to devour the coconut meat they had pried loose. The mountain natives acted delighted and talked and laughed amongst themselves as Neil concentrated on the fruit.

Finally they looked at him and began to speak. He just shook his head to indicate he couldn't understand. With sign language they motioned towards a trail and gestured for Neil to follow them. Then Morang brightened and drew his hand across his throat. "Kill Japs," and patting himself on the chest, he repeated, "Kill Japs." Then he pointed to his two companions and repeated it, "Kill Japs, Kill Japs." The small mountain man drew his hand across his throat again to indicate death.

"O.K.," Neil replied and he slowly arose, drawing his hand across his throat. Then pointing to himself, he smiled to them and said, "American fight."

They all laughed approvingly and went ahead on the trail, motioning him to follow. He hoped they would lead him to other Americans who might be fighting alongside the Filipino guerrillas in the jungles. He picked up his Colt and other gear and slowly followed them into the thick jungle darkness.

CHAPTER FOURTEEN

VALLEY OF THE SHADOW

February 13, 1945   Bataan Peninsula, Philippines

Captain Osamu Ito was livid. His men had raided the village in search of an American rumored to have stayed with local Filipino guerrillas. They had been on the American's trail for two weeks. In all the madness of the village raid some of his men had killed women, children, and were displaying the head of a suspected guerrilla fighter as a trophy. Two of his men had been caught raping a teenage Negrito girl before killing her.

"Is this the glorious Imperial Japanese Army at work? Is this our treatment of the civilian population? We expect to win their hearts and minds this way?" he shouted at the sergeant.

Sergeant Ozawa gruffly shot back, "This, sir, is the enemy. They have killed over one half of our company and wounded over one hundred more. Or have you forgotten?"

"I won't listen to your insolence, Sergeant! Tell the men we are moving out in fifteen minutes! Dismissed!" he barked in his strongest voice, now weary and weak from the orders of war he had given for four long years.

"Lieutenant Shima!" Ito called from the bamboo hut where he stood staring down at a map spread before him on a small table.

"Hai!" The slight, skeletal-looking lieutenant responded with a salute. "Yes, sir," he said waiting for orders. He suffered from dysentery and, like the rest, had been on a poor diet of rice rations and whatever meat they could get on raids of villages or from the animals in the jungle mountains. The Bataan Peninsula jungle was slowly killing the young Japanese officer.

"Lieutenant Shima. We have received a new order to abandon our search for the American and take up a defensive position against the advancing American Army in this sector." Captain Ito pointed to an old American Army map laid before them. "Our regiment is deploying along this road called Zig Zag Pass. We are to take up positions in this small valley. The rugged hills offer excellent hiding and protection for our men while exposing the Americans on the road, to our fire. The jungle and the ridges block the sun all day except the small period during the noon hour. We will use the shadows to our advantage. The sun will be to our backs and further be an advantage as the enemy tries to locate our positions. The sunlight will locate them and yet block their view of us. Our objective is to stop the enemy at these strategic points. This bridge over the Rio Sombro, then the ridges and narrow gaps. Whatever we can do to stop them, we must. These are our orders."

Lieutenant Shima asked, "The name of the valley, sir?"

"Valle del Sombro, a Spanish name, meaning Valley of the Shadow." Ito pointed to the map again.

The Lieutenant's eyes revealed a hollow, sunken look and they spoke louder than any words his tongue might relay. "Sir," implored the young officer, "the men are tired and hungry. The Americans are still more than 100 kilometers away. May I ask the Captain to allow us a day to recover, bathe in the spring, and search for food before moving out?"

The frail-looking lieutenant didn't have much left in him and the captain knew it. The young officer would never know how the captain's heart was broken over the plight of the life standing before him. His men didn't know his secret. No one knew his secret but his uncle in the War Ministry.

Ito was a Catholic, and his Christian conversion had happened years before in a school across the Pacific Ocean. He was as loyal to his faith, in secret, as he could be. And now, with so much death, disease, and more dying waiting to happen to his men, he felt a temptation to lead his men in another direction—towards the Americans with a white flag—for their sake.

One thing was certain, however. He and his men would die, before surrender. They had taken an oath to the Emperor. And as much as he loathed the idea, it was a duty, a culture, a form of honor that even he could not put aside. They were ordered to fight to the last man. The Japanese called their defensive action "Operation Sho-Go." "Operation Victory" left no option for surrender.

The Last Valentine

Captain Ito gazed at Shima standing there, waiting, hopeful, and put his hand on the lieutenant's shoulder. It was a hand of understanding and sympathy.

"We have our orders, Lieutenant. I understand the need of the men, but we are now on a defensive mission. We have no choice but to immediately carry out orders."

Lieutenant Shima cast his eyes downward. Perspiration rained down his fevered forehead as his eyes searched for an honorable escape from his misery. His soaked uniform hung on him loosely and the 115-degree heat sweltered with jungle humidity. The jungle was the enemy as much as the Filipino guerrillas. And now, the American Army had returned. He was on the verge of collapse but simply replied powerlessly, "Hai!...Yes, sir." With head bowed he took up his rifle and shuffled out of the small hut to ready his men for the march.

"Lieutenant Shima."

"Hai," he returned, facing the Captain again.

"Take the two men guilty of the rape and put them on point duty. We have no place and no time for disciplinary action."

"Hai!" came the reply. The lieutenant knew what the order meant. In this environment of danger, it was a virtual death sentence.

The two men guilty of rape would lead the company on point for a reason. They would be well separated from the body of the other men and it would make an example of them, if they should die at the hands of the enemy. The mountains were teaming with Filipino guerrillas. They were striking everywhere, now that the Americans had returned. He couldn't bring himself to execute his own men, but he knew that, given the chance, the enemy would. Justice must be met—and God would determine whose hand should do it.

Captain Ito felt an odious contempt for any of his men who engaged in the brutality of pillage, rape or unnecessary killing. And then there was the "Kempetai." He had his belly full of the Kempetai, secret police, who had brutalized the Filipino population for over three years. It was no wonder the locals were filled with such hate towards the Japanese soldiers. The Kempetai's actions against the people only made it harder on the soldiers. Their practice of terrorizing the populace through ruthless spectacles of inhumane torture and execution sickened Ito. They would take a suspected guerrilla or sympathizer and, after torture, cut his bowels out before the eyes of the villagers. Then they would behead the man or woman and cause the head to be placed upon a bamboo stake. There it was to remain, as an example. Now the tables were turning. The Filipinos were doing the same to any captured Japanese soldier.

He was the only Catholic he knew of among any Japanese soldiers in his regiment—or the entire Army, for that matter. To reveal his union to the church would immediately cause him to lose his standing in the Army, Japanese society, and might even cause severe hardships upon his wife Kyoko and son Takeichi at home in Kobe. Japanese who embraced western religions were looked upon with suspicion and ridicule, especially now, fighting a western foe. Public humiliation often followed.

Captain Ito opened his satchel and put away his map. He reached for the picture of his wife and son he kept there. He lifted out the crucifix, given him by Father Matthews, hidden in the back of the frame behind the picture, and pondered upon the events that had taken him to the Catholic college in California. With the priest's knowledge and his uncle's unwitting help, he had kept the facts of his union to the church secret.

It had been a thrill to be in America after so many years of English study at the Catholic orphanage in Osaka under the instruction of Father Matthews. And his powerful uncle, brother of his deceased father, used his influence to help assure his passport and student visa to the United States in 1935.

The motives of his military uncle were clear. Learn English, make American friends, learn their ways, and return to Japan for a commission as an officer in the Japanese Imperial Army Intelligence Corp. His uncle, General Nobuei Ito, was infuriated to learn of his nephew's ungrateful defection to the western religion, and knew that he had automatically disqualified himself for any position of importance in the Army Intelligence apparatus. He used his influence, however, to get him a position in the Imperial War College, where, in 1940, Osamu Ito had been commissioned an infantry lieutenant in the Imperial Army.

It would do the young rebel good, his uncle had thought. He would be forced to abandon his western ways. His uncle had been wrong.

"Kyoko, Takeichi, I love you," he whispered as he gently caressed the picture and raised the crucifix to his lips. His back was turned to the hut's door. He quickly returned the crucifix and the picture to its hiding place in his trouser pocket. The picture and crucifix were replaced inside the wax-type paper holding his last letter to protect them from the constant jungle moisture.

"Captain!" the husky, gruff-sounding voice announced. "The men are assembled and waiting to move out." Sergeant Ozawa stood at the hut door, awaiting orders.

"Very well, Sergeant. Have the men move out under my instructions to Lieutenant Shima."

"The Lieutenant has collapsed. He will need to be transported by gurney."

"Take me to him at once!" Captain Ito followed Sergeant Ozawa out of the hut and to a clearing outside the small village where the men had assembled. The Lieutenant was lying unconscious on a stretcher.

"His breathing is very low, Captain," offered the company medic. "I'm afraid the dysentery and dehydration have taken him to the point of death. He will not last the day."

Ito peered down at the shallow, pale face of the comatose young officer and inwardly grieved...a grief mixed with relief. This man's suffering was almost over. His stay in hell on earth would now be brief.

"Sergeant."

"Yes, sir."

"Assign two of the stronger men to carry the lieutenant."

"Yes, sir."

"And sergeant?" Captain Ito called as the cantankerous man turned to go about his task of choosing two men.

"Yes, sir?" the stubbly-bearded Sergeant queried in a tone that revealed his irritation with the captain.

"Sato and Asashi take point. I want them at least one kilometer in front. One ahead of the other with Asashi one kilometer away from our patrol leader. Understood?"

"Hai!" The sergeant scowled as he turned to carry out the orders.

"Please accompany Lieutenant Shima, Corporal Wada," the Captain commanded in gentle tones. "Make him as comfortable as possible, and when his hour to die comes, call me over."

"Hai—Yes, sir," returned the medic.

For the Captain a suddenly darkened sky held a foreboding in its storm-gathered clouds. He was tired and almost saw death as a relief from the nonstop insanity of war, sickness and hatred. He wondered if he would ever hold his Kyoko and Takeichi again. The strange foreboding, disguised in a blanket of peace, swept over him...like a voice from the past, like the sound from a verse he had learned in Catholic catechisms: "...*Peace I give you, my peace I leave with you...let not your heart be troubled or afraid...*" He took up the rear with his radio operator and walked with his men towards the enemy—the Valley of the Shadow.

***

Lieutenant Neil Thomas had been with the guerrillas for over three months. He had not yet met up with any other American. He had sent word to the American commander of the Southern Luzon region, a Colonel Boone, that he was alive and wished to join the main body of the guerrilla force as soon as possible. Whether word had gotten through, he didn't know. He wanted to make his status known, that he was alive, not "missing in action." He hoped somehow that Colonel Boone would be able to relay that to the American HQ and that, in turn, his wife could be notified. He had become acquainted with the customs of the mountain guerrillas and had earned the right to their respect by participating in several attacks on Japanese patrols and encampments throughout the Bataan region of the Southern Zambale mountains.

The Last Valentine

Ernesto Rios, a young, angry Filipino Lieutenant, led the company of ninety guerrillas and had sought Neil's approval on several forays against the Japanese. Rios was bent on revenge and justified the brutal way his men would inflict death on the Japanese, whether in battle or if captured. He spoke English, having served in the Filipino Scouts of the defeated American Army four years previous. He was fearless in his attacks and kept prisoners alive just long enough to extract the information he wanted.

Neil had a hard time with prisoner executions, and Rios knew it. It only pushed the young Filipino harder to show the American pilot that "payback" to the Japanese was justifiable. Rios would prove to the American that the Japanese got what they deserved.

Then there was young Morang and his cousins. Morang couldn't be more than fifteen or sixteen years old, Neil had surmised. He and his Negrito cousins were the indigenous peoples of the mountains whose knowledge of the terrain and skills gave the Filipino guerrilla band an added advantage over the Japanese. The three tribesmen had become Neil Thomas' unofficial bodyguards, a duty in which they took great pride. Gradually, Neil had learned enough native Tagalog and had taught Morang and the others enough words in English that they could reasonably get along. He was "Tomás" to the guerrillas in the ninety-man company. The Spanish surname equivalent for Thomas suited him well.

"Tomás," Morang gestured with a stick at the flame-cooked wild boar meat dangling from the end. "Eat, Tomás."

Neil weakly reached for the meat as he lay on the cave floor overlooking the valley called "sombro." He had been surprisingly healthy for the first month and a half, but during January, he had contracted malaria first and then dysentery. His weight and strength had dropped considerably.

"It will be over soon, Tomás. You'll see. The American Army is less than 100 kilometers down Zig Zag Pass. Japs fighting hard, but we'll kill 'em and you go home," Rios said. Rios and his staff officers, Raul Calderas and Pablo Zadillo, eyed the bearded American pilot sympathetically. They liked him and, like the Negritos, were sworn to protect him. They would be proud to meet the first American unit to arrive up the road and deliver safely, one of their own to them. It would prove their loyalty and gratitude to General MacArthur for returning to the Philippines.

It was February 13th, 1945. The American forces had invaded the main island of Luzon one month earlier. The U.S. Army Sixth Corp was fighting a stubborn enemy, one kilometer at a time, up Zig Zag Pass. The army sought to control the main artery that ran east to west across the top of the Bataan Peninsula and connected the western coast of Luzon to Manila Bay.

Neil had kept careful diary notes in his flight log, rescued from the life vest he had left on the beach the day he met Morang and the two other Negrito tribesmen. He had rounded up some paper by trading his "Zippo" lighter to a Filipino fighter, and had kept a regular letter-writing schedule to Caroline. The first thing he would do when he finally joined an American Army patrol and got back behind the lines would be to get the packet of letters, safely stored in an old .30 caliber ammo box, into the hands of the HQ mail clerk. He wanted the Valentine he was making out of a C-ration box lid to get home. He thought that maybe, by March, the letters and the Valentine could arrive, and he would not be too far behind them.

He even dreamed about it. He could picture his beautiful young wife and his little son running towards him in the tunnel at Union Station. The thought of it kept him alive. The dysentery had sapped his strength, though, and now, if he could hold out a little longer, he could make it, get pumped back up with solid American food and be home in a month or so.

He wondered about his shipmates on the Princeton. He had no way of knowing about the bomb that had sunk the carrier on October 24, 1944, just three days after he went down. The Princeton was the only major carrier casualty of the Battle of Leyte Gulf. While the Americans had virtually wiped out the Japanese Navy, a new enemy tactic called "divine wind," the *kamikaze,* had gotten through to the task force. Suicide pilots used their planes as "manned bombs," and the results were disastrous for dozens of American war ships.

In the case of the Princeton, it was one single well-placed bomb that had caused the death of hundreds of sailors and pilots and had

sunk the mighty carrier. Among the dead were some of Neil's closest comrades. Ensign Roberts was critically injured and shipped
stateside. Wilkerson had survived, but lost a leg. Chad Watson,
fighter squadron commander, died. Ensigns John Perry, Hickens,
Mallory, Phipps...all dead.

He couldn't know it, but a PBY "Blackcat" rescue plane radioed
back to the Princeton about finding Neil's raft floating empty in
Manila Bay. He was listed "missing in action," but when the
Princeton went down, the Navy couldn't confirm to his wife
whether it was before or after the sinking of the Princeton. The
matter wouldn't become clear to Caroline until the injured Ensign
Roberts paid a visit to her that very week of February, 1945.

As Neil lay in the cave, trying to muster the strength to make
one more patrol with the Filipinos, he pondered upon the last conversation he and Roberts had...the day before their final mission
together back on October 20th.

***

"Bobby?" Neil called from his lower bunk.

"Yeah, Skipper?"

"Bobby, are you a good Mormon? You know...I mean a church-
going Mormon?"

"Yeah... I guess you could say so," the younger man answered.

"Bobby, I don't know if I ever told you, but when I lived with
my parents in Ogden I went to your church a few times."

"No, Lieutenant. I didn't know."

"Yeah. My best friend was my next door neighbor, Dan Oaks.
Played a lot of basketball on the church team. Went to dances and
stuff."

"No kidding? What...what was your family doing in Ogden.
You're from Pasadena, right?"

"My dad got a transfer from Union Pacific Railroad from L.A.
Times were tough. It was the depression...you know. It was take
the transfer or lose the job. So we packed up and moved."

"Oh," mused Roberts.

Neil lay on his back with his hands behind his head, pondering.
"Bobby, I've got some things on my mind, some things that my

priest in Pasadena said to me before I shipped out. It was a year
ago today. You feel like talking about religious stuff?"

"Well, yeah, Skipper. I'm interested."

"Bobby, this may sound corny but I believe in God more now. I
mean since I've been out here almost one year."

"No, Skipper. It doesn't sound corny at all," the young twenty-
year-old pilot returned in a low voice. "I'm glad you said that. I
feel the same way."

"You do, huh? Good. I don't want you think I'm soft. I
haven't told anyone why I think I froze that day last month. You
remember?"

"Hey, Skipper... No one holds that against you. You've been
out here a long time. No one in the squadron has the record you
have. If anybody says anything about it, I'll deck 'em for you."

"Bobby, you're alright! Thanks, I needed that," Neil replied
with a muted chuckle. "Mormons... You know Bobby most people
look at your kind like they're Quakers or something. I think the
world will be surprised to find out what fighters you guys are when
this thing is over with."

"If you had as many wives you'd become a fighter, too!"
Bobby laughed good naturedly.

Neil roared. Bobby's timing was perfect. He rolled off his back
and onto the floor laughing, like a kid, for a good long moment.
"I'm not sure Bobby. Caroline is all I can handle. Man that was a
good one." He was trying to gain control and mopping at the moisture in his eyes the remark had created. It felt good to laugh...to
laugh with someone so normal, so loyal to his friends.

"I lived in Ogden for over five years—went to Weber State. I
didn't know one Mormon who looked like he had more than one
wife. Come on, Bobby, are you kidding me?" Neil finally offered
in a more controlled tone as he crawled back into his bunk.

"Yeah, I guess I am. My grandfather had two wives but the
practice has been outlawed for over fifty years now. But I'll tell
you... I was only partly joking."

"I believe... I believe you." The laughter subdued. They both
were caught up in silent thought. Neil really wanted to talk about
how he loved his wife and how she was one tough and good

woman. He'd fight for her. He'd die for her.

He knew what Bobby really had meant. His people had been kicked clear across the United States to Utah in 1847. He appreciated the spunk and fight in the Mormons he had known. They never started a fight but he had seen them finish a few. Those folks had literally fought to keep their families alive...they fought for what they had. A lot of Americans had at different times. He wondered if that was what he was doing now.

"Bobby? I've got a serious question for you?"

"Fire away, Skipper," responded the voice from the upper bunk.

"Bobby, why are you fighting in this war and what do you think God thinks about it?"

For the next three hours the two shipmates discussed deep and somewhat troubling theological possibilities about men at war— killing other men who God no doubt cared about, too.

Near the end of their probing discussion, Neil propped himself up on his elbow. He wanted one last idea from his flying companion. He asked: "What do you believe, Bobby? What do you down deep really believe life is all about? No religious rhetoric. Tell me what you really think."

"It's about finding peace, peace of mind. Knowing who you are, where you came from...where you're headed after this life. It's about a plan of God for you. It's about embracing it and living it. It's about loving a woman and your kids with a belief that you can be with them forever. Once you know that, the possibility of death doesn't rob you of your peace of mind...peace in your heart." He stopped and waited. The silence was thick with thought.

"Peace of mind...forever...wife and kid..." whispered Lieutenant Thomas. "Bobby...that thing about forever?"

"Yeah, Skipper?"

"No one should ever make a promise they don't intend to keep. I've always signed my letters to my wife, *'Forever your loving husband.'* You know, so she'll know how important she is, how much she means to me."

"I haven't found the right girl yet, Skipper, but I'm sure of the 'forever' thing. And I'll be saying it to my wife someday."

"Bobby, don't ever say it unless you mean it! God in heaven, I do love her! Bobby, *'Forever' is a promise to keep!*"

"Forever is a promise, Skipper. I won't forget it. Skipper, this is the closest I've been to a church meeting in along time. We have this habit of closing them, well, with a benediction. You mind? A little prayer? You know just to say thank you and all."

Roberts simple faith impressed Neil. "You say one. Let me see how you do it. It's been awhile since I hung around Dan Oaks and his family. I'd like it if you would." The embarrassment born of "machoness" had been abandoned by both Navy men. Roberts knelt by the bunk on the open floor. Neil followed suit.

"Sure thing, Skipper." Bobby began as he closed his eyes. Neil bowed his head but watched Bobby. He was interested, curious, needing something he didn't know how to describe.

Our Father in Heaven:
We thank thee for our lives. We thank thee for our brotherhood. We thank thee for all we have, especially our families. Wilt thou bless them? Wilt thou protect them while we are away? Wilt thou protect us on our missions? We desire to return home. And bless both Lieutenant Thomas and me. We pray for our nation and leaders, and ask thee again to spare our lives and those of our loved ones. Thy will be done, we pray, forever... In the name of Jesus Christ, Amen.

A distinct feeling of joy filled Bobby, something that gave him a bigger high than he ever remembered. He was glad he and the Lieutenant had shared their faith. He wasn't trying to convert Thomas; he was just glad the Lieutenant was his friend and had let him open up. He hadn't prayed with anyone else for months. It felt like home—it felt good.

"Thanks, Bobby. Don't tell the other men about our discussion... I'd like to...well I'd like to keep it private. I've got some things to sort out." Neil clenched his jaw in an effort to control his emotions. He stayed on his knees for a long minute in an effort to squeeze the watery reaction from his eyes. "Forever—Caroline—a promise I made...a promise I'll keep!" he swore silently.

The Last Valentine

Neil couldn't say anything for a moment. For the first time in his life he was sure that God knew who he was, where he was, and what he was thinking...feeling. Not that he didn't believe, it was just that now the meaning of a catechism scripture he learned as a kid carried power.

Where two or more are gathered in my name, there shall I be also.

Neil got up from his knees and shook hands with his friend from Salt Lake City. "Let's hit the sack, Roberts. It'll be a long day tomorrow."

"Ay, ay, Skipper," he responded as he swung himself up to his bunk.

"Skipper?" Roberts asked in a low tone after they had both retired.

"Yeah. What is it Bobby?"

"Skipper, if something happens to me...I mean...if I don't make it back, and you get home, could you call my folks in Salt Lake and tell them...you know...tell them I loved them and tell them I did my duty well. Would you do that for me?"

"On one condition, Roberts."

"You got it. What's that?" Roberts asked.

"If I don't make it back, you go see my wife Caroline in Pasadena. You tell her I said, '*I love you isn't good enough—not for you, Caroline.*' Then give my little boy a big hug for me. Agreed?"

"Roger...agreed, Skipper."

"Forever," he thought as he lay in the stillness of the small room. "Forever..."

***

Neil stretched out in the dark, dank-smelling cave. The memory was now three months old. It was turning light outside. February 14, 1945. He should have been home by today. He wouldn't make it back to L.A.'s Union Station for his anniversary as he had promised Caroline. "Forever" now had a world of meaning...meaning he never could have fathomed. He wondered... Was Ensign Roberts able to keep his word?

CHAPTER FIFTEEN

HOPE

<u>**February 14, 1945 Union Station - Los Angeles, California**</u>

Ensign Bobby Roberts got off the Union Pacific train from San Diego and strode down the concrete ramp at Track Twelve. He entered the tunnel and headed toward the main lobby, stopping at gate G to confirm his next call for Union Pacific 101 with destination to Salt Lake City. He had just arrived back to the U.S. one week earlier aboard a hospital ship that docked in San Diego. He had recovered from the burns, cracked ribs and gash to the head he had suffered months earlier. When the Princeton had been hit and sunk in the Battle of Leyte Gulf, he received more than physical wounds...he saw his friends dead and dying on a smoking carrier deck, and those wounds had not yet healed.

Bobby worked his way through the crowds of departing servicemen and their families towards the waiting area lobby. He was on a special mission today. He had a promise to keep. He promised Lieutenant Thomas he would visit his wife and son with a special message from him if Lt. Thomas didn't make it back. He had written the words down on a piece of paper so he would have it exactly as he remembered. He had no way of knowing whether Neil was alive or dead, but he inwardly believed the Skipper had made it to shore. He was there, today, to offer that hope to Thomas' wife.

Roberts mused upon the character of Lieutenant Thomas. He had known strong men before. His own parents were from a long line of self-reliant and hardy pioneering families that helped settle the Rocky Mountain valleys. He had worked side by side with his father, clearing farm land in the Salt Lake Valley as a boy and young man. Things were scarce and times were hard, but he could always count on his father. Grant Roberts was a man full of strength and energy. The work ethic personified, he seemed to be able to make the impossible, possible.

The Last Valentine

Ensign Roberts had lived an isolated life then. Then, when the world was a small-town and his whole view was deeply embedded in his Mormon roots, life was simpler. And now, he had been out in a world at war, and had met other men, strong men. They were men he could count on with his life...who could seem to take the impossible, like his father, and turn it around into a positive outcome. Men like Lieutenant Neil Thomas.

If anyone could tackle a life-threatening challenge, that man would be Lieutenant Thomas. He was strong, quick-thinking, and had a courage which made it possible for him to fly into enemy fire. He also possessed an uncommon faith in God. He recalled his last conversation with him aboard ship. The feeling—the bond of brotherhood—had been so strong during their talk that he was sure his life and that of Lieutenant Thomas were in God's hands.

The brotherhood and trust he felt for Neil had developed quickly. He had needed that kind of leadership, and Roberts felt he owed his life to his flight leader. He knew that the Skipper would have given his life for any of his men. He wished he had been able to search for him. He would have flown over every speck of ocean looking for his downed commander...if only he could have, if only the carrier hadn't been hit...if only he hadn't been sidelined from the war. At least now he could keep his last promise to the man he so deeply respected.

Confirming his next train connection for 2100 hours, 9:00 p.m., Roberts determined that he could get to Pasadena by taxi and have plenty of time to visit with Thomas' wife and son before needing to board his train for Salt Lake. It was 1300 hours, 1:00 p.m. As he headed into the waiting area lobby he checked his watch against the clock on the south wall by the patio area. Habit. Pilot's habit. Precision and timing were the difference between life and death in an air battle, and time was something he appreciated even more, now.

He passed by hundreds of servicemen with their wives and girlfriends. The Los Angeles Union Station reminded him of home, in a way. Union Pacific Station on South Temple and 4th Street West, in Salt Lake was always packed the same way...couples saying their last goodbye before separating for an uncertain future, and parents tearfully waving to their sons headed off to war. Places were different but the people were the same. He noticed the high ceiling with its massive rafter-like beams and the dark stained wood-paneled walls that surrounded the room, giving it a feeling of largeness. He wondered if the expansiveness of the rooms could ever offer enough space for the emotions that filled a place like this.

He picked up his duffel bag and headed towards the main doors on Alameda Street to catch a taxi. Following the throng heading out through the center of the large cathedral-like halls, he noticed a young woman passing him with the crowds that headed in the opposite direction—towards the departure gates. She sparked a recognition in him he couldn't immediately place. He had seen that face before but had never met her. He dropped his bag on the highly polished tiled floor and worked his way back through the crowds until he had caught up with her.

"Excuse me, ma'am," he said tapping her on the shoulder. She stopped and turned around, staring at him with an emotionless, blank look. An ambivalence showed from an otherwise beautiful face that he sensed could be captivating, if happy.

"Yes?" the young lady answered.

"Excuse me, I know we don't know each other, but...well, you look so familiar, and I..."

She cut him off, "Look, I'm married. If this is what I think it is, I'm not interested."

"Oh...no...no...that's not it...please forgive me... I thought you might be...well," an awkward pause followed. "Well, you must be on your way to meet your husband. I'm sorry." Roberts turned to head back towards Alameda Street and the taxis.

"Wait," she called. The young woman wore a flower patterned dress and her petite frame belied a strength that caused her to carry herself gracefully. Her auburn hair was neatly put up in a bun, and her brown eyes, though sad, could beguile any man—under different circumstances. She walked towards the young Navy pilot and stopped, looking at the gold wings on his uniform. She stared unabashedly. Her eyes filled with tears and a small cry escaped from her throat.

"You're a Navy pilot," she exclaimed in a soft, trembling voice.

"Welcome home," she whispered. "I'm sorry I was so sharp with you." She searched her purse for a handkerchief, the one her husband had given her the year before. "My husband...I don't know if...when...he's coming home. I just came down here in hopes... He left one year ago, and it's our anniversary, and I'm a little upset. Anyway, I'm sorry for being rude."

A smile crossed the lips of the young Navy pilot as she struggled to finish offering her apology. She wondered why he was taking time with her and her story anyway, and was embarrassed at his smile. He just didn't get it, she thought.

"Caroline?"

She looked at him, startled, with a deep questioning gaze revealed by the furrowed brow and eyes that searched his face for some reason to know who it was addressing her by name.

"Caroline, Caroline Thomas?"

"Yes," came the carefully posed response. "Have we met?"

"Not officially," he replied, extending his hand in greeting. "My name is Bobby Roberts, Ensign Bobby Roberts. I've seen your picture many times, on the wall of my quarters aboard ship...the cabin I shared with your husband, Neil."

She let out a faint gasp and put her hand to her mouth. She felt suddenly weak and gaped at him with eyes that questioned...eyes that searched.

He reached out to support the quivering wife of his shipmate. "Hey, whatcha' say we take that table over there," he pointed over at a table in the cafe that was being cleaned by a busboy. "You won't believe this," he continued as he tenderly led her through the door, "but I was just headed to catch a taxi to Pasadena in hopes of visiting with you when I noticed you walking by. I've got some information that may be of help to you."

She shook her head up and down and squinted at him with a face drawn out in a mixture of confusion and hope. He offered her a seat, pulling it away from the table and scooting it in when she had settled into it. He took a chair opposite her and noticed the confusion that had her trapped, as if in a trance, as she searched for understanding. There was a momentary awkwardness as he sought for a way to begin.

Hope

"Where's my husband?" Caroline finally asked in anxious candor, breaking the silence. Her eyelids were swollen from the crying she had already experienced, and now they were filled again and pleading at the same time.

It was almost more than he could take. His mouth struggled to form the words as his upper lip bit into his lower. He struggled to restrain the emotions welling up inside him, emotions he didn't want breaking the surface of his carefully controlled manhood. He cleared his throat and took a deep breath as he searched for the words.

"He was alive, the last time I saw him, ma'am. What did the Navy tell you, Mrs. Thomas?"

She quickly dug into her purse and pulled out two telegrams. An anxious, hopeful look filled her face as she handed them to him.

He read intently. "This is it? This is all they told you?"

"Yes," came the faint reply.

Ensign Roberts just shook his head. "I was with him on his last flight."

"When?" she asked.

"October 20th. The start of the Philippine invasion. We attacked Clark Airfield and Manila. We lost a couple of planes. Your husband's plane took a hit from some anti-aircraft fire over Manila. He was one darn good pilot, Mrs. Thomas, and an even better man."

"Thank you...but, I need to know. Was he hurt? Did his plane crash? What happened?"

The questions came rapidly and she leaned over the table, hungry for answers.

"Well, you know how the first telegram listed him 'missing in action' as of October 21, 1944?"

"Yes."

"The second telegram seems to add confusion by saying he was reported missing after the Princeton had been sunk. He never made it back to the Princeton after his plane was hit over Manila. It was like the first telegram said. He actually became missing after he ditched his plane in Manila Bay."

"Where? How? Did he survive going down?" She searched

The Last Valentine

Ensign Robert's face for any clue, any nuance that could offer hope.

Roberts' fists tightened and he rapped the table with one of them and squeezed his eyes of the moisture coming to them with his other hand. He sought for composure as a sudden rush of emotion swept over him. His mind was carried back to a moment frozen in time. He could picture the Skipper with his "thumbs up" sign to him, as he climbed into the life raft. He remembered feeling like he had abandoned him as he wagged his wings to let him know he had made the "May Day" call. It was a hopeless, gnawing feeling. He had left a friend behind to possibly die and there wasn't a thing he could do about it.

"I'm sorry, Mrs. Thomas," he said in a gravelly voice. "I had to leave him, and then all the men aboard the Princeton, good men, that died... I thought I had better control of my feelings. Just a minute..." He swallowed hard as he sought for a way to control the rush of salty moisture brimming in his eyes, and to clear the tight feeling squeezing his throat shut.

"It's O.K. I can wait." She reached across the table and tenderly patted his hand. She had waited this long. Another minute wouldn't make a difference. It warmed her to know that Neil had generated that kind of respect from other men he served with.

The waiter came to the table. "What will you have."

Ensign Roberts gestured to Caroline.

"I'll have a coffee, black, with sugar."

"A Coke. Ice cold," Roberts muttered.

"Coming right up," the waiter replied as he jotted it down and walked away.

Caroline looked at her husband's Navy comrade and waited. She was anxious, but decided not to push. Roberts was struggling. She could see he was looking for the words to tell her.

"Well," Roberts started as he cleared his throat again. "Like I was saying. After his plane got hit, he told me to take over. We had lost one guy, a new guy...Martinez. One of the other planes, Wilkerson's, had taken some hits and he was nursing his Hellcat back to the carrier. Your husband wasn't wounded—at least he said he wasn't. His plane was shot up pretty bad, though. He knew he couldn't get it back to the carrier and had only two choices. One was to bail out over the Island of Luzon and take his chances of getting captured by some angry Japs, or ditch in Manila Bay. At least in the bay there was a good chance a rescue plane or a sub could pick him up."

"So there was no way for him to get back to the Princeton?"

"No, ma'am. No way. His engine froze up."

"How did he get out of his plane?"

"Well he made a joke out of it."

"Sounds like Neil," Caroline replied, more animated now. She was feeling more positive. These were the first answers she had received in four months. "What did he say?"

"Well, he asked if I knew what two things fell out of the sky," Roberts smirked. "I said, 'Yeah, fools and bird' — well, you know."

Caroline couldn't believe that her tears could now be coming from laughter. They both laughed as the waiter brought their order. "I love him," she whispered wistfully as she pondered on his humor and the days they had together.

"Thank you," Roberts acknowledged to the waiter. "Neil didn't think it was such a good idea to jump out over the island with all the Japs we had just bombed and strafed gunning for us, so he decided to ride the plane down. He did a textbook belly landing in Manila Bay."

"So, he went down in the ocean, and he was O.K. You saw him? He was O.K.?

"Yes...he performed a classic 'tail drag' and skimmed across the water to a stop. I radioed to him and he called back that he was alright and getting into his life raft. Then, as I circled overhead, I watched him climb out of his cockpit and onto the wing. He inflated the raft and got in. I didn't leave until I saw him give me the "thumbs up" sign. I wagged my wings to let him know I had radioed in a "May Day" call and that the cavalry, a search party, was on its way to rescue him. He was alive and O.K. the last time I saw him."

"But, if he was alive, and you called for a rescue plane...why? What happened to him?"

"The weather turned bad. It was a stormy afternoon and night. The PBY, called a 'Blackcat,' it's a rescue plane, well...it couldn't find him in all of the rain and cloud cover. The next day they went out again and spotted a life raft floating in the surf near the shoreline of the Bataan Peninsula. They searched the area and didn't see any signs of him."

"So they didn't keep trying? Did they just give up?"

"No. They went out for two more days. Then our ships got attacked pretty good, the Princeton went down and the PBY crew was lost at sea. The Navy knows less than I do about this. I didn't know that they had the information so sketchy. I'm sorry, Mrs. Thomas. I would have written personally."

"I understand, Mr. Roberts."

"Please, call me Bobby."

"O.K., Bobby." Caroline stared into her coffee cup, as if an answer could come from it—an answer to a nagging question. She looked up suddenly and proposed the question plaguing her.

"Bobby? Do you think there's hope...I mean...do you think he could be alive?"

"I do. I think Lieutenant Thomas made it to shore. He was a tough man. He was stubborn and he wanted to make it back. Mrs. Thomas... Caroline—if anyone can make it, that person would be your husband."

"I know," she replied in a whispered tone as she continued to stare into the blackness of her coffee cup. "Bobby?" she asked again as she looked up at him. "What would happen to him if he made it to shore...if he was still alive?"

"Well, there are a lot of Americans hiding out in the jungles with the Filipino guerrillas. The Filipinos have rescued other pilots, I'm sure. If he made it to shore, I'm certain he found a way to locate the guerrillas and wait out the war with them. He's a fighter, Caroline. I wouldn't want to be the Jap who tried to capture him." He meant well by saying it, but sensed that he had just painted a new picture for the young wife of his friend. The picture was one both of hope and anxiety.

"Thank you, Bobby."

"It's the least I could do. He saved my life. He helped get me through some pretty tight spots. He loved you very much, Caroline. You need to hope, to hold on and to pray."

Hope

She looked at him in amazement. She thought of Father O'Donnell—it sounded like him...like something he would say to her. Maybe the prayer she offered that morning at St. Andrew's Cathedral was being answered now. Maybe Bobby was sent to answer her plea. There was silence as they both pondered on the events which had brought them there that day.

Bobby finally broke the silence. "I feel a little guilty, Caroline. I don't understand how God chooses who lives and who doesn't. I keep thinking of all those men on the Princeton. Pilots aren't supposed to die on the carrier. They're supposed to go down doing their duty, if their time is up. Up in the air, flying, I mean. Maybe...well, I was just thinking...it's kind of a crazy idea, but...maybe God spared your husband the fate of the rest of the squadron. Maybe he let him live by having him shot down before the Princeton could be sunk and possibly take his life like it did so many of the others. Well, I know this might sound way out on a limb, but maybe God has saved him, in a strange sort of way, by having him missing...for another mission. Do you understand what I'm trying to say?"

"I think I do," she responded with a faint smile and an expression that witnessed her gratitude. Caroline didn't want to leave. She didn't want the closeness she was feeling to Neil to end. She wondered if there wasn't something more. She turned again to the young pilot as he sat there, quietly sipping his drink and staring off into the crowds of passing soldiers.

"Bobby?"

"Yes, ma'am...yes, Caroline?" He returned his gaze to the table and the to the face of his friend's wife.

"Bobby... Did Neil say anything else...I mean, was there any message he might have given you, for me?" She was hopeful, looking for any signs of his love and the possibility of his survival.

Ensign Roberts perked up. "I almost forgot. I promised to give you a message if anything...well, if he couldn't make it back before I did, he asked me to give you a special message. I wrote it down so I wouldn't forget it." He reached inside his shirt pocket and pulled out the slip of paper.

The Last Valentine

"Here it is:

'I love you isn't good enough... Not for you, Caroline.'

She smiled and looked away, biting into her quivering lip, then she gratefully whispered, "Thank you."

She recalled her dream...the two nights he had come to her. Those words, "Can you do it, Caroline?" kept coming back to her.

No matter how long it took, no matter how many Valentine's Days or wedding anniversaries passed, she would wait for him. She would tend to their home and garden. He would return to her.

He had one more mission, in the dream, before he could come home to her. He was missing, not dead. "Missing isn't dead," she whispered to herself under her breath. She would wait...and hope.

CHAPTER SIXTEEN

SHADOW OF DEATH

February 14, 1945 Philippines, Zig Zag Pass—Bataan Peninsula, Luzon

Captain Osamu Ito knew his men couldn't take much more without a rest. He reasoned that they were marching into death anyway. The Americans were probably no more than 50 kilometers down the road and the reports over the radio assured him that the rest of his regiment had not surrendered.

He ordered Private Hoya to notify the two men on point duty, Asashi and Sato, that the company would be taking a one-hour break from the march.

"Captain Ito," Corporal Wada interrupted as he presented himself before the resting company commander.

"Yes, Wada. What is it?"

"It's Lieutenant Shima. I believe his time has come. He requested to see you."

"Very well, Corporal. Take me to him."

They crept through the underbrush, where the men lay dispersed, towards a small clearing and the stretcher that bore the dying young officer. His skeletal-looking frame shook from the chills as perspiration drained off his forehead. He was in a state of delirium and mumbling in broken sentences.

"Father...mother...I...I did..." he was struggling for breath and tossed from side to side in agony as he tried to speak. "I honored...I..."

"Lieutenant Shima. I am here. Look at me. Lieutenant. It is Captain Ito."

The lieutenant struggled to see clearly through the fogginess shrouding his vision. He shook as he turned towards the voice that spoke to him. "Hai," he weakly declared through a shivering strain as he sought for breath. His struggling sounds mixed with the noise of the animals in the jungle as it began to rain. A poncho was placed over him as the Captain spoke.

"Lieutenant Shima. You have done your duty well. I give you permission to take leave. You have honored your family and the Emperor. You may go home now."

The Lieutenant's breathing slowed and the chills subsided as he grew suddenly calm. He looked up towards the sky to his right as if gazing peacefully at some scene before him. His final breath released as if his body was deflating itself of the last ounce of life. His eyes were fixed open in a death-stare.

"Bury him here, where he died," ordered Ito to Corporal Wada and one of the other men near by.

Just then, a shot rang out. It came from the direction Hoya had been sent—to find Asashi and Sato.

"Sergeant Ozawa!" Captain Ito called above the noise of the rain.

"Hai." The bearded sergeant came from his resting position under a tree and presented himself.

"Sergeant Ozawa. Take another man. Look for Hoya, Asashi and Sato. Find out if the enemy has located their positions and send a message back to me at once. If I do not hear from you in thirty minutes, the company will move out and head for this sector," he pulled his map out of his leather satchel, "right here. Circumvent the river at the road and find a crossing upstream. Here. Come in from behind, here, at this point 300 meters up stream. Meet up with us at this ridge, near the footbridge."

"Hai...Yes, sir." The sergeant bellowed an angry-sounding order to one of the soldiers nearby and headed in the direction of the sound of the single gunshot.

"Corporal Hayashi!" called Ito in the direction of the machine gunner.

"Hai!" returned the young gunner as he presented himself before the captain.

"Corporal, I want you to take your squad and the Nambu gun and position yourself in the middle of the company. If we are attacked, you will automatically become the point in the wedge for-mation." He drew the formation on the wet ground with a stick.

"The other two squads will each fall back to create the wedge, leaving you exposed in the point. We count on you to lay down enough fire to give the rest of the company time to move into these defensive positions. Understood?"

"Yes, sir," the young corporal responded.

"Go ahead then, alert the other squad leaders. Have them report to me at once."

"Hai!"

The rain eased slightly. Too much time had passed already.

"Wada!" called the captain.

"Yes, sir," returned the company medic.

"Do you have the Lieutenant's personal effects? Is he buried?"

"Yes, sir."

"Very well. Wada, I want you to keep your head down. We will be needing you."

"Hai!" returned the young corporal.

"Captain Ito!" called a young soldier, out of breath, as he stumbled into the clearing. He carried a bloodied shirt with something in it.

"What is it, Private Tanaka?"

The spent private laid his cargo on the ground. "Sergeant Ozawa sent me back with this." He unfolded the bloodied cloth and revealed the remains...the head of Private Hoya. Tanaka looked on in a breathless state of shock. Horror controlled his limp and sagging features. He too looked like he would crumble under the stress of sickness and fear of the death the jungle delivered...violently, relentlessly, to one man at a time.

"What was the Sergeant's meaning in this?" growled an angry and disturbed Captain Ito. Ito knew the sergeant would press his animosity towards him in any way he could...this was just another way... He wondered if he was losing his mind...if he could retain some semblance of sanity in order to lead his men through the slaughter he sensed awaited them.

Tanaka caught his breath. "He said that the head of Hoya would answer your question about the fate of the men you sent us to find. He told me to say that he will rendezvous per plan. He suggests circuitous route."

The Last Valentine

"That's all?"

"Hai! Yes, sir."

"Dismissed."

"Corporal Wada," called Captain Ito. "Bury the remains of Hoya next to Lieutenant Shima."

"Hai!"

The rain stopped as suddenly as it had started. The sun beat down, creating a sauna effect which would further drain strength from his men. Ito looked at the high ridge that separated his company from their objective, the Rio Sombro footbridge and the narrow gap on the far side through which the enemy would have to pass. The squad leaders presented themselves.

Ito looked around him at his remaining men, in their squatting positions in the underbrush. He saw the look in their eyes as they awaited orders. Eyes of men resigned to their fate...to keep their oath as soldiers, to die honorably.

The look was one of anxiousness mixed with shock. They looked to him to lead them out of this unrelenting hell. Most of his men were mere boys when they first formed a company three years before. They should have been in school or on a job learning their first skill. Now? Now they were tired-looking old men. Too young for hell. Too old for heaven.

He redirected his eyes to his three remaining squad leaders. "We will move in this direction, towards the small valley on the other side of the ridge. Hoya is dead. Asashi and Sato as well. Matsuo, your squad takes the point. Hayashi follows. The other two squads fall in behind. Assemble the men. We march in five minutes."

He thought about Sergeant Ozawa's message. Circuitous route. Where? How? There was only one way to the objective and no doubt the movements of his company were being observed by Filipino guerrillas even now.

He knew his men could be walking into a trap. Still, it was death to go back. He had his orders and his orders were to move forward. Where would it take his men? What would it lead them into? He knew the answer lay just over the ridge. Over the ridge that lead to the Valle de Sombro...Valley of the Shadow...of death.

CHAPTER SEVENTEEN

VALENTINE'S DAY PRAYER

FEBRUARY 14, 1945 - 01200 hours Zig Zag Pass, Bataan Peninsula - Philippines

"Tomás!" Rios called. "Japs coming down ridge. Maybe one hour...we finish them off. We go in five, ten minutes." Filipino Guerrilla Commander Ernesto Rios looked into the cave where downed U.S. Navy pilot Lieutenant Neil Thomas Sr. sat hunched over a small makeshift wood table. The American was putting the finishing touches on a homemade Valentine card.

"Yeah. Sure... Just a minute more, Ernesto," Lieutenant Thomas coughed weakly. The "Valley of Shadows" was a long way from Pasadena...from home, he thought. He just wanted to make sure...make sure, if anything happened to him today, Caroline would know. If something happened...if the worst happened then she would know he was thinking about her—that his last thoughts were of her. It was their wedding anniversary, not to mention the day he promised he'd be home for her one year earlier. He hurried as he folded the carton board "C" ration box converted to a Valentine, and put it neatly with the other letters he had written.

"Ernesto!" Neil called in a muffled tone. "Ernesto, I need to speak to you."

"Yeah. What you want Tomás?"

"Ernesto. Can you make me a promise?" Neil's voice showed the strains of sickness.

"Sure, Tomás. No sweat."

"Good. This card and these letters," he pointed to the metal ammunition box where he stored the letters intended for Caroline, "If something happens to me today...will you make sure an American officer gets this box?" A desperate look greeted Ernesto as Neil looked up to him from his seated position on the dirt floor of the cavern.

"Yeah, sure. No sweat Tomás." He reached down and put his

- 163 -

hand on the scruffy-looking bearded American's thin shoulder.

"Nothin' gonna happen to you today, Tomás. We set trap, kill enemy, Americans come, and you go home. No sweat. We gotta go. Just a couple minutes more. I wait for Morang and then we go."

"Thanks, Ernesto. They'll make you general someday." Both men laughed at the remark.

Neil held up the tattered picture of his wife and his newborn son. He craved one last, hard look before he joined the guerrillas in the ambush on the Japanese soldiers closing in.

His tour in the Pacific would have been up. He had over one hundred combat missions logged in his flight diary right up to the day his plane was shot down over Manila Bay three and one half months earlier. He was due to get rotated home.

"I love you...isn't good enough—not for you, Caroline," he whispered to the picture. He smiled as he sat there in the dim light of the cave. His kid. He had never held his little boy...never kissed his cheek...never felt the grasp of his boy's tiny hand on his index finger... The hours ahead would determine if he ever would.

The thudding of artillery fire sounded in the distance. It awakened Neil to the fact that the American Sixth Army was slowly but steadily working its way up Zig Zag Pass from the coast. He reckoned it was maybe fifty to sixty kilometers away.

"Tomás! Morang coming. We go. Get ready!" called Rios from the mouth of the cave.

Neil quickly fastened the ammo box lid securely closed. His Valentine card and letters were stored inside. Now if he could just get them into the hands of a postal clerk when the Army pushed through to their position.

The diminutive Negrito scout appeared sillouhetted at the mouth of the cave. He was out of breath. Neil watched as the tribesman carried on a conversation with Rios in Tagalog. Finishing, the deeply tanned leather-skinned tribesman came over to Neil to see him one last time before the battle. Neil was weak from dysentery, and suffered from malaria. He was seated, capturing every second of rest he could before following Rios out and into the ambush location.

Valentine's Day Prayer

"Tomás!—Tomás!—Japs come!" Morang was still breathing heavily as he hurried into the cave. "Go home. O.K., Tomás? Americans come. Japs—we..." he drew his hand across his throat. The little mountain man had been the personal bodyguard for Neil from the time he found him near the beach at Manila Bay. He knew how sick his American friend was. He wanted to show he cared.

"Yeah, Morang. Maybe this last fight, then I go home," Neil returned with a cough. The place was dank and musty. The air carried a sickening scent that made it hard to breathe.

"Morang fight! Tomás no fight," the teenage native motioned with his hand. "Go home, O.K." Morang again sought to be reassuring.

Neil smiled weakly at his friend's effort to be comforting and reached out to shake the small extended hand.

"O.K. We go!" Rios exclaimed.

Neil carefully put the picture of his wife and little boy, his last letter and the Valentine card in the green metal .30 caliber ammunition box. Then he carefully removed a shiny metal object. Snapping the lid shut, he pulled Morang down to see, as he wedged the box into the crevice behind a boulder. Neil placed another flat rock over that. He wanted his letters and effects kept safe, just in case...

"Rios, please... Can you tell Morang about this box? That it's very important for you or him to get it to an American officer if something...you know, if I don't make it."

Rios called Morang over and rapidly repeated Neil's instructions to him. Neil pointed to the boulder behind him by the wall of the cave.

"No sweat, Tomás. No Japs..." He indicated death in the familiar sign language Neil had come to understand. "Tomás go home. Morang say no sweat!"

Rios gave a quick command to Morang in Tagalog and the young Negrito hurried over to Neil with his hand outstretched.

"Tomás, take." It was a hand-carved comb made from some sort of wood, possibly bone. A gift for his American friend. He beamed proudly and extended his hand to shake with Neil.

"Here, Morang. Come here." Neil motioned to the young

mountain native to help him up. In his hand was his small pocket knife. He had stored it with other personal effects he felt he wouldn't be needing, since the American Army was only miles away. It was the best thing he could find to give to the tribesman, the boy who had saved his life more than once.

Morang beamed at the gift. He reassured Neil again by hand gestures not to worry. "No sweat, Tomás." And with that, he stood stiffly erect and offered a salute, which Neil willingly obliged in return.

"Be careful, my friend," Neil called as he watched the Negrito scout hurry from the cave to his position in the jungle. Rios was busy, apparently giving last-minute instructions to another guerrilla fighter who had suddenly appeared. All he had to do now was hold out with his Filipino comrades, forty-eight hours tops. He was encouraged but jittery. The old gnawing feeling had returned. The same one he felt on the carrier deck the morning of his last mission. The same one he felt at Union Station leaving his wife one year earlier to the day.

He wished he could just lie down and go to sleep—go to sleep until the Army arrived. But he couldn't. He couldn't let his Filipino friends down. Not after all they had done for him. He had to just hold out, make it back. He took in a deep breath of the musty, thick, moist air. It made him cough.

"Tomás!" called the gangly Filipino guerrilla leader. "Tomás, we go now. Japs on ridge. Trap set. We hurry."

"Right, no sweat Ernesto," Neil coughed. "Just a few seconds...alone. O.K., Rios?"

"Yeah, sure, but hurry." Rios crouched and scanned the valley with his binoculars. They would descend to the ambush site through thick jungle foliage below the rocks and be at the bridge in a couple of minutes. The Japanese were still caught on the far side of the river making their way down the hill through the thick jungle, which obscured them from a clear view of the bridge and the guerrilla's cave hiding-place.

Neil pulled out his crucifix that hung loosely with his dog tags on the chain around his neck. It was tucked inside his ragged shirt.

Valentine's Day Prayer

He held it up to the dim light penetrating the opening to the cave. He rubbed his thumb across the top of it. He felt the crown on the figurine of the cross. The crown... It held a world of meaning for him now. Pulling it down to his lips, he kissed it and fell to his knees to pray.

Bowing his head he whispered the Lord's prayer. Then he continued:

Dear God,
If you can hear me, I want to ask something...

He paused remembering the simple and direct prayer that his flying buddy Ensign Roberts had offered all those months before on the night before his last flight. The simple prayer had stirred him then and he remembered being sure God had heard it. He needed him now.

I need to pray for some special things today. But first...first I want to thank you. I thank you this day for my life and those I serve with. I want to go home now. Please protect me and this group of soldiers, my friends. Help me make it through this battle and get home to Caroline and my little boy. Please let me keep the promise I made to Caroline...to come home to her.

I promise to seek your will the rest of my life... I just... I just want to make it back home. But God, if I don't... if I don't make it back, then your will be done.

And Father, please let my wife get these letters if something happens to me...so that she will know. So she'll know how much I loved her. And Please? Please...

Neil's frail voice broke with emotion.

If this is the final time she recieves something from me, let this last Valentine reach her. It's all I'm asking. Amen.

Neil wiped tears from his face with the back of his hand as he slowly raised himself to his feet.

"Tomás! No time to lose. We go. Now!" Rios called from the

mouth of the cave.

"I'm coming, Ernesto. No sweat," he responded tiredly—so very tired. Neil pulled out his Colt .45, checked the ammo clip, and tightened the rope that held the rotting holster to his trouser belt. He squinted back into the darkness one final time to make sure the ammo box with the letters was securely stored behind the small boulder.

A strange penetrating warmth filled him, calmed him, stifling the anxiety he had felt. Maybe God would answer his prayer. Maybe he could make it back home. Or maybe...just maybe, Caroline would get his letters and know how much he loved her. Maybe her eyes would one day gaze upon the last symbolic gesture of love he could offer from the desperation of a dirty war—his *last Valentine!*

CHAPTER EIGHTEEN

"IKEBANA"—FOR THE BELIEVERS

"Japs want the valley and the high ground. We let 'em in, then we spring trap! Like a rat to lose its head," Rios said from the mouth of the cave as he looked back at Neil.

Neil quickly undid the side-arm holster from the rope-belt and strapped his .45 over his shoulder. He had lost so much weight it was hard to keep the holster up around his waist.

"Kill lots of damn Japs today, Tomás," Rios offered.

Neil offered a grimace in place of a smile. He was tired. Sick and tired. His uniform was in shreds, a rope replaced his belt to hold his ragged pants up, his boots were cracked and falling apart, his feet suffered from jungle rot, he hadn't shaved in three months... He wasn't excited about war or killing enemies. He was hungry and worn down. But he needed to show his approval to the aggressive Filipino. He was grateful. They were doing their duty and he was alive because of them.

He offered the sign of the cross. "Do it for Caroline, and little Neil," he whispered as he followed Rios out of the cave.

"This way, Tomás." Rios motioned. They started down the jungle path which led to the river. Rios spoke in low tones. "Japs coming over the ridge. I sent Morang out with his boys to keep track of them. The Japs want to take the pass here, and the footbridge. It is a strong defensive position for them and they could hold the Americans up for weeks. Many lives will be lost if they do that. We kill 'em today. No sweat, Tomás."

"Right. No sweat," Neil answered back. He was struggling to keep up with Rios as they made their way down the slippery trail through the jungle foliage. They moved towards the rocks that provided good cover near the road and the footbridge that paralleled it.

"See, Tomás? The bridge over the Rio Sombro washes out during the rain. So the Japs think they come and take the footbridge and hold both sides of the river. Then they think they take those cliffs above the narrow pass, on our side, near the cave. They know the valley is too small for planes. The mountain's high and no space for them to fly, so they think they hold out here. It's a good idea, but we are already here. We kill 'em."

Rios had pointed out all of the strategic points and had placed his men in a position to hold each one and cut down the Japanese once they decided to cross the bridge. He had, indeed, created an excellent trap.

"Good job, Ernesto. They'll make you a general someday," Neil coughed.

The Filipino returned the praise with a broad smile and said, "You stay here. Men everywhere look out for you. The Americans, they come today, maybe tomorrow. You see. Then they make you admiral." He chuckled at his remark and left for a position closer to the bridge.

Neil observed the setting. It was almost twelve noon. The high mountains still cast a shadow over the valley. It was only at high noon that the sun offered any real light to the jungle floor and road which crossed the small but treacherous river in the narrow defile. Not much of a valley, he thought.

He could clearly see that the Japanese could hold up the advancing Americans for days, maybe even weeks, if they controlled this spot. It was like Ernesto said. It could cost a lot of American lives. They were lucky to have secured it before the Japanese did. Now he had to just hold on until the cavalry arrived.

The footbridge was made out of a hemp rope and the locals had hewn wood steps from split logs tied together, making it a single-file crossing. The footbridge straddled the river where it dropped off to a one-hundred-foot fall.

The sound of the water cascading to a pool below and the peaceful scene of the green jungle growth belied the violence that was about to take place. The rope bridge crossed the river about twenty meters south of the washed out wooden bridge on the road. The Japs would have to try to cross here.

Raul Calderas came up from behind Neil, startling him. "Tomás, you O.K.?"

"You just about gave me a heart attack, Calderas."

He smiled. "Rios told me to watch out for you."

"Raul, why haven't the Japs taken this place before?"

"We keep 'em on the run, Tomás. They think they're smart. They attack the Americans all the way from the coast on Zig Zag Pass and then they think they fall back and hold here. They make a big mistake. That's why we been one month waiting. They fall into our trap now. We kill plenty of Japs today."

"O.K., Raul. Whatever you say."

This was one of the last difficult passages the American Army would have to make on what was called "Zig Zag" Pass. It was appropriately named. The pass twisted and turned for over a hundred kilometers, and, as a main artery across the top of the Bataan Peninsula, it was essential that the conquering army control it. By controlling it, the American and Filipino Armies could cut off any Japanese retreat to the south and reduce the time it took to liberate Luzon. The shorter the conflict, the fewer lives lost. It was math. Addition and subtraction done in blood. There was no other way to do it.

Raul handed Neil an old bolt-action Springfield rifle. "You might need this, Tomás."

"Thanks. How far away are the Japs?"

"One, maybe two kilometers. They coming down the ridge. Look," and Calderas pointed to the top of the ridge. A signal was being relayed by a small mirror to Rios and the others below.

"We count thirty, maybe forty enemy soldiers. We have thirty of our men on top closing in behind the Japs. No escape. They die soon."

"Where's Morang?" Neil weakly asked.

"He's up there on the ridge. He and the other Negrito scouts making sure we know where all the Japs come from. They kill stragglers," he grimaced as he drew a hand across his throat.

Neil had seen Morang's handiwork with a machete. His small size disguised his strength and stealth. He couldn't criticize them, though. It was distasteful to him, the brutal "eye for an eye" conflict that surrounded him. In an airplane, killing was distant. You didn't have to touch or see the face of the enemy. Here it was different. It almost became a challenge to the guerrillas to see how close they could get to their enemy before killing them. And beheading had become a sport, a gruesome sport begun by the Japanese and now ending with the Filipino guerrillas.

"Just got to hold on for forty-eight hours—got to make it. Do it for Caroline. Do it for little Neil. You're almost home free." He was talking to himself in whispers. He had to be strong—just awhile longer. Calderas had slid over behind some rocks next to him and had his Thompson submachine gun trained on the footbridge.

Sweat poured off Neil's face. His weakened muscles strained to hold the old rifle in a firing position. His eyes narrowed at the sudden appearance of the noonday sun. He slid down behind the large boulder to wait. The sun would light up the valley for one good hour as its rays peaked over the tops of the mountains looming above. The entire day was cast in shadows, except for high noon. "Valley of Shadows is appropriate," he thought. "So many shadows. So many lives would be lost in them today."

*****

Captain Ito looked down the hill towards the Valle de Sombro below. He scanned the gorges, the road, and the river with his binoculars. There was the wooden bridge, submerged by the swollen river, swollen from runoff farther upstream and caused by the daily monsoon rains. To the left he examined the footbridge. Ten meters across, single file. It was suicide if the enemy was there...waiting. They must cross it. They had no choice. Whatever was left of his regiment was falling back into that position and it was up to Ito and his men to secure the area and wait. It was the only way to hold the enemy—to hold them in check until the promised reinforcements arrived.

He scanned the ridges and cliffs above the road that led to the river crossing. Tanks would have to go through there. It was an excellent offensive as well as defensive position for his men. They could knock out one tank and plug the gap for days, maybe even weeks while fresh troops arrived. At least that was the plan.

Captain Osamu Ito knew better. Deep inside he knew that no fresh troops, no reinforcements, were on their way. And, to make matters worse, he knew they were being watched. They had found the decapitated remains of Asashi, Sato and Hoya. As he had expected, Asashi and Sato paid the ultimate price for being put on point duty. It was justice, the only way he, Captain Ito, could mete it out for their brutal rape and killing of the young native girl. He let the guerrillas do it.

But Hoya. He was just one more soldier they had proved they could kill. They could do it, one soldier at a time, and not even be seen. The Filipinos held the advantage. It was their land, their mountain, and their valley. Still, he had to follow orders and take the position.

He had now halted the company for ten minutes to study the terrain. It was high noon and the valley below was lit up. It was a dense jungle, with very little open space, except for the river crossing. They would wait for the noonday sun to hide itself behind the mountains and then chance a crossing in the shadows. They couldn't wait for nightfall. Time was an enemy, now with the Americans so close.

"Hayashi!" he called in a low voice.

"Hai!" came the response from the squad leader.

"Corporal Hayashi. Take your squad and position them and the Nambu gun on the rocks overlooking the footbridge below." He pointed into the distance and handed the corporal his field glasses.

The corporal peered through the binoculars and answered, "Yes, sir."

"You will have a clear field of fire to the far side. Once the company has crossed, bring your men across and position them here." He opened the map and pointed to the high ground, the cliffs, overlooking Zig Zag Pass.

"The American Army is no more than fifty to sixty kilometers away, according to my estimate. We should soon hear the sounds of firing as our regiment pulls back into this position. We must hold it for them and for the reinforcements headquarters has promised. Understood?"

The Last Valentine

"Hai! Yes, Captain. Understood."

"Give orders to your men, and have them pass it along. We move out in forty minutes. 01300 hours sharp."

"Hai!" The young corporal disappeared into the jungle to pass the word.

Ito replaced the map in the leather satchel slung across his shoulder. He took the letter from its safely stored place in his trouser pocket. He had written it the night before but had not yet sealed it. The crucifix was missing. He searched frantically on the ground. It had fallen out as he had pulled the wax paper from the envelope. He picked the crucifix up and placed it in the envelope. Then he took the picture of his wife and child out and gazed intently at it. His son was a year older now. He wondered if they would receive this letter, his last. His feelings spoke louder than words. They told him to get ready to die, and in a strange way were peaceful at the same time.

He looked lovingly at the image of his wife. Kyoko, standing there dressed in the flowered kimono, was as beautiful as the flowers she stood next to. She was a student of the ancient Japanese art of flower arranging. He thought about "Ikebana," as it was called. Originating in the Fourteenth Century, it was an art reserved for the Buddhist Temples. Each flower, each branch, held a symbolic meaning. The Samurai warriors adopted the art later and the richness of Japanese culture became surrounded by nature's deeper nuances. The symbolism of the flowers and the plants gave to Japanese life a message and a theme.

Symbolism. His life had been submersed in it...his Japanese culture, his adopted Christian faith, the flowers, the crucifix.

He thought about the flowered arrangement Kyoko stood next to in the photograph. He considered the peach branch, a symbol of gentleness. The pine represented strength. The plum was to denote good fortune. The rose...his favorite. The *rose* symbolized love. Ikebana should be studied by the entire world, *especially* the believers. Ikebana is for *believers,* he thought.

His mind wandered back. Back in time to the days at the orphanage, before he was taken into his uncle's house. He pondered upon all he had learned from his American friend, the Jesuit priest, Father Matthews. He ached to share his feelings with someone now—someone like Father Matthews.

Ito had lived for years as a foreigner, an enemy soldier, in a Catholic land. He had been hated, despised by the Filipinos, as were all the Japanese soldiers. But he belonged to the faith that virtually all Filipinos embraced. Every town, every large village had its church, its memorials to his faith and to his God. He could not reach out and embrace the only thing that made sense to him. He longed to attend mass, to go to confession, to talk to a priest, to belong to the faith. It was a paradox to be stranded on the islands of believers and feel so lost.

Lost. He was alone. He was an anomaly among the Japanese Army. Home was thousands of miles away or as close as another believer, if he could talk to one, be friends with one. He was constantly surrounded by others, his men, or the enemy, but constantly alone. He wondered if Father Matthews had survived after he had been placed under arrest.

Death. It had separated him from so many he had loved. War. It had done the same to him. He thought about his immediate future. One hour, maybe two? But probably no more. This misery would end with a bullet. He pondered on the last words he had heard Father Matthews speak to him.

The Jesuit priest had given him the crucifix, which he had just placed in the envelope, and his words had given him strength during the dark days of war:

Never give up hope, Osamu. No matter what happens, you have a Father, a friend... Pray to him, look to him. There's always hope as long as God is there. He knows you, Osamu. He knows your heart and your soul. Remember the Proverb:

'Keep thy heart with all diligence; for out of it are the issues of life.'

No matter what happens, live so that you can see His face and receive His loving embrace...without fear and without shame. Osamu... As long as two believers live...he will be there with you.

The Last Valentine

Captain Ito hung his head, pretending to rest, along with his men. "The *issues of life*," he thought. He knew what they were. They had nothing to do with this war. "Kyoko...Taikeichi," he whispered quietly.

He silently prayed. He thought about the priest's statement, "As long as *two believers* live...he will be there with you." Would a fellow believer, a Filipino, take his life in the coming hour? Ironic. If only he had someone to talk to, another to pray with. It would be all he would ask for now.

He held the envelope in his hand. Pulling a pen from his satchel he wrote the words, "*Please* give to American Priest" in English and then: バラにはとげがある, across the top. Kyoko would understand. Kyoko would know that he loved her, and though his life was taken from him no one could kill his love! No one could take it away! No one!

He thrust the envelope into the leather satchel and hoped that whoever found it with his body would be good enough to send the letter and crucifix to his wife. It was time to gather the men.

"Corporal Hayashi. It is time."

"Hai!"

They began their descent to the valley floor—and to the footbridge at the Rio Sombro.

***

01300 hours. Rio Sombro Bridge

"Calderas," Neil whispered to his Filipino companion.

"What is it, Tomás?"

"What's the plan? Nobody has told me exactly what we're doing."

"Wait until the Japs cross the bridge. Wait till all cross. Make 'em think they safe. Then start shooting from both sides of river. They try to go back, we..." Calderas drew his hand across his throat.

"Oh," Neil grunted as he shook his head, eyebrows raised.

The first of the Japanese soldiers darted from the cover of the far side of the bridge and set up behind a log. Another two followed. Neil glanced up at a rocky outcropping on the far side of the river and thought he saw an enemy gun set up there.

"Calderas," he whispered, pointing to the rocky ledge where the Japanese had set up a Nambu gun.

Calderas nodded an affirmative that he noticed it, too.

More Japanese soldiers were coming out into the open. A small group of five began to cross. The Filipinos let them come. There was no noise. Even the animals in the jungle seemed to sense the danger. Soon, another small band came out of hiding and dashed to the footbridge to make their way across. Before long, some thirty enemy soldiers had traversed the river and set up in positions unknowingly meters away from a larger force of Filipino guerrillas, who had them outflanked and surrounded.

Raul Calderas looked for the signal. It was a call, a bird call that one of the guerrillas would give upon the signal from Rios. Neil kept his eyes on Raul and his Springfield rifle trained on the Japanese below him. He was watching for the moment all hell would break loose. He saw Calderas nod and then look up the ridge to the mirror signal.

There was a loud, shrill calling sound coming from the far bank, from behind the Japanese machine gunner's position. Then it happened. The jungle exploded in a cacophony of violence. The Japanese patrol was being slaughtered before Neil's very eyes.

***

Captain Ito crawled over to the body of his radio man, Private Harada. He turned him over and began to crank the handle to the radio that still hung from his back. It had been riddled with bullets. There was no way to contact his regiment now.

Bullets filled the air and kicked up the dirt around him. The small group of boulders, that barely protected him from the rage of the Filipino's deadly fire, offered him no way to command his men. He looked back over to the other side of the river. Bodies of his men lay scattered everywhere. He searched for Corporal Hayashi's

Nambu gun to return fire and offer cover. Nothing. It had been put out of action.

The fighting had barely begun. The lethalness of the ambush indicated that it would soon end. He searched for a white scarf, anything he could tie to the tip of his sword to raise in surrender. If he could save one of his men, he would do it. Pulling out a bandanna from his trouser pocket, he tied it to the sword. He gazed around to search for any of his men who might be firing. He couldn't see movement. Dead. All dead or wounded. He waved the flag as a grenade landed near him.

***

Ozawa had arrived at the rendezvous point, per plan. From his vantage point upstream, the sergeant had watched the enemy wipe out his entire company in an instant. The Filipinos had set a perfect trap.

Using the sniper scope attached to his bolt-action rifle, he scanned the small clearings on either side of the footbridge and counted almost thirty bodies. He searched in vain for any sign of resistance from his men. There was Corporal Hayashi and his squad, sprawled out next to the Nambu machine gun, killed by an explosion of grenades and gunfire within seconds of the first shot fired in the ambush.

Ozawa was now alone. It was up to him to avenge the deaths of his comrades and to die by the code of honor he had sworn to carry out. Death before surrender. He had a perfect position, at one hundred meters. He could take out as many of the Filipino guerrillas who ventured into the open...as many as he could before they spotted him.

He surveyed the scene again. He thought he could see an American among the Filipinos. He trained his gun at the rocks where the upper half of the American was exposed. Ozawa was well hidden by the jungle brush and he quickly chambered one round and took aim at the American—when he saw something move among his men, near the target. It was a white flag.

"Surrender!" he angrily snorted in muffled breath. It was an

"Ikebana"—For the Believers

officer's sword. He knew that it had to be Captain Ito. "The coward will die with honor, like his men," he growled to himself as he moved the cross hairs of the sniper scope to find his captain. There was an explosion near the spot and Ozawa waited to see the dust settle. Ito still waved the surrender flag.

"Stand! Stand up coward, and let me help you die with dignity!" he whispered as he concentrated on the target with one eye peering through the scope and the other eye closed. Every shot counted. Ito's back filled the sniper scope.

The firing stopped. It grew suddenly quiet. Ozawa moved quickly from the cover of the jungle canopy to a small outcropping of rocks near the river. It gave him a better field of fire. He knew he was exposing himself to certain death but he was determined to die with honor. He had no use for weaklings. To be sure, he never liked Ito. He aimed. His right index finger began to squeeze the trigger—then he hesitated. It was the American. He came out from behind some rocks with a Filipino. Now he had three targets—he could take three of the enemy with him. He would have to fire quickly.

***

Neil watched as the Japanese officer raised the flag again. The grenade hadn't killed him.

"Stop firing. Stop! Calderas, get the men to stop."

"It's a dirty Jap trick, Tomás," the Filipino sergeant called out to him.

"He's surrendering—we've killed 'em all, Raul! We could use an officer...a prisoner for American intelligence!"

Calderas signaled to Rios. Rios came out from his jungle hiding place on the other side of the Rio Sombro. He signaled for his men to stop firing. The guerrillas came out of hiding from everywhere, it seemed. Rios quickly gave them instructions as he crossed the footbridge.

"Take no prisoners and leave no wounded Japs alive," he shouted. No Japanese soldier would be shooting one of his men in the back today.

"Rios. This Japanese officer is seriously wounded. He wants to surrender. He may have valuable information for American and Filipino intelligence. I don't want him killed." Neil stood with his back to the Japanese officer, who sat on the ground, stunned and bleeding from the grenade explosion.

A dozen rifles were trained on the officer as Calderas ran to him and snatched the sword from his hand.

"Calderas, No! Stop!" Neil shouted as he reached and moved to protect the Japanese officer.

"Tomás! Get out of my way or I kill you too!" Calderas yelled in a rage. "Japs kill my brother and father. Maybe this Jap. Move, Tomás!"

"Enough killing!... Raul, enough! I'm standing here until you put the sword down. Calderas! Calderas... Rios!" Neil looked over at the Filipino lieutenant for help.

Neil turned to the groaning enemy soldier and bent over him. The Japanese officer was leaning up against the small boulders that had previously offered him protection. He was trying to stand up. The crucifix that hung from Lieutenant Neil Thomas' neck caught the startled enemy officer's eye and he mouthed something weakly. Neil carefully disarmed the officer, tossing his pistol aside as he listened to what he was trying to tell him.

The enemy officer groaned, "I Catholic. Speak English. Confession, please? I die...confession, talk...please?" The soldier's legs were bleeding badly and it appeared he had wounds to his back.

Calderas still held the sword high over his head as Rios came up behind him and grabbed his arm.

"No, Raul. Tomás is right...this time. We take Jap. If he lives, he must talk to American intelligence. If he don't talk, you can kill him."

Just then the crack of rifle fire sounded from upstream; it was followed by the sound of flesh being hit caused a smacking sound from Raul Calderas' chest as he catapulted backward.

Another shot sounded and hit the wounded Captain Ito in the upper shoulder, causing him to slump onto Neil. The jungle broke out in rifle fire as the Filipinos took aim at the lone Japanese sniper crouching in the open on boulders nearly a hundred meters upstream.

Bullets hit around the body of the wounded Japanese officer—at Neil's feet now, too. He must either leave him and get cover, or...

A strange wave of compassion ran through his body, causing him to reach for the stricken man. An image ran through his mind. He saw, in a split second, the face of the last Japanese pilot he had killed in anger...the day Jimmy Cameron was downed over Tinian.

Quickly, he scooped the wounded man up in his arms. With the frail enemy soldier in his arms, he began to run through the sand to the safety of the rocky ledges that overlooked Rio Sombro. He couldn't understand from where he was summoning the strength to do it, but adrenalin surged through him as a bullet kicked up at his heel.

"One more yard...just a couple more steps...you can make it, Neil!" The sound of the Filipino's gunfire trained on the lone sniper crackled in the air around him. He was out of breath and out of strength, staggering with his burden, the semi-conscious Japanese officer. He suddenly felt a hot sensation fill his lower back and he was thrown forward by the impact of sharp, piercing metal.

"God, no!... Not now!" he cried out as he fell forward, throwing the Japanese officer from his arms. The wounded enemy officer moaned loudly, hitting hard ahead of Neil in the sand. Neil lay face down and struggled to stand up.

Rios reached out and wrapped his arm over his shoulder, picking him up and carrying him to the safety of the rocks. Neil leaned hard against the rocks, out of breath, and slid to the ground. He felt blood ooze from the front of his lower stomach and also drain down his back. "Clean through. My God—the bullet went clean through."

"You make it, then. You be O.K.," Rios exclaimed. "I take care of this Jap."

The firing had stopped. Rios pulled out his side arm, a .38 special. He cocked the hammer and walked over to the moaning Japanese captain. "You die now, Jap," and he pointed the black six-round revolver at the head of the dying enemy officer.

Captain Ito breathed heavily, his eyes half-open transfixed on

The Last Valentine

Neil a yard away. He was completely helpless.

"No, Rios!... Please...for me... For me, Rios...please," Neil, out of breath coughed weakly, pleading with his arm outstretched, reaching for Rios. "He'll die... Let him live now...to talk... Rios?"

The Filipino let out an angry scream and fired the bullet into the sandy ground, missing the captain's head by inches. "You die soon, Jap."

Captain Ito breathed something, almost inaudible, as he lay sprawled in the sand. He seemed to be looking right through Neil...through him where his dog tags and crucifix dangled carelessly from his opened shirt. His lips barely moved as he whispered, "Domo... Domo Arrigato... Thank you."

***

Sergeant Ozawa lay in a pool of blood. He had hit all three targets before falling mortally wounded by the return fire. He could die with honor now. Blood oozed from his mouth and he coughed as he saw a shadow appear over him. It was the shadow of a Negrito tribesman. He was helpless as he lay there, watching the small mountain man raise his machete high over his head. The blade seemed to glisten from the sun's reflected light as the shadow descended with it...the shadow of death.

When it was over, Morang left the remains of the enemy sniper and ran to the footbridge and to his friend, Tomás.

CHAPTER NINETEEN

"IN THE PRESENCE OF MINE ENEMIES"

Neil looked over at the dying Japanese captain, whose mangled body two Filipino guerrillas had just carried into the cave.

"Put him next to Tomás," ordered an annoyed sounding Ernesto Rios. Rios walked over to the enemy soldier, who was bleeding, breathless from the hurried pace. "You talk, Jap. Maybe I save you, maybe I don't, but you talk!"

"Water...please?" responded the weak Captain Ito.

"Ramon!" Rios called to one of the other guerrillas standing nearby. He snapped his fingers and pointed to the canteen against the wall.

"Here, take mine," Neil broke in. With great effort, he reached next to him and held it up to the lips of the thirsty man. Ito drank greedily from the container.

"Enough!" growled Rios. "You talk now! What's your name?"

"Captain Osamu Ito, Third Regiment, Light Infantry," he weakly offered without resistance.

"How many men in Regiment? Where are they?" Rios demanded.

"Almost all dead. My company dead. Who left—fighting Americans. No more fight...please? I die... Please, I speak. No more fight," Ito pleaded through the pain that showed in his contorted facial expressions. His breathing was forced and heavy. His uniform was soaked with his own blood.

Rios was silent at the response from the Japanese captain. His hatred and bitterness ran deep, but this man possessed something—a quiet strength and attitude that he hadn't expected. He anticipated a belligerent enemy—one he would be happy to kill.

"My name is Lieutenant Neil Thomas," Neil broke the silence. "Your company has been looking for me," he offered, reaching out with his trembling left hand. Ito was no more than a foot away, but the Japanese officer was too weak to respond. He just looked back at him with a pain-filled movement of his lips. An attempt meant to reveal a smile.

Miguel Camacho entered the cave. "I brought supplies. Got some from dead Jap. Tomás, I fix you up," the Filipino medic said as he moved next to Neil.

"Corporal Wada," Captain Ito whispered under his breath. His company medic was dead, and now the Filipino medic would benefit from the dead man's meager first aid pack.

Neil grimaced in pain as the Filipino pulled open his shirt to inspect his wound.

"You shot all way through, Tomás," Camacho said as he kneeled in front of the American and ripped open a bag of sulfa powder to clean the wound. "Maybe it good, maybe it bad. We stop bleeding and get you to American Army doctor." Camacho began to wrap the stomach and back wound in a circular wrapping that became blood-soaked as fast as he could bandage.

"Not good. You hold stomach tight and lay on back now, Tomás. Pressure stop bleeding." The Filipino medic helped Neil lie back. He let out a loud groan caused by the positioning.

"We need doctor fast, Lieutenant Rios," whispered Camacho to the guerrilla leader. "He die tonight from bleeding if we don't get doctor." The medic turned his attention to the Japanese officer.

Rios examined the wounded American sympathetically. He had fought well with his men and he respected him. There wasn't the slightest of hopes of getting Lieutenant Thomas to an American Army doctor. The Americans were fighting their way up Zig Zag Pass, and they would have to punch through stubborn Japanese resistance overnight to get there in time to save him.

"This one die soon. Not much to do here," Camacho said as he washed the wounds and did what he could for the Japanese captain.

Rios took the leather satchel the Jap officer had around his neck, deciding to divert his attention from the dilemma that faced him—trying to save his American friend. He opened the satchel and started to look for any military intelligence that could be useful help. He decided to ask what he could of the Jap before he died.

"Map, nothing else?" Rios asked as he held the contents to the weary eyes of the captured officer.

"In The Presence of Mine Enemies"

Ito's eyes grew large and he reached out towards Rios. "My letter. You give my letter to Americans? They send to wife?"

Neil watched the drama as Ernesto Rios opened the unsealed envelope and pulled out the two-page letter. He found the crucifix and held it up to the light dimly glimmering from the fire in the cave.

"You're Catholic...it's true?" Neil asked with a painful cough.

"Yes...true," returned the broken voice of the dying Ito. "A long time ago, in America, I go to Catholic College...in Los Angeles. I become Catholic there. Please..." he reached towards Rios for the letter and the crucifix. Rios flung them at him. His hand moved frantically to hold the letter and, finding it, he held it to his chest as he struggled for breath. He tried to find the crucifix, searching the ground beside him, to no avail.

"Here." Neil reached beside him. He found it and held it up with his left hand, his right hand was still firmly placed against his stomach wound. He felt weak, tired, in pain, but he thought he might have a chance. Looking at the Japanese officer, he knew it wouldn't be long for him now.

"Thank you, Lieutenant Thomas. You pray with me? I say confession to you?" Ito's voice, weak and gravelly, was a gentle one—childlike—hardly the angry, stubborn Japanese officer he would have expected. His request shocked Neil.

"You say what you want, Captain Ito. I listen." He looked over at the sweaty, ragged and stubbly bearded man—frail and worn—and now bloodied, just like himself. He felt a sudden brotherhood. The feeling caught him off guard. Moisture came to his eyes as he realized things... Things the way they really were. Things the way they should be. Things...the way they once were.

"First. I say words, even though you not priest?" Ito was remembering the words of Father Matthews who he visited with before leaving Japan four years earlier. The priest had said to him:

"Osamu...as long as two believers live—He will be there with you."

"Yes, whatever you want to say, Captain Ito, you say, even though I'm not a priest," Neil returned softly as he gritted his teeth in an effort to deal with the pain.

"Then, first thing... I have sinned. I want to say much..." he struggled as his lungs forced a cough that caused blood to come up out of his mouth, "...but I... I don't know how start."

"O.K., O.K. Captain Ito. We have all sinned... Let us all..." Neil sighed heavily seeking a breath from the thick musty cave air. "Let us all," he continued, "hope we can be forgiven...for what this war has forced us to do." He looked into the ceiling of the cave, clenching his teeth as pain suddenly shot through him in a jolting sensation.

"Captain Ito—you just say what comes to you," Neil grimaced as he responded. It was crazy, he thought. Two enemy soldiers, wounded, one dying and he, Lt. Neil Thomas, possibly joining him. One is confessing to the other, where sixty minutes before they were shooting at each other.

"I do not hate American or Filipino people. I sorry I kill them. I sorry I lead men to kill. I only want peace. No more war. No more hate. No more death. Forgive me, Father, for my sins." Ito covulsed furiously for breath.

Rios looked at the spectacle with a mixture of cynicism and amazement. He reached for his canteen as he watched the Japanese officer struggle and walked over between him and Neil. He leaned down to Neil.

"Here, Tomás. Drink. I get you some rice to eat. You keep strength." He tilted the canteen to give his American friend a drink and then, in a mechanical way, turned around and offered the same to the dying Japanese officer.

"You're a good man, Lieutenant Rios. They make you general..." Neil offered with a strained smile as he coughed again.

"Yeah, sure, Tomás. You don't die. That my first order as general," he replied in frustration, returning to the other side of the cave and sitting down. He could wait and watch. He couldn't do more for his friend.

"Tomás! Tomás! Tomás, O.K?" It was Morang. He was out of breath as he entered the cave. He appeared confused and angry as next to Neil he saw the wounded Japanese soldier. Morang turned to Rios and spoke quickly and excitedly in Tagalog. He drew his hand across his throat as he pointed to Ito.

"No, Morang. No kill more Japs today," Neil called out weakly.

Morang turned and put his machete down. He looked like a puppy dog who didn't know how to help his stricken master.

"Morang help Tomás?" Neil asked. "Rios, please ask Morang to...awe, it hurts," he stammered as he clutched his stomach and looked down at the blood-soaked rags, "...to reach into the hole in the wall of the cave behind me and get the ammo box." It was becoming harder to talk. Every word was a struggle. He peered over at the weakening Captain Ito, who still fingered the letter and the crucifix on his chest.

"I do it for you, Tomás," replied Rios as he got up and went over behind him and found the ammo box containing Neil's letters to his wife. Rios set it next to his seriously wounded American comrade and opened it for him.

"Thanks," Neil offered with a groan. "I've got to write something for my wife and I..." He was out of breath and he laid his head back for a minute to seek more strength. "I want Morang and you to take care of these things. Please get this box to the first American officer you meet...if I...if I don't make it." He looked over at Rios with a pleading face and Rios repeated it to Morang.

"Tomás no die," Morang insisted, and then he spoke rapidly to Rios. They carried on a conversation, with Morang growing angry and insistent about something.

"Morang says he goes for American doctor. I tell him no way he gets through, but he says he gonna go," Rios turned to Neil and explained.

"I go," Morang proclaimed as he stood and pounded his chest. He pointed to his two cousins who had appeared moments before. He knelt down and a boyishness came over the diminutive teenage fighter. He looked at Neil with tear-filled eyes and then at the Japanese in anger. He patted Neil's face like a child would and said, "Tomás, live! Morang go now!"

"Morang! Here...take." Neil struggled as he took the chain with his dog tags and crucifix off from around his neck. It hurt to reach up with his arms.

"Morang, take and give to American. Morang take. Give

American!" the Negrito fighter replied as he wiped at the moisture from his eyes now staining his cheeks. He put the chain around his neck and then, standing at attention, saluted stiffly. Turning to his cousins, he motioned for them to follow him and quickly left the cave.

"Good luck, my friend," Neil whispered as he lay back and offered a weak salute as they left.

Rios offered him another drink and repeated the same action for Captain Ito. He ordered something in Tagalog and the medic, Camacho, came back in to check on Neil and the Japanese officer.

"I'm sorry, for you, Tomás. We take good care of ammo box," Rios said as he moved back over to the other side of the cave and took in the scene before him.

"Lieutenant Thomas," Captain Ito uttered weakly. "I need to say more."

Neil tilted his head over towards the face of Ito, a foot away. "Talk, Captain Ito."

"Please, take and maybe American Army send to my wife, Kyoko." He strained to lift the letter and the crucifix and hand it to the American.

"I take it for you." Rios came back over and lifted it from the dying Japanese officer. "We put it in ammo box. It safe there."

"Thanks, Rios," Neil smiled and added a thumbs up signal to the Filipino. "Rios, let me hold the crucifix."

"Sure thing, Tomás." The Filipino officer handed the crucifix to Neil, who examined it intently and then relaxed, holding it in his left hand. He gently rubbed the crucifix with the Christ figure, gently between his fingers, the way one does when they want good luck...or a blessing. He felt for the crown.

Captain Ito whispered in a tone barely audible, "Lieutenant Thomas. I say again, I do not hate. No more...no one...no more, forever." He coughed violently and blood issued from his mouth, this time more violently. "Thomas, I die. Psalms...you pray with me?" Ito's mouth filling with blood caused him to gurgle as he spoke.

"Yeah, sure, Captain," Neil replied in an exhausted, pain-filled voice. He knew what the captain wanted. The Twenty-third Psalm.

"In The Presence of Mine Enemies"

Neil had memorized the short verses in catechism classes as a child and had repeated them often before departing on dangerous missions. There was a comfort in them. He understood why the Japanese officer wanted to hear the words...to pray the words. Neil began with great effort as he prayed each word slowly, taking breaths as he went:

The Lord...is my shepherd... he began. He breathed heavily.
I shall not want.
He maketh me to lie down...in green pastures...he leadeth me beside still waters.
He restoreth my soul...

His chest heaved as he sought air to continue. He stopped as a sharp stabbing pain shot through his abdomen, causing him to grimace. He forced air through his teeth with a jaw clenched tight in an effort to fight the pain. He took in another deep breath and started again:

He leadeth me... in the paths of righteousness for his name's sake...
Yea, though I walk through the valley of the shadow...

Neil paused on the words... *"valley of the shadow."* A cold chill swept through him as he realized where they lay, both of them, dying from their wounds. He looked over at the deathly still Captain Ito. Tears suddenly coursed down his face and he gazed into the ceiling of the cave seeking for the words:

Yea, though I walk...through the valley...of the shadow...of death...I will fear no evil.

The Japanese soldier strained to speak as he listened, and his lips moved with every word Neil prayed. More blood spilled out of his mouth as he weakly whispered the prayer in harmony with the American:

The Last Valentine

For thou art with me...thy rod and thy staff...they comfort me...
Thou preparest a table before me...in the presence of mine
enemies...

Neil reached to touch the hand of the dying man...to let him
know...to let him know he was not alone in death. He had never
touched his enemy before. He took another breath, fighting the
exhaustion and the pain. His emotions had surfaced. He struggled
to finish:

...in the presence of mine enemies...Thou anointest my head with
oil...my cup runneth over.

Neil turned his head and looked again at Captain Ito. His
breathing had stopped. His mouth still drained blood and his eyes
were fixed open as he lay in death's stillness:

Surely goodness and mercy shall follow me...all the days of my life:
And I shall dwell...in the house of the Lord..forever.

***

CHAPTER TWENTY

LOST IN THE SHADOWS...OF WAR

Retired Colonel David Jackson, Historian—Zig Zag Pass
October 20, 1993

"Where are we, Miguel?" asked retired Army Colonel David Jackson.

"We are close to the village now. Two, maybe three kilometers. Just down road before the pass start up again. Rio Sombro is on other side of ridge," the old ex-Filipino Army Sergeant replied as he pointed west towards the jungle village.

"Are you sure the Negrito guerrilla fighter you spoke of is still living?" asked Jackson.

"To be sure, I cannot say. We'll know in a couple of minutes, though."

David Jackson studied the jungle landscape around him as he rode in the passenger seat of the old Willys army jeep. It reminded him of Vietnam and he could visualize the scenes of guerrillas ambushing the Japanese occupiers in a war now forty-nine years in the past.

"I saw him last year for the first time in forty-eight years," Miguel said, breaking the silence. "He came to the army clinic set up in the village. I was supervisor, before I retired. He looked healthy enough. Never can tell though. We World War II guys are getting old." Miguel Camacho grinned as he drove the old jeep over the bumpy dirt road section of Zig Zag Pass. "There...there over on your right, above the tree line. See the smoke. Two hundred meters. That's were we find Morang."

David Jackson anxiously anticipated the interview with the old guerrilla fighter. He had served as an infantry officer from 1962 until retirement in 1992. He had seen action as a young rifle company commander in Vietnam. He had earned the Bronze Star and two Purple Hearts. He rose through the ranks through two tours of duty, ending in 1970 with the rank of Major. Commanding a battalion in 1969, with the First Cavalry Division, he had a special appreciation for guerrilla fighters—in fact, he had been on the receiving end of their special tactics. The Japanese had been subjected to the same in the Philippines during World War II.

For the remainder of his military career Jackson had served in the Pentagon and then as an instructor at West Point. As an analyst in the Pentagon he had been instrumental in forming policies and procedures for the all new "volunteer" army. He taught history at West Point and was able to offer special perspectives to instruction in "non-conventional" warfare and military campaigns. He had been intrigued at how, so often during World War II, it was small ambushes and small company-sized campaigns that made the difference in the outcome of major battles. While the history books pointed out the successes of the larger battles, information or credit was seldom given to the down and dirty skirmishes of individual squads, platoons, or companies of soldiers that made all the difference. In timing, saving lives, securing operations zones, setting up communications and destroying enemy weapons and strongholds, these small groups of guerrillas and behind-the-lines commandos gave the larger invasion forces an important edge. Often forgotten, the relentless guerrilla attacks broke the enemy's ability to resist the U.S. and Allied Army's assaults.

Now, as a retired U.S. Army Colonel, Jackson was working for the Smithsonian Institute in Washington D.C. His natural interest in the combat roles of Americans engaged in guerrilla warfare blended well with his first assignment, which was to study small guerrilla engagements which helped shape the tide of victory in the Philippines during World War II. Perhaps nowhere like the Philippines were there more engagements that affected the successful outcome of the returning American forces under General Douglas MacArthur in 1944.

One such engagement was a little-known battle fought over a section of road on the Zig Zag Pass that ran through the top of the Bataan Peninsula. The battle for the Rio Sombro bridge was a costly one for the Japanese. The American Army's Sixth Corp had landed on the west coast of Bataan in early January 1944 to secure the road to cut off retreating Japanese Army units from the Northern Luzon regions. It was a dirty job that had U.S. Infantry units slugging it out for two months with a tenacious foe. The Japanese made them pay for every kilometer of the pass. The Filipinos, attacking from the rear, had given the American forces a much-needed advantage, one that was instrumental in saving time and the lives of many soldiers. The bridge at Rio Sombro was located in a narrow valley and pass that would allow the Japanese a strategic advantage over the Americans, if they held onto it. The Filipinos came to the rescue and it was the battle of Rio Sombro which was the focus of Colonel David Jackson's current studies.

"We almost there, Colonel," Miguel Camacho offered as the jeep rounded a bend. "See? There...Cayan. Much bigger now. Then it was just a sleepy village with Negritos...some Filipinos. We ask at the first house. Morang is well respected leader of Negrito clan. His father was leader, but killed by Japs. Everybody knows him. They take us to him."

***

The old, one-legged mountain villager was no more than four and one half feet tall. Bent with age, he ambled out of his hut with the help of his homemade crutch. He wore old, tattered khaki shorts and a shirt resembling a World War II Filipino Scout uniform, frayed with a faded, dull gray color. He looked at the tall retired American first and then at Miguel Camacho, and with the aid of his crutch, stiffened to a straight attention position and offered a military salute. Tears came freely to his eyes as Miguel came forward and embraced the aging World War II guerrilla fighter.

"Morang, I want to introduce you to Colonel David Jackson from the U.S. Army," he said in Tagalog. "Colonel Jackson, this is the Negrito guerrilla fighter, Morang. He was one good guerrilla fighter."

"I honored. I love America. I welcome American." Morang gestured for the two men to enter his small one-room hut, motioning for them to be seated on floor mats.

"I wait long. Camacho...you give Tomás," Morang said as he took a chain off from around his neck and handed to the surprised Miguel a set of old American serviceman dog tags and a crucifix. Morang pointed to the tall American. "You give now. Tomás say. You give American." He gestured with his hand anxiously as the ex-Filipino Army medic handed the chain and the dog tags to David Jackson.

Miguel's surprise quickly turned into questions as he queried the old Negrito about how he had gotten them and what he was talking about. Miguel had attended to the wounds of the American lieutenant, in his final hours and knew of Morang's attempt to get through to American lines to bring medical help for Tomás. He now wanted to know the rest of the story. He thought Morang had been killed, until seeing him the year before in 1992. He listened as the excited old guerrilla fighter's story unfolded. A rapid exchange of words occurred in the conversation that bridged a five-minute time span. Jackson was anxious to know what was being said. Miguel Camacho finally stopped and turned to him to relate it.

"I explained to Morang, why we visiting. That you study the war. Then he explains to me about our American fighter friend, Tomás. I treated his wounds at the battle of Rio Sombro."

Colonel Jackson examined the name on the dog tags. "Lieutenant Neil Thomas, USN, the serial number and religion - Catholic," he stated out loud. "Where did he get these?"

"He says Tomás—that what we call him—Tomás told him to give them to first American officer he sees. You first American officer he sees since war."

"Wait...you mean he has had these dog tags for almost fifty years?"

"Yes," replied the Filipino, Miguel Camacho.

"Then, this Lieutenant Neil Thomas was never known to have served with you until now?" Jackson was clearly excited at the discovery. An American had fought with these guerrillas...an unknown American. He gazed at Camacho and then over at Morang, who sat there proud and erect, his back straight, as he sensed he had finally fulfilled his American friend Tomás' final wish.

"Well, I think Americans know. He was a pilot. Japs shoot him down. Morang find him and bring him to us. He with us two, maybe three months. Good fighter. He was waiting for American Army. He almost make it, then the Battle of Rio Sombro. But, I think American leaders know." Camacho had been certain that Tomás was accounted for with the Americans—until now.

Morang broke in, "I take American to box."

"Box? What box? What's he talking about Miguel?" asked Jackson excitedly.

Miguel Camacho questioned Morang further and all the while the animated Negrito tribesman explained with quick hand motions, finally drawing one hand across his throat to indicate death.

"He says Tomás leave many things in ammo box. Morang told to take care of...give to Army officer. They still in cave near Rio Sombro bridge...maybe 20 kilometers over hill."

"Let's go!" Jackson was in search of history, history lost in the shadows for fifty years.

CHAPTER TWENTY-ONE

DISCOVERY AT RIO SOMBRO

Neil Thomas Jr. - CNTV Interview Pasadena - 11:00 a.m. January 9, 1995

The videotaping had progressed for two hours as I relived, for the cameras, my father's and Captain Osamu Ito's last hours of life. Susan decided it was a good time for a break.

"Stay where you are for the dramatic conclusion of American Diary's 'Valentine Day Special.' We'll be right back." Susan gave the crew the signal to stop rolling the tape. She stood up and stretched, removing the collar microphone.

"You really tell a good story, Neil. I enjoy it when I can sit back and know that the person I'm interviewing can give me an answer that will hold the audience. You wouldn't believe how many people freeze up—stone faced and scared—and how I have to coax the story out of them. It's a pleasure working with you."

"The pleasure is all mine," I responded. "What do you say we grab a drink, pastries or something. I've prepared a little of everything. Looks like the crew has found it already," I laughed, pointing the way to the kitchen. We climbed over some boxes and video cables and found our way to the kitchen table.

I offered her a cup of coffee. I had some available for the crew.

"No thanks, but I will have some of this mineral water."

I opened a cold Perrier and poured it into a clear glass. "Here you go."

"Thank you," she replied. "Water...it hits the spot better than anything after a couple of hours under the lights."

"How about a walk outside? You've never really seen the famous Thomas rose garden, have you?" I asked.

"No... No, I haven't. I'd like that," Susan answered.

Discovery At Rio Sombro

We walked out the back door, through the old laundry room and onto the covered porch where we gazed up to the snowcapped San Gabriel mountains. "It seldom stays long, but when it snows, and when the rain clears the Southern California air, these mountains and this community possess a magical feeling. Have you ever noticed how the Rose Parade is always held on a perfect winter day?" I grinned with the statement-like question.

"Amazing how you Southern Californians manage to pull that off," she replied with a laugh.

"You want to know the secret?" I asked.

"Absolutely!"

"It's the roses. Even the weatherman loves roses. I think maybe even a higher source appreciates them to the degree that we always have a perfect day for the parade. Amazing, isn't it?"

"Neil...you tell good stories, but isn't that pushing it a bit?"

"Maybe, but you come up with a better answer," I quipped.

"Can't. But I would like to see your garden," she said.

"Come on." I held out my arm. "A personal tour for the Rose Queen, Susan." I laid it on thick, but the mood was light and I wanted to take advantage of the moment.

I carefully escorted Susan down the old wooden steps and onto the gravel walkway that led in and out of dozens of rows of bushes.

"The garden, it's huge!" she exclaimed.

"Over half an acre. My mother added something every year. I grew up with most of these bushes, or their predecessors. These two right here? These are the surviving grafts from the original roses planted by my father fifty-one years ago. Over there? The greenhouse—those are the prize winners."

"What did you and your mother do with so many flowers?"

"She gave most of them away. Oh, she had some florist contracts, but the income from that barely covered watering, fertilizers and new plants. There was rarely any extra money left over. But she was happy to give the flowers away. She had this policy: If you needed a rose it was yours; no questions asked. I guess most of the roses were used by church members, school friends, or for weddings, as gifts for others...it brought my mother a lot of joy."

"Church members?" she inquired. "I'm curious. You tell in

your book how your mother was Methodist and your father was Catholic. Did your mother favor one over the other?" She looked up at me and must have noticed the furrowed brow the question brought to my face.

I paused and considered where the question might lead. I had determined that previous week to reconsider my activity in a church where my mother and I were members. I had stayed away from religious services since my wife died, I guess as a form of "mini-rebellion." With all the feelings stirring inside of me I had to end it. I attended services that very Sunday—just the day before—and found, to my relief, many outstretched hands of friendship welcoming me back. No matter what she might think, I decided that it was better sooner than later to bring up my religious ideals. The world was a funny place. Being religious, at least talking about it, seemed to turn many people off. But, I had to show integrity and now was as good a time as any to start.

"My mother favored one church in her final years more than any other. But she also had a deep respect for all faiths." I held up my right hand and looked at the little gold ring I had replaced on my small finger. "I..." Susan interrupted.

"Neil! Can I see your ring? The one on your right hand," she pointed and turned to face me. "Where did you get this?" she asked in a curious manner.

I wasn't sure what to think. Did she recognize it? Was she going to think I was a nut? I went ahead. "Oh, well—I was just about to say. My mother favored one church more than the rest. I guess I do, too. The ring is a token of remembrance, given me from my mother a year after my wife, kids and I joined in attending her church." I swallowed hard and held my breath, waiting for the possibility of a negative reaction. "It has a symbolic meaning. My kids each have one. It's a family thing."

Susan smiled and asked, "Symbolic? So what do these symbols mean?" She pointed at my ring as I fiddled with it.

"It represents a children's Sunday School class ideal that my mother taught. Each child gets a ring to remind her to do what's right."

"Neil, that's cute!" There was a pause. "So you plan on...doing the right things?" she smiled, saying it thoughtfully.

I wondered how she viewed me but responded, swallowing hard, "Yeah."

"Good. I like it when people seem to know what they want." She wandered over to a nearby rose bush. "The roses are really a magnificent commentary on your mother's devotion. What about the metaphor of the thorns? Symbolism?" Susan changed the subject abruptly and turned to look back at me.

Responding to her question I asked, "Symbolic meanings?"

"Yes, symbolism. Your ring. It has a special meaning to you. Now the rose. The rose is rich in symbolic meaning. I mean, the Rose Parade, the Rose Bowl, and, as the saying goes, 'looking through rose colored glasses.' The symbolism has become somewhat of a well-worn cliche, don't you think?" She looked up at me with a smile. I felt like I was being put through some sort of test.

"If worn, then a powerful one I suppose. Our story wouldn't be much without it." I paused to consider where her questions were leading. Leading to where? I wondered.

"You were saying?" she prompted.

"Oh yeah. Well, symbolism, cliches and such. The thorns...yes, well that's something else. Most people examine the petals of the flower and sense the fragrance of the rose and see the thorns on the stem as an unnecessary annoyance." I thought that the obviousness of the metaphor would suffice, so I didn't say more.

"Well, aren't they? I mean aren't the thorns an annoyance?" Susan was keeping the topic alive. I didn't mind so much. I just was afraid of boring her.

"An annoyance?... Yes. But unnecessary?... No. Only now do I realize how necessary they really are. The rose symbolizes love like no other flower, I guess. I suppose the testimonial of that is the perennial two hundred million of these flowers sold each February fourteenth. But flowers, statements of love alone, can't do it." Now I was beginning to sound like a preacher, so I stopped.

"Go ahead," Susan urged.

I looked at her and wondered what she wanted out of me. If I talked too much, I could turn her off. On the other hand, if I sincerely stated my feelings she would have to respect them.

The Last Valentine

"Well, I really believe what I'm about to say, Susan. I believe because of what I've seen, what I know from personal experience, what I've felt, and what I've read from my father's letters. It's this: For love to be tested...to be really forged into a lasting union of joy...for the ending of the story to be better than the beginning, then, there can be *no quick fixes. Love takes effort*, although I'd be the first to admit..." I realized I had begun to wax too philosophical. I again stopped talking.

"You'd be the first to admit what?" Susan prodded with a hint of exasperation.

"I'm sorry. I was getting carried away. I'm afraid I'm somewhat of a dreamer and a bit philosophical—I don't mean to grind a point into the ground."

"No...please. Go ahead. As you were saying."

"Well, I'd be the first to admit that I've lived my whole life among the roses, and now forty-nine years among them, I'm just beginning to notice the importance of the thorns. I grew up with them. I worked here in the garden, constantly being stuck by them, but never understood...not like my mother, anyway. Now I understand why she always smiled, as if she had a secret. Thorns never bothered her. It cost me losing Diana before I began to realize how much effort holding onto love—the rose—takes."

There was a long pause, an awkward silence. We strolled around the half acre and were headed back to the porch before we spoke again. I sensed I hadn't turned Susan completely off. She took my arm again as I offered it to her.

I wasn't sure what to make of it. No matter what the outcome would be, I was glad now that I had made my religious convictions known. If there was even a spark of a chance to get to know her better it would need to come out anyway. I was staying committed this time. This time I wasn't going to leave my faith and wander around aimlessly like I had for the two previous years.

"Profound," she finally offered quietly as she stopped at the bushes my father had planted. She touched the green stem, feeling the formations of the dull, prickly barbs. "Neil...true love—your mother—this story...choosing the right things, huh? I think I understand." She looked up to me with a seriousness that spelled opportunity.

"Hold that thought for the rest of the day," I replied with a grin. She returned the smile. "Guaranteed."

It began to rain again. We climbed back up the old porch steps and into the house. The crew was beginning to take their stations. I sensed some teasing about Susan and I was about to take place by the chuckles and the grinning of Terry towards Rudy, the audio man.

"O.K. Where were we. Terry, Rob, Rudy... You guys ready to roll?" Susan headed towards her seat by the fireplace.

"Ready when you are, Susie," Terry answered as he winked and suggestively raised his eyebrows up and down.

She give him a look that spoke "keep your mouth shut and do your job." The husky, bearded cameraman just laughed as he toyed with the camera lens.

I sat down on the sofa. I was surprised when she got up from her chair, script in hand, and came over to sit down next to me.

"Neil, I thought we should pick up on the script right here," she pointed out. "Right here, where you left off. I believe we can insert portions of the interview I taped last week with David Jackson at the Smithsonian. You led into it well during the last hour. Perhaps we could take some time and review it together before starting our interview again."

"Yeah, sure, why not?" I replied. She had moved right next to me where we could both view the television monitor together. I was hoping she wouldn't move back into her chair. I didn't care if the taped interview with David Jackson took all day—as long as she stayed right where she was.

"Terry... Will you grab that videotape of the interview with Jackson? The one we did at the Smithsonian last week?" Susan stayed next to me.

"Sure thing, Susie-Q." He started to whistle a tune from a song in the sixties by the same name that made the rest of the crew snicker. They were having fun with our growing interest in each other. I didn't care. I hoped that it wouldn't affect her, though.

"Would you like me to put the tape in the VCR or would you care to," Terry asked Susan with a grin.

The Last Valentine

"How much is your job worth?" Susan shot back, growing more irritated at the cameraman's playfulness.

"I'm union," he responded with a smile that intimated he didn't feel threatened. She glared at him. The message was louder than words. "Oh, O.K. I'll put the tape in the player." He inserted it and said, "We're rolling."

He slipped into the kitchen with the rest of the crew and flipped off the living room light as he left. I tried to act totally nonchalant about the fun Terry and the crew were having, but inwardly was grateful. I offered a "thumbs up" to Terry and the crew behind my back. A muted snicker went up in the kitchen. The videotaped interview began to play before us on the monitor.

I was intrigued. I had never met Colonel David Jackson face to face. We had corresponded and had several telephone chats over the intervening months as I sought to clarify details about his discovery at Rio Sombro. We sat in silence for about ten minutes as he described his new work which led him to the Philippines to study the guerrilla battle where my father was mortally wounded. Then he began to relate his story of meeting Morang and their trip to the cave. It was where I had left off, and as Susan had suggested, it made a perfect transition to his interview from mine for the CNTV American Diary Special.

CHAPTER TWENTY-TWO

FINAL HOUR

October 20, 1993 Colonel David Jackson - Zig Zag Pass

The old jeep wound its way up the steep mountain grade and came to a halt at the crest. The three men got out. "There. Below. There is Rio Sombro. Valle de Sombros. River is hard to see. It is more like a small stream until the rains hit. Then it overflows and washes out the bridge. See?" Miguel Camacho pointed to the area he wanted Jackson to look at. David Jackson peered through his binoculars. "The footbridge. The villagers keep it in repair. There's where the Japs crossed. There, on the far side is where we lost Raul Calderas to a sniper. Then Tomás hit. Crazy sniper." Camacho shook his head. "Sniper shot Jap officer who was surrendering. But Morang, here...he finished off the Jap sniper." Camacho patted Morang on the back and then explained to him in Tagalog what he had just told Colonel Jackson. Jackson listened but was intently searching the valley below through the binoculars.

"Kill all Japs," the aging Negrito offered proudly.

Jackson finally spoke up. "The valley is appropriately named. Valley of the Shadows. The surrounding hills, the dense jungle foliage, and the darkness all combine to make it excellent guerrilla territory. It's hard to make out anything, even at midday."

Zig Zag Pass traversed the mountains in a winding snake-like pattern for hundreds of kilometers. No doubt it had earned its name from the Americans who had won the Philippines from the Spanish in the Spanish-American War of 1898. It was slow-going in the best vehicles. It made an ideal target for the Japanese as they defended Luzon against the advancing American Army in January and February 1945. If the Japanese had captured the valley and the bridge over the Rio Sombro, they could have conceivably held the Americans at bay for weeks. It would have cost hundreds of casualties, Jackson estimated.

"Where's the cave we're looking for?" Jackson asked Miguel.
"It's over on top of ridge, above road on other side of river. See?
Look at cliff above bridge." Miguel pointed. The ledges were
draped with thick hanging vegetation, obscuring the cave opening.

"We go," Morang stated, and he turned to get into the jeep
ahead of Miguel and David Jackson.

"O.K. Let's roll, Miguel." Jackson got into the right passenger
seat. Miguel started up the engine and turned back onto the road
that led to the valley's jungle floor below.

Arriving at the bridge, Miguel stopped the jeep. All three men
got out. "Here we ambush Japs. From both sides of river. Our
men were here, over there, there..." he pointed to strategic positions
which surrounded them. "Japs had no chance. Good thing we here
first," Miguel finished.

"I agree. This terrain provides excellent defensive positions.
Good field of fire from almost any direction." Jackson looked
around him at the high looming mountains, at the jungle canopy,
and at the road called Zig Zag Pass. A few men with grenades,
mortars, and small arms could hold up a column of tanks and
armored personnel carriers for weeks. The narrow gap would be a
death trap if a well prepared enemy commanded the terrain. He
reasoned that it was indeed a good thing the Filipinos held this
ground for the advancing American Army during the week of
February 14, 1945.

"We drive across bridge and walk up to cave," announced
Miguel.

"I'll walk across. You go ahead. I want to get a feel for this
place," Jackson answered.

The shadows from the surrounding ridges cast an ominousness
that penetrated the air like a knife. Jackson could breathe the danger. Old feelings stirred—feelings he thought were long since
buried...dark, oppressing feelings. Vietnam, ambushes, instant
death, the sounds of jungle animals followed by sudden quiet, followed by explosions of violence—it all came back suddenly. He
knew what the Filipinos must have done to the Japanese company
they slaughtered there.

Final Hour

"You like our little trap?" Miguel asked as David Jackson crossed the narrow river to the other side where he waited.

"Not much hope of surviving an ambush here, unless you take prisoners," responded Jackson.

"We take one prisoner. Jap captain. Tomás say let him live. But he died anyway."

"You took a prisoner? Where? Did you speak to him? What did he say?" Jackson eagerly grilled Miguel for information.

"Wait, wait. One thing at a time. Yes. We took captain. Up to cave. He speak very little, really. He tell us all his men wiped out. His regiment all gone, then he talk about praying. Told Tomás something and they pray together, I think. He said he was Catholic, but I don't know. He lived a little. I tried to patch him up, but damn sniper put a bullet in his chest so bad, he lose too much blood. Look right over there." Miguel pointed to some boulders near the trail leading to the cave.

"Tomás, he was behind boulders during ambush. He fight good. This Jap captain almost killed by grenade, but still alive and tries to surrender with white flag. Sergeant Raul Calderas, he thinks it a Jap trick and takes sword from injured captain to kill him. Then Tomás, he comes over and stops Raul. Before you know it, Jap captain shot in back by his own man. Damn Jap sniper then kills my friend Raul Calderas, right where you stand. Then Tomás, he was standing here, he picks up Jap captain and starts to run back to these boulders for protection. I don't know what he was thinking. Jap die anyway. So, sniper shoots one more time. We all shooting at sniper now. He was upstream, one hundred meters maybe. Anyway, he hits Tomás, clean through lower back. Bad wound because Tomás bleeds so much. Too bad. We all like Tomás so much. One damn good American fighter. Well, then we shoot sniper and Morang finish him off with machete. We take Jap and Tomás to cave." Miguel looked around as if the scene, the faces and time was 1945 again.

"Did the Japanese captain live long? Tomás?" Jackson asked.

"Come, Camacho, Jackson. Come, we go now." Morang waved for them to follow him up the trail. The little man with one leg used his crutch with expert skill as he pulled himself up the steep grade. The narrow trail was overgrown, but it appeared that it was used occasionally, nevertheless. Jackson and Camacho struggled to keep up with the aging Negrito, Morang.

"He's one tough, old guerrilla fighter, Colonel Jackson," Camacho said, panting heavily. "He told me earlier that he comes three, maybe four times every year, to clean cave, check on box and cut weeds down at Tomás' grave. I was surprised. I thought Tomás was buried in American cemetery. I thought his box went to American Army."

Jackson stopped in the middle of the trail. "You mean to tell me he knows where the remains of Lieutenant Thomas are?" Jackson stared at Miguel incredulously. He had just discovered the remains of a missing World War II hero. It didn't happen. It was not an everyday, every-year—not even an every-decade—event. He wondered what else he would find. What the ammo box would reveal. He shook his head, caught his breath, and continued to follow after Morang, who had disappeared ahead of them.

After ten hard minutes of climbing, they found themselves at the entrance to a well-concealed cave. Covered over by natural jungle foliage, it was obvious that Morang had perfected the camouflage by adding palm fronds and old tree branches, which he quickly pulled away. He then took out from his khaki trouser pocket a small ivory-handled pocket knife and cut some vines away. Spreading the vines aside, he motioned for Jackson and Camacho to enter.

"Nice pocket knife," Jackson said to Morang as the diminutive man carefully folded the blade and put it back into his trousers. "Had one just like it when I was a kid."

"Tomás give Morang. Love Tomás. Good American," answered the old mountain villager.

David Jackson mused at the devotion of the aged Negrito fighter for the American, his two traveling companions called "Tomás." He watched as Morang crouched down and kindled a small fire with dry brush and wood shavings he evidently kept in supply. After a minute the fire leaped and blazed and lit the cliff side room well enough to see the size and shape of the cavern.

The height of the cave made six-foot-tall Jackson bend down as he stood there. The other two men could stand perfectly erect avoiding the jagged cave ceiling.

"Forty-eight years," reminisced Miguel aloud. "Forty-eight years ago... I have not seen this place. We leave next day after battle at Rio Sombro. Americans come. We take fight to Manila." Miguel Camacho's eyes darted around the small room as he took in a deep breath. It was as if he were observing a sacred moment of devotion. Jackson kept silent as the two aging warriors seemed to speak with thoughts of a time long since passed.

Morang began to dig behind a small boulder and finally pulled an old green metal ammunition box out of its hiding place. It was like a reverent moment for the old man. He held it as if it was a sacred treasure he was entrusted to care for. He walked over to the retired American Army officer and held the box with outstretched hands towards him.

"Tomás, say—give American. You take." There was a hint of tears as Morang nodded to the American, who nodded in acknowledgment. "Now Morang true. Now word good. I do for Tomás." Morang then spoke in Tagalog to Camacho. The exchange was brief but the tone implied to Jackson that Morang was insisting on something.

"Morang says he tell you why it take so long to give to American officer. He wants to say why, before you open box. He wants to know he is doing the right thing and that you will take care of Tomás' box."

Jackson felt astounded. Here the little man, so protective, had kept secrets to the life and death of an American serviceman locked up for almost fifty years. In keeping his word, he had also kept the survivors of the Lieutenant in the dark for all of those years. But the little man possessed honor, and Jackson respected that. "Tell Morang we sit, and listen. Tell him he should tell me his story and anything else he would like to say. Tell him he has done very good for Tomás and that I would like to see where Tomás is buried. Tell him Tomás should go home to America with his box. It is a good thing he did and the family and friends of Tomás will be very happy. Tell him that I go back to America and tell a good story to the American people about Filipino fighters. Tell him that, please,

Miguel."

Miguel Camacho began to translate to Morang, who nodded in approval. Morang neared the American and reached out his hand. Jackson gave him a warm handshake and pat on the shoulder and gestured for him to sit with him on the floor of the cave.

Morang began to tell Camacho what had happened to him after he left Tomás in the cave. The session lasted about one half hour. Miguel then added what he saw in the final hour of Tomás' life.

***

"Like Morang says, he try to go get American doctor for Tomás. Our Filipino company leader, Ernesto Rios, tells him no way. But he goes anyway. The Japs retreat between us and advancing Americans. Lots of fighting on Zig Zag Pass. Japs running around trying to set up ambush for Americans. Americans shooting at everything that moves in front of them. Morang and a cousin get through Jap lines and almost to Americans when Americans start shooting. Morang confused, gets shot in legs. Cousin shot in hand and arm. They lay there and Americans come close to finish them off. American soldier sees that it's Filipino he shoots. They hurry and get Morang and cousin to medics. Morang shot up pretty bad. He tries to tell them about Tomás, but nobody listens. Then they put him out. He wakes up with one leg gone.

He knows Tomás dead by then. He's plenty mad. He tries to tell Filipino translator about Tomás. They give him the brush off. They tell him not to worry. He can't find Tomás' dog tags and crucifix. He explains to Filipino nurse. The nurse brings American doctor who has dog tags and starts to ask him questions. He thinks that maybe they finally help. Morang tells the American that he takes them to the cave. They say yes, but do nothing. He watches American doctor go and hang up dog tags on hook by nursing room. Finally he tells his cousin to get him out of hospital and take him home. He goes at night. He takes dog tags from hook. He goes to Rio Sombro. Nobody there. He goes to find Tomás. Sees two fresh graves outside cave. He knows Jap and Tomás not make it. Morang is angry with Americans and then decides to tell

Final Hour

American officer only. He tries many times, but war going fast. Nobody listens. So he goes home. He tries many times after war ends, but always something bad happens. He says to God that when right American comes, he gives him Tomás' things and keeps word. You the right American."

"I think I understand. Tell him that he did the right thing," Jackson added. Miguel interpreted the American's words to Morang, who relaxed, seemingly satisfied.

"Miguel, ask him if he will show us the graves," Jackson said. As if Morang understood, he was up and with his crutch heading for the cave opening, motioning for them to follow.

"I think he understands English pretty good," smiled Camacho as they exited behind Morang.

They walked up the hill to a small clearing not far from the cave entrance. It became apparent to Jackson that someone kept the area clear from trees and jungle growth. The elephant grass grew over two hump-like elevations in the small flat jungle clearing. With closer inspection, a small wooden cross became visible at the head of each, with stones piled neatly, clearly marking the location of the American and Japanese graves.

The three men stood there solemnly. Miguel knelt down in front of one of the graves and began to weep. He hadn't expected to feel the emotions come out. He thought the Americans had found the place. He had just assumed that Lieutenant Tomás' death was known to them and that they had come back for the body and buried him in the American Cemetery at Clark Field, or in Manila. The Filipinos who fought with them loved them, because the Americans died with them for their freedom. Ernesto Rios was going to tell the Americans, but then he was killed two days later. Miguel offered the sign of the cross and got up from his knees. Wiping away the tears he turned to the American.

"I'm sorry. I buried Tomás and the Japanese captain myself." Just then a thunderhead appeared and rain began to pour out of the sky. "Come into the cave. I tell you about Lieutenant Tomás and then you open box. Come." Miguel started for the cave. Morang paused there in front of the grave, and then, standing stiffly erect as his crippled body would allow, saluted. They came back together inside the cave as the thunder rolled and the rain plunged in torrents.

"I tell you the story of a good man," Miguel began as they sat around the small fire.

***

Story of Lieutenant Thomas' final hours. February 14, 1945

Neil held his hand to his stomach wound. Miguel had just taken Ito's body out for burial. Morang had been gone for a few hours. Neil could hear the distant crack of rifle and artillery fire. He knew that the Americans were advancing. If he just held on through the night. But he was getting weaker, or maybe just tired. He wanted to sleep. He was sick with dysentery, malaria, and his body was thinner than it had been in his entire adult life. The wound was bad. The blood—he couldn't stop it. Sleep—he had to fight it. "Rios," he called out weakly.

Rios had fallen asleep. He rubbed his eyes and answered, "Yeah...Tomás, what is it?"

"Rios, can you help me. I don't...want to fall asleep." He fought for breath. It was an effort for him just to speak. "Could you...could you prop me up against the wall. Maybe I can stay awake. I'd like to write something to my wife." Neil strained through his teeth to get his message out. He'd never had to endure the kind of pain and torment he was going through.

Ernesto Rios came over to him and gently raised him up as he reached underneath the American to scoop him into his arms. Rios was shocked at the bony frame of his American comrade. It happened so subtly. He had forgotten what the strong healthy-looking Lieutenant he had met only three months before had looked like.

"Awe,"...Neil groaned at the pain of being moved. "Why now?" he whispered.

"Thanks...thanks Ernesto." He reached into the open ammo box next to him. He fumbled, trying to find the letter and picture of his wife and son.

"Here, let me help you, Tomás." Rios reached for the letter on top that also contained the Valentine card. He found the small black and white picture, soiled from so much handling by his American friend. "Here, Tomás." He laid them on the Lieutenant's lap where he could easily hold them.

"Thank you, Rios. You're a good man. They make ... you..." Neil struggled with the effort to talk, gasping for small shallow breaths.

"Yeah, sure. I know. They make me general someday. You rest, Tomás. Americans be here soon. You see."

Neil looked down at the picture on his lap. He squinted as he labored to focus. Miguel Camacho, the medic, had returned to the cave and could see his struggle. He put more wood on the fire so that Neil could see better.

"Thanks, Miguel. It's so cold—I'm freezing. You guys cold?"

The two Filipinos looked at Neil and shook their heads sadly. It was over 100 degrees fahrenheit in the cave. Their unsteady glances confirmed the knowledge that he was slipping away, and fast.

Miguel brought another blanket to cover Neil's shivering body. He knew that the loss of so much blood had caused the American's temperature to drop dangerously low.

"Just malaria kicking in, right Miguel?" Neil shivered, trying to smile at the Filipino wrapping the blanket around him.

"That was real nice prayer you say for Jap," Miguel answered, avoiding his question about malaria.

"You think so?" Neil shivered a response.

"Yeah, you make a good priest," Miguel returned as he helped the Lieutenant bring his picture and letter up where he could see them.

"Miguel, my eyes are not so good right now. I want to read the letter I wrote to my son." He coughed and swallowed hard as he continued, "Yesterday, I wrote it. You read English?"

"Yeah, sure. Not too fast, but I learn when I was young."

"Miguel, help me...read my letter back to me. I want to make sure it's all there." Neil's imploring eyes fought to focus as he struggled with one hand on his wound and the other to hold the picture. He laid the picture on his lap where he could see it. The

The Last Valentine

Japanese officer's crucifix hung from his neck and he gently rubbed the crown on the head of the small Christ-figure.

"Yeah, sure, Tomás. I read slowly." Camacho took the letter out of the envelope.

Rios sat across the cavern-like room and watched glumly. He knew that it was the end for Tomás. "If only he'd left the Jap alone!" he thought. He was mad about it. All he could do now was watch and wait.

Miguel Camacho, in halting words, slowly began to read:

February 13, 1945 Philippines

Dear Son,

I wanted to write you this letter even though I know that you are not old enough now to understand. I may not be able to come home after this war. Your mother will tell you all about me, about this awful World War and what happened to me—why I couldn't come home. I want you to know that, with all my heart, I do want to come home. I want to come home and play with you, be with you, take you to school, to baseball games... I want to be your Dad.

Sometimes bad things happen to good people. It's just part of life, and though it seems unfair, it's really not. I've learned that there are things more important than life...although I never thought I would. Father O'Donnell, at Saint Andrew's on Raymond Street— he will tell you what I mean if this letter doesn't make sense.

I've found some truths I want you to know about. I've written down many things in the letters in the ammo box where I store them, but especially in this one, my last, I want to explain some deep feelings of mine. I want to speak to you somehow, and right now this is the best way.

I've found the meaning of love while I've been at war. Now that I've known your mother, now that I've experienced combat and death in the air, at sea and now on ground in the Zambales of the Philippines, I think I know the meaning of the most important four-letter word in our language...love. Here's the secret:

Final Hour

Love is found when you don't have to give it. It is the emotion of generosity and kindness that is compelled by no one. It is performed on the battlefield, in our daily tasks, in the marketplace, the factories, at school, in the offices and in the halls and corridors of government... But, only when one truly gives of himself and without compulsion. No force, no law, no coercion can cause one to love... It cannot be arranged. It is freely chosen and freely given and not given only when life flows along like a song.

True love is like a metal tested in fire. Fires of adversity surround us daily. Are we to love when it is merely convenient? Like gold or silver, which very hot fires must heat to purge them of impurities, love must be thrust into the fire from time to time, to make it purer, stronger and more resilient. And in the same way, love shines its brightest right out of the flames.

The beauty of the rose and its fragrance?... There's another example of the quality that I'm trying to explain to you. The fragrance is found in the blossoms of the rose. The blossoms are found after the rose bud opens. Notice the stem on the rose bush. Notice that the bud doesn't even open until the thorns, those prickly things that can stick you and cause you to bleed, are fully formed. It's as if the rose bush is saying, "No! You can't have my beautiful flowers and the sweet smell of their petals. If you try to take one, I'll hurt you!" Is it worth risking the thorns to have the rose? It's where the blossoms dwell. Above the thorns, you will find the prize.

So it is with life. The thorns, the prickly problems of life, cause us to rise above them and then, as we do, we learn. We learn to exercise true compassion, true kindness—or the thorns, if we let them—cause us to brood, to mourn over our trials. Then we plant the seeds of bitterness, hate and ruin—weeds. We may reach up for the rose or down to the weeds...the weeds in life that tangle us, strangle us and cause us to lose hope.

The great discovery I have made is that we are all free. All of us experience disappointment—the thorns in life—rich, poor, male, female, it doesn't matter. And we may either praise God for the opportunity to reach for the prize or curse him for our fate. I've heard God's name used in a variety ways in this war. Some men praise him and others blame him, but when a man is under the gun, his life is on the line...all believe in him.

Father O'Donnell once told me something very important before I left for the war. He quoted a scripture from the Old Testament. In Proverbs chapter four verse twenty-three you will read:

"Keep thy heart with all diligence; for out of it are the issues of life."

I didn't know what he meant then, but I do now. It has to do with knowing what really matters in life...what matters most. Then as you do know what things really matter to you, you possess the key to the door of happiness and satisfaction.

The choice will be yours, Son. Never doubt that I love you. And when you face the fires, when you feel the stabbing pain of the thorns, someone will be watching, and hoping that you choose to reach for the rose—the symbol of love.

Choose love, my Son. Choose to give generously and then live with the consequences. I want you to be a good man. Love your mother. Treat others like you would have them treat you. You are always in my thoughts. I love you...very, very much!

Forever your loving father,

Lieutenant Neil Thomas, Sr. USN

***

"Tomás! Tomás!...you listen? Miguel asked as he laid the letter down next to the picture and shook Neil gently.

"Huh?... Oh, yeah, I uh...just closed my eyes to listen. It's good, isn't it, Miguel?" Neil started to rub the crucifix again as if he would hold onto life by doing it. He didn't seem to struggle so much for words now. His voice was faint and weak but the struggle was gone. The voice of Miguel reading, even with the Filipino accent, had changed him, calmed him, and he suddenly felt warm and good.

He wanted to write some more, but felt tired and needed to rest. His eyes were heavy and he struggled to concentrate as he looked down at the photo and the letter on his lap. He smiled at the prospects of seeing them. He was almost there. A few hours more and Morang would be back with help. He looked over at the cave entrance and wondered how many hours had elapsed. With the coming of the morning light, the American medics would arrive, no doubt. Miguel and Rios were nearby watching him. They wouldn't let anything happen.

He looked again toward the entrance to the cave and saw the light. It must be morning. It seemed to radiate and call to him. It was the best he could remember feeling. He was going to make it now. His hand trembled as he held the crucifix up to the light and felt his senses sharpen. *"The crown,"* he whispered, *"the crown has thorns...even he..."*

His eyes opened wide, then closed slowly. They opened again, with the look of a very tired man who deserved a rest. He smiled and whispered...almost inaudibly:

Though I walk through the valley of the shadow ...thou art with me...

There was a gentle sigh. His face went still as a shallow rush of air escaped from his lungs.

Rios and Miguel looked on. Miguel bowed his head between his knees. Rios shook his head, walked over to Tomás and picked up the picture and the letter—which now had released from Neil's hand and fallen beside him—and safely stored them in the ammo box. He would give the box to the first American officer he met. Now he had a job to do.

He motioned to Miguel, and the two of them laid the body of the American flat on the floor of the cave, wrapping it tightly in the blanket. It had turned dark outside. In the morning he would bury him, next to the Jap who had cost him his life. Rios studied the still-warm face of the pilot. A certain peace masked the look of death on the American.

"He was a good man," Rios thought. "What a waste," he said out loud in Tagalog to Miguel. "Tomorrow the Americans come. But not until we bury him and I kill another Jap. For Tomás," the angry Filipino whispered.

CHAPTER TWENTY-THREE

THE RETURN HOME

Neil Thomas Jr. CNTV Interview Pasadena—12:00 p.m. January 9, 1995

The videotaped interview with retired Colonel David Jackson had ended. I sat there, deeply moved by his retelling of the discovery of the letters and the *last Valentine*. We had them now—all of them. Several lay on the coffee table before me. My eyes caught sight of the letter, the last letter my father had written—addressed to me, his son. Tears filled my eyes as I held the pages his hands had touched. My father had been right. There were no quick fixes in life. There was a prize worth having...the power of love. The power in it—that caused him to lose his life for another person—healed me now.

Character. The word seemed to scream from the deepest recesses of my mind. "Character is the ability to make the right choice when the choice isn't convenient." He had lived his philosophy to the end. He had written it in another letter among the many we now possessed.

"Neil, what do you say we break for lunch?" The voice was Susan's. I had been so deeply engaged in thought that I had lost track of time.

I tried to hide my emotion and squeezed the water from my eyes. "Excuse me. I...I was thinking... Jackson did quite well, didn't he?"

"He really did. Come on, let's grab a bite to eat. We can talk some more. I've asked the crew to take an hour. Told them to take the van into Pasadena and find a Sizzler, Denny's or something. What do you say I make us some sandwiches?" Susan walked over to the kitchen and opened the refrigerator door.

"Sure, sounds great." I was glad I had cleaned the place and restocked the frige.

"Ohh, this looks good." It was a tray of lunchmeat I had ordered from the deli. "Some dijon and low fat mayo. A little leaf of iceberg lettuce and rye bread. Ah, you stock a good selection," she said.

"I was having company and wanted to look good," I replied candidly.

We sat down at the table and I watched as she made the sandwiches and seemed to make herself at home. It felt good to have a woman in the house. It felt good to see her relaxed and comfortable with me. I would never be able to thank Morang or Colonel Jackson enough for the joy they had brought into my mother's life at the end, and the happiness I was feeling now—with knowing Susan. I could only hope that... that there was more to come.

We began to eat. "Why don't you tell me how the information was transferred to you and your mother. I mean, how the package arrived with the *last Valentine* after David Jackson turned it over to the military. I need to brush up a bit for the taping this afternoon," she stated. Susan seemed to enjoy the atmosphere and things were definitely looking good for an "after taping get to know you better" date.

"Well," I said with half a mouth full while still managing a turkey stack on sourdough. "Between bites O.K?" I swallowed.

"Sure," she answered in a lively tone.

"Well, O.K." I took a drink from the glass of ice water she had poured me and began.

***

Caroline Thomas home - Pasadena, February 12, 1994

I had come to visit with Mom, as was my custom, just to check on her, really, after school was out. It was on my way home to my condo on Fairoaks. She was starting to forget things and had been ill. She would battle her arthritis and then catch a cold and had just gotten over a serious bout with pneumonia. I worried how long she would be able to live alone, but she was still a tiger.

There was a knock on the door. I went to open it and saw two

Navy Officers standing there with their backs to me. They quickly turned to greet me.

"Yes, gentlemen. What can I do for you?" I asked.

"Is this the home of Caroline Jensen Thomas?" the senior officer asked. He was a tall, slender man with dark hair—a strikingly modern version of what my father must have looked like in his Navy duty uniform. He bore a distinctive smile that at once silently evoked the sentiment of friendship. I was taken aback for a moment.

"Yes. That's correct," I stuttered as a warm breeze seemed to wisp past me and into the small living room.

"May we come in?" the officer in charge politely asked as they both took their hats off and moved towards the door at my gesture. "Sir, is Mrs. Thomas in? We'd like to have a moment with her. Excuse me," he extended his hand in greeting, "my name is Brady, Richard Brady, Chaplain, United States Navy and this is Chief Petty Officer Higgins." The Petty Officer reached around Chaplain Brady and offered a pleasant smile and firm handshake.

"Thomas, Neil Thomas Jr. Pleased to meet you. Yes, please come in, my mother is home. She's resting. Please..." I gestured to the living room and they eased down on the sofa by the fireplace.

"Well, Mr. Thomas," the tall officer grinned, "this is going to be a doubly pleasant visit for us today."

I smiled wondering what it all meant. "I'll go in to her bedroom and check to see if she's awake. Just a moment, please."

Crazy thoughts about my father went through my head and my heart pounded with increasing excitement. It had to be some very interesting news, but what? I tip-toed into the small hallway that lead to her bedroom and gently pushed the old raised panel door open to peek inside. She was sound asleep and stretched out on top of the covers, fully dressed. As I gazed on the most beautiful woman in my world, I wondered if someday soon I wouldn't find her there, just like she was, in a sleep that no one could wake her from.

She was fatigued from the latest round of pneumonia and the growing chronic pain from the rheumatoid arthritis that caused her joints to swell and ache. I returned to the living room.

The Last Valentine

"I'm afraid you'll have to excuse me, gentleman. We weren't informed of a pending visit. My mother is sound asleep. She's suffered from some illness and lately it's taken an especially large toll on her energy. How can I be of assistance to you?"

"Well, Mr. Thomas. This visit is a specially pleasant task for me and Petty Officer Higgins. Occasionally we are called upon, by the Navy, to visit families that have lost a loved one while in the service of their country. But, this time we..."

Just then Chaplain Brady and Higgins stood, as if at attention, and smiled in the direction of my mother's room. I turned around to see her walking slowly towards us with the aid of her cane.

"Mom, you O.K?" I asked as I rushed to put my arm around her and guide her to a chair opposite the sofa, where the two men from the Navy stood.

I gestured to my mother to sit down. "Here, have a seat, Mom," I gently said. She just stood there, still groggy, and seemed to be trying to focus on the tall man who stood smiling at her with outreached hand. Her eyes strained to focus as she grabbed my arm suddenly for support.

"Neil?" her soft high-pitched voice inquired in an unsteady tone.

"Yes, Mom. I'm right here," I replied as she stared in fixed amazement at the two men dressed in white waiting to shake her hand.

"Mrs. Caroline Thomas?" Chaplain Brady announced. "My name is Richard Brady, Commander, United States Navy. And this is Chief Petty Officer Daniel Higgins." They both reached out and shook hands with her. "We are here with some very good news for you."

"Please? Won't you sit down?" she asked sweetly as I helped her to be seated. Her attention was focused as I had rarely seen it before. I was overcome with a sense of anticipation that a special, pivotal moment, one of those rarest of occasions that happen in a person's life, was about to take shape and touch my mother and me for the rest of our lives.

She fixed her eyes on the tall Chaplain, then seemed to glow with a radiance I had rarely seen in the last few pain-filled years of her life. A broad smile graced her lips and her face seemed to lighten, adding to the dimension of energy building in the room.

"Neil," she whispered softly.

"Yes, mother?" I answered.

"Neil," she said again in a breath so low it was barely heard by anyone. I knew it wasn't me, now, she was talking to.

"Ma'am, I am delighted to extend to you some news with regards to your husband, Lieutenant Neil Thomas Sr."

A gasp rose from my mother's throat as her right hand went to her mouth and tears immediately welled up in her eyes.

The Chaplain continued with a gentleness and a smile that seemed palpable. A sacred moment was about to take place. "On behalf of the United States Navy I can offer you news that you have waited many years to hear. The body of your husband, Lieutenant Neil Thomas Sr., listed as 'missing in action' for almost fifty years, has been found." My mother and I hung onto every word that sprang from the Commander's lips.

"What's more, I am delighted to deliver to you this package." He reached over to the Petty Officer, who handed him a thick, padded manila envelope marked "Special Duty Delivery, USN."

"I believe its contents will bring you much satisfaction and offer many answers about your husband's last months of life."

The silence was broken by a muffled cry as my mother, hands shaking, received the large envelope from the gentle chaplain. She fought the tears to no avail—and I found myself also searching for a way to keep that stolid composure befitting a man in control. It was no use. I, too, was overcome as my throat suddenly burned with effort to control the tears I failed to hold back. I kneeled next to my mother and buried my face against her aging neck and shoulder to comfort her, and as people do, to just be close. The affectionate touch of a son for his mother was more defining than any words. We both knew he was coming home, and somehow we felt he knew it, too.

I looked up to my mother, who was staring far off into the distance as if she were gazing right through the walls of the small room. Her face revealed a serenity and joy that I didn't want to disturb—but I knew that there was more and I wanted her to hear it. Silence reigned for a long moment as I gently coaxed my mother back into the awareness that we needed to listen to further information from the Navy officers.

"So," I offered to break the silence. "What can you tell us? How was his body discovered?" I asked simply.

Commander Brady then went into details of retired Colonel Jackson's discovery of the ammo box. Then the startling uncovering of facts regarding my father's three and a half months of survival in the Philippine jungles as a companion to Filipino guerrillas during the liberation of the island nation during World War II.

"I'm delighted to inform you, Mrs. Thomas, that the package you hold contains letters and a special greeting from your husband, and that they will further answer all of the questions you may have regarding his last days. He was a true hero, Mrs. Thomas."

"Thank you...thank you, boys...thank you from the bottom of my heart." She emotionally pulled the package away from her chest and placed it with trembling hands on her lap.

Chaplain Brady intervened: "Before you open it, I should advise you of something that will further be a comfort and source of satisfaction to you. I have been authorized to inform you that the following awards have been recommended by the Secretary of the Navy on behalf of a grateful nation for heroic actions performed by your husband while in the service of his country." He handed me an envelope addressed to her from the Secretary of the Navy, Washington. D.C.

I opened it and began to read it aloud for her:

Dear Mrs. Thomas,

I am honored to inform you that your husband, Lieutenant Neil Thomas, Sr., killed in action during the campaign to liberate the Philippines from Japan during World War II, has been formally recommended to receive your country's gratitude in the form of military honors and decorations. For meritorious conduct in the face of the enemy and for gallantry above and beyond the call of duty, Lieutenant Neil Thomas, Sr. USN, will be posthumously awarded the following:

The Return Home

The Purple Heart
The Navy Cross
The Congressional Medal of Honor

These awards will be made to you and your family members at a special ceremony, to be announced, which will be held at the White House. Scheduling arrangements are now being made. The President of the United States has been informed of these recommendations. A personal letter, detailing the timing of the event, should soon arrive via special delivery, United States Postal Service.

In this, the forty-ninth anniversary year of the end to the Second World War, it brings the Department of the Navy special satisfaction to inform you of these awards with the knowledge that your husband did not die in vain, but as a hero, truly distinguishing himself above the ordinary man.

Truly yours,"

"Signed, the Secretary of the Navy," I finished reading. I looked up into the beaming face of my mother as she let out a heavy sigh of relief. The room was charged with a special energy.

"The Congressional Medal of Honor," I offered, looking into my mother's eyes. She nodded as happily as a child who had just made a wonderful discovery. Her smile was different than I remember ever seeing.

How can a smile be different? It loved. It was playful. It was as if she was finally with her companion. It was a connection with a sparkle in the eyes that only lovers know. It was a moment for her to savor, unlike any she had tasted for fifty years.

"He's coming home, son! He's coming home like he said he would!" She was resolute in her statement and so innocent about its surety that all I could do was agree.

"I know he will. Sure he will, Mom." There was no sense in trying to dissuade her in her fantasy. Fantasies of love, for a man lost for so many years, were well earned.

"Mrs. Thomas, Mr. Thomas." Commander Brady sought our

attention. "We want to offer you some additional information. We have received word from our forensics lab in Hawaii that all necessary work had been completed Tuesday at 6:00 p.m. Pacific Standard Time. As soon as we knew for certain the remains found were in fact those of your husband, all arrangements for transporting his body home and the other military data for processing benefits and military decorations were put into motion. Based upon the latest information I have received, his remains will arrive either February 14th or 15th at Los Angeles International. We are happy to inform you that, if you should request it, Lieutenant Thomas' remains may be interred, at no cost to you, in the Los Angeles Veteran's Cemetery in Westwood. If you have another choice for burial, you may let us know. I will leave you my card."

"I want to assure you that this visit has been one of the highlights of my military career," he continued. "As a pilot myself, I know how deeply satisfying it is to all pilots to know how hard their country strives to reunite lost men with their families. And because I know Lieutenant Thomas is alive in spirit, I sense that he must be smiling from ear to ear to know that he is finally coming home to rest. Congratulations, Mrs. Thomas, on this long-deserved good news."

She nodded and thanked both of the Navy officers as she sought to fathom what it all meant. I was still somewhat stunned and taken back by the suddenness of the surprising revelations. "I want to thank you. I can't describe what this means to us. I wish to thank Colonel Jackson as well. Would you know how I might contact him?" I asked.

"I have that right here, sir," Petty Officer Higgins announced. He opened up his briefcase and handed me a slip of paper with the Colonel's address and telephone number. I had been deeply moved by the story of the discovery and wanted to not only thank David Jackson but also turn his experience into a memorial for my father. A written memorial. I couldn't know it at the time, but my immediate interest in my father's story would turn into a book and culminate in the telling of the greatest love story I had ever known: *The Last Valentine—A Love Story.*

My mother sat there still, staring at the package in her lap. A smile lingered on her face. I was sure, that in her mind, she was visiting another time and place.

We thanked the officers once again and my mother suddenly stood up, full of vigor and enthusiasm. She reached for Petty Officer Higgin's hands and cupped hers in his. "I want you to know that you have made an old lady happier than she has been for fifty years. Thank you." She looked into his eyes and whispered it again, "Thank you." Then she moved towards the chaplain, Commander Brady, and took his hand, repeating the same phrase.

"No, my thanks to you," returned the Navy Chaplain. "You are an inspiration and I will not forget these moments we have shared."

A qualified pilot, he wore both the wings and the cross on his uniform. He had been able to bring good news to someone. He looked as grateful as he claimed to be, as he gave my mother a parting hug. I escorted them to the door.

Chaplain Brady smiled as he looked up at the fifty-year-old hand-carved sign which graced the header over the front door. *"Belief, the substance of things hoped for..."* he read, and then finishing it he said to me, "Now you have the *'evidence of things not seen.'* Congratulations again, Mr. Thomas."

He was right. I was stunned by the remarkable analogy to my father's life and the hope my mother had always maintained—that she would hear from him again—that he would keep his promise to return to her.

They had finished their visit and now it was time to view the contents of the package. I positioned my mother on the sofa and, sitting beside her, open the padded manila envelope. My mother sat there, like a child anticipating a birthday gift, or Christmas, maybe. It occurred to me that it was a gift, and I treated it with deep respect. I reached inside to carefully free the bundle from its envelope. The contents gently slid out onto the coffee table in front of us. On top of the neatly stacked envelopes was one with a message: "Open first." I obeyed.

I looked inside to see a chain with old military dog tags. I pulled it out and held it up for my mother to see. She burst into small quiet sobs as she took and held the small metal tags to her lips. Dangling from the chain was another token of my father's identity: his crucifix.

All of a sudden the passage of the years had been sealed. It was over. He had left, almost fifty years earlier to the day, and these tokens meant he was back. It was a triumphant moment for my mother, who had patiently believed she would hear from him again. And now she was going to, with the next envelope I opened.

Each of his letters had been placed in a neat, new security envelope. I slowly opened the next one, contemplating that I would be reading something written five decades earlier, and never yet revealed to us. I gently pulled out a weathered and soiled onion skin-style envelope and pulled back the flap to view the contents. It was a brown piece of lightweight cardboard with a message. I took it out and held it up to read the faint inscription, written in faded fountain pen ink. I looked at my mother, who still held the old military I.D. tags to her breast and she nodded for me to read.

An electric feeling ran through me as I held the old hand-written note. I realized that I was touching where he had touched...my father, who I had never known.

***

February 13, 1945

My Darling Caroline,

I'm sorry that on our wedding anniversary I cannot keep my promise to come home and hold you, as I did last year at Union Station. This may be my last Valentine to you. I pray that it will find you safe, and loving me still.

I wish I could somehow tell you in person how much this awful business of war has changed me. Can a man draw closer to God through the hellish nightmare and conflict I have experienced? Can a man discover what really matters most because of the contrasting experience of war? I think I have. I now believe that knowing what matters most in life is the key to happiness. You and Neil Jr. are what matter most to me, darling.

Love and hate. There's another key. I've found that I can do both—but never at the same time. I've also found that I can only "be" one or the other. Filled to any degree with hate destroys a portion of the man I am...the man I want to be. I'm not sure I'm making any sense but I am sure of what I want and who I am and what I hope to be...what I hope for the world..for little Neil.

I had the words to this poem going through my head and I thought they might describe my concern and love for you. I had hoped to whisper that Bing Crosby song, the one you liked so well, into your ear today.

I feel so alone, in this dark cave. You are my light, sweetheart. If I could just see you, feel you...if you were here, this stenchfilled cave would suddenly transform into a castle. I must go, but never doubt my deepest love for you forever! And forever is a promise to keep!

I then read the original poem my father had created, titled "My Last Valentine." It was hard for me to get through; I stumbled on every word. They were sacred and meant for her to hear long ago.

The memories she carried only made the words more delicious. For me, there wasn't enough macho in the world to hold back the welling of emotion in my eyes. He ended it with his familiar way...to try to let her know how deeply he adored her:

'I love you'...isn't good enough... Not for you, Caroline!

Forever your loving Husband,

Neil

***

My eyes were brimming with tears. I couldn't see.

My mother took the *last Valentine* from my hand, held it to her breast and repeated over and over... "I love you too, darling... I love you too... I love you, darling... I love you, forever!"

The emotions were running to overflowing. The poignancy of the moment was revealed in the miracle that had taken place. It would be their anniversary in two days—their fifty-second, had he

The Last Valentine

lived. His remains were returning, and he was to be honored as a hero by receiving the highest military decoration bestowed by our country.

As I pondered upon the strange and sudden turn of events, my mother whispered something to me. I put my arm around her frail body and asked, "What? What did you say, Mom?"

"I saw the swallow in the window yesterday. It was there again today. I'm going with him when he comes home, Son. He's coming for me, I know he is. He'll be here for our anniversary and he'll come to get me... La Golandrina."

She was smiling and rocking back and forth with the contents of the package clutched tightly in her arms. The happiness she enjoyed was as one who holds a sweetheart in her arms again, after a long separation. And the joy of the reunion is consumed in it...in the return home.

CHAPTER TWENTY-FOUR

"THE TUNNEL OF LOVE"

<u>Neil Thomas, Jr. CNTV Interview, Pasadena - 1:00 p.m. January 9, 1995</u>

I looked up at Susan. We had spent the lunch hour together reviewing the story of the discovery of my father's remains and how the package of letters was delivered to us. Susan's head rested in her hand, her elbow propping it up as she stared at me. It was as if a picture or a movie was playing in her mind—or maybe as if she was bored stiff. I felt a little embarrassed by taking so much time but reminded myself that she had asked me to retell the story.

"Well," she sighed as she straightened up and stretched. "I can't imagine a happier ending, unless he really did come for her. I wonder..."

I grinned. I had the evidence that proved the romantic ending created for the book was more than plausible, more than mere fiction. The evidence? Words from a note. It was the hand-written scrawl my mother had made in her dying moments. Having those six precious words written in my mother's shaky hand filled me with the confidence that the ending I created for my story was accurate. After all, I did have my mother's premonitions to consider, her forms of evidence...the signs of the flower budding and the appearance of "la golondrina," the swallow. Then there was the note...a treasure to me...the scribbled note found in my mother's lap by Josiah.

"You read the whole manuscript, didn't you?" I asked.

"Well yes, but how could one ever be sure. I admit that the delusions—I'm sorry... I didn't mean to imply..." Susan struggled with her reply. "Well, the dreams of your sweet mother were not only enjoyable to contemplate but inspiring as well, but really... Well, I would like to think that lovers would meet again after passing on... I mean finally be reunited like that, but...hum."

She seemed embarrassed, stumped for words. I took that as a good sign. Some deep thinking was going on and I cared what the mental struggle taking place in her mind meant. It seemed to be a clash between believing something spiritually intangible but possible, and pure pragmatism.

"Paul said, *'Belief is the substance of things hoped for, the evidence of things not seen,'*" I remarked in an off-the-cuff manner, not seeking to invite religious debate, just quoting a source.

"Paul who?" she asked.

"The New Testament Paul," I replied softly, casually.

"Oh, that Paul," she nodded in agreement as if she was familiar with the passage in Hebrews.

"Susan, remind me to show you a note my mother scribbled just before she died." I didn't have it with me. I wish I had. But it would give me a good excuse to visit with her again...to test her interest in the theological question I proposed in the ending of my book...the "happier ending" she couldn't imagine.

"You'd better not be holding out on me!" she returned, smiling and poking me in the shoulder with her index finger.

"We'll need to meet again. It's a rather important note," I said.

"Hum. Sounds fascinating. You can't give me a hint?"

"Yeah, sure. There couldn't be a *'happier ending.'*" I accentuated the last two words, smiled, and kept the secret—like a hand of cards in a poker game—carefully hidden. I wanted to see her again, without a video camera crew milling about. This was one way to get her back.

"Another meeting, huh? Well, sounds like the crew is returning from lunch. Looks like we'll be wrapping this up for today." She wasn't commiting, but by the expression on her face I could tell she wanted to know about more of what I was hinting.

"Where would you like to start?" I asked.

"Well, we left off with Colonel Jackson's story. If you briefly touch on the story you just told me and then move into the day your mother passed away, that'll be a wrap." Susan stood up and offered a quick smile. Was she being coy, indifferent? Or was she trying to get me to open up on the secret I had promised for a later meeting? I couldn't tell.

"A wrap? You mean that's it for our visits?" I probed again with a smile, hoping to get her to somehow commit verbally. Hoping she would give me some sort of signal that I could take the next step and ask her out...get to know her better and talk privately about why I ended the book the way I did...the note.

"Well, not exactly. I'm waiting for the videotape of an interview done in Kobe, Japan. We have a team over there doing a follow-up on another related story. I hope we can locate the Japanese officer's widow, Mrs. Ito, or her son. It is a touching part of this whole story. I hope to include it." She casually adjusted her collar mike, then, glancing back up at me with interest expressed by a furrowed brow, she revealed herself through expressions of which she wasn't aware.

"Then of course there will be the video tape of last year's White House award ceremony where you received the Medal of Honor posthumously for your father," she continued. "I hoped that we could get together and show you the final product before it aired on Valentine's Day." She looked at me as if she were anxious for a response.

"Good," I replied in relief. "Frankly, I was starting to feel like part of the team. And, well..." Just then the crew walked in and broke the magic of the moment. I couldn't finish my sentence on how I'd hoped she and I could get to know each other better, outside of the professional realm.

"Next time...the note. I promise to bring it along. You should read it for yourself." She nodded pleasantly, but once again without commitment.

"Well, let's begin," she smiled as she headed for the living room, giving instructions to the crew all along the way.

"I'm ready," I stated. I followed and took my seat, ready to tell the ending to the love story that would be in print and on bookstore shelves in four weeks.

"Rudy?" Susan asked over her collar mike, "Do we have speed?"

"We have speed," he replied over the sound cable that led to her hidden earpiece.

The Last Valentine

"We're rolling," Terry added. "5,4,3,2,1...speed."

For the next five minutes I answered Susan's questions about the Department of Navy's delivery of the news that my father's remains had been discovered and the impact his last Valentine and letters had had on my mother. Then she invited me to tell the story of Caroline's last hours at Union Station.

Union Station - Los Angeles February 14, 1994

Josiah had returned from checking on a disturbance in the parking lot fronting on Alameda Street.

Armando, the custodian, stopped him. "Say Josiah, I just passed the old lady. You know, Caroline? She doesn't look so good. You better go check her out."

"Thanks, Mando." He patted his Union Station friend on the back and hurried up the wide aisle to Caroline's seat.

"How we doin', Miss Caroline?" he asked. She had drifted off to sleep and he wanted to make sure that was all it was.

"Oh, Josiah. I was having the most delightful dream," she replied in her characteristic high-pitched voice, which wavered ever so slightly as she opened her eyes from her sleep.

"Sorry to disturb you, Miss Caroline, but jus' checkin' on you like I promised."

"Josiah, you're never a bother. Can you tell me what time it is?"

He had doubled his knees so he could be at eye level with her as they talked. "It's 2:35 p.m., Miss Caroline. How long you plan on stayin' before goin' back home?" he asked in a concerned tone.

"Neil should be here by 3:00 p.m.—to get me. That's when the Navy said he was returning to Los Angeles."

Josiah looked puzzled. Neil Jr. must have taken a train out of town, and knowing that his mother came here every year, he must be returning on Amtrak from somewhere. Oh, well...he'd take care of her until Neil showed up. Caroline was getting old, and no doubt living heavily in the past. After all, that's why she came to Union Station every year on Valentine's Day.

"Well, honey, I be checkin' as usual. If Neil don't come for you, I be glad to give you a ride home. You can count on it." He got up, tipped his hat and smiled as he patted her shoulder. He noticed an old weathered envelope in her lap. Must be an old letter her husband sent from the war, he thought. A note pad and pencil was out as well. He wondered what the old lady was up to.

"No need, but thank you anyway, Josiah. Please let my son, Neil, know I love him when you see him." She did look a little pale and did act unusually tired, but at the same time she seemed to radiate a serenity and a happiness he had never seen before.

Josiah scratched his head and shook it sadly. "Sure thing, little lady. Sure thing." He hated to see her lose her mental stamina, her memory and touch with reality. Her obvious exhaustion and poorer health than the previous year worried him.

"I'll be right back, little lady. You rest, I got a call to make."

"The woman's son coming to get her or no son," he thought, he was going to call the Union Station nurse to have her check on Caroline.

She looked down at the *last Valentine* and the love letter with the poem Neil had scratched quickly on a piece of carton-type paper on February 14, 1945. She had brought the reply to his poem. She had penned it that very morning before leaving from her home in Pasadena for the last time—a poem in answer to his. With the piece of note paper on her lap and the pencil, she also wanted to record her final impressions...for her son and grandchildren...so that they would know she wasn't crazy—just in love.

The excitement of the two previous days had been such that she could hardly sleep. She had read and then reread all the letters and now understood clearly why he couldn't come home fifty years ago. She understood him better, too. She understood that the war had changed him and that, like the letter from the Secretary of the Navy had said, he was not an "ordinary man." He had learned the secrets of love and had possessed the strength of character to employ the principles when it wasn't convenient. He gave his life for someone else. She was proud...so very proud.

She hadn't eaten, she couldn't sleep, and now all that was catching up with her. She had seen the swallow in the window for three days and knew she could go with him when he returned. Then the dream came back...he came back in it.

It happened the night before as she slept with his *last Valentine*, the crucifix and dog-tags held tightly to her breast. In the dream she was working in their garden. She was young, and she somehow knew that he was coming home from his last mission. She remembered how he had disappeared into the fog bank with the question on his mind, "Can you do it, Caroline?" That was a dream fifty years old, and it had sustained her for all those years. But now... Now she was an old woman, and she had done all she could, and in the new dream she appeared young again, like no time had passed at all.

In the dream, she thought about his question, "Can you do it, Caroline?" and she had strongly replied, "Yes! I can! I did!" She had survived the heartache, the disappointments, and she had been strong—for him. Now he had to come back. She had done her part; their son was raised. She was ready to go with him.

She remembered that she had looked over her shoulder in the dream. She was in the garden tending to the roses, the same ones they had planted together five decades earlier. A light filled the mist, the fog behind her. She saw him! He slowly walked out of the fog with a bright bouquet of the most beautiful flowers she had ever seen. He was as handsome as he ever had been and she let go of the roses and pierced her hand on one of the thorns. Then he ran to her and pulled her to him tenderly, kissed her hands, and the bleeding stopped. They embraced and kissed again. His smile consumed her. Then she woke up.

Now she waited. She sat in those same seats where they had earlier waited for his boarding call to go to war. They faced gates G and H, the two gates that opened to the tunnel. She was glad it was there where she would see him. Nothing, not even death itself, could hold her back from him...

"The Tunnel Of Love"

Neil Thomas, Jr. 2:30 p.m. Caroline Thomas home - Pasadena

I opened the door to find an empty house. I suspected the worst. She was in no condition to make the trip to Union Station by bus. She had worn herself out over the preceding two days...had hardly slept, hadn't eaten. Her heart was weak. She had suffered three minor heart attacks with the pneumonia over the past year.

I had made it clear to her that I would get out of school early and pick her up and take her to LAX to meet the plane.

The Navy chaplain, Commander Brady, had called the night before to confirm the time. The plane would arrive at 3:00 p.m. We would be met there by him and reporters. He suggested that we should not arrive too early. He wanted to make sure the reporters didn't cause any confusion for my mother. The chaplain also said he would be sure to allow my mother and I the space we needed to enjoy the moment...a most sacred moment. A husband, father and war hero was returning home, and we deserved the privacy to savor the moment, the chaplain had said.

I had made sure to call her in the morning to remind her, and had even left a note on the refrigerator. I could hardly believe she would misunderstand. I had gone so far as to say that on our return trip from LAX we would swing by Union Station so she could spend some moments there and keep her traditional rendezvous with the past.

As I headed back out the door to leave, I saw the note taped to the back of it. I quickly read it:

Dear Son,

I want you to know that I went ahead to look for your father. Everything is in order. I'm happier than I've been in fifty years. I love you so much. You have been my life and without you I couldn't have gone on. Look out the bedroom window. See how the yellow rose blooms early? Just like it did fifty years ago. The swallow returned today ... I'll be O.K. I'll always love you...forever! Be faithful and love the Lord. "Forever is a promise to keep!" Your father said that! Happy Valentine's Day!   Mom

The Last Valentine

I put the note gently down on the small table next to the mail drop. I wanted to know for myself that it was true. I walked back into her bedroom to see. Looking out the window, I saw a single yellow rose bud had opened.

I would have to hurry. I knew where to find her. My mother was a sweet woman, but a stubborn one when she wanted to be. I suspected that this wasn't stubbornness, however. It was confusion. Clearly, the last few years showed she was becoming more confused and forgetful, and the last few days had taken a toll on her. I would have to drive fast and hope that there were no problems on the 110—Pasadena Freeway.

As I closed the door behind me, I felt as though it would never open again to find my mother there. I knew she had found a love at the end of her life equally as exquisite as the love at the beginning. And somehow I sensed that what I would find at Union Station was my greatest fear, yet her greatest hope...an old woman who loved her life away and finally found peace.

Union Station - 2:55 p.m.

As Caroline rested there, immersed in dreams of how it had been, she recalled the days of loneliness. The sound of music suddenly attracted her attention—strains of music coming from all around her. It was a familiar tune. It was one of her favorites, one of his—he used to sing it to her. Either her mind was playing tricks on her or the sounds of the old Bing Crosby tune really did fill her ears:

Because you speak to me—I find the roses 'round my feet, and I am left with tears and joy of thee!
Because God made thee mine—I'll cherish thee, through all life and darkness, and all time to be.
And pray his love may make our love divine—Because God made thee mine!

She smiled as she looked down to see the Valentine and her poem to Neil sitting in her lap. Her dress seemed to be the red flower-patterned dress, the one she wore then. Her leg, the crippled one was young and strong looking. The shoes with the square toes were the same ones she worn that day. With eyes closed, she reached her hand up to her face. Her skin was firm and smooth. Then she opened her eyes to look again—to see if it was all just a dream. She turned to see a bright light filling the tunnel.

Quickly she reached for her note paper...to say goodbye to her son and tell him...tell him all about her *last Valentine* visit and how much love she felt for him...for everything. She strained to scribble the note until she couldn't write another word. The paper and pencil fell to her lap.

The outlined form of someone walking from the tunnel—walking towards the gate, towards her—seemed radiant, causing her to focus sharply with an ability her normal sight had never experienced.

She was surprised at the light filling the waiting area. It was unlike any she had seen and it was coming from both outside and inside the large room. She looked above her and it was there. She looked beneath her and the light was there, too.

Caroline felt drawn somehow towards the tunnel, towards the gates leading to the tunnel and the tracks. She had never felt such a euphoric sense of wellness—wholeness. Her eyes saw things differently. If it were a dream, she would refuse to wake up.

She wasn't sure what to think. She didn't care. There wasn't a word to describe the childlike sense of adventure that possessed her. Then her eyes seemed to open wider. She saw more than she had ever been able to with her aging eyes. Someone familiar was approaching the gates.

He's looking for me! *"Neil!* Here! At the end of the tunnel!" she involuntarily called out.

She could see him! "I'm here! Neil, I'm here!" she shouted as she flew from her seat to go to him. She felt light, ethereal, alive! There was no heaviness to her legs holding her down now!

He stood there, smiling, in his dress white Navy uniform, and he held the most beautiful bouquet of roses she had ever seen!

The Last Valentine

He was there! He had come for her! It was just like it was then...the love...fifty years before—but the intensity was elevated, and there was no pain!

His arms were outstretched. His smile...the same... "Oh Neil! Darling! I love you! I love you!" she cried. She threw herself into his arms and let all her emotions out as he held her tightly. She wept. "A dream, could it just be?" she wondered.

"No, sweetheart, it's not a dream!" Neil whispered earnestly, emotionally in her ear. He let her release all of her feelings as he held her, smiling down at his woman. He stroked her long auburn-colored hair that cascaded once more around her shoulders.

He whispered to her. "I'll never let you go again, Caroline! Never, darling!" He kissed her tenderly as they embraced. "I'm sorry I'm late...but I've always been there...with you and our son...watching, day after day, caring." He held her by the waist and caressed her cheeks against his, sweeping the tears from her soft face.

"You did it, Caroline! You handled the thorns...you made it!" He softly spoke to her in tones that soothed, deep resonating tones that filled her with assurance and peace. He pointed back to the waiting area and the chair. She didn't want to let her eyes leave his face...just in case it was, indeed, all a dream.

"Look, Caroline! Look at the chair. Look!" At his gentle insistence she took her eyes off him and looked, just for a split second.

There was a vaguely familiar appearance to the old woman sitting there. That was her cane, her purse, and...

Her eyes went back to his face—and she smiled, reaching around his neck and kissing him over and over. The years melted away as if the lovers had never been separated.

"You came for me... I knew you would come, darling!" she beamed as they looked into each other's eyes and spoke a language unheard—unspoken.

He handed her the bouquet and said, "Look down towards the end of the tunnel." There was light, more light than she had ever seen. It filled her with a sense of ecstasy beyond anything she could have ever dreamed. It was pure, it was real, and it beckoned.

"Caroline, we have to go now," He gripped her hand and gestured for her to come with him. The words had a familiar ring to them. He knew what she was thinking. The last time he had said those words, she had passed through the tunnel with him—and he didn't return. This time, though...

"Wait until you see where I got these roses... Wait until you see the other side of the tunnel."

"Not Track Twelve?" she thought to him as she looked up into his face.

"No, not Track Twelve," he grinned. "Remember as we stood here fifty years ago, with hundreds of service men and their wives and girlfriends?"

"Yes," she replied with a broad smile.

"You didn't want to go into the tunnel and I whispered something into your ear?" She laughed. It had all come back to her. His sense of humor, his wit. He was the same Neil, only...

"Remember?" He held her close to him as he did then. She put her face against his chest.

"Yes," she returned softly. "I remember. I remember it all, and it doesn't hurt anymore. You said, 'the tunnel of love.'" She looked up at him as their hands joined.

"Sweetheart...more love than you have ever known. More love than I can explain...and it goes on forever. I've always loved you, Caroline... I always will."

Her mind sped swiftly back in time, to the words he whispered to her then as he said them to her again, in this same place—the noise of the train engines filled the station and he shouted it. Now the words were soft and serene as he repeated them:

"I've loved you since Adams School, through the years growing up in Eagle Rock, through all the good times, and now I can't remember any bad. I think I've just always loved you!"

He scooped her up into his arms as they melted into a long-awaited kiss and embrace. He gazed into the eyes of his young wife and then whispered into her ear as his cheek felt her tender skin, "Now I know what the feeling is when I used to say those words to you...when I used to try to describe how I felt...when I used to say, *'Love isn't good enough...not for you, Caroline.'*"

She was filled with a sense of light and love...indescribable. She now knew a more powerful love at the end than in the beginning. She turned to look back one last time at Union Station and the waiting area, a scene fading into the distance. There was Josiah, gently trying to shake her awake. There on her lap was the *last Valentine* that had arrived just two days before. There was her poem to him, with the yellowed wedding photo. There was her last note...written to her son. Her last note... She tried to describe her final moments, what was happening, but...

The swallows seemed to sing to her from La Golondrina across the way, and sweet strains of music filled the air. She moved with her handsome young pilot as she watched the fading picture. She could barely still see the old lady resting there, a faint smile gracing her face, and she knew everything would be O.K.

The light was getting brighter now and they seemed to be walking into it. The warmth and glow now before them caused the dreariness of the old train station tunnel to completely disappear behind her.

"The *roses*, Neil. The place where you got them from. The stems, do they have...?"

Smiling, he gestured toward a man and woman entering the tunnel. The man was dressed in some sort of military uniform with a high stiff collar and the woman was clothed in the most beautifully flower-patterned "kimono" style dress.

The happy couple paused a few feet in front of them. Neil gestured towards them with his hand and the words "Ito," a name, and "tomodachi," a Japanese word came so loudly that she instantly knew the translation.

"Itos—our friends!" she thought, which brought a smile of recognition to the faces of the two Japanese greeters.

The man smiled broadly and bowed reverently. The small woman came forward and handed her another bouquet. The colors were beyond what she had ever seen in life.

Caroline examined the stems, then looked up to her husband and threw her arms around him. Finally, pulling back, she glanced at the bouquets in her hands and examined his face in a questioning gaze.

He smiled, stopping her, and then kissed her in a way she had never remembered. "No thorns. Never again! No... Not these. Come on sweetheart...let's go."

***

Josiah knew she was gone. The nurse had arrived. There was no pulse, no breathing, just a peaceful old lady. Her smile... It was serene, a smile in death that testified to him that she was finally at rest.

Her words came back to him. The words about her husband coming to get her. Did she know, really know? He wondered. He put in a call over the radio then looked down at the faded and worn letter resting on her lap. It was written on lightweight cardboard of some type and written with old fountain pen ink. It was a Valentine, a hand-drawn rose with a poem, homemade from Neil Thomas Sr.—from the war. There was also another letter on her lap, a poem written on fresh stationary in shaky cursive. No doubt written by Caroline, he thought. He picked up the picture, the photo of a handsome Navy pilot and a beautiful young girl taken during the war.

"Miss Caroline," he whispered under his breath. He lifted the faded Valentine, dated February 14, 1945, and began to read:

***

My Last Valentine

If this be final—the Valentine, and life is snatched away—
If war or clouds of mortal death, find me on this day—
My breath shall breathe a final vow, my wish and solemn oath—
You'll sense my kiss—the fragrance...the rose and I ...both.

The Last Valentine

Life may send its bitterness...when all is lost, it seems—
Your pained brow and fevered lips, I'll kiss...I'll fill your dreams!

You'll feel my touch when the petals bloom,
In the winter turned to storm—
I'll whisper with my silent breath—
"Peace," for when you mourn.

And like the springtime...bud to bloom, I'll wait beside the gate—
Until you come into my arms, and I beg for being late.

If death, my love, this Valentine, finds me on this day—
And these last words are sent to you, though life is snatched away,
My breath shall breathe a final vow— "I love you,"will be my oath,
You'll know the fragrance of the rose is, love, and I...both.

Josiah smiled down at the sweet, peaceful lady sitting there in death. She was satisfied. He knew it. A strange presence, something intangible, yet real, caused a warm sensation to course through him. Tears filled the corners of his eyes. Armando, the station custodian, cautiously strode over to his friend to see what was wrong, as curious passengers and "red cap" baggage handlers began to gather around.

Josiah loved this old woman. He knelt in front of her body and picked up the poem she must have written for her husband. He tried to read the words through the moisture in his eyes as the crowd now started to whisper to each other what they were discovering.

My Response to the Last Valentine

I waited, love, forever it seemed,
I waited long and prayed.
I watched where we last parted dear,
I looked each year and stayed.

"The Tunnel of Love"

You never came to rescue me,
But then I learned the truth.
The love you were surrounded me,
Sweetly, I was soothed.

For love once was, always is,
And never fades away.
Just roses do, but love grows strong,
as if it were to say:

"Love is power that breaks the band,
That loneliness holds fast.
You dear are my Valentine,
At first, always, at last!"

And like the rosebud turned to bloom,
Wait, love, at the gate!
I'm coming home, into your arms-
For love is never late!"

Josiah gazed once more at his peacefully resting friend and reverently replaced the Valentine on her lap. He noticed another piece of paper lying on the floor next to her foot.

"Must a' falled off her lap," he whispered. He noticed the small note-size paper had some words scribbled in light pencil. He held the note up to the light that streamed in from the western skylights. He could barely read the faintly scribbled words. Six words! Caroline's last words!

Josiah turned around, down towards the tunnel. An expression of surprise and amazement filled his face.

"He came back for her!" he said silently. He stiffened his shoulders as his eyes brimmed with emotion and quickly saluted towards the tunnel. Josiah put the note safely in his coat pocket, and put Caroline's belongings together for her last trip home. He then placed himself squarely in front of his sleeping mentor and friend, standing there, her guardian, as he had always been.

The Last Valentine

***

Neil Thomas, Jr. - CNTV Interview, Pasadena 1:30 p.m. January 9, 1995

A respectful quiet filled the small house as I finished reading, for the camera, the last line from my mother's poem. I had shared it from the heart, and my heart was not without its sense of deep gratitude for her, as I fought to maintain composure. I left out the secrets contained in the note found by Josiah. I was saving that for later...for Susan.

"That's a wrap, Rudy," Susan called quietly to the audio man over her collar microphone. She tried to act nonchalant, but I knew something was bothering her, or maybe the ending to the story as retold for the interview had touched her somehow.

"Neil, you did a fine job," she offered. She laid a gentle hand on my knee as she started to get up from her seat. "We'll have to do this again sometime." She was being as personal as she dared while still wearing her professional hat.

I wanted to touch her...hold her in my arms. I wasn't sure if it was the melodrama of the story taking control of me, if loneliness had so engulfed me since the loss of my wife, and then my mother's death, or if my feelings of excitement at being near her were genuine.

I gazed at her dark brown eyes, her long flowing black hair, the high cheekbones that gave a mysterious dimension to her soft, olive complexion. Her lips were full and when they parted they revealed a sense of passion that might exist somewhere...somewhere hidden deeply in the recesses of her mind or heart. The exuberance of her ready smile hinted of it, but also carefully guarded any serious betrayal of emotions. She sought to protect herself from being hurt, I sensed. It caused me to be cautious with my feelings in return.

I cleared my throat and rose to my feet. I knew I had to find someway to make her stay a little longer.

"You really were a great audience, Susan. You made it easy. You have a way that makes people feel comfortable. I don't fully understand...well, I wanted to make sure you knew...I, ah—I'll be calling Mr. Warren to tell him to give you a raise."

Susan laughed, "No... I just did my job. I'm the lucky one. I was introduced to perhaps the most romantic man and woman who have ever lived. Because of you, Neil." She flashed a coy glance that invited me to keep the conversation alive. Just then the cameraman broke in asking about the flight plans for their next shoot, scheduled for the following day in San Francisco. Again the magic of the moment was temporally suspended as she answered him. I looked for a way to regain momentum, to talk with her privately.

"Susan, please come outside with me for a moment," I invited. She nodded and followed me through the back door and out to the rose garden. She took my arm as we strolled over to the greenhouse where the prize-winning roses were carefully nurtured and bred. We entered. I picked a bright, full red rose. I carefully plucked off all but a few of the prickly thorns and handed it to her.

"This is for you," I said softly. "When you see a rose, think of us...think of me... and believe!" I handed her the rose, pointing to the prickly barbs remaining on the stem. She smiled knowingly.

"Believe?" Susan responded as she brought the petals up to smell their fragrance.

"Yes. Someone said, 'Belief is the substance of things hoped for, the evidence of things not seen.' "

She smiled, recalling our earlier conversation and since seeing the small wooden plaque over the front door. "What 'substance' should I believe in?" she asked with a full smile gracing her subtly parted and questioning red lips.

"Love—that it is the sweetest of God's endowed emotions. Love—that it can be found, held onto, and that it never needs to die...that it can be forever," I said. Her eyes questioned me. *"Forever is a promise to keep,"* I gently added with a measured grin.

She reached for my right hand and returned the flower. "The first time we met you said, 'There are many kinds of love.' I want to know more." She looked up at me with a sincerity that proved it wasn't anchor-person Susan talking now.

"Remember the note I promised to show you, the one which contains secrets to the *happy ending* you wondered possible? The ending to my parents story? Tonight, I'll share it with you."

"I believe... I've just got to find," her voice choked with emotion as she hesitated. I sensed the wall she had thrown up between us was breaking apart. "I've just got to find the 'substance,' the 'many kinds of love' you promise the readers of your book... God, a link to something that will last forever...something like you describe in the story's ending."

She stood there with her arms to her side and a "puppy dog" look, a vulnerable expression fixed toward my eyes...waiting, waiting for an answer.

I smiled, took her hand gently in mine, and made her hold onto the flower with me. One hundred questions had just been answered for me. A hope I hadn't known for years seemed to fill me.

"Where do I find this 'substance,' this kind of love?" she asked again as she closed the space between us.

I took her by the waist with my free left hand. She unlocked the hand with mine that held the symbol of love and put her arms around my neck. We embraced and our lips met. Our loneliness began to melt...among the roses.

CHAPTER TWENTY-FIVE

EPILOGUE

5:00 p.m. February 14, 1995 - Union Station, Los Angeles

I was excited. *The Last Valentine—A Love Story* had been on the book racks for a week and was selling like hotcakes. Today was the day the American Diary "Valentine Day Special" would air. The crew was already setting up. The taped portions of the program would be broadcast from CNTV network headquarters, with "live" on-the-spot commentary from Union Station.

The "forties" grandeur of the old train depot offered an extraordinary setting for the telecast. Tonight would not only spotlight my parents' love story, but also offer me a unique opportunity. It would start here, where my parents last touched—and where my mother ended her mortal journey. Susan's and my journey together would also begin here, if she accepted my proposal. I had cleared it with Mr. Warren, CNTV's owner and my publisher. He not only agreed, he personally paid for the one-carat diamond engagement ring. His gift to us, he had insisted.

The proposal was prearranged to take place during the last sixty seconds of the program. The worst that could happen is she would leave the audience hanging for the next broadcast. If she didn't accept, she wouldn't say it on the air. She was too classy for that. But, she would accept—I knew in my heart she would.

As a matter of fact, she had hinted of it. We had spent the weekend before with my kids, Eric and Rachel, at Disneyland. The next day we attended church services in Pasadena and then went back to the house for a Sunday meal. Susan cooked; I cleaned. It was a "test" for the kids and a needed "get to know you better" date for Susan and me. I wanted my children to like her, but they needed to feel that way for themselves, not just to make me happy. I loved them with all my heart. I needed to know how Susan would handle my deep commitment to them and their happiness.

The Last Valentine

In marrying me, she would marry all of me...my children and
my devotion to them as well. I wasn't disappointed at the outcome.
She took to them and they allowed her to be their friend. And religious values...my church affiliation? She came alive by the strength
of what she saw there. We talked for hours about beliefs, God, and
the note...my mother's last words written in her dying moments.
Having the precious words of her note was as if a hand from the
other world was touching ours. The truth it hinted at was deep yet
simple, powerful and joyful at the same time. Susan accepted it
easily. She stated she knew that two people who had any hope of
making something last should possess the same goals concerning
something as important as religious faith. It was the answer I was
looking for and the *"substance"* she was searching for.

Now I waited for her to arrive for the airing of the show from
Union Station. I kept the engagement ring in my blazer coat pocket. I had been pacing the floor. Suddenly I felt a hand on my
shoulder.

"Sir, you'll have to move all of this stuff. We got important
people comin' tonight."

I turned. It was Josiah Williams standing there smiling at me.
An old man stood next to him.

"Josiah!" We shook hands vigorously and slapped each other on
the back. "Josiah Williams! It's been a year, hasn't it?"

"It sure 'nough has, Mr. Thomas. I bought your book today.
You gonna sign it for me?" he asked, holding it up.

"Of course! Here, let me do it now," I said, taking it in my hand
and reaching into my pocket for a pen. I noticed the old man still
standing there. He smiled and I returned the smile, wanting to greet
him. I opened a copy of *The Last Valentine—A Love Story* and
wrote: " *For Josiah Williams, the best guardian angel in Los
Angeles. A true friend who has handled the thorns and possesses
the secret of the rose. For all your love to my mother and my family, I shall forever be in your debt."*

I handed the book back to him and thanked him again for all he
meant to me.

"Thank you, Neil. I sure do miss your mama. I jus' wishin' she could be here ta see all this. Oh, this man says he knows you. I told him ta follow me and meet Union Station's favorite author," Josiah grinned. "I gotta make some rounds. See you in a while, Neil." Josiah was happier than I'd ever seen him—he seemed to walk with two feet off the ground. He was an exceptional man and I was glad to have given him such a mention in my book.

"Hello, I'm Neil Thomas Jr. I'm sorry it took me so long to greet you formally. You were very patient to wait," I said to the older man. He wore a neat blue suit with a cowboy style "bolo" neckwear piece. He possessed a warm smile that accented a kindly old face. "Fatherly," I thought. He stood tall, straight, and proudly wore a blue and white ball cap with an insignia of a naval vessel or fighter squadron. An old World War II Navy man, I thought. American Diary reportedly had found some veterans from my father's ship, survivors of the Princeton, and they had been invited to fill the audience. Probably read the book and wanted an auto-graph.

"It's been a long time, boy. Too long," the old man said with a shaky voice as he sought to contain emotions that now appeared in his eyes. "You were only ten the last time I saw you. Your mother and you made a special trip up to Salt Lake City on the train. Remember?"

I examined his face in a questioning way. He was my first con-scious contact with Mormons, Utah, and someone who had actually been with my Dad in the war. "Bobby? Bobby Roberts, is that you?" I gasped in wonderment. He had never aged in my mind. I received his warm fatherly greeting with a strong hug.

"All these years. I always meant to come back and visit you. Oh—the memories of that week on your farm...they're still strong. I've meant to call...to come and see you!" I pulled back from the warm embrace. "Life has a way with us, it seems. I'm so sorry to let forty..."

He held his hand up in a gesture of understanding. "No need for concern. Now's what counts. It's so good to see you." He stood back, looking at me like a father might. A father inspecting a son. "Your father would be very proud...very, very proud. I can't get over the resemblance. You look exactly alike!" He just stood there and shook his head.

"Bobby, I'm so happy you came. I guess you've read the story."

Emotion came to his eyes and filled his voice. "I was overcome to find out, well, to find out that your father's remains were discovered. I knew it! I knew he had survived after we left him. I knew it!" he said with a gesture of a hand swinging down and up that emphasized his feeling. "If only I could have stayed with him. It's hurt all these years wondering if I had let him down, and now with your book..." Now the old man broke down and quietly sobbed. I came forward with both arms open.

He straightened up and with rough, work-worn hands, wiped the tears from his eyes and coughed as he sought to continue. "I'm proud of you, boy. You've honored your parents real well by telling their story. Your father was a great man."

I was astounded at the emotions the story was bringing forth and amazed at the devotion old World War II warriors, like this, had for one another. "He wouldn't have wanted you to hurt, Bobby. You kept your promise to him. That's all a man can ask," I said.

"I would have given my life for him," he sniffed, trying to clear the evidence of the tender respect that flowed down his kindly old face. I noticed a profound sense of relief sweep over the man as he inhaled deeply, releasing his breath in a quiet sigh. I stood back and waited as the old ex-Navy fighter pilot regained his composure. I wondered at the anxiety I sensed he was releasing. A burden he carried for fifty years seemed to be suddenly lifted from him.

Bobby finally raised his head and cleared his throat again. "I can't tell you what hearing that means to me. Fifty years...it seems like yesterday. I remember answering questions about my faith to your father the very night before the attack on Manila. We prayed. He was a good man...such a good man. And now. To find this out. Your father's remains and letters! Your mother and you...and Lieutenant Thomas finally together! Well..." He shook his head in amazement as a thousand thoughts seemed to fill his questioning mind.

I could see as him a twenty-year-old again. Our conversation had taken him back in time. He searched for words. His voice was soft and hesitant. "I prayed many times...after leaving your father out there in Manila Bay. I prayed... I prayed that he would be spared. The war. It was so awful. So many good men." He looked up at me. "I loved him like a brother," he finished, looking into my eyes for evidence that I understood what he was trying to say.

I placed my right hand on the old man's shoulder. He was noticeably in charge of himself again. In charge like he'd found his friend once again and was connected in a brotherhood...one which spanned time past and would live on into the future.

"Well." Bobby looked me squarely in the eyes. "I want you to know that I would have given my life for him. I'm proud to have served with him and full of happiness at this wonderful outcome. My flight leader...home!" He nodded his head with me as I smiled in return.

"Come on. Let's go. Let me introduce you to some others gathering up in the lobby. All surviving shipmates. You never know. Maybe we'll find someone else...someone else who's joined up with our flight group." He smiled as I led him up to the seating area.

"This place is exactly as I remembered it." Bobby stopped suddenly and looked around. "Right here! It was right here where I bumped into your mother on February 14th, 1945!" I allowed him to savor the memory. "Being in this place is like going back in time!" he said as he gazed around at the walls, the high ceiling, the old wall clock, the stiff leather chairs. "Nothing has changed. Nothing has changed at all!"

Arriving at the seating area in the center floor of the main lobby area, I bade him farewell for the remainder of the show. I promised to see him soon in Salt Lake. And this time I meant to keep the promise. This time I would be with my kids—and hopefully with Susan.

We gathered with other members of the crew as invited guests now continued to stream in. Bobby turned to talk to an old Navy man who tapped him on the shoulder. I watched and waited for Susan.

We were locating the telecast in the wide aisle, between the empty rows of leather chairs that filled both sides of the waiting area. The camera would have Susan with her back to the tunnel that leads under the tracks and the old 1940s signs that read "Gates G & H." The audience then would have the same view as the camera. Many of these men, veterans, would have no doubt passed through these same doors, down the same walkways, through the same tunnel.

It was inspiring to see them as they walked in, all shaking hands and slapping backs as if congratulating each other on having survived that terrible day on October 24, 1944 when the Princeton went down in the Philippine Sea. It was good to see men humbly show their deep and poignant feelings. I had learned from my father's letters the meaning of love and of being a decent human being. Those secrets evoked emotions, and were no doubt discovered through his thoughtful ponderings under the stress that came from combat.

Bobby was talking it up with other veterans as I waited near the cameras for Susan to arrive. Then I saw her, coming in from the Alameda Street entrance. I waved and started to stride in her direction.

"Susan, I was beginning to worry about you!" I said as I gave her a quick hug and kiss.

"I was getting worried, too. You wouldn't believe the traffic I ran into in Denver and then getting here from LAX. Whew! You look nice," she said, patting me on the cheek as I escorted her with my arm lightly on the small of her back.

"Yes!" I thought. "She's going to say yes!" I was happier than I could remember being in years.

I watched Susan immediately take control of the scene. She had an amazing way of creating order on a set...telling people what to do and all the while having them like her for it. I enjoyed watching her.

"Well, it's good to have you all here," she announced as she directed the audience to be seated. Her aide, Kathy Clark, handed her the outline for the program.

"Mr. Bobby Roberts, Josiah Williams, Neil Thomas Jr. and Chaplain Brady, USN?" If you're here, could you all take a seat on the stand with me?"

I hadn't seen Commander Brady yet. He came out of the crowd

where he had been sitting, talking to one of the old veteran pilots. I shook hands with him. "Chaplain, good to see you again!" I said.

"Good to see you, Mr. Thomas. Congratulations on your wonderful book." He held up a copy.

"Thank you. Thank you very much!" I returned. "You sure helped make it possible," I added. We shook hands as we took our seats.

"Well," Susan began as she cupped her hands together. "It is an honor to be surrounded by so many veterans of the aircraft carrier U.S.S. Princeton. We are also delighted to have family and friends of Neil and Caroline Thomas here tonight to share the airing of a special segment of CNTV's American Diary. We have two large monitors, as you can see," she said pointing to the television screens on either side of the audience, "to afford you total viewing capability. We will now outline our program for you. We are scheduled to begin in fifteen minutes."

She handed the program to her assistant, who proceeded to outline it for the audience and call out last-minute instructions.

"Neil, can I speak with you privately for a minute?" She came up behind me, whispering in my ear.

"Sure," I replied as I followed her off the stage and over to the south exit under the old wall clock.

"Things get kind of crazy, people interrupt, and I just wanted to make sure we could have some time together afterward. I've got some things on my mind, and, well, I'd like to talk them over with you." She looked up at me in a personal way, revealing that she looked forward to some private time together.

"I've got just the place," I said, smiling.

"Good. You'll really like what we've done with the videotaped segments from the White House and then from Kobe, Japan. This program is going to help sell a zillion books," she said, squeezing my face with one hand and giving me a quick peck on the lips.

"Hold that thought," I said as I put my arm around her and marched her back to the stage. We were about to begin the final episode of a journey that had started fifty-one years earlier. I hoped my mother could appreciate—maybe somehow even know—what was happening here at this, her "special" place, her rendezvous location with the past—Union Station.

American Diary Valentine's Day Special - 7:00 p.m. PST
February 14, 1995

Susan's lips parted as she offered her famous welcoming smile into camera number one and began:

"Welcome to this Special Edition of American Diary! Tonight we are going to take you back in time. You are going to meet two lovers who last saw each other here, at Los Angeles' Union Pacific train depot, fifty-one years ago today.

"Today, Valentine's Day, is the day reserved for sweethearts. It is said that over one billion Valentine cards will be exchanged today. It is fitting that we should celebrate that great showing of affection by sharing a romantic love story that took five decades to fully mature.

"Lieutenant Neil Thomas Sr., World War II hero, last saw his beloved wife, Caroline, here on their wedding anniversary, February 14, 1944. On that occasion he gave her a Valentine, promising to return one year later. As they held each other they made a vow to be true and faithful to each other. The day that would bring him back to her, here in this place, never came. But, what did finally come was his *last Valentine*. This story will surprise you, thrill you, and leave you to never doubt again the meaning of true love."

Turning to camera two, she added, "It took fifty years for *The Last Valentine - A Love Story* to arrive," she held up the book, "but when it did, it brought with it a new understanding of enduring love and believing that love could last forever.

"Don't go away! The secrets to true love will be unearthed in this Special Edition of CNTV's American Diary. I'm Susan Allison. We'll be right back after these messages!"

The audience was silent. They waited through the break. Susan's ability to promise an audience a rewarding experience for waiting kept them on the edge of their seats. The telecast would switch to the taped interviews interspersed with unrehearsed commentary from those of us on stage, once the break was over.

Camera one's light flashed back on. Susan readied herself and then introduced the story. The taped interviews at my mother's home began. It flowed like the book. The story twisted and turned with the heartache my mother felt fifty-one years ago as she bade her farewell to my father. Susan stopped the taping at the pre-arranged times to introduce Josiah, Bobby, and ask for brief commentary from me. Soon we were ending with Colonel David Jackson's interview and the discovery of the *last Valentine* and my father's long-lost letters.

Now it was time for the segment of videotape I hadn't seen. Susan told me it would be a surprise. It was.

White House - May 29, 1994

"This is Jonathan Newell coming to you live from the White House Rose Garden. We're pleased to broadcast a special CNTV 'American Diary Moment.' Today, May 29th, Memorial Day, offers a special opportunity for all Americans to reflect upon the sacrifices of those heroes who willingly gave their lives in the service of their country.

"Every now and then, a story of an American hero surfaces to raise our consciousness. A story so powerful, so full of virtues and values which Americans everywhere hold dear comes to the fore to remind us what this country stands for and what price has been paid to ensure our liberties and freedoms. Today we will be invited to remember one such American who will be awarded, posthumously, the Congressional Medal of Honor for his valor during action in World War II.

It was fifty years ago this month that Lieutenant Neil Thomas Sr. fought in some of the most famous sea and air battles of the War's Pacific theater. He was to become an ace with over one hundred missions against Imperial Japan's sea and land forces as the United States Armed Forces liberated island after island in the South Pacific. It was on his last mission, October 20, 1944, on the opening day of the liberation of the Philippines from the Japanese, that his plane sustained damage which forced him to ditch in

The Last Valentine

Manila Bay.

"Lieutenant Neil Thomas Sr. was listed 'missing in action' following his forced landing at sea. Unknown to his superior officers, he survived, and for three months fought on the Bataan Peninsula with Filipino guerrilla forces awaiting the arrival of U.S. Army landings to liberate Luzon Island. Facts surrounding his survival and participation with the guerrillas recently came to light through military studies conducted by retired Colonel David Jackson, U.S. Army. During Colonel Jackson's investigations surrounding facts of a key battle between Filipino guerrillas and Japanese forces, he was able to make a startling discovery: the remains of Lieutenant Thomas, along with his diary and letters he had written, stored in a .30-caliber ammunition box and hidden safely in the wall of a cave near the site of the last battle he participated in. It was there, while fighting that battle, that Lieutenant Thomas rose to the greatest level of sacrifice one can render...the surrendering of personal safety and life for the safety and life of his fellow man. What makes this story so extraordinary is that Lieutenant Thomas risked—and ultimately lost—his life trying to save the life of an enemy soldier. Because of his devotion to his country, but also because of his sense of mercy and justice, he paid the ultimate price. For this reason, his country will present his survivors, this day, the highest homage and honor it can bestow.

"The President is now approaching the podium. Ladies and gentlemen, The President of the United States:

" 'Distinguished guests, friends and family of Lieutenant Neil Thomas, Sr. Our respected colleagues of the United States Armed Forces, White House staff and media. It is with great pride that I address you this day...'

For the next few minutes the President explored the courage and actions my father displayed and the circumstances that compelled him to bestow the nation's highest military honor on him. Then he continued:

'A bridge of friendship has been built over the last forty-nine *years with our former enemy. Japan, once one of this country's greatest foes, has since become one of this country's greatest allies. That bridge of friendship was begun in remote places, small unknown locations.'*

The President stood silent for a moment; he seemed to be genuinely touched. He cleared his throat, took a drink from the glass of water on the podium and continued:

'One such bridge of friendship was a small footbridge in a little-known battle high in the Zambales Mountains of Luzon Island, Republic of the Philippines. It was there, on February 14, 1945, that Lieutenant Neil Thomas made the ultimate sacrifice for his fellow man and thus, in my mind, qualifies for the greatest human virtue as defined by the teacher from Nazareth, the greatest teacher of all time, when he said:

Greater love, hath no man than this, that a man lay down his life for his friends.

'Twenty-six-year-old Lieutenant Thomas sought to save the life of a surrendering Japanese soldier, who, ironically, was being needlessly shot at by one of his own men to keep him from surrendering. The outpouring of mercy that the frail, tired and drained young American pilot showed, when he reached out from his position of safety and picked up the wounded man, at the peril of his own life, most of us will never know.

'I quote the following passages...words written almost fifty years ago by Lieutenant Thomas in a final letter to his son, in hopes that his son could have them and benefit from them someday. I share them with you so that we all may benefit. I quote:

"Love is found when you don't have to give. It is the emotion of generosity and kindness compelled by no one. It is performed on the battlefield, in our daily tasks, in the marketplace, the factories, at school, in the offices and in the halls and corridors of government...but only when one truly gives of himself and without com-

pulsion. No force, no law, no coercion can cause one to love...it cannot be arranged... Love shines its brightest right out of the flames."

'*Lieutenant Neil Thomas Sr. typified the best in American spirit, and it is with singular pride and satisfaction that I invite his son, Neil Thomas Jr., to accept The Congressional Medal of Honor on behalf of his father.*

'*Mr. Thomas, on behalf of a grateful nation, I wish to posthumously bestow this award, The Congressional Medal of Honor, to Lieutenant Neil Thomas Sr., USN, for the bravery and courage demonstrated by him while in the service of his country. His sacrifice was willingly made, above and beyond the call of duty, and as a nation we share particular pride in the greatness of his spirit and humanity.*

'*Congratulations, Mr.Thomas, on the return of your father, Lieutenant Neil Thomas Sr. and on his name going down in the records of our country as one of its great heroes.*

***

I sat there in Union Station watching the video clip with the rest of the audience. The flood of memories it caused created a deep surge of love and pride to spring from the innermost part of me.

What and who taught my parents the principles of virtue and the values that so uncommonly guided their lives? It was a selfish, self-centered world we were living in. And here, before me, the love story of my parents was being unfolded before the twenty-some-million viewers of the "American Diary Valentine Day Special." I was more deeply moved than I had ever been, even in the writing of *The Last Valentine—A Love Story.* Susan's voice pulled me back from my musings to a sense of the present.

"Don't go away. We'll be right back after a pause for these commercial messages."

Epilogue

Two commercials ran for the next several minutes. Very appropriately, American Greeting Cards, which sells tens of millions of Valentine cards every February, was one of the sponsors. Hallmark was the other. The themes were touching. One depicted scenes of World War II soldiers returning home to their sweethearts. I looked out over the audience of old World War II warriors and didn't find a dry eye.

Love is the most powerful of emotions. Appropriately packaged, love will sell any product to anyone. But, the only product being pitched tonight was a simple one. To greet those you loved—to tell them how you felt. I mused upon the fact that my father, hidden from the view of the world as he wasted away for three desperate months in the sweltering heat of the Philippine jungles, followed those basic instincts of a man who loved. He preserved his deepest feelings for us. He wrote them down. He sought to let us know. That was the greatest gift he could give to me. It was the greatest gift any man could give to his son, daughter or wife. It was time for the "Valentine Day Special" to continue.

"Welcome back to American Diary's 'Valentine-Day Special.' This is Susan Allison, and tonight you have been witness to an unusual story of an uncommon American hero, and his sweetheart.

"But there is another side to this story, one recently revealed by our overseas correspondent Tori Lewis. Upon investigation, Tori learned that a letter from the Japanese officer contained startling similarities in substance to the lovers' story that is portrayed in *The Last Valentine—A Love Story*...the story of Caroline and Neil Thomas. It seems to be a sequel to their story—and the sequel is the legacy of Lieutenant Neil Thomas Sr. When Lieutenant Thomas saved the Japanese officer from a sniper's bullet, he also rescued a letter of love—a Japanese soldier's love letter to his wife.

"Preserved because of the heroism and valor of Lieutenant Neil Thomas Sr., the message of love has reached across the Pacific to touch another family. There was no way for Lieutenant Thomas to know that in trying to save the enemy soldier's life, he would preserve precious words of devotion...the heartfelt final desires of a dying man for his wife and son, to be read fifty years after the war would end.

The Last Valentine

"It is ironic that what you are about to witness came from its safe storage—an ammunition box—to come forth in this anniversary year of the end to a war in which millions of Japanese were killed and hundreds of thousands of American men lost their lives. A box formerly storing bullets, now stored messages of love, hope and inspiration of not only our American hero, but also those of the enemy the bullets were manufactured to kill.

"What you are now about to see, our guest and author Neil Thomas Jr. will see with you for the first time. What you will now hear will encourage and inspire you as the final secret of *The Last Valentine—A Love Story* finally becomes revealed."

We all turned to look at the television monitors on cue and the videotape shot in Kobe began to play for us.

Kobe, Japan—American Diary Valentine Day Special Assignment with Tori Lewis

"Hello, Susan, and greetings to our viewers from Kobe, Japan, the site of the terrible January 17, 1995 earthquake.

"It's been only a month since a devastating earthquake destroyed much of this port city, killing over 5,000 of its inhabitants in a matter of seconds. There is no way to describe the devastation that can occur when the forces of nature are unleashed, as happened here, other than to say it must resemble a war zone. No doubt you, Susan, and our viewers are familiar with the scenes of destruction we broadcast on CNTV in these last weeks following the quake.

"One of the things I have learned over the past month is how resilient the Japanese people are. I am impressed as I watch them pick up their lives and start over with renewed energy to rebuild their shattered city. Tonight's tale includes a story of resilience, hope and love. It is a story of resilience in a rose that has sprung from the ashes of a home, the ashes of a home destroyed by the fires of the Kobe quake. The home? It was the dwelling of the "Flower Lady of Kobe," Kyoko Ito.

"It is a story of hope—hope that no matter what the fires of adversity may bring to us, hope in our future yet lures us to overcome, to rebuild our lives and dreams.

Epilogue

"Likewise, it is a story of love—love contained in a letter which arrived almost fifty years after her husband's death in the Second World War.

"Behind me stand the ruins of the home of Kyoko Ito. To the side, as you can see, is the small garden plot that had become a memorial to her husband, Captain Osamu Ito, killed in the Philippines on February 14, 1945. The garden had become a famous shrine in Kobe…one to which many would come, for reasons often unknown to them. But as it has been explained to me by her son, Takeichi Ito, who is also with us here tonight, the people came. The widows of soldiers killed in the war came year after year, to light candles for their fallen loved ones, here, in the flower garden-turned shrine. They seemed to sense an indescribable feeling of closeness as they came to the flower garden, and the garden was always open to whomever sought peace in it.

"Kyoko Ito had been a student of "Ikebana," the ancient Japanese art of flower arranging which goes back five hundred years to the days of Buddhist Temple worship and the Samurai warriors. She became a teacher of the art after fifteen years of study. Takeichi tells us that "Ikebana" brought Kyoko Ito much joy and peace as many would come to her to ask for arrangements symbolizing the virtues each plant, flower, or tree branch possessed according to Japanese custom.

"The striking similarities between "The Flower Lady of Kobe" and our own "Flower Lady" of Pasadena, California, Caroline Thomas, are too far-reaching to dismiss lightly.

"For a brief moment in time, fifty years ago, two men met on the field of battle. Lieutenant Neil Thomas and Captain Osamu Ito. In that brief moment at a firefight for a bridge, time and love became placed in an empty .30-caliber ammunition box, to come forth with its secrets fifty years later.

"For a brief moment in time tonight, we will witness the hand of fate—or, as some suggest, the hand of a much higher source—as we share the contents of the last love letter of Captain Osamu Ito saved among the letters and the *last Valentine* of Lieutenant Neil

The Last Valentine

Thomas.

"Perhaps this single rose behind me that has sprung from the ashes of Kyoko Ito's home can say as much as the letter, but I will let you be the judge. The letter begins:

February 13, 1945
My dearest Kyoko,

By the time you receive this letter I will have entered into my rest. I am so sorry to not come home—home to you and my dear little Takeichi. It has been hard for you, I know, and I wish I could be there to dry your tears, to see your smile, to hold you forever! To watch, with you, our little Takeichi grow to manhood.

My heart aches for you and it aches because of this awful business of war. I am in a country full of Catholic believers. I see their hatred, anger and fear of me and I want to shout out, "I AM ONE OF YOU!' But I have my orders, always my orders.

Today we are ordered to hold a bridge against advancing Americans. I fear this will be the last bridge I cross in this life... I fear that today I shall cross another bridge. But, my love, I cross where no man may kill me again! I, Osamu Ito, will watch over you—I will be your guardian angel... I will be with you and Takeichi always!

When you water the roses, think of me! When you smell the roses, think of me! When you hand out the roses, think of me! Hand out the symbol of our love—and where you go, I go. Where you give, I give. As long as there is a rose to bloom, you will know that I am there...to care for you, to be the ocean breeze to cool the warm summer's night, your shield against the storms. Look to the roses, my love, my life! When the roses bloom no more, I will come for you. I wait for you on the other side of the last bridge—with a handful of flowers! I love you!

Forever your devoted husband,

Osamu

Epilogue

Tori Lewis began again:

"Susan, I don't know about you, but I have been deeply moved by this letter. It arrived in time for Kyoko Ito to realize the full measure of joy that comes from a devotion such as hers. The letter to Caroline Thomas did the same. This has been such a warm and poignant love story, and the ending to it is best symbolized in what lies behind me...the single-stem rose that has grown out of the ashes of this disaster...testifying to the memory of the "Flower Lady of Kobe" who passed away two days after receiving the lost letter from her husband.

"Some say she even now waters the rose; others say she *is* the rose. I like to think of the rose, like two people's gift for each other—Americans and Japanese—as a symbol of friendship, springing from disaster and reaching out across the waters, healing an enmity, the scars of war which years ago ran so deep.

"Some have said only time can heal old wounds. Others that there is a bridge that spans time. While both sayings may contain truth, there seems to be something more coming out of this story. 'The Flower Lady of Kobe,' Kyoto Ito, understood something else. That something else was summarized in the words Captain Osamu Ito scribbled on the back of the envelope which contained his last letter. The words, written in Japanese kanji characters, are:

バラにはとげがある 'Roses have thorns!'

"Some say the rose represents the soul of Kyoko Ito. It may be so, but to me the rose with all of its thorns is the final bridge...the bridge to friendship and love.

"Back to you in Los Angeles, Susan."

***

The silence at Union Station was palpable. My heart raced and my eyes stung as I sought every remedy to control my emotions. I could not. It was more than the hand of fate that brought my father and Captain Ito together. It was a higher source. I was now convinced of that.

"Even roses have thorns!" The impact of my father's statement in one of his early war letters to my mother and then this Japanese officer's last words to his wife, held me spellbound for the remainder of the show.

I must have managed to say the right things during the interview segment. People applauded as I finished my statement to Susan about love never dying. I just hoped they read the book, *The Last Valentine—A Love Story,* and enjoyed it, participated in it, and celebrated love, the way it was meant to be. My awareness ran deep and consumed me in an inexpressible feeling of peace and satisfaction as I pondered on the amazing events of the previous year.

I couldn't have written a better surprise ending to my book. I had never known the contents of the Japanese officer's letter. I had never asked. I would like to meet this Takeichi, son of Captain Ito, some day. Two men couldn't have more in common. He would know of my faith in the *Gospel of Peace* that our fathers had shared.

I surrendered my musings to return to the present, as the camera and the lights were turned off and Susan's words rang in my ears:

"Thank you for watching American Diary's 'Valentine Day Special.' The book, *The Last Valentine—A Love Story* by Neil Thomas Jr., is available at bookstores everywhere. If every man and woman decided to grasp hold of the *rose,* no matter how painful the *thorns,* every day would be Valentine's Day…and love would rule the world. Good night everyone, and happy Valentine's Day."

***

The show was over. I said goodbye to all the audience members who gathered around and enjoyed a warm and final chat with my friends Josiah Williams and Bobby Roberts. Soon the crew had loaded the equipment and Union Station was itself again…a half deserted forties-looking train station—a place frozen in time.

Epilogue

I was immersed deep in thought, my hands in my pockets, as I finally looked around me to find Susan standing there, by the chair where my mother had sat each year on Valentine's Day. I walked over to her and she held out a single-stem rose to me.

"No thorns," I stated as I reached out gratefully for the flower.

"I took them off," she replied.

"I hope we haven't 'rosed' people out tonight," I smilingly suggested as I ran my hand over the stiff leather cushion of the high-backed chair. I wanted to feel my mother's presence there. I felt something, and it felt good. Perhaps she knew, perhaps they both knew that I had done my best to honor their memory and that I, myself, was willing to share the rose with another person...to give love another try.

I took Susan's hand and we began to walk. It was 9:00 p.m. as we headed towards the doors that led to the parking lot on Alameda Street. I reached into my coat pocket with my free hand and realized that I had forgotten to do the surprise engagement ring announcement on the air. I realized that I had just been too overcome with surprise at the story of Captain Osamu and Kyoto Ito.

I held the small velvet-covered box in my left hand as I held Susan by the right. I noticed a small piece of paper in the pocket as well. "The note," I smiled knowingly to myself. I decided not to waste another minute. I had a special place in mind for my proposal to her: the place where my father had given my mother her engagement band fifty-two years earlier.

"Hungry?" I asked as we reached the front exit.

"Sure!" came Susan's reply. "Do you have someplace *special* in mind?"

I nodded across the street. You could see Olvera Street through the glass entry doors. We stopped for a moment and looked at each other.

"La Golondrina?" she asked delightedly.

She was beautiful. Like an excited young woman on her first date. I embraced her, kissed her, and answered in an assuring tone, "Yes, La Golondrina."

I wondered if I wasn't moving a little too fast, but the feelings were good and right. As we walked down the wide corridor towards the exit and Alameda Street, we started passing the photographs from the World War II era. I motioned with my arm, which was now linked with Susan's, for her to accompany me to one very special photo. There it was. Susan released her arm from mine as I reached out and touched it—just as my mother had fifty times since last seeing my father here.

"Goodbye Mom, Dad," I said as I pulled my hand away. I realized at that moment, that fifty two years earlier my father had walked out these same doors, arm in arm with my mother, and had proposed just outside. Suddenly I knew for certain that everything would work out as it was supposed to. We headed for the doors as I mused upon it and recognized that Susan was being quiet, in a respectful way, knowing my thoughts were deep and poignant.

Just then I stopped to listen. I thought I heard music, a familiar song...*their* song over the Union Station PA system.

"Susan, do you hear that?" I asked.

"Hear what?"

"That song!... Do you hear it?... It's faint..." I cocked my head as if in so doing my ear might pick it up better. "It's my parents' song!" I exclaimed, looking down at Susan for an answer.

"Tonight might have had a more dramatic effect on you than you know. I don't hear a thing sweetheart."

That was the first time she had personalized an address to me without using my name. I liked it. "Yeah, you're right," I laughed. "I guess I feel like I just threw the winning touchdown in the Superbowl. The cheers are still ringing in my ears."

We headed out of the empty train depot for our night at La Golondrina. "She would accept. She'll say yes," I thought, my arm around her waist. I pulled out the velvet box containing the engagement ring and tried to imagine my father holding my mother in his arms here so long ago. As I pulled the small container from my pocket, the note my mother had written in her last moments of life came out with the ring box. It blew down towards Alameda Street. I was about to chase it.

"Naw," I thought. "I've got her last words locked deep inside and I've got something eternally important to do right now." I stopped Susan, looked down at her, opened the small velvet box and held it up to her. "We were going to do it on the air." She

Epilogue

threw her arms around my neck and whispered an answer to a question I hadn't verbalized. I pulled away and surveyed her expression. One look into her eyes said it all.

"I love you," I said softly.

She looked up into the night sky and fought the emotions that seemed to be flowing over into me. Why was I so unable to maintain my composure? Why couldn't she?

"I love you...isn't good enough—not for you, Neil Thomas," she said with a certainty that filled her usually anchor-woman controlled voice.

Our sensitivities suddenly turned from serious "romantic" drama to joyful, almost playful laughter. We had transformed our questions about one another's feelings into affirmations—affirmations of love. We wouldn't fill our nights in loneliness any longer. If this could happen to me... Well, I knew God never meant for anything but the greatest of gifts to come to his children.

I would never be able to forget the joy I had just experienced, and the incredible good fortune of having Susan with me. I knew there never needed to be a *last Valentine* as long as love grew...as long as two people worked to make it last... As long as *"forever was a promise to keep."*

And, as my mother had said to Josiah and others long ago:

It's not in the end alone that we love, but along the way... A love that endures the thorns... It calls out to us, it lights the ground upon which we tread and we know that we are not alone...

***

Josiah lost the signal for only a moment. He played with the radio dial, trying to tune in to National Public Radio's "Nostalgia Night." Los Angeles 89.5 FM. He finally had it and plugged the music back into the PA system, then walked away, satisfied listening to the music from the forties. It was Bing Crosby singing:

The Last Valentine

Because you speak to me—I find roses 'round my feet, and I am left with tears and joy of thee!

Because God made thee mine—I'll cherish thee, through all life and darkness and all time to be.

And pray he may make our love divine... Because God made thee mine!

***

Armando was walking along Alameda Street returning from dinner for his nightly custodial duty at Union Station. He mused upon the CNTV television show which, for a night, made his work-place famous. A small piece of paper blew across his path and he reached down to pick it up without thinking. He never did that. He wondered what was on it. It looked like a note. He held it up to the streetlight. It looked like the handwriting of an older person, shaky-looking cursive letters, but distinct enough to make out. He started reading each word, slowly, deliberately...

Neil! Wonderful... Beautiful... Light... Neil... Forev...